PRAISE FOR *A DOOR BETWEEN US*

"A vivid, thrilling story of clashes and collisions, between
tradition and civil liberties, between families, between
individuals and institutions, between reform and reaction...
You will not forget these scenes and these characters."

—ROBERT MORGAN, *New York Times*
bestselling author of *Gap Creek*

"In a riveting story, Sadr captures the lines that
divide Iranian society and the specter of tragedy that
haunted it. She cuts right to the heart of life in 2009 and
its consequences in a deeply understanding story."

—NAZILA FATHI, author of
The Lonely War: One Woman's Account of the Struggle for Modern Iran

"A deeply compelling story about the struggle
for democracy in Iran. The broken dreams of a
generation poised for change are brought vividly
to life in this powerful and haunting tale."

—AUSMA ZEHANAT KHAN, author of *Among the Ruins*

"Ehsaneh Sadr vividly tells the story of one...divid d nily
that brilliantly captures th   d
dreams, the betrayals and   :d
in the multitude of stru

—TRITA PARSI, author
and the Triu.   ..,   .ъvmacy

"Ehsaneh Sadr's insightful debut, with its thoughtful social justice message, paints a very human and, at times, harrowing picture of a complex nation and a group of people rarely present in Western fiction."

—HOLLY DAGRES, Atlantic Council

"A powerful story that illuminates both the personal and the deeply political aspects of contemporary Iranian society…An impressive and relevant work that adds to the richness of our Iranian American literary canon."

—PERSIS KARIM, director, Center for
Iranian Diaspora Studies & coeditor,
Tremors: New Fiction by Iranian American Writers

"Politics, family frictions, and divided loyalties collide in Ehsaneh Sadr's engrossing novel…Intense, emotional, and rich, *A Door between Us* is a stirring novel about the importance of conscientiousness and truth."

—FOREWORD REVIEWS

"An enthralling story of hope, courage, and the powerful ties that bind families and communities together… From start to finish, the story held me rapt, its poignant message of interconnectedness lingering with me long after I turned the last page."

—AMANDA SKENANDORE, author of *Between Earth and Sky*

"Captivating and heartbreaking…With a fresh, compassionate voice, Sadr reveals our inherent closeness beyond the divisions and separations. An assured, immersive debut."

—MARJAN KAMALI, author of
The Stationary Shop and *Together Tea*

"An intimate, personal story set within a pivotal period in Iranian history, and Sadr deftly shows how political unrest affects ordinary people in unexpected ways. Readers who enjoy Etaf Rum and Elif Shafak will appreciate this promising debut."

—BOOKLIST

"Family secrets, unexpected liaisons, and relationships figure into this cultural tale…The final confrontation of the religious and political forces is riveting in its unpredictability, violence, and redemption. It is a celebration of our connectedness, in spite of our best efforts to sort each other into Us and Them."

—NEW YORK JOURNAL OF BOOKS

"[A] graceful debut…This is a brave, intelligent novel, a story of difference overcome by love."

—SHELF AWARENES

A

DOOR

BETWEEN

US

A

DOOR

BETWEEN

US

EHSANEH SADR

**BLACK
STONE**
PUBLISHING

Copyright © 2020 by Ehsaneh Sadr
Published in 2021 by Blackstone Publishing
Cover and book design by Zena Kanes

All rights reserved. This book or any portion
thereof may not be reproduced or used in any manner
whatsoever without the express written permission
of the publisher except for the use of brief quotations
in a book review.

The characters and events in this book are fictitious.
Any similarity to real persons, living or dead, is coincidental
and not intended by the author.

Printed in the United States of America
Originally published in hardcover by Blackstone Publishing in 2020

First paperback edition: 2021
ISBN 978-1-6650-8804-6
Fiction / General

3 5 7 9 10 8 6 4 2

CIP data for this book is available
from the Library of Congress

Blackstone Publishing
31 Mistletoe Rd.
Ashland, OR 97520

www.BlackstonePublishing.com

To Niloufar,
whose love and beauty will always be remembered,
and the 175 individuals with her on Flight 752.

LIST OF CHARACTERS

HOJJATI FAMILY

- MEHRI—sixty-year-old matriarch of the family
- SADEGH—Mehri's adopted son who was born to her husband's second wife
- SUMAYEH—Sadegh's half-American wife
- ZAINAB—Mehri's oldest daughter and confidant.
- FATIMEH—Mehri's younger daughter
- ALIREZA—Mehri's son

BAGHERI FAMILY

- SARAH—nineteen years old and engaged to marry Ali Rahimi
- MAHDIYEH—Sarah's mother and Mehri Hojjati's sister
- ABBAS—Sarah's father

RAHIMI FAMILY

- AZAR—thirty-five, a divorce lawyer, mother to Hossein and Muhammadreza
- IBRAHIM JAFARI—Azar's husband, an economist
- ALI—Azar's brother, engaged to marry Sarah
- MR. & MRS. RAHIMI—Ali and Azar's parents

TABIBIAN FAMILY

- ROKSANA—Azar's secretary
- LEILA—Roksana's daughter

BASIJIS

- GANJIAN—Sadegh's former teacher and friend, leads a Basij unit headquartered in Sa'adat Abad
- HEYDARI—member of the Revolutionary Guards

PART ONE
THREE DAYS IN JUNE

While there was intense attention to the June 12 presidential election and its potential impact on Iran's internal balance of power and foreign policy, no serious analyst or scholar predicted the series of events that has transpired in the wake of that ballot.

—Suzanne Maloney, Iran Expert at the
  Brookings Institute, June 26, 2009

CHAPTER 1

Thursday, June 25, 2009—thirteen days after the election

> Baton-wielding riot police in thigh-length black leg guards
> swarmed from the shuttered Interior Ministry in the early
> hours of June 13. They went to work beating people.
> —Roger Cohen, "Iran: The Tragedy & the Future"[1]

Sarah was bored at her own wedding.

The blind mullah apparently couldn't pass up an opportunity to lecture a captive audience on an obscure topic nobody cared about. He'd been flown into Tehran at great expense, ostensibly due to the prestigious nature of his association with the Imam Reza shrine, Iran's most important pilgrimage site and also, Iranians were fond of noting, the largest mosque in the world. But what Sarah cared about most was the man's blindness, which meant that as soon as the *sigheh* marriage contract was finalized, she could immediately remove the slippery satin bridal chador that covered her like a white cocoon from which only her face was visible. Sarah was eager to stand before Ali uncovered for the first time so he could admire the way her thick black ringlets grazed her bare shoulders and be even prouder of the wife he'd fought for. If the mullah took much longer before getting to the *sigheh*, Sarah's ringlets were going to go flat and frizzy and the four hours spent doing hair and makeup that morning with one of Tehran's most sought-after beauticians would have been entirely wasted.

As the blind mullah rambled on about a happy family life, which could be preserved by taking care to enter various rooms with the right or left foot—bathrooms with the left, bedrooms with the right—Sarah admired the exquisite *sofreh aghd* wedding spread laid out on the floor before her and Ali like an ornate picnic blanket. There were the Swarovski candlesticks and a rhinestone-encrusted Venetian mirror her mother had purchased for her on a trip to Austria back when Sarah was still a toddler. A Quran on a hand-carved wooden *rehal* was open to Chapter 30, Verse 21, about the love between spouses being another sign of God's mercy. There was a bowl of honey for when Ali and Sarah would use their pinkies to feed each other a small taste of what would hopefully be a life full of sweetness. The rest of the spread was filled with decorated candies, eggs, nuts, herbs, gold coins and other symbols of piety, fertility, and prosperity.

All the female relatives from Ali and Sarah's families had left their tables and were crowded around the *sofreh* in a semicircle with Sarah, Ali, and the mullah seated on a raised platform at one end. Sarah recognized some of the women from their shoes. She wished she could look at everyone and enjoy their congratulatory and admiring glances or even a few teasing eye rolls. But she knew Aunt Mehri, the family matriarch, wouldn't approve, and Sarah wanted to be particularly respectful of the old woman's feelings today. Best to stick to the role of the dutiful, shy bride with her head firmly bowed.

"So now we come to the marriage contract," the mullah said.

Finally, thought Sarah.

"In Islam, of course, there is no compulsion in marriage just as there is no compulsion in religion. See how advanced Islam was at a time when little girls were being buried in the desert? The Prophet, peace and blessings be upon him and his family, was the first person to recognize the rights of . . ."

The mullah launched into yet another lecture. Was there no way to stop the man? Sarah was sure her father would have prodded him to finish thirty minutes ago. Baba had no patience for grandstanding. But Maman-joon was too timid to ever consider interrupting anyone, let alone a respected mullah. And Aunt Mehri, who might have stepped in under normal circumstances, had washed her hands of the whole affair.

They were lucky she'd even agreed to attend the wedding.

"So now it is time to ask this young lady if she will give me permission to perform this marriage to enter her into a marriage contract with—"

"Yes!" Sarah exclaimed, cutting the mullah off before he even finished asking the question. Sarah was determined to move things along, and she hoped the mullah would get the hint.

There was a beat of silence. What was the mullah waiting for, Sarah wondered. Why didn't he get on with asking Ali to accept as well?

Then Sarah heard a sound that started off as a cough but turned into laughter that spread across the group of women gathered around the bridal spread. Sarah realized that she'd answered the mullah much too soon. In this part of the ceremony, the bride wasn't supposed to answer the first or even second request to marry, let alone cut him off before he'd completed the question. Sarah should have remained silent, playing hard-to-get, as the female wedding guests answered the mullah in a traditional singsong chant that the bride was out picking flowers, *Aroos rafte gol bechine*. Then the mullah would have to try again, three times, before she finally consented.

Sarah's cheeks grew warm at her too-quick response. How embarrassing!

Yet even as her cheeks burned, Sarah wished once again that she could lift her head and join in the laughter herself. After the mullah's long sermons the ladies needed some entertainment, and Sarah didn't mind providing it, even at her own expense.

Had Ali been amused as well? Provoking his amusement had become one of Sarah's chief goals and unexpected pleasures during the few months they'd been engaged. The first time she'd accomplished the feat had been entirely unintended. In their only private moment during the traditional first meeting of *khastegari* courtship. Sarah had primly announced that she had no intention of marrying Ali or anyone else and that she'd only agreed to meet him because of her parents' pressure and Aunt Mehri's insistence that he was a good match from a good family. It was Ali's surprised chuckle and friendly encouragement that she should pursue what she wanted independent of her family's wishes that made her notice his honey-colored eyes for the first time.

Straining her eyes to the left as far as they'd go with her head still down and constricted by her chador, Sarah could just see Ali's profile in her peripheral vision. Ah, there it was—his clean-shaven cheeks, so unlike those of men in her own family in the way they revealed every facial expression, had a slight fold that meant he was definitely smiling.

Sarah felt a rush of love, joy, and pride. She would gladly endure much worse embarrassment to amuse her sweet, stubborn Ali, who had wanted her, and only her, so much he refused to let Sarah go, even when the whole mess of the election brought their families' political differences to light. Sarah wished she could look directly at him and admire how handsome he was in the Brioni suit her father had purchased for him in Italy. The suit's light-olive color made Ali's honey eyes look almost green, and its tailored design narrowed his oddly thick neck so that, if not quite elegant, at least it didn't look wider than his head.

Yes, Sarah was happy to have amused everyone. She was in love with her husband-to-be. And she was proud of the opulent wedding party her parents were throwing in one of Tehran's most expensive hotels. The banquet hall was stunning, with its gold-trimmed ceilings and oversized chandeliers. And the food was exquisite. Earlier, when guests were settling in and waiting for the ceremony to begin, they'd been served a variety of flaky pastries that exploded a cool sweet cream with every bite, along with cardamom-infused black tea and a variety of fruits like strawberries, kiwis, peaches, plums, grapes, and small cucumbers. If the mullah ever finished, they would be treated to succulent dishes of lamb shank with dill-flavored rice, chicken, beef, and lamb kabobs, and, of course, the traditional sweet rice of weddings with slivers of orange peel, almonds, and pistachios.

Aunt Mehri's sudden reversal regarding Ali's suitability as a groom had been accompanied by dire warnings about the bad omens associated with insisting on marrying someone who'd fallen out of divine favor. But thus far, the wedding party itself had been a spectacular start to Sarah and Ali's life together and a fine testament to God's blessing on their union.

The tittering died down, and the mullah cleared his throat to announce, ahem, that he was starting over. As he took a breath to launch into his next lecture, Sarah heard Aunt Mehri's sotto voce insult, *"Che ajale dare* . . . she's certainly in a rush," that was predictably followed by Cousin Zainab's *tsk* of distaste over Sarah's too-quick response and its implied eagerness for her husband's bed.

Sarah knew without looking that Aunt Mehri would be standing next to her eldest daughter and confidante, Zainab, who by virtue of her domineering personality as well as the seniority of being two years older than Sarah's mother, was the family's deputy matriarch who supported and enforced all her mother's decrees. The mother-daughter pair would be wearing matching rose-colored indoor chadors, pulled tight around contrasting body types that were as different from one another as their characters were alike. Tall and rail-thin, Cousin Zainab made a perfect number "1" whereas short and round Aunt Mehri was a "0." The "10" they created together had ruled the family for years, and Sarah knew Aunt Mehri's remark was her way of meting out punishment over the unusual experience of having been disobeyed.

"We're in a rush too," someone said.

It was Ali's mother, Mrs. Rahimi. "We just can't wait to have such a lovely daughter-in-law," she said, her voice beaming with warmth.

Sarah was touched by these generous words and would have smiled her thanks at her soon-to-be mother-in-law if she hadn't been worried about further angering Aunt Mehri. Mrs. Rahimi was so loving, gentle, and kind, just like Maman-joon. The two womens' statures and speaking voices were so similar that, in their black chadors, shopkeepers kept mistaking them for one another during the many joint excursions where Sarah got to pick out one beautiful wedding item after another. In the drama of the past few days, Sarah had forgotten how well the two women had initially taken to one another.

The mullah cleared his throat again. "Now, Miss Sarah, take your time and think carefully about this important decision. Do you or do you not allow me to conduct this marriage contract for you with the honorable Mr. Ali?"

This time, like millions of Persian brides before her, Sarah sat quietly as the ladies crowded around the *sofreh aghd* answered for her.

"Aroos rafte gol bechine! The bride is picking flowers!"

It was a funny phrase. Sarah had heard it and even shouted it hundreds of times at other weddings. Where had the tradition come from? It might have made sense in, say, a village where the bride's relatives were teasing the groom by pretending she was out picking flowers when he came for her. But in modern times when the bride was obviously sitting right next to the groom, it was a little silly to pretend she wasn't there. It did, however, give the guests a way to participate. Maybe that was the point.

In the midst of the women chanting, Sarah heard someone shouting something different. She strained to catch the words. What else could anyone be saying? It wasn't as if there was another version of the ceremony.

The mullah asked a second time whether Sarah would consent to the marriage. The ladies sang out, "*Aroos rafte golaab biyare!* The bride is bringing perfume!" ostensibly referring to the rosewater the bride was now making out of the flowers she'd picked.

This time, Sarah could hear the discordant voices more clearly. "*Marg bar diktator!*"

Death to the dictator? Sarah was so shocked, she lifted her head immediately to see who would dare utter such treasonous words in present company. Ali's devilish nephews, nine- and ten-year-old Muhammadreza and Hossein—who, unfortunately, were young enough to be in the ladies section—had their little fists raised as they chanted words they'd surely heard at one of the street demonstrations that had racked Tehran over the past two weeks. Even more unfortunately, they were sitting cross-legged on the floor right in front of Aunt Mehri and Cousin Zainab.

At another time or in a different context, Sarah might have thought it was funny to see two little boys alleviating their boredom by disrupting a wedding ceremony. But now she felt something bordering on panic. She didn't need anyone, least of all

Aunt Mehri and Cousin Zainab, to be reminded of the political differences that had almost derailed the wedding.

Two months ago, it had been Aunt Mehri herself who'd decided Ali—the nephew of her childhood friend Mina, the friend who'd always brought Mehri sweets from her father's chain of bakeries and who grew up to marry a diplomat that was currently representing Iran at the United Nations in New York— would be a good match. Over Sarah's objections, Aunt Mehri had convinced Baba and Maman-joon that Ali's family was too good a prospect to pass up and that they should agree to at least one courtship *khastegari* meeting.

On that *khastegari* day that would change the course of Sarah's life—when she met Ali and started falling in love with him within minutes of having turned him down, and had furtively given him her email address so they could circumvent Aunt Mehri's overzealous rules about whether and when they could communicate—the upcoming presidential election was the last thing on anyone's minds. Sarah would have been hard-pressed to name all of the candidates vying to defeat the brash populist President Ahmadinejad, who was favored by the country's supreme leader.

But after Sarah and Ali were formally engaged and the election neared, surprising political differences began to emerge. Sarah's family were all Ahmadinejad supporters due to their longtime loyalty to supreme leader Khamenei. But Ali's sister Azar and her husband Ibrahim, the parents of the little boys now disrupting the wedding, were outspoken supporters of Mir-Hossein Mousavi, the candidate who repeatedly implied that the supreme leader and his favored candidate had led the country astray from the original intent of the Islamic revolution. Azar's husband even began working directly for Mousavi's campaign during his hours away from Sharif University, where he taught economics.

Still, it wasn't until the actual election that things got really tense. Aunt Mehri's youngest and favorite child, Sadegh, started spending every spare moment with the Basij volunteer militias that were trying to keep security in the streets and protect the nation from violent rioters. Aunt Mehri, beside herself with worry over Sadegh's safety, had been deeply offended to learn that Azar's husband had led a mass resignation of 120 university professors to protest the supposed ill treatment of students by government forces.

But the final straw was when, at a ladies-only party hosted by Cousin Zainab, Azar had insisted that the election had been rigged, that the Green Wave protesters were simply standing up for their rights, and that the government crackdown was violent and immoral.

"Did you see what happened just yesterday?" Azar had asked, waving a picture on her phone in the air. "A young woman, a peaceful protester, Neda Soltani, shot in the chest with live bullets. I have the video right here. Any human being would be outraged."

What made things worse was that, Mrs. Rahimi, who Aunt Mehri had known since she was a child, who was the youngest sister of one of Aunt Mehri's oldest friends, hadn't bothered chiding or even trying to quiet her daughter when she was so obviously insulting their hosts. Not only were the family's politics wrong but its members were ill-mannered to boot.

That night, after the party, Aunt Mehri had informed Sarah's mother that the wedding had to be called off. "It breaks my heart to see this from Mina's family," she'd exclaimed, her hand pressed to her chest as if holding her fragmenting heart together. "And I'm sure that if Mina were here, she would set her sister straight. She's been in New York far too long. But, praise God, it just goes to show how right I was to take things slow and keep the young people away from any temptation. Praise God, we found out what this family really is in time to break things off with no harm done."

Had Aunt Mehri noticed the boys' antics beside the *sofreh aghd*? And where was Azar? Why wasn't she controlling her unruly sons?

Sarah spotted Azar on the left side of the bridal spread, almost exactly opposite her sons and Aunt Mehri on the right. As sister of the groom, she was one of the few women at the gathering who didn't have to cover up her revealing wedding dress while Ali was in the ladies section of the banquet hall. Azar's thick black hair was pulled into a severe updo, and her makeup was limited to a bit of lipstick and mascara. She wore a black sheath dress and dark-green jacket with black accents at the lapel and upturned sleeves. Even in a dress, Sarah had noticed earlier, Azar managed to look as if she were working.

Azar really was a strange woman for their *tabaghe*, or class of wealthy religious families. For one thing, it was rumored that she'd refused her husband's bed for the first few years of marriage. For another, she worked outside the home at her own law practice in the morally suspect field of helping women obtain divorces. And she wasn't at all interested in the typical things that ladies enjoyed. Once, in an effort to bond with her soon-to-be sister-in-law, Sarah had confided her difficulties in completing purchases of furnishings and linens for the home she and Ali would share. "I just can't sleep at night thinking how I'm going to find towels to match the bathroom accessories my father brought from London," Sarah had complained. Admittedly, Sarah might have been a bit melodramatic but she hadn't deserved Azar's rolled eyes and contemptuous question that if mismatched towels kept Sarah up at night, how on earth would she handle a *real* problem. Since the towel incident, Sarah had felt a bit prickly toward Azar.

With all her manly attitudes and behaviors, one might have thought Azar wouldn't have any trouble controlling two young boys. But, in this area, she seemed to be at a loss. Sarah had seen Azar plead with Hossein and Muhammadreza in the same manner, but with less success, than when Sarah pleaded with her father for more spending money.

Azar met Sarah's eyes and gave her a small smile. She looked surprised to see Sarah looking so pointedly at her. Was it possible she hadn't heard her boys? Sarah tilted her head and narrowed her eyes toward Hossein and Muhammadreza, but when Azar followed her gaze, she still looked confused.

Exasperated, Sarah turned her attention to Aunt Mehri, hoping that she might have missed the boys' chanting. But from the way Aunt Mehri's pursed lips radiated angry lines through her papery skin, it was clear she'd heard the boys' offensive words all too well. Sarah felt her corset winch another notch around her waist as she wondered what her aunt would do.

Despite Aunt Mehri's sarcastic remarks about Sarah's blundered response to the mullah, Sarah actually felt a little sorry for her. Sarah couldn't think of another time when Aunt Mehri's decision about a family matter hadn't been the final word, and a part of Sarah still couldn't believe she'd managed to convince her parents, Maman-joon especially, to defy her older-by-twenty-years sister who was more like a mother to her and a grandmother to Sarah.

Aunt Mehri hadn't taken it lightly. In the past few days she'd railed at Sarah's parents for making a monumental mistake. She'd threatened to boycott the wedding and forbid other family members from attending. And she'd warned tearfully that her poor heart couldn't take being treated this way and that no one should be surprised if God in his infinite mercy took her from this world before she had to witness her niece marry into the "family of traitors and infidels"—a family she didn't seem to remember having once been so enthusiastic about that she'd literally forced Sarah to meet their son.

In the end, however, Aunt Mehri had swallowed her pride, attended the wedding, and had, mostly, been quite gracious. It was unfair for Aunt Mehri to have these awful chants thrown in her face.

Sarah wanted to bow her head back to its proper position before Aunt Mehri noticed. But she was transfixed by the sight of Aunt Mehri's arm as it began to stretch, amoeba-like under the veil's draping, toward Hossein's shoulder. When Aunt Mehri's reaching appendage grasped the startled boy, Hossein grimaced in pain from what Sarah knew from experience to be a surprisingly strong grip for a woman whose cloistered body enjoyed even less exercise than it did sun. Aunt Mehri held him firmly as the boy squirmed. But as the awkward strain of her bent position became too difficult to maintain, she suddenly pitched forward. Sarah tensed and squeezed her eyes shut just as Aunt Mehri crash-landed into the middle of the bridal spread on the floor, scattering flowers, eggs, and other decorations on her way.

When Sarah opened her eyes again, it was to the sight of her mother, Cousin Zainab, and some of the other ladies, Mrs. Rahimi included, valiantly trying to help Aunt Mehri get upright while holding their rumpled chadors in place over their revealing wedding gowns. Aunt Mehri's rounded proportions made the job an extra challenge as the ladies struggled to roll her up over the girth of her belly while keeping her veiling secure and without damaging any more of the fragile bridal spread accouterments. When Hossein and Muhammadreza started laughing, Nafiseh, Aunt Mehri's teenage granddaughter, the one Sarah always thought would one day inherit her mother Zainab's position as enforcer of rules, gave Muhammedreza a swift kick that set off another physical tussle. The adults momentarily abandoned Aunt Mehri on the bridal spread as they tried to pull the children apart. Azar, finally cued in to the havoc her boys were causing, ran around the bridal spread to get to the melee. At first, she tried to help the forgotten Aunt Mehri, but when the old woman slapped at her extended hands, Azar turned to grab and pull her boys away.

"What's going on?" the mullah shouted. "Ladies, your

attention please. It's time to ask the bride one more time if she will permit me to perform this marriage ceremony." The man didn't seem to realize he had entirely lost his audience.

Cousin Zainab, Sadegh's scarred wife Sumayeh, and a few other ladies of the family finally managed to get Aunt Mehri on her feet. Aunt Mehri's chador was snug again but off-center so that one side trailed on the floor while the other ended at her shins, making her stockinged legs and wide-heeled black shoes visible. "*Khodaya, ghalbam vaystad!* Lord help me . . . my heart can't take this," Aunt Mehri aspirated, taking trembling breaths between words. "Those . . . little monsters! I have never . . . ever . . . Zainab, dear . . . get me out of here . . . I can't . . ."

"*Biya beshin.* Come, take a seat," Sarah's mother pulled at her sister to move her toward the chairs and tables where she could sit away from the bridal spread. Maman-joon looked as if she was going to cry. All of the engagement and wedding drama had been hardest on her. Maman-joon was the one who'd had to break the news to Aunt Mehri that the wedding would proceed as planned and then bore the brunt of anger and hurt from her beloved and revered older sister, who'd taken her in and raised her along with Zainab and her other children when their parents had passed. It was all made worse by the fact that Maman-joon was too embarrassed to admit that Sarah had been secretly talking to Ali all along and had fallen in love with him. So Aunt Mehri had little context for why she was being disobeyed. Even more than Sarah, Maman-joon had hoped that a successful wedding party would mollify Aunt Mehri by demonstrating God's favor as well as the finality of the decision.

"*Na!*" Aunt Mehri pushed Maman-joon away as she righted her chador, centering it correctly around her. "I won't stay another second. What kind of people teach their children such lies about our supreme leader, who has spent his whole life guiding us toward God and protecting us from our many enemies? What kind of people teach their children to attack an old woman? They're just like those violent rioters in the street. Zainab dear," Aunt Mehri called, "Get me out of here!"

Sarah knew she had to do something. Gathering the folds of her awkward bridal chador around her, she stood and called, "*Khaleh-joon, koja mirin?* Dearest Aunt, where are you going? The wedding party hasn't even started."

Aunt Mehri turned, and the ladies parted to allow an unobstructed visual tunnel connecting the bride at one end and the family matriarch at the other. Suddenly everyone was silent. Even the forgotten mullah seemed to have tired of trying to get everyone's attention.

Aunt Mehri's lined skin was damp and her voice shook. "My mistake was that I came in the first place and agreed to mix with people who teach their children to insult someone I would die for. I knew I would regret it. I wanted to help and guide you, as is my duty, but you turned your back and ignored me and treated me as if this decision was none of my business. After all I have done for your mother and your family, how could you treat me this way?

"I shudder for you, my child," Aunt Mehri went on. "You can't imagine the wrath you and your parents have called upon yourselves. These people threaten our Islamic Republic, even at a wedding. Nothing is sacred to them! God doesn't forgive such traitors."

Aunt Mehri turned her back on Sarah and pulled away from Maman-joon. Her entourage—including Cousin Zainab, Zainab's two daughters, Zahra and Nafiseh, who had kicked Azar's son, and Aunt Mehri's two daughters-in-law—closed up around her and the ladies exited the ballroom.

Sarah felt the weight of expectant gazes upon her as the remaining ladies looked to see what she would do. She searched her mind for some quip or joke or segue back to the ceremony that would shift the mood and make everything okay.

Sarah glanced at Ali for help. But he seemed frozen in place with his head down and eyes low. Had he seen what had happened? What was he thinking? Ali didn't have any interest in politics, and Sarah knew he didn't share his sister's affinity for the Greens. But Azar was his sister. And although he'd known of Aunt Mehri's opposition, it was another thing to hear with his own ears the way she talked about his family. Would it change how he felt about marrying into hers? What were Mrs. Rahimi and Azar thinking about Aunt Mehri's scene? Would it prompt them to oppose the marriage as well?

Before she had time to decide on her next move, Sarah felt a hand on her arm. It was Maman-joon.

"Sarah," she whispered, "come with me."

Sarah had never been a rebellious child. Unlike many of her school friends she had generally felt loved and understood and, in turn, sought to please her mother and father. Yes, she had a reputation for some mischief-making, but even that stemmed from her knowledge that her parents were secretly proud of her high spirits. She never crossed a line into outright defiance.

When Sarah and Ali had begun emailing and then calling one another, Sarah hadn't really seen it as disobedience. She and Ali were engaged after all. And Sarah knew her parents didn't entirely agree with Aunt Mehri's overly strict insistence that the engagement period was for families to get to know one another and ensure they were a good match, and that there was time enough *after* the wedding for the young people to fall in love. If it weren't for Aunt Mehri, Sarah was sure she and Ali, like many other engaged couples from religious families, would have done the *sigheh* early on so they could even spend time together alone. Whispered conversations in which Sarah tried to make Ali laugh with funny stories about her latest scrapes felt innocent and so right that it was hard to imagine anyone being upset about it.

When Sarah heard from her mother that Aunt Mehri had changed her mind about Ali's family and had decided that the marriage should be called off, it was as if someone had told her that her name wasn't Sarah or that she wasn't really Iranian and didn't belong with her mother and father. Ali already felt like such an immutable part of her life and identity that Sarah couldn't believe he could be ripped away and erased as if their relationship had never happened.

On the other hand, if Aunt Mehri had made a decision, Sarah couldn't imagine any way around it. The matter was out of her hands. All Sarah could do was pray that God would change her aunt's mind again or intervene in some way to allow Sarah and Ali to be together after all.

It was Ali who had refused to accept her aunt's decision and convinced Sarah to fight for their marriage.

"Sarah," he'd argued, "this is our life. We can't let your aunt or my sister or anyone else make decisions for us. Especially for stupid political reasons that have nothing to do with us. We don't care about a Green revolution. Or a blue or purple one for that matter. We just want to live our lives!"

When Sarah asked what they could possibly do, Ali made it sound easy. "We tell them that we've been secretly talking and that we're already in love and we refuse to change our minds. If it comes to it, we lie and tell them that we've been seeing each other too and, well, we could even tell them you're not a virgin anymore."

Sarah had been shocked by the scandalous suggestion but also a little pleased at how far Ali was willing to go. He made her promise, before God, that she would marry no one but him. It was a thrilling moment. It almost felt as if they were married already.

It was that promise she held onto in the face of her parents' disappointment when they learned of her clandestine contact with Ali. It was her promise that steeled her to withstand Aunt Mehri's outrage as the wedding went forward more or less as planned.

And it was that promise she held onto now. When Maman-joon gave her hands a squeeze and prompted, "So? Should I go tell everyone?" Sarah managed to make her voice and her resolve sound stronger than they felt. "Maman-joon," she insisted as she returned her mother's squeeze, "Ali is the only one for me. I love him and hope you can love him too."

Maman-joon dropped her hands and looked so sad that Sarah almost regretted her answer. Was this feeling of being torn between her family and Ali to be a recurring feature of her life from now on? Sarah hated having to make choices that would hurt one or the other. Was it possible to make it all go away?

Sarah imagined for a moment how easy it could be to agree with Maman-joon and let her take care of everything. Her father would be delighted. Aunt Mehri would forgive her. And she wouldn't have to deal with an unpredictable sister-in-law and her awful children.

But what of Ali and his clean-shaven cheeks and honey-colored eyes? What about the way his tongue ran over the chip in his front tooth whenever he was distracted?

It was lucky Maman-joon didn't press any further, as Sarah's delicate and divided will might have been crushed by the weight of her desire to please her parents. Maman-joon pulled Sarah into a fierce hug that painfully pushed the bands of Sarah's corset even further into her ribs. "Oh, my daughter," Maman-joon said. "I love you so much it scares me sometimes. I don't know if we're doing the right thing in allowing this to go forward. When I was your age, our elders made all the important decisions. It didn't cross our minds to even have an opinion. But I don't have it in me to tear you from someone you love. May God help us all understand his plan and play our part in it. Tonight, I will pray for my beautiful daughter and my new son-in-law as you start your lives together."

"Mahdiyeh, what's going on?" Cousin Fatimeh asked as she

lumbered into the alcove. Cousin Fatimeh was a large woman with her sister's height and her mother's round build. She was a year younger than Maman-joon and her closest friend. The two of them had grown up together under the watchful eyes of Aunt Mehri and Cousin Zainab, and it was a sign of their devotion to one another that Cousin Fatimeh had stayed at the wedding despite the departure of her mother and sister.

"The *hajj-agha* is complaining and wants to know if you're coming to finish the ceremony or if he should go," Fatimeh reported in a voice that was as lumbering as her build. Sarah noticed a line of sweat beaded across Fatimeh's upper lip. It probably hadn't been an easy decision for her to stay.

"We're coming," Maman-joon said as she released Sarah and helped her wrap into her chador again. Then Maman-joon walked Sarah back to the ballroom, where Sarah responded to Ali's quizzical look with what she hoped was a reassuring smile. Azar led the ladies in joyful ululations to get the ceremony back on track, and this time when the mullah asked whether Sarah would agree to marry Ali, she answered immediately and with a strong voice that, she hoped, didn't betray any of her confusion or doubt, "Yes, with my mother and father's permission, I do."

*   *   *

The rest of the evening passed quickly, if somewhat awkwardly, as the two families strained to conceal their dislike for one another from both the cameras and their 412 guests. The only moment Sarah truly enjoyed was when Ali—finally seeing her bare-headed and bare-armed with a hint of cleavage rising out of the heart-shaped neckline of her Marchesa wedding gown, her ringlets still intact—shook his head with besotted wonder, as if he couldn't quite believe how lucky he was.

By the time the banquet hall started emptying out and Sarah and Ali were escorted to Ali's white Mercedes Benz, Sarah was exhausted. Her feet hurt and her corset hadn't let her take an easy breath all night.

It wasn't easy negotiating all the fabric surrounding her body. As Sarah sat in the car, the sheetlike chador started pulling back, and she had to awkwardly bump her bottom up a few times to pull it over her head while trying to keep her dress from riding up along with it. Warmer than she liked to be, she asked Ali to turn on the AC.

"*Chashm, azizam.*" Ali turned it on full blast. Then he backed out of their parking spot and pulled over to wait for their families. Traditionally, close friends and relatives would accompany the bride and groom in a long procession of cars to the new home, where yet another party would be thrown before the exhausted couple was finally left to enjoy their first night together. Ali and Sarah had convinced everyone to forgo this additional event, given the strained relations between the two families as well as the many street demonstrations that had made it increasingly difficult to travel about Tehran. Their parents would accompany the newlyweds to ensure their safe arrival home but would then take their leave at the door.

"What a night!" Ali exclaimed as they waited.

"Oh my God," Sarah was ready to focus on the hilarity of the evening. "Aunt Mehri, poor thing, rolling around on the *sofreh aghd*!"

Ali chuckled softly and then took Sarah's hand. It was the first time he was touching her, and Sarah was surprised by how soft his thick fingers felt.

"I hope she's okay," he said, his voice subdued. "Those boys . . . they've been worse than usual since Ibrahim left the house."

Distracted by the tingling sensation Ali's touch had ignited, Sarah asked absently, "What do you mean?"

"So many of his friends have been arrested, Azar told Ibrahim to leave town before he got picked up too. The boys are taking it hard. Akh!" Ali rubbed his forehead with his free hand. "I don't know why they had to mix themselves up with all of this. It just causes problems for everyone."

Sarah didn't know what to say. She agreed with Ali's sentiment but didn't want to seem overly eager to criticize his sister and brother-in-law. She opted for what she hoped were sympathetic listening noises as she played with Ali's fingernails

"When your mother pulled you away . . ." Ali's tone softened as he squeezed her hand. "I thought I might never see my *gollam*, my little flower, again."

Ali pulled Sarah's hand to his lips for a sweet kiss, his breath on the back of her fingertips jolting something in Sarah's belly.

"I love my sister," Ali went on after a pause. "But I don't know if I would ever have forgiven her if I'd lost you because of her."

"Don't be silly," Sarah said, conveniently forgetting how close she'd been to complying with Maman-joon's request. "You could never lose me."

As Ali smiled at Sarah in response, flashing headlights behind them announced that their parents had arrived. Ali started off with the two cars behind them.

The parking lot's exit onto Khodami Street was blocked by a huddle of unkempt young men gesturing to a tall, slim man Sarah recognized as her cousin Sadegh, Aunt Mehri's youngest child.

Sadegh held out a hand to command Ali to stop as he continued listening to the men around him.

"What's up?" Ali asked Sarah as he traced delicious circles on the inside of Sarah's palm with his thumb.

"*Nemidoonam.* I have no idea. These must be some of Sadegh's Basiji men. Maybe something's happened."

Ali rolled down the window, let go of Sarah's hand, and leaned his head out of the car. *"Agha Sadegh, ejaze mifarmayid?* Would it be possible for us to pass by?"

No answer.

"Agha Sadegh, I'm sorry to interrupt you. Would you mind stepping to the side?" Ali tried again.

Sadegh glanced toward their car and lifted a long finger to signal they were to keep waiting as he carried on with his men.

"What exactly does he do with them?" Ali asked Sarah.

"Who knows? One of his friends, an old teacher of his, I think, is with the Basij and Sadegh helps out. Sometimes they do checkpoints or break up those parties with alcohol and drugs and stuff. These days I guess they're doing things related to the demonstrations, but I don't know why they're outside a wedding. Did you see him in the men's section, or has he been outside the whole time?"

Ali shrugged. "I can't remember, azizam. There were so many people in there."

Sarah wished Ali would take her hand again. She could still feel a slight tingle from where his fingers had been interlaced with hers.

After a brief pause, Sarah continued, "Sadegh would probably go full-time with the Basij if he didn't have to run the family shops. He's just like Aunt Mehri." Sarah shook her head with irritation. "He loves telling people what to do."

"Shhh. *Mishnaveh* . . . he'll hear you," Ali warned, reminding Sarah that the car window was still down.

But Sadegh was still busy with the men, who were now listening as he gave orders. Sarah watched as he leaned into an aggressive posture and suddenly grabbed the man in front of him. Sadegh bunched the man's shirt into his fist and pulled him close as he yelled something that Sarah couldn't make out. Then he pushed the man away and stalked toward their vehicle.

Sadegh leaned into Ali's window. "Sorry to keep you waiting," he said in a gruff voice that belied his slim frame. Then he took a breath and changed his tone. "I wanted to give my congratulations to the new couple."

Ali answered, "*Mersi*, Mr. Sadegh. Thank you so much."

Sarah didn't like how deferential Ali's voice sounded. She bit her teeth and kept quiet.

Noting Sarah's silence, Sadegh congratulated her again, "*Mobaraket*, my cousin, may the two of you grow old together."

Sarah nodded her head slightly and managed a cold smile, "*Mersi, mahremat ziyad*," she said, using the overly formal words of thanks to indicate her irritation in a subtle Iranian way. She was desperate to get out of the parking lot and to her new home where she and her husband could begin their life together, and she was furious with Sadegh for delaying them further. It was hard to remember that there was ever a time that she'd actually had a crush on her cousin. She'd been fourteen years old, and Sadegh seemed so smart and handsome, not to mention the fact that he was one of the only marriageable males she regularly interacted with. The crush had been short-lived. When Sadegh complained to his mother, Aunt Mehri, that Sarah was flirting with him, the ensuing humiliation was enough to transform her budding attraction into a dislike bordering on hate.

Sadegh continued looking at Sarah in a pointed, almost inappropriate manner. Sarah returned his gaze steadily. In the dark, the pale green eyes that Sarah had once found so mesmerizing seemed to give off a light of their own. Sarah silently cursed him as she held the stare defiantly. Couldn't he just let them go?

Sadegh stroked his beard. "My mother and Sumayeh left early. What happened in there?" he asked.

Perhaps if the day hadn't been quite so long, if she'd managed to eat or drink something, or if her corset wasn't trying to strangle her at the waist, Sarah's answer would have been more typically polite. As it was, she surprised herself and her new husband by snarling. "Nothing happened! Aunt Mehri ruined my wedding, that's all. Now can we go?"

Ali laughed nervously, "*Ey baba* . . . the wedding wasn't ruined. There was a . . . misunderstanding. And I hope the poor *bandeye khoda* didn't get hurt when—"

Sadegh's eyes had darkened to a deep teal. He cut Ali off abruptly. "*Kheyle khob*, okay. I'm sorry to have taken your time."

Sadegh backed away from the car and signaled to his men to move out of the way. Then he turned back to the new couple. "Be careful out there tonight. Avoid Modarres Highway and take Valiasr Boulevard and you should be fine."

"Mersi, agha Sadegh," Ali responded as he bowed his head repeatedly.

Sadegh inclined his head in farewell, and the small caravan exited the parking lot.

*   *   *

But Sadegh was wrong. Just north of Vanak Square, traffic slowed to a snail's pace.

"If we can get to the next alleyway," Ali said, "I'll head into the neighborhoods and see if we can find a way around this mess. Call our parents and let them know."

Cellphone service had become unpredictable since the election unrest, and none of Sarah's calls would go through. They turned to use hand signals to communicate their intent and realized that the car behind them belonged to neither set of parents.

Ali decided to try the shortcut anyway. Their parents would be able to find their own way through the snarl, and they'd meet up again at the home they were being chaperoned to.

Theirs wasn't the only car to ditch the main streets for the alleyways. Traffic was still heavy, but at least moved forward by yards instead of mere inches. For almost ten minutes, they weaved and wound through one side street after another before coming to a full stop on a one-way alley just south of Esfandiar."

Ali switched off the car.

"We're low on gas," he explained.

The night's heat began to seep into their air-conditioned bubble. Sarah tried to distract herself by flipping down the sun visor and examining herself in the mirror. The makeup artist had done a good job. Sarah liked how she'd used shading and false eyelashes to make her small slanted eyes look so much bigger. With her mother's eyes and her father's flat nose, Sarah had an almost East Asian look, like that Japanese Iranian girl, Roxana, who'd been jailed for spying.

She flipped up the sun visor and loosened her chador to let some air in. Sarah had never been a particularly sweaty girl. Even in black coverings on a simmering August day, a bit of dampness under her arms was all her body produced. Tonight, however, she seemed to be suffocating in rivers of perspiration. The soaked silk of her corset wrapped around her like a boa constrictor intent on squeezing the breath out of her, and the awkward satin chador added another layer of insulation hugging the heat to her body. She envied Ali, who had not only shed his suit jacket but also rolled up his sleeves and undone the top buttons on his shirt.

The muggy air was made more oppressive by the fact that they were hopelessly stuck in this narrow alleyway with cars and buildings pressing against them from all sides, blocking any conceivable escape route. For a moment, Sarah wondered if she might faint.

She was distracted by the sight of a young woman hurrying in their direction from up ahead. The girl didn't wear a chador but had a black *maghnaeh* head covering, the type Sarah had worn in high school, that was paired with a black, relatively long manteau worn over jeans and white tennis shoes.

Sarah wondered whether the girl was a driver who'd abandoned her trapped car in frustration. But why was she breathing so heavily, moving in such a hurry, and looking over her shoulder so frequently? And then, suddenly, she wasn't the only one. Dozens of young people were now moving swiftly through the alleyway, turning sideways to squeeze between vehicles, leaping over hoods, and maneuvering the mashup of cars like water over a pebbled surface.

With a jolt of adrenaline, Sarah realized they were afraid. They were running from something. Or someone.

It didn't take long to identify their pursuers. Looking further up the street, Sarah could see the black-clad riot police, batons swinging, moving methodically down the alleyway.

As the police came closer, the stream of runners became eddied and confused. The girl Sarah had first seen, who'd run past them seconds earlier, passed them again but in the opposite direction.

"Ali, what are they yelling?" Sarah asked.

Ali cracked the window to listen, but visual clues proved to be more enlightening. Through the rear window, Sarah saw a new group of police rounding the corner into the alleyway from the southern end. The demonstrators were trapped.

The newlyweds watched in silence as the young people's faces registered their situation and they began searching the walls, the alleyway, the skies, for some escape. Sarah watched them pound on doors—some of which eventually opened—begging for admittance. A garbage dumpster became sudden home to three young men, while others tried to hide under cars. The girl in the black manteau and *maghnaeh* simply stood still in front of their Benz, resignation mixed with defiance settling on her face. She saw Sarah watching and nodded her head slightly in greeting.

The girl was beautiful. Her light-green eyes shone in the dark much as Sadegh's had just an hour ago. But hers were further accentuated by well-sculpted eyebrows, cheekbones so prominent they left hollow spaces beneath them, and perfectly shaped lips. How could someone so exquisitely beautiful have gotten mixed up with these rioters? Sarah felt certain it must have been a mistake or a bad twist of fate. Maybe she was in love with one of the young men. Or maybe she was just in the wrong place at the wrong time. All Sarah knew with absolute certainty was that the girl didn't deserve whatever the security forces would be meting out. The panic that the girl refused to show began to rise in Sarah's own throat.

"Ali," Sarah whispered with urgency, "let her in the car!"

Her husband's eyes were wide as he looked at her. "What? Are you sure?"

"Yes, yes! Hurry, oh God, please hurry!"

Ali unlocked the doors, and Sarah used her eyes and eyebrows to direct the girl, who was still looking at her calmly, toward the car's back door. The girl took a moment to comprehend the lifeline that had been extended before dropping to the ground, crawling along the length of the Benz to reach the back door, and then clambering inside.

"Mersi!" she whispered.

"Stay low," Ali warned the girl. "The windows are tinted, but someone still might be able to see you."

Outside, the scene proceeded with surprising calm. The police at the south end of the alley were sweeping the operation, flushing the runners out of their hiding places and prodding them forward. At the north end of the alley, their comrades were lining the young men and women up against the wall and escorting groups of them back toward the intersection where, Sarah assumed, police minibuses were waiting to take them to Evin Prison.

The southern line of police moved northward, ever closer to their car. Sarah looked to the back seat and saw the girl crouched down with Ali's jacket over her face. She wondered how well the inside of their car was concealed and whether it would be obvious that the girl was one of the demonstrators. She wondered, with a start, whether the danger she'd feared for the girl was now a possibility for herself and Ali. Surely, even if they found the girl, the police would realize they were simply newlyweds on their way home and had nothing to do with these rioters. Perhaps they could claim they hadn't even noticed her crawling in to begin with? Was it too late and too cruel to ask the girl to leave? What had she been thinking, Sarah admonished herself, to insert herself and her husband into this mess?

Black sleeves and baton-wielding hands could be seen out of the driver's-side window. A twin pair of sleeves, hands, and batons passed on the right. Both were followed by more of the same as the police line streamed around their car. Sarah tensed, waiting for a rap on the window or door that would indicate one of these black-clad men had noticed the girl.

But they all moved on without stopping.

Relieved, Sarah released the breath she hadn't realized she'd been holding.

"*Raftan*," Ali announced with his own exhale. "They're gone."

"Oh my God," the girl whispered from the back seat. "Thank you so much. God bless you both. Okay. I'll slip out now."

"Why don't we give you a ride?" Sarah offered. She was feeling generous again now that the danger had passed.

"No thanks," the girl declined as she opened the back door. "I don't live far. I'll get there faster walking. God grant you a long and happy marriage. Thank you again."

When she was gone, Sarah wished she'd asked the girl's name. It would be nice to have a name when telling this story. Sarah could already imagine how impressed her school chums would be by her brush with danger.

"You okay, azizam?" Ali reached over and pinched her cheek softly.

"Is life with you always going to be this eventful?" Sarah teased her husband. "What a wedding night!"

"Just you wait and see what I've got planned once we get—"

Ali's rejoinder was interrupted by the sound of the door opening again. Sarah looked to see if the girl had returned to the car before realizing that it was actually the driver's door that had opened.

A burly man with an ample belly, unkempt black curly hair, and disturbingly red eyes had opened the driver's-side door and was looking in.

His voice was soft and respectful. "*Agha befarmayeed payeen.* Please get out of your vehicle."

Ali protested "*Yanni chi?* What do you mean? What for?"

"*Befarmayeed payeen!* Out! I don't want to ask it again."

Ali stepped out, still protesting "This is crazy. We're just trying to get home from our wedding, and we got stuck in traffic that you people created. And now you're giving us a hard time over nothing. *Vellemoon kon.* Leave us be!"

Sarah watched the red-eyed man pass Ali on to another plain-clothes Basiji and return to the car. Her heart raced as he sat in the driver's seat, fiddling with levers to move the seat back and make room for his belly. Sarah noticed food stains on his beige button-up shirt and dirt-colored pajama-like slacks.

"*Bebakhshid khahar.* I'm sorry, my sister," he finally addressed Sarah, "but who was the girl that just left your car?"

Sarah's heart beat so violently against her corset she thought it might snap. She wasn't prepared for this. She'd never been a good liar, and even if she was, she and Ali hadn't coordinated a story. Should she take a stab at making something up? As she thought through her options, the man spoke again.

"You should know that my friend is asking your husband the same thing."

What could she say? What answer would deliver them? She couldn't breathe. She really was going to faint.

A long sigh from the red-eyed man. "*Khob*. I think I understand."

The man rubbed his forehead. "But what should I do with you two? A bride and groom. Why did you have to involve yourselves?"

Sarah didn't have an answer. She had no idea what had possessed her to think letting that girl into their car was a good idea. It had been an impetuous decision. There was something about the beautiful girl's gaze that had mesmerized her. And it was the first time Sarah had felt connected to one of the nameless protesters she'd heard so much about. But it wasn't as if she had any sympathy for what the protesters were doing to their country. She just felt sorry for that one girl.

The man opened the door, set one foot out and then turned back to her.

"Do you know how to drive?"

Yes, Sarah did.

"Once this traffic clears up, head straight home. Mobile phones won't work tonight, so just go straight home to your family."

"What about my husband?" Sarah asked in a small voice. A part of her wanted to shriek at this dirty, unkempt, and uneducated man that he had no right to detain her husband and that under normal circumstances he would be lucky if Ali hired him to be his office water boy. But she was scared. She didn't want to make things worse.

"Listen to what I say," the man sighed. "Just go straight home. Don't wait for him."

Sarah did as she was told.

CHAPTER 2

Friday, June 26, 2009—fourteen days after the election

If after every election, the losers take to the streets to protest and then the winners take to the streets in response, then what is the point of holding an election?

The use of force in the streets since the election is wrong. Because it goes against the principle of democracy and the will of the people. I want everyone to put an end to this behavior. If they do not, then the consequences are theirs to bear.

—Supreme Leader Khamenei in his first Friday prayer speech after the 2009 election

Sadegh's mother greeted him at the door.

"Sadegh-joon, *kojai*? Where've you been? You're late."

Maman-Mehri held the house phone delicately within a folded Kleenex, as she often did as a protection against germs. She wore a breezy sky-blue house chador draped loosely around and framing a black headscarf, long-sleeved blouse, and skirt. As always, the air around her carried the saffron smell of her kitchen and the rosewater of her prayer rug.

"*Bebakhshid*, Maman-Mehri," Sadegh answered his mother as he helped Sumayeh and the kids inside. "I'm so sorry. Traffic is awful. Everyone's headed to Friday prayers."

"It's okay, azizam. I'm just glad you could take time to visit your mother. Between your work at the shop and with your Basiji friends, you don't seem to have time for me anymore." Sadegh tried to protest but Maman-Mehri kept talking over him as she greeted Sumayeh and the children, but not her son, with kisses. "*Salam*, Sumayeh-joon. Salam, little ones. Everyone's in the living room. Go on in while I finish talking to your Aunt Mahdiyeh. Don't forget to wash your hands!"

Sadegh's mother walked back toward the kitchen, returning the telephone to her ear.

"She's talking to Mahdiyeh?" Sumayeh asked. "Praise God, maybe Sarah and her mother called to apologize," Sumayeh said as she awkwardly removed her heavy black outside chador and unfolded her green-patterned house chador, all while balancing their baby daughter Sana on her hip.

Sadegh knelt to help five-year-old Mahdi remove the Nike shoes Sumayeh's mother had purchased for her grandson during her most recent visit with family in Ohio. "Maman-Mehri is too forgiving for her own good," he said. "Aunt Mahdiyeh better make a proper apology. I swear, If I'd known the full story last night, I'd have . . ." Sadegh got stuck as he tried to figure out what he would have done and simply frowned and shook his head to indicate it would have been bad.

The baby in Sumayeh's arms was now throwing her body weight toward the floor in a suicidal attempt to get down to where she could practice her new toddling skills. Sadegh took her from Sumayeh so his wife could settle into her new wrappings. Mahdi zoomed off to find his cousins, while Sadegh, Sumayeh, and the baby proceeded toward the living room, where the rest of the family was gathered around a coffee table laden with fruit, nuts, and Iranian baklava made with pistachios. Sadegh's three older siblings and their spouses rose and offered kisses, handshakes, or nods of the head, depending on the gender composition and relationship of each greeting duo.

"So did you hear?" Sadegh's eldest sister Zainab practically crowed. "Ali got arrested last night."

Sadegh's eyebrows rose. "Sarah's husband? When? What did he do?" Sadegh's mind flashed on a picture of Ali, still in his wedding finery, throwing a Molotov cocktail.

Zainab angled back into her chair and grabbed a handful of pistachios. "Ah, that whole family is involved with this Green group. It was only a matter of time before they caught up with him."

Sadegh's second sister, Fatimeh, spoke up. "It might not be that. Mahdiyeh said that they got stuck in a group of protesters. Maybe it was a mistake." As usual, Fatimeh's voice was hesitant as if afraid permission to speak might be withdrawn at any moment.

Sadegh grunted his disagreement. "People don't get arrested by mistake. He must have done something." Sadegh took a few juicy nectarines from the big bowl of fruit on the coffee table and started cutting them in pieces to share.

"God! I can't believe we're related to these people!" Zainab exclaimed.

Sadegh couldn't help cringing at his sister's words even as he agreed with her sentiment. Calling God's name in this way was common practice in Iran, even among religious families. Sumayeh, however, in what was perhaps a holdover from her mother's Christian upbringing, felt strongly that it was disrespectful, and Sadegh and his family generally tried to respect her wishes in this regard.

But Zainab was right. It was incredible that Sarah would insist

on marrying someone whose family had been stoking the very fires
that Sadegh's friends were risking their lives fighting. Sadegh had
heard firsthand accounts of the violent mobs who had dared to
attack Basij safe houses. Even Sarah, a girl who was known to make
jokes during mourning ceremonies commemorating the deaths of
religious figures, should be able to see that this was serious.

"Maybe not," Fatimeh spoke up again.

Zainab narrowed her hawk eyes on Fatimeh. "How's that?"

"Well . . ." Fatimeh looked to the right and left as if to ensure
children's ears weren't present. "Mahdiyeh said they never got to
his house. Sarah slept at her parents' last night."

The sisters exchanged meaningful glances and Sadegh thought
about the implications of Fatimeh's words. Sadegh was pretty sure
the marriage would have been formally registered into Sarah and
Ali's identification documents. But if the new couple separated
before—well, Sadegh didn't like to think about it, but—before
they consummated the marriage, Sarah should be able to remarry
easily enough with little harm done. Sadegh wondered whether
Ali's arrest would be enough for Sarah to finally understand what
her husband was mixed up in.

"Where were they when they got picked up?" Sadegh asked
as he arranged the pieces of nectarine on a small appetizer plate,
took a couple for himself, and then passed them around to share.

Fatimeh was clearly pleased at her inside information. She
blinked her bovine lashes as she answered. "In the alleyways,
across from Park Mellat. *Bichareha*, the poor kids hadn't even
gotten five kilometers from the hotel. *Albate*, I don't know why
they went that way. Valiasr Street is always a mess on weekends,
even without the protests."

Sadegh took a moment to digest this along with another piece
of nectarine. He'd been irritated with Sarah when he'd suggested
she and Ali take Valiasr to get home from the wedding. He knew

from reports coming in that it was flooded with protesters and figured sitting in snarled traffic would serve Sarah right for whatever
had happened to make Maman-Mehri leave the wedding early,
not to mention the disrespectful way she'd spoken to him. But
perhaps the impulse had been more divinely inspired than he'd
known. Clearly it had created the opportunity for his comrades
to arrest Ali. Sadegh wondered what Ali had done or what he'd
been wanted for.

"*Bacheha*, I'm so sorry. That took longer than I thought."
Maman-Mehri's phone call had ended, and she joined them in the
living room as she spoke. "Let's eat. You all must be starving."

"*Hala* . . . what did Mahdiyeh say?" Zainab asked what
everyone was wondering.

"At the table," Maman-Mehri promised.

*   *   *

The children were called from various corners of the house.
Sadegh washed Mahdi's hands and got him settled at the children's table in the kitchen, where Fatimeh and Zainab's girls, as
the oldest cousins, would watch over the little ones with the help
of Soghra-*khanoom*, Maman-Mehri's live-in servant. The baby,
too young and difficult to be left in the kitchen with her cousins,
was already in the dining room with Sumayeh.

Sadegh left the kitchen and followed his mother through
the short hallway into the dining room. Just inside the entryway,
Maman-Mehri's indoor sandals caught on the fringed edge of
the thick carpet. She might have successfully righted herself, but,
instead, she twisted violently away from Sadegh's instinctively out-
reached hand. She toppled over—carefully protecting the knee she
had hurt in the previous night's fall—and Sadegh's brother Alireza
jumped out of his chair and pushed forward to help her up.

"Oh! What did I do!" Maman-Mehri straightened her scarf and chador as Alireza brought her slowly to her feet.

"Oh my goodness! What can I say?" she gasped. "Look at me, I'm such an old lady now. I can't even walk right! *Mersi, Alireza. Sadegh-jaan, mersi, azizam.*"

Maman-Mehri dropped Alireza's hand as soon as she was stable. She continued to thank Sadegh profusely. And as soon as they sat to begin their meal, she made a point of serving him first.

Sadegh understood. But, as always happened on those rare occasions when the difference between himself and Alireza was forced to the surface, he was stung by the reminder that he was not, in fact, Maman-Mehri's son.

*   *   *

Maman-Mehri shook her head and said, "Mahdiyeh is a mess, poor thing," in answer to Zainab's repetition of her earlier question about their aunt.

The nine of them sat around the French-style rococo dining table in their usual configuration. Maman-Mehri was at the head of the table where she could observe and converse with everyone and also call orders to Soghra-khanoom in the kitchen as needed. Along the right side of the table sat Sadegh and Alireza flanked by their wives, with Sumayeh sitting beside Maman-Mehri. Zainab sat to Maman-Mehri's left followed by her husband, Fatimeh's husband, and then Fatimeh who sat across from Alireza's wife. The chair at the very end of the table was empty but, as always, a place was set in memoriam of Maman-Mehri's late and beloved husband who had died nearly fifteen years ago.

"Mr. Ali's parents have been looking for him all night," Maman-Mehri continued as she filled plates with the delicious *lubia polo* of lamb, green beans, and tomatoes mixed into lightly spiced rice. She used a silver *kafkir* rice-serving spoon that came from the new shipment of utensils Sadegh and his brother had just imported for sale at their kitchenware stores. "They went to Vozara, Evin, and police stations but haven't been able to get any information. Mrs. Rahimi, Mr. Ali's mother, and her daughter went to Mahdiyeh's house this morning to pressure her into letting Sarah go with them—Sadegh, hand me Alireza's plate. They think people might be more sympathetic to a new bride looking for her husband. But I told Mahdiyeh"—Maman-Mehri paused to shake her finger for emphasis—"not to allow it." Maman-Mehri resumed filling plates. "And she was smart enough to keep Sarah sleeping, so she didn't even see them. Our only chance of ending this thing is to keep Sarah away from that family."

With no more dishes to fill, Maman-Mehri set the serving spoon down and lifted a hand to her chest. She closed her eyes briefly and took a deep breath. "Oh, my children, God is big. Never doubt it. Last night I was heartbroken! Mahdiyeh was making a horrible mistake. These Green Wave people are a danger to our society. A danger to Islam! And, not that it's important, but naturally I was a little hurt about the way I'd been treated. But see how God"—Maman-Mehri pointed to the ceiling—"intervened to save Sarah and make things right. And Mahdiyeh called this morning to beg my forgiveness. It is all due to faith and prayer. The one thing I ask of you—as your mother, who has the right to ask anything—is to hold tight to your faith and worship and never forget God, so that you will always enjoy his protection the way that I have throughout my life. Now, what are you waiting for? Eat, eat, before the food gets cold."

Sumayeh was touched. "Mersi, Maman-Mehri. I feel so blessed to have such a mother-in-law, whose only request of us is for our own benefit."

Sadegh agreed and felt ashamed at his momentary hurt.

Maman-Mehri was a devout and devoted servant of God who had done more for him than he deserved to expect. He had been only a little older than Sana, who was playing in Sumayeh's lap, when his own mother, his father's second wife, had abandoned him. But Maman-Mehri had raised him with so much love and special attention that his older siblings had sometimes resentfully referred to her as *Maman-e-Sadegh* or "Mother of Sadegh." It was only out of an overabundance of religious caution that she began avoiding physical contact with him once he became a man at the age of fifteen. And it was only then that Sadegh had learned she wasn't his mother by blood.

Under the table, Sadegh squeezed his wife's knee discreetly to indicate his thanks and approval of her words. She looked at him and smiled. The baby in her lap was unusually calm, sucking her thumb contentedly and reaching her other hand up, as had become her habit, to trace the jagged and jarring purple scar that dominated the right side of Sumayeh's face. Sumayeh took hold of the pudgy hand and put it to her lips for a kiss. Again, Sadegh reproached himself for his childishness. With such a woman by his side, how could he ever feel sorry for himself?

Sadegh's attention turned to Zainab, who was asking questions as everyone else dug into lunch. "I still don't understand what made Mahdiyeh change her mind. Last night she acted like she couldn't care less about us when she sided with that Azar."

Maman-Mehri pointed skyward again to indicate it was God's intercession, but it was Fatimeh who answered, "Zainab dear, I'm not sure you're being entirely fair." Fatimeh's slow, soft voice had become strained and high-pitched as it always did on those rare occasions that she dared to disagree with her older sister. "She couldn't just leave all her guests and go with you. But she did talk to Sarah and tried to convince her to call things off even in the middle of the wedding. It's just, well, Maman-Mehri, I'm sure she explained to you that Sarah, well," Fatimeh appeared a bit flustered as she went on, "she and Ali were . . . well, Sarah thinks she's in love with the boy. She refused to listen."

Zainab's eyes narrowed on Fatimeh in a way that cinched her narrow face even further. "She and Ali were . . . what?" she asked.

Fatimeh didn't say anything but stared at her sister stupidly for a long second.

Maman-Mehri intervened with a disapproving look at her younger daughter, "You shouldn't have brought it up in front of everyone." Fatimeh started and ducked her head. "But, yes, it's true," Maman-Mehri continued. "Mahdiyeh told me all about it just now. Sarah was *talking* alone on the phone with this boy all along and had gotten . . . attached."

Sadegh shook his head in disgust. He shouldn't be surprised. Sarah's character in this regard was obvious from the time she was barely a teenager and had flirted so shamelessly with him that he'd felt obliged to tell his mother. He would have hoped she'd have learned some propriety since then, but clearly she hadn't.

"I know it isn't easy Zainab dear," Maman-Mehri continued. "Especially after the way I was treated, but we must be forgiving. I can truthfully say that I am completely over my hurt feelings and am only worried for Mahdiyeh. Up until last night she was willing to tolerate that family for Sarah's sake, but now that she can see what they are, she is looking for any way to end it. Oh, I forgot to tell you. That horrible woman, Ali-agha's sister, that divorce lawyer, actually implied that I had something to do with her brother's arrest and that his being taken in was a way of getting revenge for my treatment at the wedding. These people are crazy!"

Sadegh felt the blood rush to his face with anger. He wasn't sure what he found more disgusting. The implication that the Basij would arrest someone for no good reason, or the woman's pretension that her family had done nothing worthy of arrest;

this despite the fact that everyone knew her husband had been involved with Mousavi and his campaign.

"Clearly, I've been disappointed with Mrs. Rahimi," Maman-Mehri was saying. "I'm heartbroken to see how she's allowed her children to fall under the influence of these Western ideas. But I absolutely won't allow that rot into our own family!" Maman-Mehri slapped the table with her crooked fingers.

Then she softened. "But I do feel for her. Sadegh, maybe you could ask and see what the story is. Where are they keeping Ali? What exactly did he do? And when and where will there be a trial?"

Sadegh didn't like the idea. "What difference does it make? And why should we involve ourselves to try to help these people? Anyone involved with this Green group deserves what they get."

Maman-Mehri reached out and stroked Sumayeh's arm as a proxy for touching her adopted son. "We must be compassionate my dear, even to our enemies."

Sadegh shook his head. "I don't know . . ." Sadegh was interrupted by the sound of the cuckoo clock. He looked up at the hand-carved home out of which a little bird flew three times to announce the hour as the weight driving its movement traveled down the wall. Sadegh's father had bought the clock for Maman-Mehri during a business trip to Switzerland almost thirty years ago. With its warm wooden color, Sadegh thought it looked out of place in the formal white marble dining room. But Maman-Mehri adored it and dusted and wound the clock herself every week without fail. Besides, Sadegh knew he didn't have much of an eye for decorating.

The cuckoo bird returned to its home for the last time just as Sadegh was deciding it wouldn't hurt to ask a few questions about Ali's whereabouts. "Okay," he said, "I'll go see Ganjian this evening and see what I can find out."

Ganjian was Sadegh's old high school teacher at the K–12

private school he'd attended with the sons of other wealthy, religious, and politically connected families. He was one of Sadegh's favorite teachers, and his good nature, sincere devotion to Islam, and life of service had inspired Sadegh's own piety. He'd left full-time teaching a few years back to rejoin the Basij unit he'd worked with during the war, which was now tasked with ensuring security in Tehran, but he kept in touch with Sadegh and some of his other former students. Sadegh supported Ganjian's unit financially as much as he could and also liked to pitch in and help the men on the ground whenever possible. Since the election, that had been most nights and weekends.

Maman-Mehri squeezed Sumayeh's hand as she smiled at Sadegh. "Thank you, my son," she said gently before resuming her usual tone. "Now eat something. You're as skinny as a light pole."

* * *

It was late afternoon before Sadegh and his little family got in the car to head home. Lulled by the hum of the engine, the children promptly fell asleep in the car seats Sumayeh's mother had brought from the US, where it seemed, children used them until they were nearly old enough to drive.

Sumayeh reached across the gearshift and laid a gentle hand on his thigh. Sadegh covered her hand with his and smiled at his wife. He enjoyed watching the dimple in her unmarred cheek appear as she returned his smile, and he admired her small Western nose with the slightly upturned end that betrayed her mixed heritage. From this perspective, Sadegh couldn't see Sumayeh's scar but knew it was still there as a silent reminder of the strength of his wife's devotion.

It had happened near the end of the long war with Iraq when a wailing siren indicated that the evening's installment of Scud missiles was arriving earlier than usual. As was her habit, twelve-year-old Sumayeh refused to interrupt her prayers to head to the basement shelter. Her face was turned up in *dua* and supplication when the windows shattered and a particularly large shard of glass sliced her forehead, but—in a clear sign of divine favor—narrowly missed her eye on its way through her cheek, mouth, and chin.

Many years later, when Sadegh heard Sumayeh's story from his sisters, he recognized the same self-sacrificial obedience to God that he had seen in the war heroes he looked up to and the Basijis he worked with. Like Ganjian and his colleagues, Sumayeh had put her body and even her life in jeopardy as she worshiped God and sought to implement his will. Sadegh determined immediately that this was the woman he would marry and refused to be dissuaded by warnings that Sumayeh was older than him by four years, was likely to have picked up some strange habits from her American mother, and would have that ugly scar long after Sadegh's initial fancy had passed.

In seven years of marriage Sadegh had never regretted his choice. He trusted and respected his wife and was happy to let her take the lead in determining the shape of their domestic lives together even when—as in the case of her strictness with the children—he disagreed. She was a benevolent dictator who loved him and their children fiercely and was the spiritual heart of the family. Sadegh felt himself truly blessed.

Sumayeh shifted in her seat. "Mahdi noticed what happened with Maman-Mehri today," she said.

Sadegh removed his hand momentarily from Sumayeh's to shift to a lower gear and then returned to stroking her wrist and fingers, which were even more thin and delicate than Sadegh's own.

"What do you mean?" he asked, though he suspected he knew the answer.

"When she pulled away from you," Sumayeh explained

patiently. "It's only a matter of time before he starts to ask why his grandmother won't touch his father."

Sadegh shrugged to indicate he didn't think it was a big deal. "So we'll just explain it to him."

Sumayeh pulled her hand from his and turned sideways in her seat to face him. Sadegh could tell she didn't appreciate her concerns being dismissed. "Sadegh, how is he going to feel when he grows up and Maman-Mehri starts avoiding him too? And it just doesn't make any sense. There is absolutely no religious reason for Maman-Mehri to be avoiding physical contact."

Sumayeh was right. According to Islam, all of a man's children were *mahram* to all of his wives, meaning that since, like brother and sister or father and daughter, they couldn't marry, there was no risk from or prohibition on their nonsexual interactions. Sadegh had pointed this out to Maman-Mehri himself when the story of his unusual parentage had come out.

Maman-Mehri had been more flustered and uncomfortable than Sadegh had ever seen her before or since. "You're right Sadegh-jaan." She pressed her lips together as she spoke and swallowed several times as if chewing her words first would make them easier to spit out. "It's just that I can't be sure your father, God bless his soul, was actually, well, officially married when you were conceived. Or even, forgive me, that you were really his. That woman," Maman-Mehri's voice hardened as she changed topics, "was poison, Sadegh-jaan, pure poison. She bewitched your father, tricked him into feeling sorry for her, and attached herself to him to get at his money." Maman-Mehri frowned and shook her head in disgust as she spat, "I can only imagine what else she tricked him into."

Sadegh turned onto Hemmat Highway and came to an abrupt stop in the bumper-to-bumper traffic it contained. He leaned forward and hugged the steering wheel to stretch his back.

Their Honda Accord was roomier than most Iranian cars but still wasn't entirely comfortable for Sadegh's long frame.

Sadegh turned to look at Sumayeh. "Sumayeh, you know how Maman-Mehri is with all her extra prayers and fasting," he said. "She always likes to do more than is required just to make sure she isn't inadvertently violating God's will. And . . ." Traffic started moving again, so Sadegh sat back and put the car in gear. "Well, I think she's afraid I might be *haramzadeh*."

"What?" Sumayeh gave a small laugh of disbelief.

"She thinks my birth mother may have already been pregnant when my father married her. Does it bother you that you might be married to a *haramzadeh*?" Sadegh teased his wife. His voice was light, but there was a time when he'd been terrified at the thought that he might be a bastard and had started doing additional prayers and *duas* to scrub his soul of whatever sin might have been passed down from his uncertain parentage.

"Don't be silly," Sumayeh answered. "That's an Iranian thing not a Muslim thing. No one is to be judged for the sins of another, least of all an innocent baby."

Sadegh smiled. Sumayeh's mother often claimed in her American-accented Farsi that true Islam was more easily found in America, where it was shorn of cultural influences that polluted its pure essence. While Sadegh sometimes found her comments on the topic to be irritating, now he was grateful for her influence on his wife's thinking.

"Sumayeh, azizam. Have I told you that I love you?"

"Twice so far today."

"So you're tired of hearing it then?"

"Never."

He told her that he adored her, and she leaned across the gearshift to rest her head on his shoulder.

But Sumayeh wasn't finished.

"It doesn't matter to me Sadegh, but it will matter for Mahdi and Sana. I'm going to talk to Maman-Mehri about it myself. Maybe she just needs some help to think this through."

Sumayeh's head still rested on Sadegh's shoulder and he twisted his neck to give her chador-covered forehead a kiss. Sumayeh and Maman-Mehri were extremely close, and Sadegh figured she had as good a chance as any to change Maman-Mehri's mind. But he had his doubts.

There was something in the way that Maman-Mehri had talked to him so many years ago that made him think her choice to observe the *hijab* in front of him stemmed from something more than her usual overzealousness. "Sadegh-jaan," she'd said quietly, "you are the greatest blessing of my entire life. Your father's betrayal . . . well, it almost broke me. But you healed our family in so many ways. The years after you came and before your father's death were the sweetest of my life. You can't imagine how good he was to me. How sorry he was for his mistakes. Oh, I miss him!

"So you see, you were the answer to my prayers Sadegh-jaan! As painful as this separation is, this distance I have to keep from you, it is a small price to pay for the joy of having you. Do you understand? *Vagh'an*, truly, God is big! He knew I needed you and chose to deliver you in this way to test and strengthen my faith. I would endure much more than this silly hijab to prove my gratitude."

If Maman-Mehri thought of this physical separation from Sadegh as necessary remuneration for God's blessings, Sumayeh was going to have a hard time convincing her to let it go.

Sadegh turned the car into their alley.

"Sumayeh, I'm going to go in tonight. Things are still crazy. And I want to ask about Sarah and Ali. I'll help you get the kids inside and then go."

"No, it's okay. Just drop us off at the door. I can manage the kids."

"But they're asleep. I'll carry Mahdi up."

"No, my love. We'll wake him and he'll walk up on his own two feet. He's a lucky child if this is the worst of his troubles."

Sadegh stopped the car in front of their apartment's garage entrance and got out to help Sumayeh get situated. Mahdi, displeased at being woken from his deep sleep, started crying piteously. Sumayeh spoke to the boy in her typically firm but kind way. "Let's go, my son. Into the house. You can lay down when we get inside."

As Sadegh returned to the car, he wondered briefly whether his wife's ability to tolerate their children's pain stemmed from her mother's American culture or whether her passionate love for God had interrupted and left less room for maternal instincts. Last week when Mahdi had come home from school heartbroken over having lost his brand-new soccer ball, Sadegh had thought he was handling things well when he yelled at his son for being irresponsible but promised to buy him a replacement. Sumayeh, stepping in, had actually hugged their son and expressed sympathy but refused to purchase or allow Sadegh to purchase a new ball. "How will he learn if we protect him from his own mistakes?" she had pointed out. But Sadegh wasn't so sure. Wasn't protecting children from mistakes part of the basic job description of being a good parent? And he was pretty sure that his scolding had made an impression so wasn't that learning enough?

Sadegh turned on the radio and flipped through channels, stopping for what sounded like a replay of the Friday prayer sermon he had missed.

"Anybody who fights against the Islamic system or the leader of Islamic society, we will fight him until complete destruction!"

Yes! Sadegh was glad to hear such stern words. The enemies of the beloved supreme leader should know his defenders were not afraid to spill blood. Mousavi would deserve whatever he got!

Sadegh's heart burned for Iran and Islam, which had so often been sacrificed and betrayed by self-interested politicians pandering to foreign interests. It was unbelievable that Mousavi, who'd actually led the Islamic Republic as Prime Minister during the brutal years of Iraqi attacks, could turn around and serve the very Western powers that had provided Saddam Hossein with the missiles and chemical weapons that had been used to kill and maim millions of Iranians like Sumayeh. Sadegh wondered what the man had been promised for changing his loyalties and what price could possibly be worth the hellfire that was surely awaiting him.

What bothered Sadegh most about Green Wave leaders was the way they perverted Islam to lead people astray. Last week Sadegh had spent an evening with his Basiji comrades banging on doors and warning people against shouting 'Allahu Akbar! God is Great!' from their rooftops in support of the demonstrations. Sadegh would never forgive the leaders of this *fitneh* for putting him in the position of having to prevent people from chanting such a blessed phrase by making it a rallying cry in support of the Green Wave.

Traffic was unusually light, and Sadegh arrived at the Kaj roundabout quickly. He parked in front of the bank that was housed in the outer arm of Sa'adat Abad Mosque on Sarv Street. As he walked toward the entrance, he took a moment to appreciate the beauty of the various shades of blue in the mosque's dome, minarets, and tile work that were set against the slightly dingy yellow bricks out of which the structure, like so many in Tehran, was built. Sadegh's artistic tastes tended toward the *dahati* or unrefined. He loved color, the brighter and more varied the better. When he was twelve and had chosen bright-red village *qelims* to decorate his bedroom, Zainab had complained that it hurt her eyes to go into his room.

Sadegh removed his shoes at the mosque's entrance and moved briskly through the main prayer hall toward the stairs leading to the small rooms and offices in the basement. The downstairs corridor was less chaotic than it had been in earlier weeks but was still packed with scruffy-bearded men and assorted boxes of clothes and equipment. The smell of sweaty feet and hairy armpits mingled with that of the weak black tea that was being served and the rosewater that must have been sprinkled recently as part of someone's prayer ablutions. Several young men stood near the doorway of Ganjian's office. Recognizing Sadegh they murmured greetings and stepped aside for him to enter.

Ganjian's thick bare feet were crossed and resting on a battered desk that reminded Sadegh of the one Ganjian sat behind when he was his high school math teacher. Ganjian had been unusual among the staff at Sadegh's elite school for having actually served and even having been injured at the war front. He would sometimes illustrate various math concepts with stories about his experiences. Sadegh remembered a complicated word problem having to do with the amount of gas in a truck's tank, a leak in said tank, and whether much-needed supplies would reach their destination. In real life, apparently, the truck got stranded, and a severely dehydrated Mr. Ganjian desperately took to drinking radiator fluid and almost died.

Ganjian was talking into a cellphone. Seeing Sadegh, he nodded his head briefly, waved him in, and rolled his disturbingly bloodshot eyes to share his irritation at whomever he was on the line with.

"Look, I don't care whose fault it is or what the problem is," Ganjian exclaimed. "You tell him I can't keep these kids another night! We don't have room, and we don't have enough people to guard prisoners. He either sends someone to come get them or I let them go. Simple!"

A pause.

"No! That's not an option! We already got identification on all of them. You can round them up again later if you want. Otherwise, you send a bus by eight p.m. to pick them up. Got it? I have to go."

Ganjian let out a heavy sigh, set the phone on the desk, and stood to shake hands.

"How's the weather up there?" Ganjian teased as Sadegh bent to offer the standard three-cheek kiss of the Basijis. "Every time I see you, you've grown another two inches and gotten thinner around the middle. Doesn't that American wife of yours feed you?"

"You don't look so good yourself," Sadegh teased his mentor back. "Why are your eyes so red?"

"Goddamn pollution and allergies," Ganjian said. "What are you doing here? I told you I'd call if we needed y——"

The cell phone rang.

"*Bebakhshid.* Sorry . . ."

"*Allo?*" Ganjian spoke into the phone as he sat heavily into his chair and gestured that Sadegh should do the same. He roughed a hand through a thick head of curly black hair that had clearly not seen scissors or even shampoo for a while. Not for the first time, Sadegh thought his friend ought to remarry. It was a shame about his first wife. Sadegh thought it was some type of cancer. But that was almost eight years ago. Ganjian should have someone to look after him. Someone to have children with. Sadegh would be lost without Sumayeh.

"What? I can't understand you," Ganjian was saying. "What's that noise? Calm down and tell me what's going on."

Pause.

"Yeah? So go scare them a bit." Ganjian dug a knuckle into his right eye as he spoke. "Show them who's in charge. Figure out who the leaders are and separate them out. Remember, you have all the power. Don't be such a baby."

There was a pause. Sadegh figured Ganjian must be talking to Basijis who were having trouble at the safe house a few blocks away.

He was glad he'd come in.

"Yes, I know. They may have to fast a bit today. These spoiled brats don't have much experience with that, but they'll be fine. You can't let yourself feel sorry for them, or they'll sense weakness. You'll be okay. I'll send a couple guys to help out."

Ganjian set the phone down again and called to the boys by the door. "*Bacheha!* Take one of the motorbikes and go up to the house to help out your buddies. Hurry!"

He turned back to Sadegh. "What a mess! We're still stuck with the guests we brought in on Wednesday."

Sadegh was surprised to hear Ganjian had held several dozen prisoners for almost forty-eight hours. The facility was a small house in a residential neighborhood and had only ever been used to process people before quickly moving them elsewhere.

"They're still here?" Sadegh asked.

"Yeah, it's been a real pain in the ass. No one has room to come get them. But neither do we in that tiny house. And we're out of cash. This morning I bought breakfast for all thirty of them with my own money. Anyway, it doesn't matter. They'll be gone tonight."

"You're out of cash? And you didn't tell me?" Sadegh asked. "How many times do I have to tell you to let me know if funds get low. Especially with what's going on these days, there are a lot of people in the Bazaar who want to help. I'll make a few calls and make sure you've got enough by tonight."

"Mersi, Sadegh-jaan. You're too generous." Ganjian stood up and tucked his cellphone and a small pistol into his pants. "I should go up to the house and check on things. The guys up there don't know what they're doing. You want to come? Why'd you come in anyway?"

"I figured you could use the help," Sadegh said. "And I have something to ask you. Come on, I'll drive you up to the house, and we can talk on the way."

Sadegh told him about Sarah and Ali as they left his office. They climbed the stairs up to the Mosque's main floor and began crossing the deserted prayer hall. As Sadegh described Ali's arrest on the night of their wedding, Ganjian stopped walking, looked at him intently, and cracked a smile.

"Unbelievable! I'm the one that arrested him."

"Really?" Sadegh asked. "What did he do? Or had you already been looking for him?"

"He and his wife were hiding protesters in their car." Ganjian answered. "You know, things have been so strange out there I actually wondered if the bridal clothes and car were some sort of disguise. Damn! I almost arrested her too!"

"Sarah's just a kid." Sadegh said dismissively. "But this family she's married into . . . well, they aren't what we thought they were. I wouldn't have been surprised if you were after Ali for questioning. Anyway, where's he being held?"

Ganjian's doughy face became serious. "We were working with Heydari's group that night. You remember him, right?"

Sadegh had only met the small, trim man with strange-colored lips once, but he'd left an impression. Several years back, Sadegh had joined a few of the Basijis from Ganjian's team to help Heydari respond to a call about an alcohol-fueled party in the Fereshteh neighborhood. When Sadegh arrived, Heydari explained that, rather than enter the home, he had his man stationed outside to arrest the drunken guests as they left. They had just detained a group of three young men and a girl. Sadegh watched one of Heydari's men separate the girl and direct her into a dark alleyway. When one of the young men protested, Heydari immediately punched him in the gut. The boy doubled over, and Heydari twisted his ear, shouting angry obscenities as he continued to pummel him.

Sadegh wasn't worried about the girl. He knew she was being ushered to join the other females that had been detained.

But he was taken aback and also a bit impressed by how quickly Heydari had lashed out. Ganjian wasn't shy about using force or even violence if necessary, but he had strict rules about keeping one's emotions in check and expected his crew to take action for the sake of Allah and not for the satisfaction of their own anger. Clearly Heydari didn't have the same expectation, and Sadegh was left to wonder which approach was right. These partyers they had to deal with were corrupted by sin and, allowed to continue, would rot the moral underpinning of the Islamic Republic. Perhaps a bit of righteous anger was justified.

"I thought Heydari left to be a specialist for the Guards." Sadegh said. The Revolutionary Guards was a more professional force of security and intelligence specialists that often oversaw the volunteer paramilitaries of the Basij.

Ganjian continued. "Yes, but with all this going on, we needed more experienced people in the streets, so they sent him back to oversee his old team. Anyway, we already had too many guests at our station, so Heydari took all the detainees that night. If he's had as much trouble as we have getting them transferred, your cousin's husband might still be with him."

Sadegh considered this. He hoped for Ali's sake that he hadn't actually done anything to warrant arrest and that he'd behaved respectfully and obediently since his arrest. Heydari and his men weren't likely to tolerate much.

Ganjian's cell phone rang again.

"Akh! They won't leave me alone. Sorry."

Ganjian answered and began walking again toward the Mosque exit. "What is it?" he demanded. "Can't you leave me alone for five minutes?"

Sadegh wasn't paying much attention to Ganjian's conversation as he followed him outside, although he did notice his former teacher's increasing agitation. Just beyond the mosque's arched doorway, Ganjian stopped so abruptly that Sadegh almost bumped into him.

Sadegh backed up and moved around Ganjian to the top of the mosque's stairs. He noticed an old woman in a black chador limping around his car. A beggar?

"Pedarsaghay Ahmagh!"

Sadegh turned back to Ganjian, who was swearing into the phone, calling whomever he was talking to a son of a dog as he kneaded his right eye with his flattened palm.

"What the hell is wrong with you? Okay, just shut up. Look, there's a doctor's office in the alley across from ours. Run over there and get someone to come take a look at him.

"Wait! No, actually, take the kid there directly. I don't want anyone coming to the house. Got that? Do *not* bring anyone to the house. Take the kid there, see if you can fix him up, and if not, take him to Modarres Hospital. I'll be right there. And don't you dare lay a finger on another one of those kids, dammit."

Ganjian flipped his cellphone shut and turned to Sadegh.

"Shit! Look, I'm just going to run up there. It'll take twice as long going through the roundabout with the car."

"Are you sure?" Sadegh asked. "It's all uphill. I can take you. What's going on?"

Ganjian squeezed his eyes shut and massaged them both with the thumb and middle finger of his right hand. "One of the prisoners might need a doctor. Damn it! No, I'm going to go. Meet me there, okay?"

Ganjian took off at a slight jog up Sa'adat Abad Avenue.

Sadegh moved toward his little car. The woman he'd noticed earlier was still standing there. She wasn't as old as he'd first guessed from her limping walk. Her outermost coverings were draped loosely, revealing a black headscarf and modest tunic under the chador that cascaded casually from the middle of her head and around her shoulders before being tucked under an elbow. When she noticed Sadegh moving purposefully toward his car, she began rearranging her coverings to stand more formally. The folds under the elbow were dropped as she leaned forward to pull the top of the chador toward her forehead, smooth the sides along her lined, but surprisingly attractive, face and unite the two sides of the material like a theater curtain closing across the stage of her body.

"*Befarmayeed, madar.* What can I do for you, mother?" Sadegh used a gruff voice to indicate that, despite the politeness of his words, she'd better move along.

But his words had an unexpected effect. The woman's shapely eyebrows lifted as she inhaled sharply and her breath came in sharp ragged bursts. She swayed as if she might fall and reached a chador-covered hand toward the car for support.

"Are you ill?" Sadegh asked, alarmed.

"No, my dear. No. I'm fine. I just . . . I didn't expect . . . You can't imagine how I've longed but never expected to actually get to hear you say . . ."

The woman could barely speak for crying. Her grimaces, tears, and shiny sweat had greatly diminished whatever beauty she possessed. Sadegh felt distinctly uncomfortable.

"Do you need help?" Sadegh asked. "I'm in a hurry and have to go, but there are ladies in the mosque. I could . . ."

"No. Azizam. I'm so sorry. I'm okay," the woman replied and took a deep breath before going on. "Sadegh, my sun, my moon, my stars, do you have no idea who I am?"

And that was when Sadegh knew exactly who she was.

CHAPTER 3

Saturday, June 27, 2009—fifteen days after the election

Truly, why do we women have to sit around and wait for someone to tend to us? We have to be the ones who step forward. We can learn much from the stories of great women in history.

—Zahra Rahnavard, artist, professor, and wife of 2009 presidential candidate Mir-Hossein Mousavi[2]

What you have done, Mazi, makes my blood boil. I don't want to raise my hand against you, but what do you suggest I do with someone who has insulted the Leader?

—Revolutionary Guard interrogating journalist Maziar Bahari[3]

"Good morning, Maman," Azar greeted her mother in the kitchen, where she was drinking tea at the round table with uneven legs and worn varnish that had been slowly decaying since Azar was a child.

"*Sobh bekheir*, my dear," her mother answered with a warm but concerned smile. "Did the television wake you? I told the boys to keep it down."

"No, it's not that," Azar said. "I have to get them ready. There's going to be a lot of traffic from your house to their day camp."

In fact, Azar had been woken before sunrise by the flock of crows that seemed to favor her parents' home as an early morning conference hall. Azar and her boys had been staying with her parents since Ali's arrest two nights ago. But Azar wasn't sure she could take the squawking another day.

Azar opened her mother's freezer and pulled out a bag of *sangak* flatbread that had been cut into single-serve pieces. She popped the bread into the toaster and then went back to the refrigerator for butter, cheese, walnuts, and the quince jam that was her mother's specialty.

Her mother rose and began opening cabinets for plates, cups, and silverware to set the softly rocking table.

"Did you hear from Ms. Tabibian last night?" her mother asked.

"No. I don't know what's going on," Azar answered. "Even if she wasn't able to get any information about Ali, she should have at least answered my calls. And I have to talk to her about this week's court cases too."

"And Ibrahim? Did you hear from him?"

"Oh, yes," Azar lied. "He wanted to talk to both of you, but you were already asleep. He's doing fine, just worried like the rest of us about Ali."

Azar busied herself with checking the bread. She didn't want to worry her mother, but she hadn't heard a word from her husband since he'd left last week. They'd agreed it would be safer for him to stay away from the house and off phones until there was a change for the better. It was the right decision—several of their friends had been taken in, probably to Section 209 of Evin as political prisoners. But, except for those early tumultuous years, it was the longest they'd gone without talking. Azar felt the pain of his absence like the reed flute in Mawlana's famous poem whose melancholic notes cry out for the reed bed from which it has been separated. "*Beshno az ney chon hekayat mikonad / az jodayiha shekayat mikonad.*" Ibrahim loved poetry and would often recite verses like these spontaneously and apropos of nothing.

Azar quickly blinked back tears as she took the warmed *sangak* from the toaster and put it in the bread basket. "Do you mind pouring the tea?" she asked her mother as she set the bread basket on the table. "I'm going to get the boys."

Azar announced breakfast once, twice, three times, before turning off the TV herself and ordering Hossein and Muhammadreza into the kitchen over cries of indignation about being in the middle of a show and not being hungry for breakfast anyway.

"Shhh!" Azar hissed. "Your grandfather is still sleeping. Selfish boys! Don't you know we're all exhausted from worrying about your uncle and all you care about is your show? In the kitchen, now."

Still grumbling, the boys moped into the kitchen, where a quarrel erupted over the fact that nine-year-old Hossein kept pointing his index finger at his younger-by-a-year brother, Muhammadreza. Azar's threats of punishment ended the visible provocations, but Muhammadreza continued to complain that he was certain his brother was still pointing at him from under the creaky old table, which registered its own objections to the commotion by rocking so violently it threatened to unload their breakfast onto the floor.

Thankfully, the doorbell rang, indicating the driver's arrival. The boys scrambled for shoes and bags before chasing each other out the door and into the courtyard only to return and report that it wasn't the driver but their mother's secretary who'd rung the bell and was now standing outside the courtyard door.

Azar was surprised. Ms. Tabibian was here? Why hadn't she just called? Perhaps she had news that couldn't be discussed by telephone.

Azar threw on a house chador and a pair of brown plastic outdoor sandals before heading downstairs. As she crossed the courtyard, she noticed her boys throwing pebbles at a stray cat stalking atop the wall separating their building from the neighbors'. She opened her mouth to object but then decided against it. Surely the cat had escaped worse torment, and at least the boys were occupied for a moment.

"Ms. Tabibian? Is that you?" Azar asked.

Azar opened the door to see her secretary standing before her in a tightly drawn black chador held in place with a fist under her chin.

"Salam, Ms. Rahimi," Ms. Tabibian said with a bow. "Are you well? I'm so sorry to impose on you this early in the morning."

"Don't be silly," Azar answered. "I've been waiting for your call. Where were you last night?"

"Forgive me, Ms. Rahimi. I lost my cellphone, and by the time I got home it was too late to call. Also—" Ms. Tabibian leaned closer and lowered her voice. "—I thought it might be better to talk in person."

This could only mean she'd gotten some useful information from Mr. Sadegh. Azar pushed the door open wider and invited her secretary inside.

Ms. Tabibian limped through the door with her usual pattern of one long step followed by the short half-circle swing of her left leg.

As Azar closed the door behind her, the sound of pained cries came from their neighbor's courtyard.

"Ow! *Vwah!* Where the hell did that come from?" a male voice shouted from the other side of the wall.

Azar glared angrily at her boys who had clapped their hands

over their mouths to prevent their laughter from escaping. Clearly, the pebbles they'd been throwing at the cat had hit another target.

At that moment, a squeal of brakes and quick *beep-beep* announced the driver's arrival. The boys grabbed their bags and ran out of the courtyard and away from their mother's hisses that they should be ashamed of themselves.

Azar sighed as she shut the door and turned to show Ms. Tabibian across the courtyard. She didn't like having her secretary witness her boys' bad behavior. Azar had always made a point of keeping her home and work lives as separate as possible. The office was a place where she felt calm and confident, strong and in charge. She had no desire for her clients or employees to have knowledge of the weaknesses and insecurities that were usually stored safely at home.

Indeed, it was only the combination of strange coincidence and present danger that had led Azar to invite an office worker into her parent's home today. The wellspring of this unusual event was the discovery, ten days ago, that she and her secretary were about to become relatives.

*   *   *

"*Befarmayeed*, Ms. Tabibian. Please, take a seat," Azar directed the woman toward the couch. "Shall I bring some tea?"

"Oh no," Ms. Tabibian said as she shifted her weight to her good leg, sat down, and relaxed her coverings so that the scarf and mandatory manteau tunic she wore under her chador were visible. "I won't be staying long. Again, forgive me for not getting in touch earlier."

Azar decided against removing her house chador. All she had on underneath was a long nightgown which was not the sort of thing she wanted an employee to see her in. So she hitched up the light cotton cloth and sat facing Ms. Tabibian.

"Yes, I can't tell you how disappointed I was not to hear from you last night." Azar chided. She was not one to mince words with an employee—or anyone else, for that matter. And berating her secretary was a way of unconsciously compensating for her own embarrassment over her sons' behavior in the court-yard. "It's a very sensitive time, and we need to find him as soon as possible. You should have called or come here immediately."

Ms. Tabibian looked pained. "You're right. I'm sorry. It was just that it took so long to—"

Azar cut her off. She wasn't interested in excuses. "Were you able to get any useful information?"

"I think so," Ms. Tabibian said as she nodded. "I—"

"Wait," Azar cut her off again. She didn't think they would be talking about anything sensitive. If anyone was listening in, all they'd learn is that she was looking for her brother, which would be no surprise to anyone. But she'd promised Ibrahim she'd be careful. "You said you lost your cellphone. So you don't have a phone with you?"

"Oh, well, I got a . . . um, a replacement this morning," Ms. Tabibian answered.

Azar held out her hand and Ms. Tabibian rummaged through her purse before handing over a Samsung phone with a sliding keyboard. It was much nicer than the flip phone Azar had seen her using previously.

Azar powered the phone down. Then she turned it over and slid off the back cover to remove the battery like Ibrahim had taught her to do.

"It's a nice phone," Azar remarked as she set the disassembled phone on the coffee table. "The shops were already open this morning?"

Ms. Tabibian's olive skin tone deepened in a way that caught Azar's attention. She watched closely as her secretary mumbled, "Well, actually, a . . . friend got it for me."

A friend? In the four years Ms. Tabibian had been working for her, Azar couldn't recall her ever mentioning friends or even family other than her daughter Leila and, more recently, Mr. Sadegh. From Ms. Tabibian's discomfort, it seemed to Azar that this 'friend' might be a romantic interest. Ms. Tabibian was, after all, an attractive woman with those light-green eyes that were so prized in Iran. Azar made a mental note to investigate further to make sure her employee wasn't involved in anything untoward. She had to be particularly sensitive about the moral rectitude of her office and employees given the controversial nature of her work.

For now, however, Azar needed to focus on Ali.

"Okay," Azar said, "tell me what you learned."

Ms. Tabibian brightened at the change of subject. "Yes, I have an address for where they took Mr. Ali. And the name of the station commander is Mr. Heydari. Here, I wrote it down for you."

Ms. Tabibian set a scrap of paper on the coffee table between them.

"Oh! That is *very* helpful!" Azar exclaimed as she picked up and examined the paper. The address scrawled across it was in an upscale neighborhood not too far away, which meant Ali hadn't been processed into Evin. With luck, and possibly a small bribe, they could get him within the hour!

Azar smiled at her secretary as she congratulated herself for thinking to arrange yesterday's reunion. It'd been several weeks since Ms. Tabibian had come across Mehri Hojjati on a list of names Azar was inviting to a party in honor of her brother's upcoming wedding. Recognizing the name, Ms. Tabibian had come to her with the shocking suggestion that the woman, Sarah's Aunt Mehri, might be the woman who had destroyed Ms.

Tabibian's marriage and stolen her son more than two decades earlier.

Azar had heard Ms. Tabibian's story before. The loss of her son was part of what drove her secretary to help Azar serve clients facing similar custody and other divorce battles. But it was an unwelcome twist to hear Ms. Tabibian name Ali's future in-laws as the family responsible for her loss. Ms. Tabibian begged Azar to investigate her claim and, if proven correct, put her in touch with Sadegh.

The request had made Azar extremely uncomfortable. She didn't like the idea of meddling in the affairs of a family she was about to be linked to. And what if the Hojjatis had good reason to have dissociated from Ms. Tabibian? Azar had come to depend on and even like the woman. She didn't want to learn anything that might make it difficult to continue working with her.

Azar had reluctantly agreed to help Ms. Tabibian. But it wasn't until the relationship with the Hojjati's had frayed to the point that Azar concluded that Sarah's family might have had something to do with Ali's detention, that she'd taken any action. The previous evening, Azar had driven Ms. Tabibian to Mehri Hojjati's home, where they saw and followed Sadegh to Sa'adat Abad. Azar's desperate hope had been that Ms. Tabibian's sudden appearance and plea for Ali might help jar loose some useful information from her newly found son. But at the very least, she didn't mind causing some disturbance and embarrassment for a family that had hurt her own. It was hard to believe that this long shot born of anger, desperation, and a need to make good on a promise to her secretary had actually worked.

"Did Mr. Sadegh say why they took Ali?" Azar asked.

Ms. Tabibian's eyes dropped, and she shook her head. "No, he didn't say."

Her secretary's discomfort made Azar wonder about Mr.

Sadegh's reaction to his biological mother's reappearance. She'd clearly managed to get some important information out of him. But perhaps he hadn't been as welcoming as Ms. Tabibian had hoped.

"I'm sorry," Azar apologized. "I'm in such a rush to get information about Ali that I forgot to ask how things went yesterday. Was Mr. Sadegh surprised to meet you? Did he realize we'd been following him? Did you spend much time together after I left?"

Ms. Tabibian looked at Azar and shrugged her shoulders. "*Alhamdulillah*, praise God, I suppose it went as well as one could expect. But, you know, for so many years I'd hoped and dreamed about the day I would get my son back. And seeing him, I realized, well, I'm never really going to get him back. I'm a stranger to him. Worse than a stranger . . . That woman has influenced his mind about me the same way she did to his father."

"What exactly happened with Mrs. Hojjati?" Azar asked. Now that things had gone so badly with Ali's marriage, Azar didn't mind inviting some gossip about the family he'd almost married into.

Ms. Tabibian shrugged again and shook her head as if not sure where to start. Then she went still and looked steadily at Azar. Her eyes were the color of drying grass with yellow and brown blades mixed with the green. They stood out even more due to the heavy wrinkles and dark half-moons under her eyes. Ms. Tabibian was at least ten years older than Azar.

"Your husband, Mr. Ibrahim . . . your parents chose him for you?" Ms. Tabibian asked.

What a question! Yes, in fact, Azar's parents had chosen Ibrahim for her over her strenuous objections. She'd been only fourteen. A baby. And all she knew of Ibrahim, her seventeen-year-old second cousin, was that he'd made a practice of terrorizing Azar and her closest girl cousins when they were children. In one particularly memorable incident, he'd trapped the girls, then eight years old, behind the big willow tree in his family's garden by threatening to shoot them with his BB gun if they tried to escape. When, after what felt like hours of tears and pleading, Azar decided to make a break for it, the threatened shots never came, but in her panic she'd tripped and twisted her ankle. Ibrahim ran to check on her and Azar kicked him in his face, hard.

When her mother had told her it was all arranged and Ibrahim would be her husband, Azar responded that she would die before marrying that boy. "Azar!" her mother had scolded, "Don't joke about such things. I'm your mother. I know you better than you know yourself, and I'm telling you this is a good match. You're a smart and ambitious girl. We didn't even have to ask permission for you to continue your studies, because Ibrahim himself said he expects his wife to go to university. University! This type of boy among families like ours isn't easy to find. If Ibrahim gave you a hard time when you were kids, it was only because he liked you even at that age. Just you wait a few months, and you'll see how right I was."

It had taken years.

In the end, of course, it had all worked out. Ibrahim was a good man, and Azar had actually gained more freedoms as a wife than she'd had as a daughter. Still, the first case that drew her into divorce court was that of another fourteen-year-old bride that hadn't been so lucky. The girl's petition for a divorce was denied, and so far as Azar knew, she was still living with a man who refused to let her leave the house by herself.

Anyway, this was none of her secretary's business, and Azar expressed her disapproval of the inappropriate question with a sharp "Excuse me?"

It seemed, however, that Ms. Tabibian's question was rhetorical, as she had continued without waiting for an answer.

"An eighteen-year-old girl needs parents to help her make that most important decision," Ms. Tabibian said, her voice tight.

"But me . . . I was all alone. And when a kindly older gentleman wanted to marry me and take care of me, I agreed to be his second wife. How could I know that his first wife objected? How could I know she would never forgive me and would seek to deprive me of the only real family I had ever known. How could I know that she would take my son . . . my little Sadegh!"

Ms. Tabibian clenched her jaw. She was clearly struggling to keep her composure. Azar hoped she would be successful but pushed a box of tissues toward her just in case. Ms. Tabibian took a deep breath and went on. "She put it into my husband's head that I was unfaithful. When he divorced me, he told the judge he didn't want—" Ms. Tabibian paused and looked up at the ceiling to, Azar guessed, prevent pooling tears from overflowing. "—his son to be raised by someone like me." Ms. Tabibian finally abandoned her valiant efforts to keep from crying. Her face seemed to fold in on itself as her clenched eyes pulled her forehead down while her chin pulled up toward her downturned mouth. Ms. Tabibian began to sob. She pulled several tissues and pressed them to her face.

Her secretary's tears made Azar uncomfortable, and she regretted having opened the door to them with her question about Sarah's aunt. Azar was a good lawyer who battled the courts successfully more often than one might expect given the stacked deck Iranian women were facing when it came to divorce law. But she'd never enjoyed the part of her job that entailed comforting or even just dealing with the emotions involved. It was always heartbreaking when a young mother lost custody of her children. Ms. Tabibian, going up against a powerful man like Mr. Hojjati wouldn't have had much of a chance.

Aloud, Azar tried to be comforting. "There, there, azizam, don't cry. Crying never solved anything. Besides, now at last you're reunited with your son, and that's good, right?"

Ms. Tabibian nodded and took several deep breaths.

"Well, I suppose I should go see this Mr. Heydari as soon as possible, right?" Azar said, hinting that it was time for the woman to go.

"Right," Ms. Tabibian said. She picked up her disassembled phone, put the pieces in her purse and leaned forward onto her good leg to stand.

"Thank you again for your help with this," Azar said as she walked her secretary to the door. "And thank you for running things at the office today. I almost forgot to mention," Azar turned to office business. "Ms. Jalili's court date is Wednesday. Her only chance is to prove her husband is infertile, so check to see if he still hasn't gotten the test. We have to file an official complaint by tomorrow. Also, I need you to call Ms. Raisdana to tell her we need another man willing to testify that her ex-husband beats their daughter. If we can convince the judge that the ex isn't fit to make decisions for her, he might be prevented from marrying the girl off to his cousin. I'll be back in the office tomorrow. Everything else can wait until then. If you have any questions, talk to one of the associates, and if they can't help, call me."

Ms. Tabibian nodded as she walked to the door. Azar knew her capable secretary would probably have known to take care of these things even without her reminders. Ms. Tabibian, like Azar, was zealous about using every possible loophole and ruling to give their clients the best possible shot at having a say in their futures. In the office at least, Ms. Tabibian had never let her down.

Ms. Tabibian paused at the door. She turned slowly to Azar.

"Just one thing," Ms. Tabibian said. "You should take Mr. Ibrahim with you. These sorts of places, it's better to have a man. Mr. Ibrahim is here with you, right?"

"No, he's not. He's—" Azar stopped herself. There was something about the pointed way Ms. Tabibian was looking at her that reminded Azar it was best not to share anything about Ibrahim having gone into hiding. "He's not here. But, well, it's good advice. I'll be sure to take my father."

"It would be better to take your husband," Ms. Tabibian repeated. Then she bowed slightly and hobbled out the door.

*   *   *

"*Ya'allah, ya'allah.*" Azar's father warned of male entry from behind his cracked bedroom door.

"Come in, *pedaram*, my father," Azar called in response as she hung up her chador. "It's okay, she just left."

Her father entered the living room yawning. He wore a baggy white T-shirt tucked into striped cotton pajamas, the drawstring tied snugly above his waist.

"Good morning, *pedar*," Azar said and she greeted her father with a warm kiss on his grizzled cheek. "Can I get you some tea? I have good news."

"I'll get my own tea," her father said and moved toward the kitchen. Azar followed him and took a seat at the wobbly table that, she noticed, had been cleared of all dirty dishes but still held the bread and other breakfast items that her mother must have left out for her and her father.

"Guess what," Azar said as she heaped butter and jam on bread. "I just got the address for where they're holding Ali. Have your breakfast and then we should go as soon as possible."

"I don't need breakfast," her father said as he opened kitchen cabinets, "just my morning tea. Where are the teacups?"

"Did you look in the dishwasher?" Azar set her bread down and popped up to retrieve a teacup and saucer from the machine. "Here you go."

"Thank you, my dear." Her father lifted the steaming teapot

off the samovar and poured its hot, dark contents into the teacup, filling it about a third full and spilling more than a few drops in the process. He placed the teapot back on its perch and opened the samovar's spigot so the boiling water pouring into his cup lightened his tea to the right color. His teacup full, he turned the spigot again but didn't manage to close it all the way, so small drips and drops continued to escape the vessel's spout.

"So," he said as he sat and set the teacup and saucer on the softly rocking table, "your secretary gave you an address for where they're holding Ali?"

Azar, still standing, had quickly tightened the spigot, wiped drops of tea off the counter, and was now cleaning up the small puddle that had formed on the floor under the samovar's spout. Azar often resented her father's proud insistence on serving himself. It usually caused a great deal more work—which he was entirely oblivious to and unappreciative of—than if he'd simply allow himself to be served. Azar knew it was a small thing to care about in a country where a woman's life was valued at half a man's, but she found it increasingly difficult to resist the impulse to point out to her father the many unacknowledged ways he was propped up by the women in his life to look stronger, wiser, and more self-sufficient than he really was. Azar wondered whether Zahra Rahnavard, Mousavi's charismatic firebrand of a wife, played the same role for her husband as well.

"Yes," Azar answered as she tossed the wet paper towels in the garbage and washed her hands before joining her father at the table. "She even gave me the name of the station commander."

Her father lifted the teacup from its saucer to his thin lips and blew, forming cooling ripples in the steaming liquid. Azar noticed that the saucer was dangerously close to the edge of the table, where the slightest bump would result in a crash landing. She nudged it inward as her father asked, incredulous, "She managed to get all this information within minutes of reuniting with her long-lost son? Didn't they have other things to talk about? And why would he give that information out so easily? Did she tell Sadegh that she worked for you?" He took a sip of his tea and set the cup in the saucer, pulling it back toward himself and the edge of the table before fixing a critical gaze on Azar.

It was a good question, and Azar felt a little stupid for not having thought to ask her secretary the same thing. Particularly since Mr. Sadegh, by Ms. Tabibian's own account, hadn't been especially happy to see her.

"Well . . . I don't know exactly how she did it," Azar said. "But she's a loyal employee, and she's smarter than you might think for someone without any education. Maybe she tricked the information out of him somehow. Or maybe Mr. Sadegh was already feeling guilty about putting poor Ali away."

"Akh!" Her father waved his hands in the air, jostling the table as he did so. "Whatever their failings and whatever our disagreements, I refuse to believe that boy or anyone else in that family arranged Ali's arrest."

Azar closed her eyes. She suspected her father was implying that Ali's arrest had something to do with Ibrahim and Azar's political activities. He'd warned strongly against their involvement in Mousavi's campaign and had been apoplectic about Ibrahim's role in encouraging mass resignations at Sharif University, where he worked as a professor of economics. Since Ali's arrest, he kept muttering about how no one had listened to his warnings that political activities like that always led to misfortune.

Azar didn't disagree with her father about the risks. It was just that she and Ibrahim felt compelled to join in putting their shoulders to the wheel of history and offering what small efforts they could toward moving the country in a better direction now that there was a real opportunity to do so. And despite the tumult of the last few weeks, Azar was still certain that the Green Wave would ultimately prevail.

Ali, however, shared their father's philosophy and had steered clear of the conflict that had embroiled the nation. There was absolutely no reason for anyone to go after Ali for political reasons.

It was much more likely, in Azar's opinion, that her brother's misfortunes stemmed from his unlucky entanglement with the Hojjatis. The family's behavior since Ali's arrest had been shocking. Sarah's mother hadn't even let Azar or her mother talk to Sarah directly to hear the story of Ali's arrest firsthand and ask questions about what had happened. Sarah was much too upset and delicate to talk, Mahdiyeh-khanoom had insisted when they'd called. And when Azar and her mother had decided to simply drop by in hopes of seeing the girl and convincing her to help them look for Ali, Mahdiyeh-khanoom told them Sarah was sleeping and couldn't be disturbed. Sleeping! While her husband was being held God knows where.

At the very least, it was obvious that Sarah's family was trying to use Ali's arrest as an excuse to end the marriage. But Azar thought it was possible that the family had arranged Ali's arrest to begin with and had angrily hinted at her suspicions to Sarah's mother. Wasn't Sarah's Aunt Mehri exactly the sort of vengeful woman who would do such a thing, especially after the humiliation of her fall at the wedding and the experience of being so openly defied? Didn't her son work for the Basij? Hadn't Azar seen Sadegh outside the wedding venue with his Basiji friends? And didn't his provision of information about Ali to Ms. Tabibian prove that he knew something about it to begin with?

But Azar didn't want to have a fight with her father right now. Eyes still closed, Azar took a breath to calm herself and managed to avoid the bait. "Whether or not they arranged the arrest," she said, "we have an address, and I'm going to go check it out. You don't have to come if you don't want to."

"Who said anything about not coming," her father responded gruffly. Azar relaxed and opened her eyes.

The first thing she saw was her father's empty teacup teetering on the edge of the table. She jerked to save it from falling but, in her haste, jarred the wobbly table instead. The teacup and saucer tumbled off the table and Azar tensed in anticipation of their smash on the stone floor. Her father, however, managed to snatch both items from the air, one in each hand.

"Be careful," he chided. "You almost broke my cup!"

*   *   *

By 9:00 a.m. Azar and her parents were driving toward the Niavaran neighborhood, which was less than four miles—but more than forty minutes in current traffic—from her parents' home in Darrous. Azar drove, her mother uncomfortably sitting sideways in the passenger seat after having lost the battle over who should sit in the back and not wanting to disrespect her husband by putting her back to him.

"I just can't believe these people!" her mother was complaining about Sarah's family. "Who could have thought it would come to this? It seemed like such a good match. Mehri-khanoom and my sister were school chums. Imagine! Just like me and Nargess."

Nargess was her mother's closest childhood friend. She was also the daughter-in-law of Grand Ayatollah Montazeri, the man who was once designated as Khomeini's heir but who had now suffered for years under house arrest for his dissenting views. The mullahs running the country were hard on the people they ruled but even harder on objectors among themselves. Montazeri had been unable to participate directly in politics for years. But after the contested election, he'd noted publicly that no one in their right mind could possibly believe the official results. Azar, Ibrahim, and many other supporters of Mousavi and the Green Wave considered him to be their primary spiritual and political leader. God willing, he would once again have an important role to play in healing the nation once the Green Wave was successful in making the regime respect the will of the Iranian people.

Azar swung a wide arc to turn right onto Dolat Street from one of the leftmost lanes and bypass the crush of cars inching through the same turn on her right. In doing so, she momentarily blocked oncoming vehicles. A young man with glasses and a mustache pulled his SAIPA close to Azar and rolled his window down to curse at her, further slowing west-going vehicles, which began to toot their horns impatiently.

Azar refused to look in his direction as she maneuvered her car into another lane. "*Ajab ollaghiyeha*. Stupid donkey!" she exclaimed. "I blocked the way for less than two seconds, but he wants to sit there all day wasting everyone's time with a stupid fight."

"You shouldn't have blocked traffic to begin with," her father reprimanded from the back seat.

Azar grimaced and considered retorting that this was the only way to get anywhere in Tehran these days given its steadily worsening traffic. But before she could say anything, her mother went on with more complaints about their new in-laws.

"Besides, at this point," she said, "the *aghd* has been read and the marriage has been registered. Do they think that just because they haven't spent the night together, people won't think of Sarah as a divorcée? Is marriage, and divorce, taken so lightly these days? Imagine if we'd behaved the same way toward you and Ibrahim?"

Her mother was right. If marriage wasn't official until its consummation, Azar and Ibrahim's marriage hadn't started until three years after she'd moved in with him and his family.

She'd refused his bed and slept on the floor of their room for three years. At first, her poor Ibrahim had chivalrously tried to get her to trade so that he would be on the floor instead, but she'd so clearly enjoyed refusing and foiling his various attempts that he'd finally stopped giving her the pleasure.

They'd settled into a long cold war marked by silent treatments, fierce competition, and a few real or imagined jabs.

The first year saw the worst of it. There was a period of several months when neither of them could ever find their shoes, keys, or wallets as the other would hide them whenever they got the chance. Another time, the weapon of choice was alarm clocks set to go off at all the wrong times. And using their own bathroom became a perilous activity once they discovered that a flaw in the doorknob allowed it to be locked from the outside.

The last year or so of this was fueled more by habit than real anger. More and more frequently, Azar found herself admiring Ibrahim for his passionate arguments that democracy and Islam are entirely compatible, for his quick wit and laughter, and for the way his biceps bulged whenever he lifted his arms in prayer.

One night, rather than change in the bathroom as was her habit, Azar turned her back to the bed on which Ibrahim was reclined, and began unbuttoning her shirt. As she slowly slipped off her clothes, her ears strained for the squeak of bedsprings or rustle of sheets that might indicate the direction of her husband's reaction. She was heartily disappointed to hear nothing at all and wondered, as she pulled on her soft nightdress, whether he'd already fallen asleep.

Turning around, Azar was startled by Ibrahim's hungry stare. For a long moment, he looked her over and Azar felt the blood rush inward from her extremities to her loins like a flower closing its petals to a single point. When Ibrahim pulled her insistently, triumphantly onto the bed, she didn't resist. And she never slept on the floor again.

*   *   *

Reluctantly, Azar abandoned the still-arousing memories of that first night with a husband she loved. It was time to focus on the upcoming confrontation. As Azar negotiated the car into the alleyway, she wondered what their approach should be. Should she do most of the talking, or should she leave it to her father, who though male, was perhaps too elderly to be taken seriously? Or, alternatively, would it be best to have her mother speak in hopes that they might be softer with her? Should Azar be deferential and seek to flatter their sense of importance? Or, as was her preference when representing cases at court, should she seek to confuse and intimidate them by refusing to be cowed by their bullying?

It was hard to know who or what one was dealing with in the Basij. Like everything else associated with the revolution, it was a beautiful concept that had been badly distorted by corrupt leaders after the death of Imam Khomeini. The original Basijis were faithful young men and women who had responded with pure hearts to Imam Khomeini's call for volunteers to defend the nation from Saddam's brutal invasion. These days, however, the Basij had been unleashed on Iran's own population and they weren't shy about using force to control or even kill peaceful protestors, like the beautiful young Neda. Azar had been moved to tears by the disturbing footage of her final moments that had been shared throughout Tehran and the world.

Azar was sure that nowadays most Basij "volunteers" were simply poor and uneducated men looking for the perks and paychecks associated with membership. The involvement of someone as wealthy, educated, and connected as Mr. Sadegh was a surprise to Azar and increased the mystery surrounding this shadowy paramilitary force. What would this Heydari be like, Azar wondered.

Once again, she wished she could talk to Ibrahim. He would know how to handle the situation.

Azar found the house number she was looking for. From the outside, there was nothing to indicate that the beautiful villa served as a Basij station, and Azar wondered whether any of the neighbors in this upscale area were aware of the building's true use.

Azar parked the car, stepped out, and opened the back door to help her father. Of late, he was not always steady on his feet, and the deep gutter she was parked beside could prove a hazard. As usual, the challenge lay in helping him without being so obvious about it that her father, who detested any form of coddling, would snap at her to get out of his way.

As they crossed the street, Azar said "Listen, let me start off doing the talking. If it doesn't go well, then you take over, okay?"

Azar pressed the intercom buzzer outside the gate.

No answer.

Azar pushed again, this time holding the buzzer longer.

"*Befarmayeed.* What do you need?" The voice didn't come from the intercom but from the other side of the wall where, apparently, a guard was waiting.

"I need to speak with someone." Azar said with the loud voice she often used to project more confidence than she felt.

"What is your business?"

"Let us in and I'll tell you," Azar answered.

"Tell me now."

Azar thought for a moment. She needed to say something that would get her past this guard so she could talk to the people who made the decisions. "We're here to see Mr. Heydari. He asked us to come."

"Ah. Come in," was the immediate response.

The door swung in. Azar wondered briefly whether she ought to go in first to place herself protectively between these people and her parents or whether she should follow the usual protocol of politely standing aside to let her parents enter first. As she hesitated, her father moved through the door so Azar turned to guide her mother in ahead of her as well.

They crossed the courtyard on stepping-stones spaced too close together to correspond to a comfortable gait so that every other step was in the cracks. The path was lined with stunning, sturdy orange and red tulips, the kind Azar had heard was being imported from Holland. God, it was disgusting how this government was burning through cash for things like tulips when so many Iranian children lacked proper medical care or schools. God willing, their days were numbered, and soon experts and economists like Ibrahim could steward the country's economic resources in a more responsible manner.

The villa's door opened onto a hallway lined with closets. There they were greeted by a small man with a short white beard trimmed neatly around full lips that were the deep purple color of a three-day-old bruise. He introduced himself as Heydari's assistant and politely ushered them into a waiting area, where they sat on uncomfortable chairs. The man wore a thick silver agate ring that he twisted around his finger as they spoke.

"My friends, I'm afraid that Mr. Heydari is busy this morning," he said. "I wonder if there's anything I can do to help. Can you tell me why he asked you to come in?"

Azar, a bit ruffled by this man's politeness and friendliness nonetheless responded firmly. "No sir, we will wait for Mr. Heydari." She knew it was always best to talk to the person in charge.

"Of course. I understand madame." Heydari's assistant responded politely. "Well, why don't you write down your names for me so I can let him know you're here."

Azar thought a moment. By writing down their names, Heydari and his assistant would surely realize she'd lied about Heydari inviting them to come in. On the other hand, he would know their names eventually.

The man handed Azar a pen and notepad. She wrote her name and her parents' names.

"Write down your husband's name as well," the man prompted.

Azar paused. Like most Iranian women, she hadn't changed her name after marriage so her connection to Ibrahim, who she feared these men might recognize, wasn't yet obvious. She really didn't want to bring her husband into this.

Noting her hesitation, the man softly said "It's not important. Perhaps your business doesn't involve your husband."

Azar nodded brusquely. "Our business with Mr. Heydari has to do with my brother, not my husband."

"Ah, then write his name down."

But Azar was done with writing. She widened her stance and projected her voice "I'd rather speak directly to Heydari."

The man licked his strange lips and pressed them together briefly before smiling as he twisted his ring again. "Of course. I'll let him know. In the meantime, please tell the guards if you need anything at all."

"How long will we have to wait?"

"Don't worry. I'll hurry things along." The man said something to the guard that Azar couldn't hear and then left.

* * *

An hour later, they were still there. Both of her parents had been to the bathroom, and Azar was starting to think she might need to go too. Where was Heydari? Or even his assistant? Azar wondered if it had been a mistake not to tell him why they were there. He had seemed willing to help.

Azar used the time to study the interior of the building. The grimy walls and cheap furniture contrasted sharply with the beautiful outdoor landscaping, and Azar wondered whether the exterior upkeep was simply meant to conceal the Basij presence from the neighbors. She turned her attention to the small waiting room and tried to guess at what the building's architect would have originally intended it for. It was too small to be an entertaining salon or living room. Perhaps it was supposed to be some sort of cozy den or television room? Azar wondered when the home had last been inhabited by civilians and when it had been taken over by the Basij. Probably, she thought, the last residents were west-toxified *taghootis* who had fled the 1979 revolution, leaving their home and belongings to be taken over and administered by government bodies.

While they sat, Azar didn't see anyone other than the guard, who was flipping through a newspaper at a battered wooden desk, and the errand boys who kept bringing everyone tea. She wondered what these young men thought about what was going on in the country and their part in it. Did they have any idea what the powers they served were doing?

In the weeks leading up to the election, Mousavi had clearly been in the lead. Everyone knew President Ahmadinejad had been a disaster. Ibrahim and his colleagues had been particularly disturbed by the man's inflationary and utterly wasteful spending of oil windfalls that, in an unfortunate twist of fate, coincided with the man's rise to power. Azar had been more disturbed by the family-law legislation Ahmadinejad had pushed to, among other things, make it even harder for women to get a divorce. As the election had neared, Tehran was awash in the deep green color of Mousavi's campaign. With cries of "Ahmadi, bye-bye!" the capital seemed to rejoice in the opportunity to rid itself of this absurd little man who'd embarrassed the country with his ridiculous claims about the absence of homosexuals in Iran, his special relationship with the hidden imam, and the creation of nuclear power in a young woman's backyard.

When Ahmadinejad was declared the victor, shock quickly turned to anger as the Iranian people realized the regime had rigged the results. Millions of citizens poured into the streets for silent protests bigger than any demonstration since Iran's 1979 revolution. Azar and Ibrahim had taken their boys to several of these gatherings so they could witness and be a part of history being made. That was before the violent government crackdown and all the mass arrests. There was no way she'd take her boys into the streets anymore.

Sitting now in the station house, Azar wondered whether these young guards had any idea that the regime's days were numbered. No matter how they tried to suppress the Green Wave, they couldn't change what was in people's hearts, and the Iranian people would not allow their voices to be silenced this time.

Azar was tired of waiting. She stood and moved toward the guard.

"Could you please call Mr. Heydari's assistant?" Her words were deferential, but her tone communicated that she expected him to comply immediately.

The guard didn't move except for his eyes which he rolled away from his paper to look at her. "Mr. Heydari is busy. He'll see you when he has time."

"No." Azar leaned onto the desk so she loomed over the boy. "If Mr. Heydari isn't available, I want to talk to his assistant."

The guard exhaled a quick burst of air that sounded like a chuckle and then turned his eyes back to his paper. "His assistant will see you when he has time."

* * *

Another hour passed. Azar's father thumbed through the book of prayers he always carried. Her mother leaned her head against the wall and dozed. Azar was livid but unsure how to proceed. Maybe they should leave and go home. Heydari would have seen them by now if he had any intention of doing so. On the other hand, surely this couldn't take much longer. If they left now, they might lose their chance.

Her mother's head jerked as she caught herself from sleepy relaxation.

Azar decided.

"*Pasho*, Maman. Baba, let's go. I'll drop you at home and come and wait myself. There's no reason for all of us to be sitting around here."

Azar stood and started helping her parents up.

Noticing their movement, the guard spoke up. "*Kojaa?* Where do you think you're going?"

"Clearly Mr. Heydari doesn't have time for us."

The guard neatly folded his newspaper and dropped it on the table. Then he stood and walked around his desk so he was standing in front of them. "Take a seat," he directed. "He'll be with you soon."

"No thank you," Azar spat. "I'm taking my parents home. They're too old to have to sit in this place so long." Azar shepherded her parents toward the hallway.

The guard blocked their path. "Sit down."

Azar lost her temper. "Get out of my way!" she boomed. If Heydari was anywhere in the building, she was sure he could hear her. "I'm taking my parents home. What is wrong with you people making elderly grandparents sit around like this!"

The guard said nothing but gestured for them to wait as he called to one of the errand boys. "Hey, go tell Mr. Heydari his guests are ready to see him now."

Azar was confused, angry, and unsettled. Perhaps she should have tried to walk out earlier as that's what seemed to finally spur these people to action. She had no clues as to the best course of action and was simply running on emotion. She remained standing to indicate they weren't willing to wait much longer.

Azar heard her father murmur quietly behind her, "Stay calm my dear. We don't know who these people are." For a brief second, Azar's heart expanded like a balloon with more hate for her father than she thought it could hold. When would he learn that sometimes one had to take a stand?

The errand boy returned and indicated that they should follow him. Finally. Azar hoped this would be a lesson to her father. If she'd stayed calm, they would likely be waiting several more hours.

Azar stood aside to let her father go first. But the errand boy looked at the guard and shook his head.

"No, there isn't room for everyone. Just her."

Azar's father pushed forward. "I'll go. Azar, you stay here."

The guard looked confused a moment. Then he shrugged. "Look, Heydari's assistant said she could go. If you want to go instead, I'll have to ask and I don't know how long that will take."

Azar took her father's forearm. "It's okay, *pedar*, I'll go."

He ignored her. "It's not right," he said to the guard. "My daughter shouldn't be by herself with all these men."

Azar's heart ballooned again, this time with love for her elderly father, who still sought to protect her.

"Don't worry hajj-agha," the guard reassured him. "There are other women in the back."

Azar took his hand and squeezed gently. "I'll be right back. With Ali, *insha'allah*."

*   *   *

The boy led her past a long row of file cabinets set up, it seemed, to divide the big living room of this converted house into different office spaces. Azar noticed a few hallways as well as a staircase leading to a second floor. Where would they be keeping Ali? Oh, Ali. Her serious and often irritatingly self-important little brother. They were too far apart in age to be truly close, especially since she'd gotten married when he was still a child. But he was a man now. It was impressive how he'd managed to revive her father's business by switching from the import of high-end men's luxury goods to more affordable Chinese knockoffs. He was a wonderful brother, her sons adored him, and Azar's heart ached at the thought that he was alone and frightened and abandoned by the ridiculous wife he had chosen. With luck, this would all be over soon.

The boy stopped and knocked on the door of what must have once been a bedroom.

"*Befarmayeed.* Come in."

Azar entered. The small room contained an ugly sofa and coffee table at one end, a desk and row of chairs at the other, and a couple cheap card tables pushed together in the center. Mr. Heydari's assistant seemed to be finishing a conversation with a few younger men who were gathering what looked to be maps and other papers off the card tables. There were no other women in the room.

"Salam." Azar greeted the man.

In contrast to his earlier friendly demeanor, this time, Heydari's assistant barely looked at her as he gestured impatiently for her to sit on the sofa. He wrapped up his conversation and then ushered the men out but left the door open. He took a pad of paper from the desk and pulled a chair up to sit near the sofa. As he did before, he twisted the agate ring as he spoke.

"*Khob.* Okay, now tell me why you're here."

This time, Azar got right to the point. "It's my brother. He was taken in by mistake on his wedding night. I was told that he might be here."

"What's your brother's name?" Heydari's assistant asked.

Azar told him, and he took notes on his pad.

"And who told you he might be here?"

"A family member suggested it," Azar answered, not wanting to bring up Ms. Tabibian or her son.

"And where is your husband today?"

"Excuse me?"

The man looked up from his notepad and spoke contemptuously. "Why didn't he come with you? Why did he send you here by yourself?"

"I'm not by myself. My father is with me."

"Where? You're here, alone, with an unrelated male. A *namahram.*" The man's purple lips curled with contempt. "I had to leave the door open for common decency!"

Azar was lost. What did he mean by this? Surely he knew that his own guards had prohibited her father from joining her.

Azar spoke slowly. "Hajj-agha, I think I've answered enough questions. I'd like to speak with Mr. Heydari now."

He snorted a wheezy high-pitched chortle that was entirely incongruous with his trim and controlled appearance. "Oh yes, Mr. Heydari. Let me call him now." He stood up and walked toward his desk.

It was then that Azar understood. The man wasn't Heydari's assistant. He was Heydari himself. A fear that seemed centered in Azar's bowels began to root upward, stroking her intestines and lungs with tiny tendrils. The deception itself wasn't so important. What scared Azar was that she had underestimated her adversary. She had assumed she was dealing with a simple Basiji. Now she wasn't so sure. Tactics like keeping people waiting for hours or lying to them about who they're speaking to were likely meant to keep targets off-balance and trip them up into revealing things. Tactics like these were more advanced than what a traditional Basiji needed or used.

But it wouldn't do to let on that she'd been rattled. Like animals, these bullies would pounce at any sign of fear.

"*Khob*, I see, Mr. *Heydari*," Azar enunciated his name with additional emphasis to convey she had noted his lie. "I'm here to take my brother home. The poor kid was arrested on his wedding night! And he's never been involved in any political activities. He has no interest in it."

Heydari twisted his agate ring and pulled it off his hand. He placed it on his desk and picked up a thick dictionary-sized book that Azar recognized. *The Open Society and its Enemies* by Karl Popper had become popular reading among many of her friends for its arguments against totalitarianism. Azar herself had never been able to get through the heavy philosophical treatise.

"But you, Mrs. Jafari." He gave her a meaningful smile as he used her husband's last name. "You do have an interest in politics, don't you? You must know this book well."

Azar struggled to keep her face neutral. His use of her married name, her husband's last name, meant he knew exactly who she was. But she still had no clue as to who or what she was dealing with. Did the Basij have its own intelligence capabilities? She was sure the answer was no. But it was possible this man was actually with the Revolutionary Guards, a more professional force that often oversaw the Basij. Or could he even be with the Ministry of Intelligence? These men would stop at nothing to protect the power and privilege the Islamic Republic created for them.

She said nothing.

Heydari absently fanned the pages of the book. "It's surprising you even had time to come in today. Don't you have to be in court to help another one of those depraved women leave her family so she can pursue her own pleasures? Isn't that what you are after with your One Million Signatures campaign?"

How did Heydari know so much? Azar, like many others active in the area of women's rights and divorce law, had been a strong supporter of the campaign to get one million signatures in support of equal rights for women. She'd hosted several events to gather signatures from friends and family, and she often mentioned the campaign to clients who were on the receiving end of Iran's discriminatory laws.

Again Azar said nothing.

Mr. Heydari's voice was soft, his face smiling. A casual observer might have thought he was making friendly conversation.

"Where is your husband right now?" He hefted the book up and down in his hand like a baseball.

A new thought formed in Azar's increasingly cloudy brain like the sudden appearance of an oncoming vehicle out of thick fog. Ms. Tabibian. She had to be a part of this. Why else would she have insisted Azar bring Ibrahim? How else could Heydari be so familiar with the details of her court cases and her involvement with One Million Signatures?

"Who is he working for?" Heydari demanded.

Her father was right. They were after Ibrahim.

Azar clenched her jaw defiantly and narrowed her eyes with contempt. If they thought arresting Ali and threatening her would be a way to get information about her husband, they were in for a disappointment.

Heydari pursed his lips so tightly their color changed from the weird purple to a more natural light pink. Azar was gratified to note that he looked frustrated. She hated him and all he stood for and would take her small victories where she could.

"Your boys . . . Hossein and Muhammadreza are both at Adab school, right?"

The fear in Azar's gut traveled up her esophagus, and for a moment she thought she might vomit.

He clucked sympathetically as he walked toward her. "Poor kids. You and your parents stuck here. Their father not around. Who'll be there to open the door when they get home? Perhaps we should pick them up for you. Bring them here until we can finish our conversation."

Azar released her fear and anger in a roar. "How dare you talk about my children. How dare you threaten them! What kind of animal are y—"

As she yelled, Azar vaguely noticed the newly concentrated focus of Heydari's eyes as well as the way he shifted weight to his back foot and raised the arm holding *The Open Society*. Still, somehow, she didn't recognize these as warning signals for an attack until her angry outburst was interrupted by the heavy spine of the book making contact with her nose.

Her instinctive inward gasp of air brought the blood streaming from her nose into her lungs. She coughed on the thick blood as a second blow landed on the back of her head.

Heydari screamed over her as he continued beating her with the book. "Shut up! How dare I threaten your children? How dare you even ask that question! How dare you threaten this country? How dare you mislead all these poor young people out in the street to threaten the *rahbar* and Islam? I would do anything to protect Islam! I would sacrifice my own children. You think I would hesitate for one second to sacrifice you or the children unlucky enough to have you as a mother? Answer me you cowardly, God-hating traitor. We will eliminate all of you!"

Azar, who had never in her life been struck, was slow to find a position that would protect her face. Heydari swung sideways and the corner of the book tore into Azar's eyelid before crunching into her nose again. Azar would have screamed for pain, but with all the blood pouring into her throat, the only noise she produced was a gurgling cough. She pressed her bloodied face into the sofa and raised her arms and knees to create a protective cage around her head. Her chador had slipped and she instinctively clutched at her head scarf to make sure it was still in place.

The beating continued. Azar heard Heydari's heavy breathing and grunting as he pumped the book into her huddled body. Her last thought before a wallop to the base of her head brought welcome blackness was that her worrying had been so misplaced. She had worried for Ibrahim. She had worried for Ali. She had never thought to worry for herself.

PART TWO

TWO AND A HALF MONTHS OF FALL

US support for Iran's newly born civil rights movement, the Green Movement, was seen by the Iranian leadership as clear evidence of US interference in the internal affairs of Iran.

—Seyed Hossein Mousavian, former Iranian diplomat and nuclear negotiations team member, in his book *Iran and the United States: An Insider's View*

CHAPTER 4

Monday, September 21, 2009—three months and twelve days after the election

Hundreds of students have staged an antigovernment demonstration at Tehran's Sharif University, the second such protest in two days.

Many students were chanting "Death to the Dictator" and "Political Prisoners Must Be Released," in reference to the more than 100 people still jailed in Iran.

—Golnaz Esfandiari, senior correspondent at
Radio Free Europe / Radio Liberty[4]

Sarah didn't recognize the man she'd married three months ago.

She was at a window table in Yassi Café by Laleh Park with a crowd of her university friends. Minoo, her highlighted hair barely covered with a gauzy yellow scarf was regaling the group with a story of being stopped by an Afghan Basiji while on a date with her boyfriend Sam in Chitgar Park. The Basiji had offered to let them go in exchange for a kiss from Minoo but readily agreed to the couple's counteroffer to give the man a ride in Sam's Audi S4 instead.

Sarah had just quipped that Minoo ought to have been offended that the Basiji seemed to value a car ride more than a kiss from her. The table erupted in laughter, and that was when Sarah noticed the man standing in line at the cash register with a briefcase in one hand and a phone in the other.

There was something about him that looked familiar, and Sarah tried to place him. He was a bit young to be a friend of her father's, but perhaps he worked at Baba's office. Or maybe he was a distant relative she'd met at a family party. It wasn't until the man, looking up at the menu of choices before him, ran his tongue over the notch in his front tooth that Sarah recognized Ali with a jolt that both thrilled and terrified her.

It wasn't just the passage of time but also several physical changes that had lengthened the gap between seeing and recognizing the man she'd loved. Ali had lost quite a bit of weight, and his suit hung on him. He'd grown a beard and looked older and quite serious as he gave his order and handed over several bills.

Minoo went on with her story of the Basiji, but Sarah couldn't hear, her pulse beat so loudly in her ears. Would he see her? How should she respond to this man who had abandoned her? She had just gotten used to hating him, but the sight of Ali's still-thick fingers reminded her of the way he'd caressed hers during the only time they'd ever been alone together.

The girl at the counter delivered Ali's drink. From the frothy green liquid gleaming through the transparent plastic, Sarah could see it was a melon smoothie. Ali took it and turned to leave. But he turned the opposite way, so he never faced Sarah's direction. Then his phone rang, and Sarah watched him pass his drink to the hand also holding his briefcase and awkwardly crook the phone between his chin and shoulder so he could push the door open and exit. As the door swung shut behind him, she heard the beginnings of his greeting to whoever had called. He was gone.

What were the odds, Sarah wondered, that in this sprawling city of ten million people, they would be at the same café at the exact same time? And how strange and almost tragic that God should bring them so close without creating an opportunity for them to actually interact. She wondered whether they would ever cross paths again. Perhaps the next time, Ali would be the one to see her, and she would carry on with her day like he was doing now, entirely unaware of having been so close to the one he had once loved.

"Sarah!" Minoo called.

Startled, Sarah pulled her attention from the café door Ali had just exited to her friends that were calling her name. Then she followed their pointing fingers to the other side of the window, where Ali was standing, staring at her.

*   *   *

He came back inside.

As she stood to greet him, Sarah's heart beat so hard she wondered whether it might bruise her ribs from the inside.

"Sarah-khanoom . . . salaam." He set the briefcase and smoothie down and jammed his thick hands into his pockets. He looked shocked and maybe even a little scared but also pleased to see her.

Sarah dipped her head in formal greeting. She was aware of her school chums' curious eyes. None of them knew the real reason she and Ali weren't together. And Sarah did not want to be humiliated again.

"I . . ." Ali paused and looked around the table at all the young women listening in. "It's so . . . nice to see you."

Really? Sarah thought. It's so nice to see me, and yet you've made no attempt to do so? What kind of man gets out of prison and doesn't bother to contact his wife?

Aloud, Sarah responded with stiff Persian pleasantries, asking about the health of his parents and other family members in a way that she hoped would convey indifference and also a little anger.

Ali looked disappointed as he responded to her tone. "Oh, well," he said finally, "I don't want to bother you. I guess I'd better be going anyway."

He picked up his briefcase but kept standing there tapping it against his shins and pulling at his beard with his free hand. Sara decided the beard looked good on him because it narrowed his neck. Although, perhaps that was really the result of his weight loss.

"If you're in the neighborhood," Ali said finally, "I'll be here at the same time next week."

Then, almost before he'd finished his sentence, he nodded farewell and left.

As Sarah sank into her seat, she noticed Ali's untouched melon smoothie sweating on the table where it had been left behind. Without warning, Sarah burst into tears.

*   *   *

All week, Sarah agonized over whether she ought to return to meet him. She had so many questions about what had happened and would love the chance to tell him off. On the other hand, perhaps the best way to hurt him the way he'd hurt her would be to let him sit alone at the café waiting for her. The thought was satisfying in a vengeful sort of way. Plus, she wanted to move on. After all the pain and heartbreak of the summer, things had finally started to feel a little normal, and she didn't want to disturb her fragile stability.

Her parents, she knew, wouldn't approve. Her family viewed Sarah's aborted nuptials as a divine blessing that had protected her and the rest of them from a politically and religiously suspect alliance. But even if they liked Ali, they wouldn't think it appropriate for Sarah to be meeting a man at a café. Although, Sarah reflected, she was pretty sure she and Ali were still technically married. Her parents would have told her if they'd managed to finalize the divorce.

It wasn't until she was stuck in traffic, on her way to the café but already forty-five minutes late, that Sarah knew for sure that she had to see him. It was as if an internal magnetic bar had finally identified true north after having circled the face of a compass erratically due to interference. But was it too late? Would Ali still be waiting for her? She had no way of contacting him. But if he left, it might really and truly be over. It was this realization more than anything that had sparked her change of heart. Because, mixed in with the anger and fear of what he would say was the certainty that a part of her still loved him. She wanted to understand and explain. She wanted to give him the notebook, just as she'd planned. The only thing worse than having the conversation she'd been dreading all week would be not having it at all.

Traffic was at a standstill, and the car was moving forward only inches at a time. As many people as vehicles seemed to be in the streets as pedestrians weaved between the slow-moving cars. Sarah noticed flashes of green and wondered whether all these people were headed to some sort of event or demonstration. Sarah shook her head. What would compel people to take to the streets yet again? The early protests might have been fun, with millions of Tehranis turning out like they did when the national soccer team won an important victory. But since the supreme leader had endorsed the election results, protests had been small, sporadic, and heavily policed. Where was the fun in that? And what was the point even, since the numbers of people turning out was too small to make any difference.

"Is there no way to get around this?" she asked the driver. "Couldn't we try the alleyways?"

"*Na*, khanoom," the driver said. "This is the only way to get to the park from here. It looks like something is going on at the university."

"Then I'm going to get out here," Sarah announced.

"Wait!" he protested. "I'm sure traffic will open up soon."

"No, I'll get there faster if I walk. Don't bother trying to get to the sidewalk. The cars aren't moving so I'll get out right here."

"Be careful, madame."

Sarah paid and then grabbed her purse and the notebook and hopped out of the taxi. She wended her way through the cars in the street and then the pedestrians on the sidewalk. She held her chador carefully to avoid trampling on it in her haste. Her shoes—chosen for fashion, not comfort—rubbed against her heels, and her purse bumped awkwardly against her hip with each step. Why, oh why, hadn't she left the house earlier? She would never forgive herself—or God, who should have been more helpful—if Ali wasn't still at the café when she got there. Assuming, that is, that he'd come to begin with. What if he'd had his own change of heart?

Sarah turned onto the side street on which the café was located and began jogging down the slightly sloped hill. Two blocks away she saw a man exiting the café. Was it him? He raised his arm to signal for a cab.

Sarah hollered as she redoubled her speed. "Ali!"

The man turned. As did the other dozen or so pedestrians on the sidewalk.

Sarah was running hard now. "Ali!"

It was Ali. He dropped his arm and stared.

Sarah knew she must look a sight. Running and yelling in the streets was entirely unexpected behavior from a well-bred religious girl like herself. But she was too happy and relieved to care about what passersby might think. She tried to slow down and catch her breath, but the momentum of her downhill run tripped her up, and she fell, rolling knee over arm, shoulder, and back until she came to a sitting stop on her other side. More dazed than hurt Sarah tried to regather her chador, purse, notebook, and dignity as Ali came running up to her.

"Are you okay?"

She looked up at him and gingerly rubbed her knee where it had hit the pavement. "Yeah, I'm fine."

Ali shook his head and made a strange expression.

Sarah asked, "What?"

"Nothing. It's just . . ."

Sarah realized he was trying to suppress laughter as he continued.

"You should have seen yourself!" Ali was laughing openly now. "You were streaming down the hill with your chador trailing like a superhero cape and screaming like a banshee and then, *boom*, down you go."

"Yeah? Maybe I should have just let you leave?" Sarah tried to look offended but was sure her twitching lips were giving her away. She'd forgotten how much fun it was to make Ali laugh.

"No!" He smiled warmly and offered her a hand up. "I'm so glad you're here. It just . . . surprised me, that's all."

Sarah paused a moment before taking his hand and standing. She let go as soon as she was upright and asked, "You don't like having a superhero wife?"

Ali took a deep breath before answering.

"Actually, I'm quite delighted."

*   *   *

"So why didn't you get in touch when you were released?"

They were inside the café where they had already been talking for almost an hour, catching up on the current events in one another's lives. Conversation was so easy and intimate that Sarah felt ready to address the main topic on her mind. After considering several subtle ways of bringing it up, she had decided to be direct.

Ali sighed deeply. "Sarah . . ."

"Do you know how I heard you were free?" Sarah cut him off. "I ran into Mr. Shirazi's daughter, and she asked how you were doing. Do you have any idea what it feels like to learn, from someone I barely know, that my husband had already been out of jail for two weeks and hadn't bothered to come see me?"

Rather than looking apologetic, however, Ali looked irritated. "Well," he said, "I honestly wasn't sure you wanted to hear from me, since you completely forgot about me while I was in prison. Prison! I thought maybe you finally agreed with your aunt that marrying me was a bad idea. My parents said you never once called to ask about me. Why?"

This wasn't right, Sarah thought. How was it that she was the one being put on the defensive?

"Why didn't your family call me?" Sarah turned the question on Ali. "Why didn't they call, even once, to see how *I* was doing after those men ripped my husband away from me the night of my wedding."

"They did!" Ali insisted. "They even came to your house to see you."

"No!" Sarah knew her voice was too loud but couldn't help herself. "I never saw them. I never heard from them. Never!"

Ali didn't say anything but looked at her expectantly, as if waiting for her to figure something out.

"No," Sarah said again but this time in a whisper. She shook her head as if the movement would stave off a truth that Sarah did

not want to accept. "My parents wouldn't have . . . I don't believe
it, I . . . How could they have managed it?"

Even as she asked the question, unbidden memories arose of
the small pink sleeping pills her mother had insisted she take that
first night and for several days after.

"My God!" Sarah breathed. "I just can't believe they would do
such a thing. I . . . I need to talk to them. Maybe it was a misunderstanding. Or they were worried about upsetting me. Or . . ." Sarah's
mind searched for an explanation that would absolve her parents.

"Anyway, I don't know exactly what happened," Sarah said,
unwilling to speak ill of her parents. "But, you have to believe me.
I never knew that your family visited or called. My mother told
me your family blamed us for the arrest. I didn't think they would
want to hear from me."

"All you had to do"—Ali's eyes were unyielding—"was pick
up the phone one time and call my mother, and this would have
all been cleared up. Why didn't you?"

He was angry with her! Sarah couldn't understand it. Didn't
he see that it wasn't her fault?

"I don't know," she stammered, lips trembling. "I was afraid, I
guess. I didn't know they had called me, and I thought they were
angry at me and my family. And my parents, well, they told me it
would be better not to call."

Ali leaned forward, elbows on the table, his eyes locked on
hers. "Sarah. This is important. I can't be married to someone
who will put her parents above me. Look, I love my parents too,
and I want them to be happy, just like you want your parents to
be happy. But there are times when the best decision for us isn't
going to please anyone else, and I need to know that my wife
will stand by me. Otherwise, there really is no point in this."

Sarah was weeping with anger. She wiped at her cheeks with
scratchy café napkins as she responded. "That's not fair! We didn't

make a decision together that I could defend to my parents. You were in jail and I was all alone, trying to figure out what to do. Maybe I didn't make the best choice. Maybe I should have called. But when you aren't around, you shouldn't be surprised if I listen to my parents. They've cared for me my whole life. You and I hadn't even known each other for three months when you were arrested."

Sarah blew her nose and tried to calm her breathing.

"It doesn't matter how long we've known each other," Ali insisted. "I need to know I am my wife's first priority, and she needs to know she is mine. I need to know that when I'm dragged into jail, her heart is with me and she's thinking of me and trying to help me and my family."

"I *was* thinking of you! You have no idea what it was like for me. Every day, from the moment I opened my eyes to when I finally fell asleep at night, I was praying and begging and crying for God's intercession. I couldn't eat. I didn't talk to anyone. I sat in my room all day except for the few times we went to the shrines to pray for your release. And then, after a month and a half of this, I find out from some stranger that you've been out for two weeks . . . How do you think that made me feel?"

Ali rocked his head slightly from side to side as if to consider her words.

Sarah knew what she had to do to make him see her side of it. She slid the yellow notebook across the table. It wasn't pretty. Just a standard A4 notebook left over from the previous school year. But it would make him understand.

"What's this?" Ali asked.

Sarah kept her eyes on the notebook. "When you were gone, I felt so alone. I was so used to talking to you and emailing you. And I was afraid everything would be monitored, so I, well, I wrote to you in that notebook. If you read it, you'll see I didn't forget you."

Ali thumbed through the notebook. "You filled almost the

whole thing," he commented. Then he flipped to the front and started reading Sarah's first entry which was written four days after Ali's arrest, when she'd finally stopped taking her mother's sleeping pills and had a clear head but no idea what to do.

Sarah waited, trying to remember what she'd written in that first entry and wondering what Ali would think. As he read, his tongue returned to the jagged edge of his lateral incisor.

Ali looked up from the notebook. He smiled at her. "You still sleep with my jacket?" he teased.

Ali had left his wedding suit jacket in the car when he'd been arrested. In the days and weeks that followed, Sarah used it as a covering at night to feel closer to him. She remembered having sworn in her first notebook entry that she would sleep with that jacket until it was replaced by her beloved.

Sarah narrowed her eyes at Ali. "I burned it when I realized you hadn't contacted me after your release."

Ali looked startled for a moment and then, realizing she was teasing him back, broke into a loud guffaw. Sarah let her mask of feigned anger drop and joined in with laughter of her own.

"Oh Sarah-khanoom," Ali said shaking his head. "You're too much!"

He glanced at the grimy clock on the café wall. "I actually have to go. I'm already late for a meeting."

"Really? But I came early so we could have plenty of time together." Sarah couldn't help teasing again.

Ali chuckled. "Yes, it's terribly inconsiderate of me," he said with sarcasm. "But I do have to go. Can I take this with me to read?" He gestured to the yellow notebook.

"Yes, of course," Sarah said. "It's yours now. You can do whatever you want with it."

Ali slipped it into his briefcase and gathered his things but remained seated at the table.

"I want to see you again," he said in a low voice. "Let's meet at the house next time so we can have some privacy."

"What house?" Sarah felt her cheeks grow warm, but she pretended she didn't know what he was talking about.

"Our house," Ali said. "The one we were going to live in . . . the one we were driving to on our wedding night."

Sarah tried to answer coolly. "Sure. Why not?"

They decided on a date and time, and he gave her his new cell phone number so she could call or text if needed. They stepped outside the café, where Ali chuckled again in the midst of their final goodbyes.

"I'm going to have that image of you running down the hill"— Ali gestured to the hill in question—"in my head all day long."

Sarah made a face at him, pretending to be offended as internally she relished the accomplishment of having made him laugh once again.

"You're constantly surprising me, Sarah. I . . ."

Ali's voice trailed off, and the smile on his face stiffened. Sarah followed his gaze across the street to the front gate of a shabby apartment building from which a small, neat man with a trim white beard was exiting. The man looked up and down the street before motioning to a car that quickly pulled up before him. The man licked his unusually dark purple lips and then pulled out his telephone and punched at it with his thumb as he got into the car. Sarah and Ali watched as the car drove off down the hill, the man inside with his ear pressed against his phone.

Sarah asked. "Who was that?"

Ali's entire affect had changed from the relaxed, teasing posture of a few seconds ago. He was breathing hard and put his hand up to rub his forehead.

"Ali," Sarah called his name with alarm. "Are you okay?"

"I'm sorry," Ali answered, still rubbing his forehead as if to erase something from it. "It's just . . . He was one of the people . . . in jail. He . . ."

"He was one of the protestors?" Sarah asked.

"No . . . he was . . . God! These people won't let me alone!" Ali shook his head. He looked angry.

"I don't understand," Sarah said.

"Nothing. Never mind. I'm okay. I just . . . Let's forget it." Ali took a deep breath and turned away from her and then back in a slow circle. When he faced her again, he looked calm.

"Okay, Sarah dear, I really need to go," he said. "You can get yourself home from here, right?"

"Yes, yes, of course," she answered.

Ali turned to go, and Sarah watched him walk down the hill, one hand holding his briefcase, the other in his pocket. A light wind blew into his suit jacket so that it ballooned around behind him. At the bottom of the hill, Ali turned and smiled at her before heading east on Keshavarz.

Sarah couldn't wait to see him again. She was sure he'd suggested they meet at their apartment so they could . . . Well, she wasn't sure how she felt about that. It might be best to stick with public places for now. At least until they were 100 percent sure that their parents would let them stay married. Although now that she and Ali had reconnected, she supposed it wasn't up to their parents anymore.

Lost in these happy thoughts, Sarah turned to start walking up the hill, feeling the blister on her heel protest as she did so. She glanced across the street and was surprised by the sight of a familiar face in an unfamiliar setting.

At the building from which Ali's jail acquaintance had exited. Sadegh.

What was her cousin doing here? Sarah watched him buzz and speak into the intercom system. She noticed that Sadegh was holding a bouquet of yellow and purple flowers. He must be going to someone's house. Sarah watched as Sadegh waited for what seemed like a long time until the gate was opened, manually it seemed, by a girl who greeted him warmly. Sarah gasped as she recognized yet another familiar face. It was the beautiful girl she and Ali had saved on their wedding night.

*   *   *

"You're sure it was the same girl?"

Ali questioned Sarah as they sat at their small kitchen table eating delicious kabobs he had picked up from Nayeb restaurant. Sarah had overcome her qualms about meeting him at their condo. He was still her husband after all, so there were, technically, no religious grounds for concern. But, although she removed the long black chador when they came inside, she kept her headscarf and manteau on.

Sarah had looked forward to seeing their condo again. It looked almost exactly like it did the last time she had seen it, shortly before the wedding, when she and her mother and a few cousins had worked on the final decorative touches. Sarah did notice, however, that the beautiful embroidered kitchen hand towels her mother had picked out had been replaced with a plainer variety she did not recognize. And the few dishes in the drainer to the left of the sink were not from the collection of Italian dishware her family had stocked the cabinets with. Probably, she noted with approval, Ali had been spending time here but didn't feel right about using all the beautiful things her family had purchased for them to use as a couple.

Sarah considered Ali's question as she chewed her food.

"Well, I only saw her for a moment, and she was all the way across the street. But . . . I remember her face. And her eyes were so unusually light. It was definitely her. I just can't imagine what Sadegh would be doing there."

Ali cocked his head as if to chide her for not catching on. "I think it's actually pretty clear. She was probably working with your cousin that night to get me arrested."

Sarah was confused. "How could that be possible? She was one of the protesters. I was the one who invited her into our car."

"I don't know, Sarah. Maybe she stopped right in front of our car knowing we would try to help her. Maybe they paid her off afterward in return for her testimony. All I know is that my arrest was no accident. It was a trap to get at my sister and her husband through me."

"Ali, that doesn't make sense," Sarah protested. "Why wouldn't they just have gone after your sister directly? And how are you making all of these connections just because Sadegh was with this woman? Maybe it has nothing to do with that night."

"It has everything to do with it!" Ali cried. "Sarah, remember the man that left the same building just before I said goodbye? That man . . . he was one of the people that took me in. He was in charge of them, actually, and he was . . . a terror. He never laid a finger on me, but I saw him do some things that . . ."

Ali shook his head and took a deep breath before continuing. "Anyway, if it had been just Sadegh and that girl, okay, it might have been a coincidence. But how do you explain three people from that night coming together again. That building must be an undercover station for the Basij. They use residential buildings so no one can guess where their stations are. And I'm starting to think they actually wanted us to see them."

"What?"

Ali's voice quavered. "They want me to know they're watching me. God! What am I going to do?"

Sarah was shocked to see Ali cover his face with his thick

fingers and begin shaking with what looked like sobs. She'd never seen her father cry and felt a bit embarrassed for Ali. She reached tentatively across the table to pat his arm.

"Don't cry. Nothing has happened. It's okay," she tried to comfort him.

Ali grabbed her hand and squeezed hard as he continued to cry. After a moment, he took a few deep breaths, calmed himself, and wiped at his eyes. He raised her hand to press it against his scratchy cheek and then smiled sheepishly.

"I'm sorry," he apologized. "I've been under so much pressure."

"I know," Sarah reassured him. But her mind was on the feel of his breath on the back of her hand. "Prison must have been awful."

"No. I mean, yes, prison was . . . worse than you can imagine. But that's not what's upsetting me. Sarah, I need to tell you something. I haven't told anyone, and you can't tell anyone. I know we haven't settled everything between us, but I know I can trust you. And I need your advice."

"What is it?" Sarah asked.

Ali brought his hands down to the table, but held on to Sarah's. He opened her fingers and traced circles on her like he'd done in the car on their wedding night.

"I've been telling them about my sister," he said.

Sarah was distracted by the feel of Ali's fingers but managed to ask, "What? Who do you mean? What are you telling them?"

"I don't know who it is. Every few weeks they call and ask questions. The thing is, as part of my release, I agreed to give them information about her. They said they just wanted to know things like her daily schedule or whatever."

"They want you to spy on her?"

Ali stopped tracing circles and looked at her.

"See . . ." He paused and swallowed. "I didn't think of it as spying. They made it sound like I would just be helping them confirm that Azar and her husband aren't really up to anything. And I was so sure about Azar that I figured this was a good way for me to get out and help clear her name in the process and that they would get bored with us soon and it would end. But now . . . I don't know what's going on. They're asking questions about a 'Foundation' I don't know anything about. And, well, Azar has changed too. Or maybe I'm noticing for the first time. I never would have thought it . . . My sister always cared about women and their rights. But I thought the goal was to fix the system, not to work with foreigners to overthrow it. And now . . . I don't know. She's been banned from working, and yet she always seems to be leaving the boys with my parents to go into her office. What is she doing there?"

"You think she's involved with the *fitneh* to overthrow the government?" Sarah asked. "But what's the point? No one even goes to their demonstrations anymore. The best they can do is show up at government events and have a few people shout the wrong slogans." Sarah was referring, among other things, to the Jerusalem Day event of a few weeks earlier. Every year, people poured into the streets for a government-sponsored demonstration of the country's commitment to the Palestinian people. This year, the few remaining Green Wave supporters had used the opportunity to gather and shout tired slogans such as "Where's my vote?"

"I don't know for sure what she's doing. But, if she's involved in some sort of plotting, well, I'm so angry with her and Ibrahim. How dare they jeopardize their family and endanger our lives and livelihoods? What about their boys? What about me and my parents? Just between us . . . when I took over my father's company it was a mess. You wouldn't believe it. I couldn't believe it myself. But we were close to bankruptcy. Over the past five years, I've built the company so we have contracts with some of the biggest Chinese manufacturers. And it can all go up in smoke within twenty-four hours if we anger the wrong people. Already, business has been affected by my imprisonment. But none of that matters to Azar. For her, it's all about democracy and women's rights, and I admire that, but what good is it if your family goes hungry?"

"Have you told her?" Sarah asked.

"Told her that these people are asking about her? No!" Ali looked at Sarah as if he couldn't believe she was asking the question, but he also looked as if he'd asked himself many times if he should do just that.

"I mean," Sarah clarified, "have you tried to get her to stop some of what she's involved with?"

"Oh, yes, of course," Ali said, nodding. "Well . . . ," He reconsidered, "not directly. But we do talk about politics, and she knows how I feel about it. It's not worth bringing up again. She's . . . well, you know they took her in too. She's out now, *alhamdulillah*, but they've got Ibrahim, her husband."

"Oh my God," Sarah said. "I didn't know." Her anger flared as she wondered what Azar and Ibrahim had been arrested for. Ali was right. They were incredibly selfish people. If she and Ali were going to try to rekindle something, and she still wasn't sure that they were, it was going to be even harder to convince her parents and Aunt Mehri to accept Ali with his sister directly involved in efforts to overthrow the government.

"Yeah, they're something else," Ali said, shaking his head. "So far as I'm concerned, there's nothing in the world that's worth risking another second in prison. But the two of them are so stubborn. And I'm afraid of what it's costing me . . . my freedom, my business, my—" He looked at her intently. "—my wife."

Sarah didn't say anything but noticed his fingers were tracing circles again, this time on the back of her hand.

"Sarah. I don't know what's going on with my sister. And now the security forces are following me. I have no idea how this is going to play out. But"—He looked at her with a hungry need—"I know I want you with me."

Sarah felt her whole body pulse like a single nerve transmitting an urgent message.

"I read your notebook, Sarah," Ali said as he pulled her hand to his lips for a kiss. "I'm sorry I ever doubted you." He kissed her hand again, his scratchy beard tickling the back of her fingers. "I realize you were in a sort of prison too." Another kiss. "Can you forgive me? And can I count on you now? Can we be a team and stand together no matter what my family or your family says? I need to know."

Ali had stopped kissing her hand and held it against his cheek, waiting for Sarah's answer.

Sarah locked eyes with Ali and, without any hesitation, said, "Yes. So long as you don't doubt me again, I'm yours."

Ali reached across the table and tugged at her head scarf. He spoke in a low growl.

"Then what are you still wearing this for?"

*   *   *

Sarah saw Ali as often as she could manage. She started skipping classes, and Ali took long lunches to accommodate their all-too-brief visits to the condo. They talked about when and how they should break the news to their families but agreed to keep it a secret for now. Ali didn't want to further burden his parents, who were already overwhelmed with helping Azar and her kids deal with her husband's absence. Sarah made similar claims about her own family but, truth be told, simply didn't have the stomach to confront her parents with the lies they'd told her or deal with the hailstorm of fury that would come once they learned about her rekindled relationship with Ali.

Besides, keeping the secret was fun. The condo was a separate reality, all the more precious for being unknown and inaccessible to the outside world. Sarah was in no rush to expose their happy cocoon to outsiders whose unappreciative gaze might bruise its magic.

But keeping the secret was also harder than Sarah might have thought. It wasn't that she had to lie. Sarah was a horrible liar, so she was grateful that her university schedule was sufficient to justify her comings and goings. What was hard was containing the joy that bubbled forth unceasingly in the form of dreamy smiles and distracted attempts to keep up with conversation, when all she really wanted to do was sit and think about Ali.

Which was what she was doing at her aunt's home, almost two months after she and Ali had started seeing each other again, when the conversation took a turn that captured her full attention.

It was after Friday luncheon, and the whole extended family had retired to the formal living room for tea. As usual, the men had congregated in one corner of the room, while the ladies bunched around several coffee tables on the other side. Sarah, exhausted and lost in her plans to see Ali the next day, ignored the ladies' chitchat. What should she wear tomorrow? How should she do her hair? It wasn't easy thinking of clothes and a hairstyle that would stay presentable under the layers of coverings she would be wearing on the way over. Maybe Ali was right and she should keep a key of her own. That way, she could arrive earlier and change into whatever she wanted to wear for him.

Sarah yawned. She was so sleepy these days. Wasn't love supposed to energize you?

Suddenly her aunt reached over and snapped her rheumatoid fingers in front of her face.

"*Kojaee?*" Aunt Mehri demanded in her shrill voice. "Where are you, Sarah?"

Sarah was irritated at having been jolted out of her own thoughts but forced a smile and apologized. "*Bebakhshid.* I was distracted."

"I can see that," Aunt Mehri harrumphed. She turned to Sarah's mother and asked "Mahdiyeh, did you get things straightened out for this girl of yours?"

Her mother shook her head to indicate that the answer was no. "We're working on it," she said. "I called his mother again this week."

Her aunt rolled her eyes. "*Khodaya.* My God! You're still working on it? You should have taken care of this immediately. How are you going to find someone else for her if she's still legally attached to this boy?"

"I know. We wanted to but . . ." Her mother glanced at her before continuing. "Sarah wasn't ready and Ali was in jail, so there was really nothing we could do."

"*Azizam,* come on!" Aunt Mehri's voice was disbelieving. "He's been out for months!"

"I know," Sarah's mother agreed. "But that family . . . I just don't know what to think."

Sarah interrupted. "About what? What do you mean?"

The ladies ignored her, and her mother went on. "Before now, I didn't want to press them too much. Their daughter was still in jail, and now their son-in-law . . ."

Sarah was surprised to realize her mother had known about Azar and her husband. What else had they kept from her?

Aunt Mehri jumped in. "You're worried about *their* daughter? Mahdiyeh, you need to worry about your own daughter!"

"You're right—you're completely right." As always, Maman-joon swiftly capitulated to her older sister. "They're giving us such a hard time. I talked with Ali's mother again yesterday, and now she says that he refuses to agree to a divorce."

"What?" Aunt Mehri clucked. "It's about the *mehriyeh*, the dowry, isn't it?"

"I don't think so. We told them we don't want it. We'd gladly forfeit the whole thing just to get this over with. I don't know what the problem is, but without their agreement, it won't be easy."

Sarah's aunt shook her head again, and her voice trembled as she spoke. "The problem is who these people are. They're parasites! They destroy everything good and clean and holy that they come near. It's just like these protesters who hijacked the thirteenth of Aban commemoration of our victory over America to turn it into a Green demonstration. It makes me sick just thinking about them. Mahdiyeh dear, you know I never like to say I told you so, but it just breaks my heart . . . I can't help but think that so much needless heartbreak could have been avoided if only . . . Well, I suppose there is no point dwelling on it."

Sarah's mother was penitent. "You are absolutely right Mehri-joon. I'm truly horrified and ashamed that we ignored your counsel, and you can be sure it won't happen again."

Aunt Mehri was mollified. "Well, anyway . . . we need to figure something out for Sarah soon. She's so distracted . . . It's almost like she's in love with some college boy. You need to be more careful about the way you let her come and go."

Sarah protested. "I'm not in love with a college boy!"

Her aunt ignored Sarah altogether and continued talking to Maman-joon.

"But seriously, I have a few ideas for Sarah. You know the family that we went on Hajj with? They have a boy that is suitable. He's not very good looking. He's got some sort of acne infection. But he's from a good family and we can't be too picky now."

Sarah felt sick to her stomach.

It was at this moment that her cousin Sadegh broke into the conversation from across the room.

"You're talking about Massoud? He's a very good boy. A thousand times better than that scum, Ali. It's a very good idea."

Sarah was enraged. How dare he!

"Scum?" Sarah challenged her cousin, "You don't even know him."

The living room suddenly quieted as the emotion in Sarah's voice registered.

Sadegh looked at Sarah in surprise before answering. "Well . . . I know his family. I know what type of people they are. Look what they're trying to do to our country. Look how they encouraged people into the street again. If we don't stop them, they'll invite the Americans in tomorrow and turn us into another Iraq."

Explosions went off in Sarah's head.

"Oh my God! It *was* you. All this time I couldn't believe it, but you are the one that got him arrested. You're the one that ruined my life!"

"Sarah!" Her mother interjected with a nervous laugh. "Don't be silly."

Sadegh looked irritated. He stroked his beard with his long thin fingers. "What are you talking about? I'm just trying to help. Where do you get these crazy ideas?"

Sarah felt the weight of her family's eyes watching for her response. She decided she wouldn't back down and shouted, "I know you were involved! I saw you."

Sadegh rolled his green eyes condescendingly and pulled his thumb and forefinger along the sides of his mouth. "When did you see me dear cousin?"

"I saw you! With that girl near Laleh park. You had flowers."

Sadegh froze. He opened his mouth as if he wanted to say something. Then he closed it and swallowed.

Sarah's aunt spoke up. "*Chi migeh?* What is she saying Sadegh?"

Sarah repeated. "I saw him! Don't try to deny it. What were you doing with her?"

Sadegh looked at his mother. He looked at his wife. His face was flushed. He rose from his seat and walked out of the room. After a brief moment, his wife went after him.

Sarah's mother hissed. "What is wrong with you? What are you doing?"

It was only then that Sarah thought about the small detail of the flowers whose significance she had previously overlooked. Sadegh hadn't gone to that apartment building for work or to spy on someone. He was taking flowers to a beautiful woman who was not his wife.

CHAPTER 5

Friday, November 27, 2009—five and a half months after the election

> Iran's Revolutionary Guard has confirmed that five British sailors have been detained after apparently straying into the country's coastal waters.
> —Stephen Adams, *The Telegraph*, December 1, 2009[5]

Sadegh stepped into a pair of sandals on the back patio and jogged down the three wide steps to the garden, where he began walking the path around its perimeter, trying to calm himself.

How could Sarah have seen him with Leila? Laleh Park was nowhere near any place Sarah needed to be . . . What was she doing there? It was incredible how little control Sarah's parents had over her.

At the far corner of the garden, Sadegh grabbed a broken broom handle from among the shovels and rakes leaning against the wall. He lifted the long handle and brought it down on the trunk of his mother's massive walnut tree. The stick vibrated at the contact and generated a painful and satisfying warmth in his hands. Sadegh raised the broom handle and struck the tree again. Crows squawked and vacated the tree. He lifted the handle for a third blow but stopped at the sound of footsteps. He guessed it was his wife and didn't want to further alienate her with his display of temper.

Sadegh turned around. He held the broomstick horizontally with his hands joined together and resting on his thighs. With his head bowed, he felt like a disgraced servant awaiting judgement. He had no idea what he would say to Sumayeh.

Complete honesty was a core tenet of their relationship. One of Sadegh's first conversations with Sumayeh during their *khastegari* had been about dishonesty and how it was akin to idolatry in that the liar feared another person's reaction more than they feared God's. Since they'd been married, whenever Sadegh had felt even the slightest unholy attraction to a woman in the streets, he'd admitted it immediately to Sumayeh. How was she going to understand his deceptions about Leila?

Sumayeh finally spoke. "*Khob, chi shode?* So, what's going on?"

Sadegh fixed his eyes on his wife's thin and delicate feet shod in black plastic men's sandals that were much too big. Sumayeh must have stepped into whatever shoes she'd first found on the back patio.

"Nothing, azizam." He answered. "Really, there's nothing to worry about. I just . . ." He didn't know where to start, so he shrugged his shoulders and shook his head again.

"What's that supposed to mean?" Sumayeh snapped.

Sadegh looked at his angry wife. The afternoon shadows played with her scar, making it look like a long and strange extension of her frown.

"Nothing. I'm so sorry," Sadegh tried to communicate just how sorry and ashamed he was with his voice, his eyes, his posture. "I wasn't sure . . . but then I couldn't say no. And I thought if I saw her once that would be enough, but then it was even harder."

"Sadegh. I don't understand." She emphasized the last conso-
nant of each word, as if speaking in time to the thump of an ax
hitting a tree. "What are you talking about? Who is she?"

"Her name is Leila."

"And you're . . . She's . . . I know it's not possible . . . but Sarah
made it seem as if she was some sort of . . . Well, who is she?"

Sadegh was confused by these halting questions from his
usually unflappable wife. He'd expected calm and cold condem-
nation. Why did Sumayeh look so disconcerted?

"Leila"—Sadegh saw Sumayeh's black eyes flinch as he said
her name in the familiar way without a *Ms.* or *khanoom*—"is my
sister. It's kind of unbelievable really. My birth mother, well, she
found me in the summer, the day after Sarah's wedding. And,
well, Leila is her daughter. From her second husband."

Sumayeh's eyes reflected her relief. "Oh," she exhaled. "Yes,
that makes sense now. She's your sister, not . . ."

Sumayeh didn't finish the sentence, but it was enough to make
Sadegh finally understand. "Wait, you thought she was some sort
of . . . girlfriend?" Sadegh was astounded that his wife could even
consider such a thing and relieved that his actual sins were so
much more benign than what he'd been suspected of. He bounced
the broken broomstick in his hands and almost started chuckling
at the misunderstanding, but swallowed his laughter in the face of
Sumayeh's angry expression.

"What am I supposed to think?" she demanded. "All I know
is that you've been hiding something. That's a betrayal whether it
involves a girlfriend or not."

Sadegh answered with sincere penitence, "I am sorry,
Sumayeh-joonam. Let me explain."

Sadegh gestured to a small stone bench where Sumayeh sat
and listened as he told her about the woman he'd met outside the

Sa'adat Abad mosque who'd turned out to be his mother. She'd asked questions, that Sadegh had refused to answer, of course, about Ali. He'd cut the visit short as quickly as he could, but not without agreeing to another meeting. He'd been introduced to his sister, Leila, for the first time at Valiasr square, near the women's clothing shop where she was employed. Since then, he'd seen her and their mother only three more times, once at their flat near Laleh Park, where Sarah must have seen him.

When he finished his story, Sadegh waited for Sumayeh's response as she picked apart a dry autumn leaf so that only its bony veins remained attached to the stalk.

"It's incredible that she found you," Sumayeh finally said. "And I can't imagine how you must feel about meeting her after all this time. But I still don't understand." Sumayeh dropped the remains of the leaf on the ground and looked up at Sadegh with wounded eyes. "Why didn't you tell me? Why did you keep this a secret for so long?"

Sadegh dropped Sumayeh's gaze and fiddled with the broom handle as he thought about what to say. The fact was that Sadegh had put off telling his wife in a childish attempt to preserve his uncomplicated life by willing away and ignoring things he didn't want to deal with. He wasn't sure how the sudden appearance of a new mother and sister would change things. He didn't know what the impact would be on Maman-Mehri and his siblings. He resented the intrusion of these women and wanted to minimize their contact with and impact on his real life for as long as possible. But trying to pretend they didn't exist was such a childish and cowardly response that he knew it would only increase Sumayeh's disappointment in him.

"Well," Sadegh spoke slowly. "I wanted to see what type of people they are before involving our family."

Sadegh watched Sumayeh's reaction as he spoke. She was

listening intently, trying to understand, maybe even hoping for an explanation she'd find forgivable.

Sadegh continued. "And, frankly, I'm not sure it's a good idea to have too much contact with them."

Sumayeh cocked her head. "If it isn't a good idea to have contact with them, then why are you still seeing them?"

Sadegh leaned on the broom handle, twisting its broken end into the dirt. "I'm still trying to figure it out. See, the last time I saw them, about a month ago, she . . . my mother started talking about Leila getting married. It came out of nowhere, and since then she's been calling and hounding me about helping them find a good match and—well, I can only think of one reason why there would suddenly be so much urgency about getting married."

"You think she's pregnant?" Sumayeh understood immediately. She wrinkled her American nose as if she'd seen a cockroach in the kitchen.

Sadegh stopped fidgeting with the stick and shrugged. "I'm just guessing. I don't know about this type of thing. But it's been hard for me to decide how involved to be. I'm not going to trick some young man into marrying her if that's what's going on."

"No, of course not." Sumayeh was quiet a moment and then asked, "How old is she?"

"Nineteen. The same age as Sarah. And she seems to be a good girl but . . . well, she doesn't have a father around, and I don't really know how *mughayed,* observant, they are."

"I see." Sumayeh frowned as if she was working out a problem.

"Sumayeh, dear, what should I do?" Sadegh sincerely wanted his wife's opinion. But he also hoped that Sumayeh might get so busy figuring out and telling him what he should do that she'd forget about being angry with him.

"What you should have done, Sadegh," Sumayeh eyed him as she answered, "was to come to me immediately."

Sadegh's attempt at diversion hadn't worked. He pulled the broomstick toward himself and tensed behind it as if to make himself small enough that it would protect him from his wife's disapproval.

"I know, Sumayeh-jaan, azizam," Sadegh said. "I'm so sorry I hurt you."

Sumayeh cut him off. "No, not because of that. My feelings aren't important." Sumayeh waved her hand in the air as if erasing her feelings from the equation. "I can see you were trying to do what is right, and that is the most important thing. The point is that you should have come to me because I could have helped you figure out this whole mess a long time ago. If something strange is going on or your sister really is pregnant or in some other type of trouble, I'm the one that can figure this out. Women are much better at this sort of thing."

"Really?" Sadegh took a deep breath of relief. "Oh, Sumayeh, you're so right. I should have come to you from the beginning."

Sadegh tossed the broomstick aside, sat next to his wife, and took her hands. They were ice cold.

"Azizam," he said as he pulled her close and rubbed her back and arms. "You're freezing."

The air was crisp but not especially cold for a late November afternoon, and Sadegh, warmed by his anger and shame hadn't felt a thing. But he should have noticed that Sumayeh was getting cold.

"I'm fine," Sumayeh insisted. And she pushed him away, motioning to the patio.

It was Maman-Mehri. Moving heavily, she came to the top of the stairs and leaned against the railing.

"Sadegh-jaan, Sumayeh-jaan, *ye lahze biya, karet daram.* Come here, I want to say something."

Sadegh and Sumayeh stood and walked toward his mother,

Sumayeh in front on the narrow path. Sadegh whispered as they approached. "Just don't say anything to her about this."

He hoped Sumayeh would understand. There was no need to lie. But there was also no need to share the full story. Sadegh wasn't sure exactly how Maman-Mehri would react to the news of his mother and sister's reemergence. But he was sure it wouldn't be good. Why not spare her as long as possible?

Sumayeh turned and looked at Sadegh as if she was about to say something. But she was cut off by Maman-Mehri.

"Thank you, my dears." Maman-Mehri was breathing hard as she spoke. With her house chador wrapped tightly around her spherical body, she looked like a sky-blue balloon that was rapidly inflating and deflating with each breath.

"You know, I never like to meddle in my children's marriages. So far as I'm concerned, you always know best. But sometimes, well, us older folks have some experiences of life that we have an ob-li-ga-tion to share." Maman-Mehri rapped the rail to emphasize each part of the word. "It's my duty, even though it is hard for me, to give advice that can keep you on the right path and save you from sorrow or sin."

Maman-Mehri put a hand, wrapped in her chador, on her heart, "Sumayeh, my *aroos*, I could not ask for a better daughter-in-law."

"And I couldn't ask for a better—" Sumayeh began but was interrupted.

"You're an angel! A rose!" Maman-Mehri's voice quivered with emotion. "For me, there is absolutely no difference between you and my own daughters. I love you just like I love them. Every time I say my prayers, I thank God for you and do extra prayers for your safety and happiness."

Sadegh knew it was true. Maman-Mehri had initially been skeptical of his interest in Sumayeh, with her odd family background.

Sumayeh's mother was not only American but was a former nun whose yearning for a cloistered life devoted to God that could also incorporate children and a family had led her to Islam. She'd met and married Sumayeh's father at UCLA, where he was a leader in the campus Muslim Student Association, and the two of them became increasingly involved in anti-Shah and pro-Khomeini activities until they moved to Tehran in November 1978.

But once Maman-Mehri had seen how determined Sadegh was to win Sumayeh, she quickly got on board and did everything within her power to convince Sumayeh's parents that her family would be a good match. And she'd been a generous and loving mother-in-law ever since. She and Sumayeh had taken to each other naturally, bonding over their shared devotion to God and family. So when Maman-Mehri said Sumayeh was like a daughter to her, no one could doubt it.

"Mersi, Maman-Mehri," Sumayeh said, but Maman-Mehri had turned her attention to her son.

"Sadegh,"—Maman-Mehri's tone was sorrowful—"if you have done something that has hurt Sumayeh in any way, you have made a grave mistake. And if you persist in this, you must know that God will not forgive you and that even I, your mother, will not forgive you."

Sumayeh looked hard at Sadegh. He could tell she wanted him to correct Maman-Mehri's misunderstanding and explain that Leila was just his sister. But Sadegh shook his head to indicate that he wasn't going to. He hoped Sumayeh would understand enough to keep quiet as well. Maman-Mehri might be disappointed to think he'd engaged in some sort of illicit relationship. But he was sure she'd be devastated to learn that Sadegh had reconnected with his biological mother. Sadegh cursed his cousin once more for putting him in this position. Sarah was such a selfish girl.

Taking Sadegh's motion as an attempt to interrupt her, Maman-

Mehri started speaking more loudly. "I am not finished, Sadegh!" she barked. "And there is nothing you need to say anyway. It's none of *my* business. You have to make this right with God. You have to make this right with your wife. *They* are the ones whose forgiveness you must beg."

Sadegh nodded in what he hoped was a penitent manner. But Maman-Mehri had turned back to Sumayeh. "Sumayeh, my darling girl, I know the pain you are in, believe me, I know better than you can imagine. And I know that, even if it seems impossible, the only way forward, the only way to soothe your deep hurt, is to forgive."

Here, Maman-Mehri paused, and it became clear she was fighting back tears.

Sadegh noted with alarm that Sumayeh was trying to interject as she walked up the steps to take her mother-in-law's hand. "Maman-Mehri, it's okay, it's just a mis—"

Maman-Mehri spoke passionately through her tears. "No! I don't want to hear the details. It is too much for a mother to witness the mistakes of her children." Maman-Mehri's voice was so high-pitched, she was practically squeaking. "And it's none of my business anyway. I just need you to understand that there is beauty in forgiveness. So much beauty! I'm not only saying this. I know! I know because I lived it. My husband, God forgive and bless him, made mistakes too. And I saw with my own eyes that when you are willing to forgive, all-merciful, all-loving God rewards you a thousand times over. Whatever has been taken away will be returned with more than you can even imagine! Don't let pride or hurt feelings keep you from such rewards my dear. Promise me."

Maman-Mehri wiped at her eyes with the sides of her chador.

Sumayeh started again, "Maman-Mehri, please don't be upset. Sadegh didn't—"

Sadegh rushed up the stairs and grabbed Sumayeh's elbow but she'd already been interrupted by Maman-Mehri.

"Just promise me!" Maman-Mehri begged as she stroked Sumayeh's hand. "Oh, my dear beautiful child."

"The woman Sadegh has been seeing is—" Sumayeh began.

Sadegh barked sternly, "Sumayeh!" How could she not understand that Sadegh's reunion with his birth mother would cause Maman-Mehri much more pain than any assumptions she might be making now about possibly infidelity.

"She needs to know," Sumayeh insisted.

Maman-Mehri replied through her tears. "No, I don't need to know. I'm going inside now, and we never have to speak of this again. I've done my duty in warning you both. Now it is up to you. All I can do is pray."

Maman-Mehri turned to head back into the house, but Sumayeh held tight to her hand.

"Maman-Mehri, please listen. It's all a misunderstanding."

Sadegh was panicking now. He broke his wife's hold on his mother's hand and shouted, "Sumayeh, let her go! You aren't helping!"

But Sumayeh would not be deterred. "Sadegh! What's wrong with you? You'd rather your mother believe a lie, when all you were doing was seeing your sister? Maman-Mehri, Sadegh has been contacted by his . . . other mother."

There was nothing more Sadegh could do to protect himself. As he looked at Maman-Mehri's confused face, Sadegh realized that this was what he had most feared all along. This was the real reason he'd kept his mother and Leila a secret all these months. Because to tell Sumayeh would mean telling Maman-Mehri. And what would it do to Maman-Mehri's love for him if there was suddenly another mother in the picture and if they were forced to talk about things they preferred to keep hidden?

Yes, perhaps it was a form of idolatry to fear the loss of Maman-Mehri's love more than God's anger over dishonesty. But it was Sadegh's decision to make. Sumayeh had no right to force this conversation.

Maman-Mehri looked ill as she choked out her words. "What? What are you talking about?"

Sadegh kept quiet. Sumayeh had insisted on this. Let her deal with the fallout.

Sumayeh answered slowly. "Yes. I didn't know either. Sadegh's mother got in touch a few months back, and Sarah must have seen him when he was meeting his half sister. You see, it's all a misunderstanding. Sadegh would never, could never, do anything to hurt his family."

Sumayeh smiled comfortingly at Maman-Mehri, who looked desperately at Sadegh.

"Why?" Maman-Mehri demanded. "What does she want with you?"

Sadegh wished that he could take his mother's hand and kiss her cheek and ease her pain with some physical demonstration of his love. Instead, he tried to convey all of this with words that fell flat even to his own ears. "I don't know. It's not important. *Maman-e aziz*, my dearest mother, I am the dirt under your feet. You are everything to me, and you have done everything for me, and you will always be my mother. My only mother."

Maman-Mehri still looked stricken. She whispered, "How did she find you?"

Sadegh grimaced. "She was working for Ali's sister."

Maman-Mehri clutched her chest. "Ah! That family again. They'll stop at nothing!"

Sadegh didn't know what to say. Sumayeh remained silent. Perhaps now she recognized her mistake.

Maman-Mehri's breath caught. "I don't feel well. This is too much for me to bear. I need to go inside."

Maman-Mehri turned to go but stumbled lightly at her first

step. Sumayeh grabbed her and supported her inside with a backward glance at Sadegh that he couldn't quite read.

Alone in the garden, Sadegh looked up at the blue afternoon sky and prayed.

*   *   *

By the time Sadegh walked back in the house, the family luncheon had broken up. Sarah and her family as well as his brother's family had already left. His brothers-in-law were quietly conversing in the family room, but he didn't see his sisters, Sumayeh, or Maman-Mehri. Sadegh walked down the hallway toward the bedrooms. As he passed the guest room, he heard women's voices, Sumayeh's among them, speaking quietly.

Sadegh knocked lightly at the door and called, "Sumayeh?"

"*Janam*. Come in."

Sadegh pushed the door open and saw Sumayeh sitting on the bed with his two sisters, who looked up at him with more interest than usual.

"We should go," Sadegh said. "Where's Maman-Mehri?"

"It's better not to disturb her," Sumayeh answered. "She went to her room to sleep."

"Are you sure? I think maybe I should talk to her," Sadegh said.

"No, trust me, azizam. Let her rest and give her some space for now."

Sadegh might have protested further, but his sisters' vigorous nods suggested that all three women were in agreement about the best course of action. "Well, okay, then I guess we should go."

"Yes," Sumayeh agreed. "Can you take the baby out to the car? I'll get Mahdi and join you in just a minute."

Sadegh bade his sisters goodbye and picked up Sana, who'd been toddling around the bed. He made his way out of the house and into the car, where he waited impatiently for Sumayeh and Mahdi. The baby entertained herself with the steering wheel, gear shift, and other knobs and switches, managing to turn the radio on in the process, just in time for the top-of-the-hour news report.

President Ahmadinejad's office was promising a thorough investigation into the possible "evil intent" of five British sailors that had entered Iranian waters the previous week. Sadegh felt glad to have strong leaders protecting the country during these dangerous times when outside powers kept trying to meddle in Iranian affairs. Just this morning, Sadegh had read about the US pressuring other International Atomic Energy Association board members into a resolution condemning Iran for uranium enrichment in violation of nuclear agreements. He was certain this was an American plan to foment more support for the flailing Green revolution by getting other countries to go along with additional sanctions, thereby weakening Iran's economy and increasing dissatisfaction among the general public. The supposed yacht club "sailors" were probably spies sent to gather information and coordinate plans with Green Wave leaders.

The baby started fussing, and Sadegh dug through the diaper bag to find some treats to distract her with. By the time Sumayeh and Mahdi finally made it to the car, Sadegh was thoroughly irritated.

"Sorry you were waiting so long," Sumayeh apologized. "Mahdi was hiding, and I couldn't find him."

Sadegh was sure that hadn't been the only delay and wondered how long Sumayeh's conversation with his sisters had taken. But he didn't say anything and simply waited for the kids to be situated in their car seats and his wife to settle in beside him before starting the car.

"Okay," Sumayeh said. "I talked to your sisters, and we've got it all figured out. You'll invite Leila and her mother over for lunch sometime this week, and Zainab and Fati will come too, so we can figure out what these women are up to."

"What!" Sadegh had already guessed that Sumayeh was filling his sisters in. But he couldn't believe she was making all these decisions without consulting him. Before he could say any more, Mahdi piped up from the back seat.

"Who did you invite?"

Sumayeh ignored him and turned to Sadegh. "You're upset? I thought you would be happy."

Mahdi asked again. "Who's coming to lunch?"

Sadegh answered his wife. "Happy? For what? That you're telling the whole world about this?"

Sumayeh looked disbelieving. "How are your sisters the whole world? Of course, I told them. What am I supposed to do? Just let everyone go on thinking that you were having some sort of . . ."

Mahdi, unused to being ignored, was now kicking at the seat in front of him as he complained. "Tell me who's coming!"

Sumayeh sighed and turned to answer their son. "Mahdi-jaan, it hurts my back when you kick my chair. We're talking about having some ladies over. There won't be any kids, and it will be while you are at school."

Mahdi stopped kicking the chair but pouted. "Why don't you invite kids? You never invite kids!"

"We can talk about that another time," Sumayeh answered calmly. "Right now, your father and I are having an adult conversation."

But Sadegh, who didn't feel like talking anymore, said quietly to his wife. "It's okay. We can talk later. Just so long as Maman-Mehri isn't involved." Then he looked at his son in the rearview mirror and asked more loudly. "So tell me. Who would you like to invite?"

*   *   *

It wasn't an easy week. As Sumayeh busied herself with plans and preparations for the upcoming luncheon, Sadegh was reminded of another reason he'd avoided telling her about things in the first place. Sumayeh was always so sure she knew exactly what to do and proceeded with complete confidence that God would ensure the outcome. Sumayeh's only concession, and this due to his sisters' insistence combined with his own, was to avoid mentioning the get-together to his mother.

The luncheon was set for Wednesday afternoon. By Tuesday night, Sumayeh had almost everything ready. A delicious stew of beef, beans, and various green herbs was in a pot to be warmed up the next day. The house was clean, and the table was set with the elegant English dishware that Sadegh had showcased in the family's stores a few years back. All that was left was to make a salad and rice and pick up the kabobs that would round out the meal.

They were in the midst of these final preparations the following day when the doorbell buzzed.

Sumayeh looked at Sadegh in surprise. "Could that be Ms. Tabibian? It couldn't be your sisters. Their prayer meeting won't be over until noon at the earliest."

"I don't think so," Sadegh answered. "It's still early."

Sumayeh picked up the intercom handset and asked. "Yes? Who is it?"

Sumayeh's eyebrows tugged at her scar as they flew upward in surprise. "It's your mother!" she said as she buzzed the door open.

"Really?" Sadegh said. "I thought I told Leila to come at—"

"No, Sadegh," Sumayeh interrupted him, shaking her caramel-blond hair and looking at Sadegh with a mix of worry and compassion that delivered her meaning along with a jolt of adrenaline.

"Maman-Mehri?" Sadegh asked, his heart racing. "Since when does she drop by unannounced in the middle of the week?"

Sumayeh gave Sadegh an encouraging smile that dimpled her unmarred cheek and said "I don't know. But don't worry. Maybe she won't stay long. Let's trust in God's plan and figure this out together. *Tavakol be khoda.*"

Sadegh immediately repented for all his complaints, voiced and unvoiced, against his wife. Here she stood, his faithful partner in all that would come, helping him remember that the outcome was not in his hands. Perhaps she was right. Perhaps there was a reason for all of this. Perhaps he truly did need to trust in God. He took a deep breath to try to slow his racing heart beat and said, "*Kheili dooset daram.* I love you so much."

Sumayeh smiled at him again but didn't answer, as Maman-Mehri had now reached the door.

After walking up the flight of steps to their unit, Maman-Mehri was breathing heavily. She didn't seem particularly surprised to see Sadegh home in the middle of the day.

"Salam Sadegh, Sumayeh-joon. How are you?" Not waiting for an answer, she continued. "Sorry to drop in on you. I was on my way home from the prayer meeting. I left a little early because it was so crowded and hot today I just couldn't bear it. I haven't been feeling well, you know, so I thought I'd go home and lay down. But then," Maman-Mehri cleared her throat, "I thought I'd stop by . . . to say hello."

Ignoring the awkward note in Maman-Mehri's voice, Sumayeh thanked her for coming and kissed her in greeting. "Come sit down." Sumayeh invited Maman-Mehri into the living room.

Maman-Mehri shuffled in and lifted her black chador slightly around her so she could sit on the edge of the couch. Her short legs barely reached the floor. The coffee table before her held fruit, nuts, and small plates arranged in a perfectly centered row. Sadegh watched as Maman-Mehri took in the formal layout that was clearly meant for guests and then looked over at the dining room table, carefully set with the rose patterned china that had been part of Sumayeh's dowry.

Sumayeh gave Sadegh a pointed look. Sadegh opened his mouth but couldn't think of what to say. Maman-Mehri looked at Sumayeh, and then at the coffee table, and then at Sadegh, and then the coffee table again.

Maman-Mehri cleared her throat again. "Where's the baby? Is she sleeping?"

"No," Sumayeh answered. "She's with my mom today."

"Oh," Maman-Mehri said.

Sadegh, Sumayeh, and Maman-Mehri looked at one another.

"Did you hear the news about the British sailors?" Maman-Mehri asked, clearly straining to make conversation. "They were released this morning."

"Yes, I heard," Sadegh said. "They've already landed in Dubai."

"Well, I hope they were actually innocent. Our leaders are too trusting and compassionate sometimes."

Sadegh nodded but he wasn't really thinking about the sailors. He was trying to figure out the best way to explain about the luncheon.

Before he could say anything, Maman-Mehri, gesturing to the dining room table, said, "You must have guests coming. Did I come at a bad time? I should go." But she stayed in her seat.

"Maman-Mehri—" Sadegh began, but he was cut off by his mother.

"Actually, it was quite strange," Maman-Mehri puzzled. "When Mr. Namazi from the taxi *agence* picked me up from the prayer meeting, he asked if we should wait for Fati and Zainab before heading to your house. He said the *agence* told him the ladies from the Hojjati family were coming here for lunch. I told him that your sisters would still be a while and then he just headed here without even asking where I was going."

Sadegh silently cursed Mr. Namazi and the stupid taxi service that had served his family for years and had ruined their plans. Aloud, he said, "Yes, they're coming by after the prayer meeting."

"Well then," Maman-Mehri said, hurt quickly replacing the confusion on her face at this confirmation that she'd been purposely excluded from their gathering. She rocked forward off the couch and onto her feet. "It seems Mr. Namazi has made a mistake. I should go. I certainly don't want to be in the way. Us old people can be a burden. It's good for you young ones to have these get-togethers without us. Don't worry about walking me downstairs. I know the way."

"How could you say you're a burden?" Sumayeh objected as she got to her feet to stop Maman-Mehri from moving toward the door. "We're always grateful for your presence. It's just—"

Sadegh jumped in, wanting to be the one to tell the truth. "Maman . . . Ms. Tabibian is coming for lunch."

"Who?" Maman-Mehri peered at him sharply.

"Ms. Tabibian . . . the lady that . . . gave birth to me. I'm sorry we didn't tell you. We didn't want to upset you."

It seemed to take a moment for her to understand. But as she did, his mother's mouth went flat, so she looked like the baby refusing a new food. She sank back onto the couch, readjusted her chador around her, and lifted one hand under it in question. "She's coming here?" Her voice was weak. "To your house?"

Sadegh nodded.

"But why? What does she want with you? What does she want with Zainab and Fati?"

"Nothing, Maman-joonam," Sadegh answered swiftly. "I just needed them with me to see what type of person she is."

"You want to see what type of person she is?" Maman-Mehri's voice gained strength but still shook. "I can tell you that. This is a woman who abandoned a baby for her own lustful desires! She doesn't deserve a second of your time!"

Sadegh was surprised. He'd never asked Ms. Tabibian directly why she'd left. But from her references to having lost Sadegh, he'd gotten the impression she hadn't had much choice in the matter. But Maman-Mehri seemed to be implying she'd left of her own accord. And that she'd left to be with another man.

Maman-Mehri licked her lips and continued. "That's right. I've never wanted to mention it, but you should know. After all your father did for this woman . . . after all that she put us through . . . it turned out that all along she'd been with some gutter scum like herself. What kind of woman does that sort of thing? And then after all these years, when I've done the work of raising you to be the perfect young man you are, she comes along and wants to interfere in our family again?"

Maman-Mehri's voice was teary. She reached for a tissue from the box under the coffee table and continued.

"How could you do this to me Sadegh? Did I not do enough for you as a child? Did I not care for you and send you to university and find you a beautiful wife and love you and your children? What did I do that would make you want to break my heart and humiliate me like this?"

As she spoke, Maman-Mehri seemed to squeeze her chador tighter and tighter around her face so that her cheeks and forehead bulged, angry and red, out of the small opening.

"You have no idea what pain I went through," Maman-Mehri continued. "That woman . . . she is a devil! A devil! Thirty years ago, it took all I had to protect myself and my family from her. I can't do this again!"

Maman-Mehri looked up, released her chador and raised her hands to the ceiling. "*Khodaya!* My dear God, help me. Give me death, my Lord, give me death!"

Sadegh was shocked. He'd never seen his mother like this. "Maman! What are you saying!"

"Death would be better than this! Your poor father . . . this is the first time I am grateful that he isn't here to witness this." Here Maman-Mehri broke down into loud wracking sobs.

Sadegh looked desperately at Sumayeh, who seemed to have nothing to say but kneeled next to Maman-Mehri to try to comfort her.

Sadegh tried to reason with his mother.

"Maman-joon, you're making too big a deal out of this. She's no threat to our family. She can never replace you. The truth is, I could never see her as a mother."

"Then why, my son, why?" Maman-Mehri pleaded. "Why do you have to see her?"

"Well . . ." Sadegh thought about how to explain. "It's her daughter Leila. I think she may be in some sort of trouble because . . . I don't really know, but I feel an obligation to figure out what's going on and try to help. The lunch was actually the ladies' idea."

Maman-Mehri was still sniffling but had calmed down a bit. Sadegh continued.

"I'm sorry we didn't tell you from the beginning. But I'm glad you found out. It's better this way. Why don't you have lunch with us? You'll see how Ms. Tabibian is for me . . . no more than a distant aunt or cousin."

"No!" Maman-Mehri shouted. "I don't want to see her. I need . . ." Maman-Mehri's voice lost its angry edge and took on an almost childish whine. "I need to go home and rest. I'm not well. I'm really not well."

Sumayeh stroked Maman-Mehri's arm and said. "Why don't you rest here? Our guests won't arrive for another half hour at least. When you feel refreshed, you can decide to leave or stay and join us. It's not for me to say, but it might be good for this woman to see you here so she'll know there's no hope of coming between you and Sadegh."

Maman-Mehri seemed to consider the idea. "Traffic is quite atrocious. I suppose it might be better to take a quick little nap here. And then I'll be up and out of here before anyone arrives."

Sumayeh helped Maman-Mehri up, and the two of them walked toward the bedrooms. At the hallway entrance, Maman-Mehri paused and turned to face Sadegh.

"I'm sure I'll be gone before anyone arrives. But just in case . . . don't tell anyone I'm here. If I feel up to joining you, I will. But I don't want everyone pestering me if I decide I just want to stay in the room saying my prayers."

"*Chashm Maman*," Sadegh agreed as Sumayeh led his mother off toward the guest room.

*   *   *

"So, Leila-khanoom, why do you want to get married?" As was typical in Maman-Mehri's absence, Zainab took charge of the gathering.

Leila smiled shyly and looked down. She had barely said a word for the thirty minutes she'd been in Sadegh's home. Sadegh wondered what she thought of Zainab, Fatimeh, Sumayeh, and his aunt Mahdiyeh. They were all good, devout women that she could learn a lot from.

Ms. Tabibian prodded her. "*Javab bede*, Leila. Speak up." Ms. Tabibian's nut-brown hair grazed her shoulders in a layered bob that neatly framed her light eyes and pretty features. She wore a long-sleeved scoop-necked purple tunic over wide-legged pants with a green paisley pattern that Sadegh actually thought was quite nice but knew his sisters would find garish.

Sadegh had seen Leila and Ms. Tabibian without their coverings once before, at their home. They were the first new women he'd seen uncovered since marrying Sumayeh seven years earlier, and he'd felt intensely uncomfortable. But today, with his uncovered wife and sisters with him, it didn't feel so unnatural.

Leila looked at her mother before answering slowly, "I just feel like I'm ready."

Zainab's hawk eyes observed the girl closely. "But why the rush?"

Ms. Tabibian jumped in. "It's better for her to get life started with a good man as soon as possible. Who knows how long I'll be around, and the older she gets, the harder it will be."

Leila was looking down again. She seemed intensely uncomfortable at being the center of attention and Sadegh wondered whether she might cry. She really did seem like a good girl, and Sadegh wondered what sort of mess Ms. Tabibian had allowed her to get into. Whatever the story, Sadegh was grateful he'd grown up under Maman-Mehri's strict religious guidance.

Warmhearted Fatimeh, who was sitting next to Leila, reached over and hugged the girl to her as she said cheerily, "Oh, I'm certain Leila-khanoom will have plenty of suitors and *khastegars* whenever she wants them. Just look at this beautiful girl."

It was true, Sadegh thought. Leila was unusually pretty. The striking contrast of her light-green eyes against her brown skin combined with perfect cheekbones and a strong nose to create a stunning effect. Her skin was a bit darker than his own, but otherwise, she looked a lot like himself, except the combination of features looked much better on a girl than on a balding, bearded, overly skinny man.

Fatimeh continued, turning to Ms. Tabibian, "Actually she reminds me so much of you." Fatimeh's voice was almost shy as she went on. "I remember the first time I met you, I thought you must be some sort of royalty. You looked just like the girls in my mother's sewing magazines."

Sadegh was surprised. Fatimeh had met Ms. Tabibian? He didn't think his sisters had had any contact with her, even when she'd been married to his father. He wondered whether his mother was following the conversation from the guest room, where she was still resting.

This was apparently news to Zainab as well, who broke into Ms. Tabibian's modest demurrals to demand, "When did you meet?"

Fatimeh grinned and blinked her big cow eyes. Sadegh thought she looked almost proud to be the subject of their often-dismissive older sister's curiosity.

"Mahdiyeh was with me sometimes too," Fatimeh said.

Heads turned to the other side of the table, where Sadegh's aunt nodded and asked Ms. Tabibian. "It must have been shortly after you were married, right? Were you already pregnant with Sadegh then? It seems like you were sick a lot."

Ms. Tabibian nodded and said, "You have no idea what a comfort you two were to me. I was so alone. Your father, God bless his memory, was a good and kind man. But he had so many responsibilities. He couldn't be around much, and he didn't like me to leave the house or have many visitors if I was alone."

"And you didn't have much family in Tehran, if I remember," Fatimeh said.

"That's right. I'm from the north. The only family I had in Tehran was my great-aunt. I'd actually only just moved here to help take care of her when I met your father."

Sadegh had already heard this story. But he enjoyed watching the ladies struggle with their curiosity. He was sure they were dying to know the details of Ms. Tabibian's first encounter with his father. But it would be crass to press for details too obviously. Would their sense of propriety win out?

Perhaps aware of their internal conflict, or maybe simply eager to explain that the circumstances were less lurid than they might have imagined, Ms. Tabibian continued without being asked.

"It was a car accident. I was crossing a busy street, one lane at a time, and someone pushed me into the lane your father was driving in, and he hit me, through no fault of his own. I woke up in the hospital, barely able to move. And my hip never did fully heal, as you can see from the way I limp around. But your father . . . well, I suppose he felt responsible. He took care of everything. God bless him, he was a good man."

There was a pause as the ladies of Sadegh's family seemed to wait for more. But Ms. Tabibian did not continue, so Zainab asked her question of Fatimeh and Mahdiyeh again. "So, when did you two meet Ms. Tabibian? Why didn't I know anything about it?"

Chatty Aunt Mahdiyeh would have normally been the more likely candidate to tell a childhood tale. But perhaps she felt shy about commenting on a family drama she had become a part of only because she was living in her sister's home at the time.

Fatimeh finally spoke up. "I'm not sure how it happened," she said apologetically to her sister. "I think Father just took me and, later, Mahdiyeh to her house sometimes. Maman-Mehri was so . . . unwell. And you were busy taking care of her and Ali-reza. Probably, Father just wanted to get us out of your way, or maybe he thought we could help Ms. Tabibian. But he never even explained who Ms. Tabibian was. Although he did say we weren't to mention our visits to Maman-Mehri. Or you."

"Humph," Zainab digested this information with a sour look.

Fatimeh went on, addressing Ms. Tabibian. "You were so good to us. I never had a chance to thank you. And I only really understand now, as an adult, that it must not have been easy having a thirteen-year-old girl dumped on you. But you went out of your way to make visits fun. Your house was the first place I heard Googoosh's music, and I've been a fan ever since. I looked up to you so much, sometimes I even pretended my name was Roksana!" Fatimeh tittered loudly.

Sadegh thought he heard a noise coming from the hallway that led to the bedrooms and winced as he wondered again whether his mother was hearing all of this. He was sure it would hurt her to hear her daughter speak so highly of a woman who had only caused her pain. And Sadegh felt it *was* rather disloyal of Fatimeh to gush on like this, even if Ms. Tabibian had been good to her. He looked across the table at Sumayeh who'd been following the conversation with interest while making sure everyone's plates were filled and refilled. They made eye contact, and Sadegh tilted his head toward the hall to ask Sumayeh silently to check on his mother. Understanding his request immediately, she pushed back her chair and excused herself.

The conversation at the table continued. Ms. Tabibian was speaking now.

". . . honored to have you." She seemed to be getting emotional. "Truly, that was a lovely time in my life. You two felt like the little sisters I'd always wanted. Sadegh arrived, and motherhood brought more joy than I could have imagined. And your father was so . . . good to me."

"Why did you leave?" Fatimeh asked.

"Fati!" Zainab admonished her sister with a jab of her sharp elbow.

"Oh, I'm sorry," Fatimeh apologized immediately as she rubbed at her pillowy upper arm where Zainab's jab had landed. "It's none of my business. I just always wondered. It was all so abrupt and no one ever explained."

"It's okay Fatimeh dear," Ms. Tabibian assured her. "I can try to explain, although to this day I'm not sure I understand exactly what happened. You see . . . your father asked me to leave." Ms. Tabibian looked down. "It seems that the neighborhood grocer, well, it's embarrassing really, but he'd developed some . . . feelings for me. And your father, well, someone put it into his head that I was encouraging this man. Can you imagine? Someone gave your father love letters that were supposedly between me and this grocer. He . . ."

Fatimeh gasped and clapped her hand over her mouth. Sadegh wondered what she thought of Ms. Tabibian's story since he wasn't sure what he thought of it himself.

"Yes, it was unimaginable to me, too," Ms. Tabibian said. "I laughed at first and didn't take it seriously. But then one day, when your father had taken me out to eat, we came back and found the grocer actually inside the house. It scared me to death . . . I thought he was a burglar or some crazy killer. But he told your father I had arranged it. He even had a key."

Fatimeh looked at Ms. Tabibian with her big eyes widened so much they seemed to occupy the entire upper half of her face.

Zainab cocked her head suspiciously, "How did he have a key?"

Ms. Tabibian puckered her lips to one side and shook her head. Then she sighed and said, "I honestly don't know. I must confess I always wondered whether . . . You see, I didn't realize your mother was so opposed to your father taking a second wife. Now that I'm older and understand the world better, I can imagine she must have been terribly hurt, and I suppose it's understandable that she might have wanted to end it somehow. Although, I must say that it is hard for me to understand how anyone could take a child away from their mother." Ms. Tabibian's voice dropped to a whisper. "It nearly killed me to lose—"

"That's enough!"

Ms. Tabibian froze midsentence, and the rest of the ladies looked shocked and confused as they tried to digest the sudden appearance of Maman-Mehri, shuffling in like a short, plump ghost in a too-long white house chador she'd borrowed from Sumayeh.

Sadegh felt he should explain his mother's presence. "Maman-Mehri stopped by right before—"

But Maman-Mehri cut him off. "He was *my* husband!" she shouted as she leaned heavily on an armchair for support. "*My* life partner! You were nothing to him. He felt sorry for you, that's all."

Sadegh looked at Sumayeh, Zainab, Mahdiyeh, and even Fati for a clue as to what he should do, but all eyes were on Maman-Mehri and her tirade against Ms. Tabibian.

"You weren't worth the dust under his feet! After all the pain he caused to make a home for you, I can't even speak of what you did. Disgusting! And yet you stand there in front of my family not only denying your treachery but trying to blame me for it!

"I don't have the words to describe the sort of filth you are," Maman-Mehri spat. Her face was bright red against the white cotton chador. "But I promise I will not let you infect this family again. Get out! Get out and don't you dare come back!"

Maman-Mehri had long ruled the family and their wider community of religious friends and relatives as an absolute matriarch. On those occasions that called for a public scolding, the hapless recipient of her wrath was well aware that the only acceptable response was either submissive silence or apologetic bleating.

So it was a shocking contravention of expected norms when Ms. Tabibian interrupted Maman-Mehri with a defiant slap on the table and shouted, "How dare you?"

Maman-Mehri was rattled into silence.

Ms. Tabibian went on. "It wasn't enough that you turned my husband against me with your lies and manipulations? It wasn't enough that you took my only son, my beloved Sadegh, away from me? It wasn't enough that you ruined my life? On top of all this, you stand there in front of my children accusing me of unspeakable things! How dare you?"

Maman-Mehri's face went purple with rage. "Quiet! You

disrespectful vermin. Don't you dare deny it. I saw the letters with my own eyes. Letters to your lover! I still remember his disgusting name. Babak Islami."

Fatimeh let out a strange squeak.

Ms. Tabibian refused to back down. Her grassy eyes flashed yellow, like hornets buzzing through a meadow.

"I deny everything! And I tell you that on the Day of Judgement, when the truth of your lies becomes known to everyone, I will insist upon my right to see you fully punished as God promises for liars and spreaders of false gossip. You stand there so self-righteous and act like you're better than me but mark my words, on that day everyone will know who the true vermin is."

Maman-Mehri swayed as if she might fall. Zainab jumped up to join Sumayeh in helping Maman-Mehri into a seated position.

Maman-Mehri protested breathlessly through sobs. "No! I won't stay here with her. Take me into the bedroom. And call the driver. I can't listen to this devil tell these brazen lies any longer. Oh, my heart, my heart!"

Ms. Tabibian laughed an ugly laugh. "All these years later, you haven't changed a bit, have you? Just like he always said, anytime you want attention you pretend you're sick or dying."

Maman-Mehri gasped. Sadegh felt as if a vein were bursting in his left temple as he heard his mother beg her children to help. Ms. Tabibian had gone too far. He stood and roared. "That's enough!"

The room quieted. Sadegh tilted his head toward Ms. Tabibian. "*Shoma dige befarmayeed.* It's time for you to go."

Ms. Tabibian seemed to have recognized that she had crossed a line and began apologizing. "I'm so sorry. She pushed me too far, my son—"

"Don't call me that!" Sadegh shouted. "My mother . . . the woman who stayed by my side and cared for me and raised me is in that chair . . . decimated by your hurtful words!"

"I'm so sorry. But you have to understand what she—"

"That's enough! I want you to leave now."

Leila, already standing, pulled Ms. Tabibian out of her chair.

"Okay, we'll leave. We can talk later about—"

"No! Don't you dare call or contact me again. I'm finished with you. This has been quite enough already!"

"Sadegh-jaan, please!" Ms. Tabibian begged as she limped toward him. "Don't say that. Think of your sister! She needs you. We both need you!"

"I want you to leave. Right now."

Leila tugged at her mother.

Ms. Tabibian waved Leila off and turned to Sadegh, her mouth a thin line.

"I won't go until you promise to help Leila."

Leila grabbed her mother's arm. "Maman! Stop it, let's go!"

"No! I won't go until he promises!"

Sadegh felt trapped with the sound of Maman-Mehri's tears in his ears. He pushed himself away from the table, stood up and stalked toward Ms. Tabibian as he shouted. "GET OUT! Get out before I throw you from the window!"

Eyes wide, Ms. Tabibian finally started hobbling toward the door. Sadegh stood where he was, breathing with all the anger of fire-starting bellows. Sumayeh came forward to calm her husband and help the two ladies retrieve their shoes and outdoor coverings.

As the ladies made their speedy exit, Sadegh gave his final instruction. "Don't you dare contact me again! Or I'll tell the authorities you're harassing us."

CHAPTER 6

*Thursday, December 10, 2009—five months
and twenty-seven days after the election*

In a letter to former president Akbar Hashemi Rafsanjani,
Mehdi Karroubi said senior officials had informed him of
the "shameful behaviour" taking place. Mr. Karroubi wrote
that both male and female detainees had been raped, with
some suffering serious injuries.
—BBC News Online, August 10, 2009

Azar's panicked shriek was entirely inappropriate to the circumstances. The collision between the back of her head and the open
file drawer had been little more than a tap.

What is wrong with you? Azar scolded herself as she massaged
her head. It'd been almost six months since her encounter with
that man, and still she lost control anytime her head made contact
with something harder than a pillow.

Azar took the file she'd been looking for, closed the open
drawers, and returned to her desk. She opened the file to review
its contents, but her hands were still trembling so badly she could

barely flip through the pages. Azar finally gave up and let the papers fall to the desk. She stretched her hands wide and then clenched them, repeating the motion a few times in an effort to stop their shaking.

On her left pinky was a jagged scar where *The Open Society* had ripped through her flesh.

She'd been luckier than many who'd been taken in during the government crackdown. The case file on her desk was enough to tell her that. Azar had been beaten only that one time and had received medical attention promptly. When she was transferred to Evin's Section 209 for political prisoners, her cell had been relatively spacious and even had a window. Besides, at this point she'd been home with her boys for almost four months. So why were her hands still shaking? Why was she so weak when others had to survive so much worse, or hadn't survived at all?

And all of it for what?

It was hard to believe there was a time when there had been any hope. The brutal crackdown that had followed the Green Wave uprising had been cruel, efficient, and much more effective than Azar, Ibrahim, and their friends had believed. The authorities had said openly that they would not repeat the Shah's mistake of softness that had resulted in the 1979 revolution. Thousands were imprisoned, many were killed or injured, and the streets were emptied of Iranian citizens, who were too tired, scared, and disempowered to continue the fight. Ahmadinejad remained president, free to continue destroying the economy and any hope of progress toward women's rights. Grand Ayatollah Montazeri, the Green Wave's most important spiritual leader, remained under house arrest, where the most he could do was issue meaningless and entirely irrelevant statements such as his most recent one that the 1979 occupation of the American embassy had been a mistake.

1979? Who cared about 1979?

Azar shook her head to clear her thoughts. She had to focus on her work. Maybe a cup of tea would help. She got up and made her way down the hall, past the vacant offices, and through the empty waiting room to the kitchen. She filled the tea kettle, set it on the electric stove, and waited for it to boil.

Most days she missed the bustle of the busy office she used to head, with three junior associates, two secretaries, the office tea boy who kept liquid and solid refreshments coming at a quick pace, and the clients and their families milling about. But at times like these, solitude was welcome. Azar could almost be thankful for the court order that had barred her from working for a year.

Well, not quite. Azar took that last thought back. Still, she'd been lucky, she reminded herself. She'd been lucky.

Her first substantial memories of her imprisonment began in a medical facility where she awoke in pain and shackled to the bed. The doctors wouldn't say what all her injuries were but seemed to be sincere in their attempts to reassure her that she'd be all right. She guessed she probably had a concussion and a couple of broken ribs. Her nose was obviously broken, and she had a patch over her left eye. She feared she'd lost its function for good and was greatly relieved when the patch was finally removed to note that she could see just fine, although splitting headaches plagued her at random moments. She asked her caregivers about the searing pain in her right hand and was told she may have sprained a finger but that nothing was broken. She was severely bruised and tender all along her left arm, back, and buttocks but was actually surprised at how minimal the permanent damage was given the ferocity of the beating she'd received. Of course, she wasn't exactly an expert on beatings and their accompanying injuries.

Regular visits from Intelligence agents began while she was still in the medical facility. This time, she'd anticipated them and tried to prepare by deciding on and mentally tucking away the parts of her life she wished to keep hidden. But her amateurish efforts were completely overwhelmed by their professional arts.

It wasn't that they ever actually hurt her or even threatened further physical pain. On the contrary, they asked after her health and comfort with real or well-feigned concern. One of them even apologized for the events that led to her hospitalization.

No, it was her human impulses rather than fear of further physical pain that they were able to use against her, especially when they transferred her to a solitary cell in Evin. She'd already heard enough about the prison experience not to be entirely surprised by the way her craving for autonomy and predictability created a barely controllable desire to cooperate in any way necessary to secure even small freedoms such as access to pen and paper. What was astonishing and humbling to witness, however, was the way her primal need for human connection could be so easily manipulated.

Azar knew it was by design that one of her two main interrogators was warm and friendly while the other was accusatory and insulting. It was a classic "good cop / bad cop" strategy. But understanding the calculations behind their behavior did little to mediate the instinctual emotional response it elicited. Isolated, bored, and in continued discomfort, Azar found herself almost looking forward to visits with the kindly older gentleman who expressed his faith in her loyalty to the Islamic Republic, apologized for the gruffness of his counterpart, and gently urged her cooperation so that he could get her home to her family as quickly as possible. To her shame, she found herself torn between a deep-seated emotional desire to please him and an ever-diminishing intellectual awareness of the man's actual role and intent.

Then there was the sheer mental exhaustion produced by the barrage of continual questioning on topics ranging from the political and personal to the inane. The same questions would be asked repeatedly in different ways by different people and even slight variations in her answers, all of which she was forced to write out on school paper, would result in accusations that she was lying. She learned that they often operated like bargain hunters in the bazaar seeking to throw the shopkeeper off by appearing to have their hearts set on one item while feigning indifference to another in order to drive its price down. Not infrequently, after a particularly intense session where her questioners would seem to be determined to learn as much as they could about, for example, a particular client's case, Azar would surmise from subsequent interactions that they'd really been looking for something else entirely, such as her whereabouts on a given day.

The whole experience was mentally and physically grueling. Bit by bit, Azar became increasingly adept at dealing with her interrogators. She learned to hide her panic when she feared she might have given something away. She learned the critical importance of congratulating herself on each and every minute she managed to stay silent rather than lamenting those when she'd said too much. She learned not to spend time thinking of her boys, how they were doing with her parents, whether her studious Hossein was still determined to be the top of his class, whether Muhammadreza was still beating all his friends at Ping-Pong. And she learned to use the excuse of her concussion and splitting headaches to repeat the phrases "I don't know. I don't remember."

But any progress on this front was entirely undercut by her growing restlessness and depression over being caged and shorn of the friend and family relationships that had always anchored her identity with necessary human reflections of who she was. Her memories of the strong and confident woman that bore her name and once strode powerfully among the living started to seem like distant dreams, and she'd started to ask herself what difference it would really make to tell her interrogators all they wished to hear.

After two weeks in solitary, Azar had been allowed to join four other women in a cell. The interrogations became much less frequent and, when they occurred, had a pro forma feel, almost as if the men were doing them to be polite and so as not to disappoint her expectations of a prison experience.

Once her nose had healed and the visible marks of Heydari's beating had disappeared, Azar had been let out on bail. At her court hearing the following month, she'd been sentenced to a year for "colluding with intent to harm national security." But the sentence was suspended, meaning that she wouldn't have to serve the time unless she repeated her offense during the two-year suspension period. She'd been so thankful that her boys wouldn't be orphaned with both parents in jail that she'd barely registered the judge's additional ruling that she couldn't work for a year.

She'd had to close down her practice, although she'd kept the office, saying goodbye to everyone, including Ms. Tabibian who'd had the nerve to cry duplicitous tears. It wasn't until the following week, feeling more bored and restless than she had in solitary confinement, that Azar truly understood what it meant to be deprived of the activity that had once defined her entire identity. Thank God for the Foundation. She'd have gone crazy without it.

The tea kettle hissed. Azar turned off the stove and poured hot water into a crystal teacup with a short pedestal bottom. She dunked a bag of dark Ahmadi tea into her cup a few times and then discarded it in the garbage before heading back to her office.

She wasn't sure if it was the tea or the short trip to the kitchen that calmed her nerves, but this time she was able to leaf through the file on her desk without any trouble. As she'd suspected there wasn't an autopsy report. The file was for Bahman Sanandaji, a twenty-two-year-old Kurdish Iranian student who'd died in custody. Azar had just come from a meeting with his parents at Mellat Park, where they sat on a bench and watched a young couple play badminton as they told her about his life and what they knew of his death.

They'd been told he'd had a seizure. But, his father told Azar, when they'd washed and prepared his body for burial, they'd noticed obvious signs of torture, including bruising and blood around the ears and head. They wanted to file a complaint. When Azar gently explained that such evidence wouldn't hold up and asked whether they'd had an autopsy performed, the family looked confused. They didn't seem to know what an autopsy was, but said that perhaps it was among the papers in their file. Having now confirmed that there was no autopsy, Azar knew there was little that could be done for them. Even with a formal autopsy it would have been hard to force the courts to hold someone accountable for the death of this young man who, his mother had tearfully recounted, had once liked to build miniature skyscrapers out of milk cartons and had aspired to be an architect.

Azar rolled her chair back from her desk in frustration. These cases were worse than the divorces she'd worked on for years. In family court, there was always a chance, however remote, one could convince the judge that a client had valid grounds for divorcing a man who was crazy, or infertile, or had abandoned or hit her. But with human rights cases, the entire weight of the system was designed to compel silence. Once again, Azar marveled at the discipline and fortitude of the Foundation's lawyers and staff who toiled to bring human rights abuses to light despite serious personal risks and very rare successes.

She'd known of the Foundation to Defend Human Rights for a couple of years as several of the One Million Signatures campaign leaders were associated with it. But it wasn't until they helped with Azar's, and then Ibrahim's, cases that she gained a better appreciation for the vital services they performed.

The Foundation didn't engage directly in any overtly political activity, but they defended the rights of those who did. As a result of their work on behalf of clients involved in the Green Movement, the Foundation itself had become a target, and several of their leading attorneys were serving jail sentences of their own. Even now, however, the overwhelmed remaining members continued to work, serving clients and documenting abuses. When Azar, needing something to fill her days, offered to help, they gratefully agreed. Given her suspended sentence and the prohibition on working, Azar couldn't officially represent clients or appear in court. But she could do intake meetings—carefully, in the park—and help with writing reports and other tasks. She was learning so much about this new area of law that she thought she might want to work openly with the Foundation, despite the risks, once Ibrahim was out of jail and she was allowed to practice again.

Ah, Ibrahim . . . Azar's eyes traveled to the gigantic empty vase on her desk. She reached out to stroke the engraved crystal and thought once again to her last day with her husband and the few hours they'd had together between the time she'd gotten out of Evin and he'd been taken in.

When she'd been released, blinking in the bright light outside Evin, she'd found Ibrahim waiting stiffly by the gate, holding a ridiculously large bouquet of at least two dozen red roses in a crystal vase that looked exactly like the one on her desk.

She hadn't seen Ibrahim since he'd gone into hiding several weeks before her arrest, and she wondered how she looked to him. Even when they were feuding as teenagers, she'd always been careful to pluck, thread, and wax her eyebrows and any other embarrassing facial hair as it appeared. But she hadn't seen a pair of tweezers for two months and knew she must look a sight. She pulled the chador a bit tighter around her face so less of it would be visible.

He'd been so eager to give her the flowers, he didn't seem to realize how awkward it would be for her to manage the heavy package as they walked to the car. Ibrahim carried several clear plastic bags with a dozen foil containers that he started opening as they walked to show her the foods he'd purchased from Tehran's finest restaurant and ask what she felt like eating. By the time they got to the car, Ibrahim had four open containers balanced in his hands while the remaining food dangled in a bag from his pinkie finger.

It was then that the heavy vase started to slip from Azar's fingers. As Azar and Ibrahim struggled to catch it, he lost hold of the food so that the rice, kabobs, tomatoes, and herbs rained into the street around them, soon to be followed by the slippery vase that shattered into a thousand small pieces, mixing prettily with the rose petals and different colored rices.

Azar had burst into tears.

Ignoring cultural taboos against touching in public, Ibrahim had pulled her close and held her tight. As Azar had calmed down, she'd been surprised to realize that his body was shaking in a way that could only mean he was crying too.

They'd stood together, holding on through their tears until someone hissed that they should be ashamed of themselves for such a public display of affection.

In that moment, they'd dared to believe their ordeal was over. Throughout the weeks of Azar's imprisonment, Ibrahim, who'd immediately returned home to the boys, had been subject to numerous visits and interrogations of his own. Surely, after all the questions they'd answered, the authorities realized that Azar and Ibrahim's actions stemmed from a love for, and concern about, Iran and its Islamic ideals, and not from any cooperation with outside Western powers. Surely, their family could now get back to normal.

They took Ibrahim the next morning. Had she known how little time they would have together, Azar would have endured far greater chastisements for a few additional moments in her husband's arms.

The day he was sentenced to a year in prison, Azar had found and purchased a replica of the vase they'd broken. When Ibrahim's sentence was complete, she planned to meet him outside Evin with the vase full of flowers once again.

*   *   *

Azar's cellphone rang. It was Ali.

"Salam, Ali," she said.

"Salam Azar-jaan," he responded. "*Kojaee?* Where are you?"

"At the office," Azar swiveled to look at the clock on the wall. It was almost five thirty.

"Still?" Ali asked. He sounded exasperated. "What could you possibly be doing there? Where are your kids?"

The sharp point of his words pricked her. It was true that she'd been leaving the boys more and more frequently with her parents as she'd been taking on more work for the Foundation. The fact was, they exhausted her. They were constantly bickering or getting into mischief, and she could never figure out the correct parental response. Without Ibrahim to provide a steady counterbalance to her fluctuations between anger and overindulgence, she was often afraid she did them more harm than good.

She also felt incredibly guilty about what she and Ibrahim had put them through. When the Guards came for Ibrahim, Azar's screams and pleadings had woken the boys who'd immediately hurled themselves at the men taking their father. Azar had managed to grab and hold on to Hossein but Muhammadreza's attack had hit its mark with all the fury of a nine-year-old boy. The security guard he started punching laughed and said, "This one's got a strong arm, *mash'allah*." Then he pinned Muhammadreza's arms to his sides as his colleague dragged Ibrahim away.

How did trauma like that affect a child?

Defensively, Azar answered Ali, "They're with *Maman*. I'm getting ready to go get them right now. *Hala*, did you need something?"

There was a pause.

"If you're going to pick them up, I'll meet you there. I need to talk to you."

Azar hoped it wouldn't be another lecture from her little brother about being more careful not to give the authorities any additional reasons to doubt her.

Aloud, Azar answered, "Okay, I'll see you there."

Azar hung up but didn't get up immediately. She wanted to jot down a few notes from her meeting with the Sanandajis while the conversation was still fresh in her mind. She worked with concentration and finished her task swiftly. Then, eyeing the clock and wishing she could slow it down, she shoved the file back in the cabinet, grabbed her purse, and turned out the lights to leave.

* * *

Bzzzzzz.

The doorbell sounded just as Azar was about to walk out of the office. Azar hesitated before answering. She'd become increasingly paranoid about being watched. Someone always seemed to be calling or buzzing her doorbell, but when Azar answered, there would be no response. Were security folks trying to keep tabs on where she was? Or had she just been the victim of more of Tehran's infamous prank callers than usual?

Azar slowly picked up the intercom.

"*Baleh?* Who is it?"

"Ms. Rahimi?" came the answer. "This is Leila, Ms. Tabibian's daughter."

"Leila? What are you doing here?" Azar asked with more bluntness than Iranian culture generally permitted.

"I'm sorry to impose on you, Ms. Rahimi. I need to talk to you. It's important."

"I was just on my way out," Azar said. "Why don't you come back tomorrow?"

"Please," the girl pleaded, "I promise not to take more than five minutes."

Azar sighed, buzzing Leila in and waiting for her to make her way through the courtyard and up the elevator to her floor. She didn't know Leila well and had only seen her a handful of times over the four years Ms. Tabibian had worked for her. What could she possibly want? And what bad timing . . . Ali wasn't going to be happy.

When she heard the elevator ding, Azar opened the door and ushered the pretty girl into the waiting area, where they sat across from one another, Leila on the couch, Azar on a high-backed chair, the coffee table between them.

"So, Leila-khanoom, *befarmayeed*, what can I do for you?"

Leila opened her mouth but didn't say anything. She blinked her beautiful eyes. They were green, like her mother's. But whereas Ms. Tabibian's eyes always reminded Azar of an earthy and grassy meadow, Leila's were a more ethereal, crystalline green. Like the light-green emeralds in the crown jewels kept at Iran's Central Bank Museum, which Azar and Ibrahim had visited shortly after they'd found out she was expecting their first child. Ibrahim had whispered in her ear that the intricate tiaras, jeweled necklaces, and gem-encrusted thrones were nothing compared to the beauty of his pregnant wife.

"*Befarmayeed*," Azar interrupted her thoughts of Ibrahim to prompt the girl again. "I really have to go."

"I'm sorry," Leila said, "I was just thinking of where to start."

The girl pulled a battered manila folder from her bag and pushed it across the coffee table. "I wanted to show you this and get some advice about what to do."

Azar opened the folder. Inside were a dozen or so papers of different sizes and weights. Several of them had areas that were warped with brown stains as if someone had spilled tea on them.

"What is this?" Azar asked as she looked through them.

"They're medical records for—" Leila began.

"Stop!" Azar commanded as her eye caught the patient's name. "Do you have a cellphone on you? Let me see it."

Leila obediently handed over her cellphone and Azar removed the batteries. Then she did the same for her own cellphone so they would be safe from listening ears. She wasn't worried about any additional listening devices in the office. The Foundation's technicians had just swept it and confirmed it was clean.

"Where did you get this?" Azar demanded. "Do you know who this is?"

Leila nodded. "I think so. Isn't it the same Arman Tamimi whose uncle is in parliament? The one they said died of an epileptic seizure?"

In fact, Tamimi's case was one of the only ones that had been reported on as his uncle had publicly questioned official accounts of his death during a live session of parliament.

"Where did you get this?" Azar asked again.

"From a friend. Of my mother's," Leila answered.

Azar remembered Ms. Tabibian's mysterious friend who had purchased a phone for her so many months ago. She wondered whether this was the same person.

"He works with the Revolutionary Guards," Leila continued. "He was at our house last night and had a bunch of folders like this in a big box. Anyway, this is a big deal right? He wouldn't want this to get out, right?"

Azar didn't answer but continued flipping through the papers until she found one that seemed to summarize the medical

findings. Among other things, the examiner had found significant bruising, swelling, and lacerations around the head and neck.
He'd also reported "bruising on both sides of the hips and outer
area of the anus caused by a hard and hot object." On another
page was an autopsy report. Cause of death was "trauma to the
head by a blunt object."

"My God," Azar exhaled, "if this is real, this would be hard
evidence that Arman didn't die of a seizure. He was beaten to
death while he was in custody. You said this friend had more of
these medical files?"

"There were other files in the box, but this was the only one I
saw," Leila answered.

"He just left this one?" Azar asked. It was hard to believe
anyone would be so careless.

Leila shook her head. "No, not on purpose. I spilled tea
on his things when he was saying his prayers. I tried to clean
everything up but I panicked and hid this folder since it was on
top and the most damaged. I didn't actually see or understand
what was inside until this morning.

"Do you think this sort of thing could be used to, well . . .
See, this man, Heydari, has been trying to get me and my mother
to do things that we don't want to do, and when I saw this, I
thought maybe there was a way to get him to leave us alone."

At the name of the man whose beating had imprinted its
memory on her body, Azar felt as if her stomach were flooded
with ice water. Could there be another Heydari that worked with
the Guards?

"This man," Azar breathed, "what does he look like?"

"What does he look like?" Leila repeated, surprised. "He's,
well, he's old. He has white hair and a short beard. His lips are a
strange color. He's kind of small. Not much taller than me."

As Leila described him, Heydari's image appeared before Azar so strongly it was almost as if he was standing over her again, *The Open Society* in his hand.

"Leila," Azar asked in a low voice, "what exactly is your mother's relationship to that man?"

"Mr. Heydari?" Leila asked, "He's from her village up north."

Azar's stomach tightened. In prison, where she'd had plenty of time to think it through, she'd concluded Ms. Tabibian must have been recruited by her son, Sadegh, to get to Azar and Ibrahim. Azar had never imagined the woman had a relationship with Heydari.

"And how long has your mother been working for him?" Azar asked the question that was foremost on her mind. How badly had she and Ibrahim been compromised?

Leila's crystal-green eyes looked clouded and confused. "What do you mean? She's never worked for him. She's been looking for work since—"

"Don't lie to me," Azar snapped. "I know this—" Azar couldn't bring herself to say his name again. "—man. Your mother sent me to him. And he knew everything about my life and my work. Clearly your mother had been giving him information about me and my husband. I ask you again, How long was my secretary spying on me for this old friend of hers?"

"No," Leila protested, waving her hands in the air. "It's not like that! It couldn't be true. My mother hadn't been in touch with him for years. She only saw him again in the summer."

Azar didn't say anything but continued looking at the girl in disbelief.

"Believe me, Ms. Rahimi. See, over the summer, I got arrested at a demonstration, and when they processed me, Mr. Heydari was there, and he recognized my mother's name. Before that, we didn't have anything to do with him. I'd never met him before in my life. And, you have to believe me, I curse myself every day for having brought this man into our lives. He's a horrible, evil man, and I despise him. My mother despises him. There's no way she would work for him."

Azar tried to process what the girl was saying and decide whether she was being honest.

"You're saying you and your mother didn't have anything to do with this man until you got arrested?" Azar asked. "When was that exactly?"

"June twenty-fifth," Leila answered promptly. "It was the same night your brother was taken in. I remember because the evening after I was released was the first time Mr. Heydari came to our house. My mother was trying to get information for you about where Mr. Ali might be. She'd tried asking my brother, but Sadegh wouldn't say anything."

Azar thought about this. When Ms. Tabibian had brought her information about Ali and where he was being held, she'd assumed that she'd learned everything from Sadegh. But it had been Heydari all along.

"What exactly did your mother tell Heydari about me?" Azar asked pointedly.

"Nothing important," Leila insisted. "Nothing political. Just a little about your work and your kids and your husband . . ." Leila's voice trailed off as she seemed to be considering a new thought.

"Leila, what did your mother say about my husband?" Azar demanded.

"Nothing!" Leila insisted, but she looked nervous. "It was just that Heydari kept bringing him up and telling her that you should take him with you when you go to get your brother."

"Yes," Azar said. "My husband was the one they were after. And they used every detail your mother gave about my kids and work and life against me. Why didn't your mother tell me about this man? She let me believe she got the information from her son, Mr. Sadegh."

"I . . . I don't know," Leila cried. "But you have to believe me. My mother never intended to create problems for you. She only wanted to help. She was so proud to have gotten information for you. And maybe she was embarrassed to admit that Sadegh wouldn't tell her anything. This was all before we realized . . . You see, Heydari seemed so kind and helpful. He got me out of jail, he gave us information about your brother, he bought things for my mom. How could we have known? My mother would never have breathed a syllable if she thought it might hurt you."

Azar thought about Leila's story. If the girl was telling the truth, this would mean that Heydari had known much less about Azar than he'd pretended. That was a comforting thought. And it wasn't hard to believe the man could have gotten information out of Ms. Tabibian without her realizing it. He'd done the same to Azar when he pretended to be his own assistant. Besides, even if Ms. Tabibian's role had been more sinister, Leila probably wouldn't have known.

"Thank you for explaining, Leila. I'm sure you're right and your mother wouldn't have purposely tried to hurt me."

Leila looked relieved. She thanked Azar and assured her once again that her mother would never have spied on her for Heydari. But Azar didn't want to talk about that anymore.

"*Begzarim.* It's in the past," Azar said. "Let's talk about this file. This is extremely important information. You say there may be more of these? Can you access them?"

"Well, I don't know," Leila said. "I suppose so, but why would I need to? Isn't this enough?"

"No," Azar insisted. "We need to show that these sorts of cover-ups are happening regularly. One case isn't enough."

Leila looked uncomfortable. "I didn't bring this to you to try to prove something about the government. I just wanted to use it to threaten Heydari and get him to back out of our lives. I thought we could, like, threaten to release this to a newspaper or something if he doesn't leave us alone."

Azar didn't understand. "What are you talking about, Leila? If you and your mother don't want to see him, then don't see him. How is threatening him going to help?"

"You don't understand," Leila looked close to tears. "He won't leave us alone. He says he wants to help us. He says two women shouldn't be alone. And that his . . . wife is too ill to have normal relations with him."

"He wants to marry your mother?" Azar asked. "And you're opposed?"

Leila looked at her with reproach.

"Oh!" Azar exclaimed, as she finally understood. "I see. I should have guessed. But still . . . The man is more than twice your age."

"I told you, he's evil!" Leila took a deep breath. "He likes us to be . . . scared. My mother had hoped that Sadegh could help somehow . . . that he could find me a good husband quickly so I'd be protected, but he . . . well, Sadegh doesn't deserve to be her son. You'll never believe it but he actually kicked her out of his house. His own mother. She has loved him and pined for him all these years. And she wanted nothing of him for herself. It was all for me!"

Leila covered her face with her hands and started to weep.

"There, there, don't cry," Azar slid a box of tissues across the coffee table. Her words sounded awkward even to her own ears. She'd had plenty of crying clients over the years, but they always made her nervous, and she never quite knew what to do for them. It was too bad Mr. Sadegh hadn't been willing to help these women. A speedy marriage for Leila arranged by a powerful family like his would have been a good solution.

Leila took a few tissues and wiped at her cheeks and nose. The tears made her eyes shine even more brightly, as if the emerald of each iris were surrounded by diamonds.

"Leila, dear," Azar said, "you know he can't actually force you to marry him. It's your right by law to refuse."

Leila nodded. "Yes, but he can make life miserable for us until I agree. And, well, he knows some other things about us that he's holding over our heads. When I saw this file and what it contained, I thought maybe we could use it in the same way against him. He wouldn't want anyone to know about this, or even that he was so careless with his files as to bring them to our home, right?"

It was a desperate plan. If Leila and her mother tried to threaten Heydari directly, Azar was sure the man wouldn't hesitate to do them real physical harm. Still, maybe there was a way to help Leila while also striking a blow at the organs of state responsible for the worst abuses.

"Leila, dear," Azar said, "the best way for you to deal with this man is to diminish his power without him ever learning of your role. I know people that can use these reports to help Arman Tamimi's family file a complaint. Or maybe we could get this out to the international press. And if there are similar files for a few other cases, well, that would suggest systematic mistreatment of prisoners. Who knows, maybe Heydari himself could end up in jail for his crimes. There are still people in government who can't tolerate this sort of thing."

Azar stood up. "Let me make a copy of these," she said. She walked to where her ancient copier squatted in a corner and powered it up.

Leila followed her. "What are you going to do?"

"Well," Azar replied. "Here's what I'm thinking. I'll make a copy and keep it in a safe place. You take the original and get it back to Heydari without him realizing. And then you try to find more files like these. I'll talk with some of my friends at the

Foundation and see when and how we should proceed with filing complaints."

The creaky machine blinked that it was ready, and Azar began making copies. She wondered what the chances were of this actually working and felt impatient to talk to some of her friends. Where was she going to keep these documents safe in the meantime? Her home and office could be raided at any time. Her father, she knew, would never willingly keep them for her.

"But how am I supposed to do that?" Leila asked. "It won't be easy to even return this file, let alone try to find more."

The path forward seemed so clear to Azar that she felt a bit impatient Leila wasn't getting it. "The best thing you can do for now is to go along with him," Azar said. "You don't have to marry him. Just act like you aren't opposed to the idea. Try to gain his trust and confidence. That'll give you more time and opportunities to look for more of these sorts of documents."

Leila shook her head. "I can't do it."

Azar took the originals off the machine and handed them back to Leila. The copies she stuffed into another folder, which she then slipped into a large white envelope.

"Look, Leila, it's up to you. But . . ."

BZZZZZZ.

The sound of the doorbell startled her. Azar looked quizzically at Leila. Had someone followed her?

BZZZZZZ, BZZZZZZ.

Heart pounding, Azar walked to the intercom to answer.

"Baleh?" she inquired into the speaker.

"Open the door," Ali directed.

"Ali? What are you doing here?"

"I'm the one that should be asking you that question," he said angrily. "You were supposed to have left your office almost an hour ago! I brought your boys for you. Remember them? My god, if you care nothing for your own children, at least think of our parents. They're too old to be looking after these little devils!"

"Ali-jaan, I'm so sorry. Someone came by and . . ."

"Just open the door," Ali repeated.

Azar buzzed them in and turned to Leila.

"I'm sorry, but my brother is here, so you need to go. Like I was saying, this is up to you, and I don't want you to do anything you're not comfortable with. But you should realize that what you're doing may be bigger than your own situation. Maybe this is a step toward forcing the government to confront the ways the system has allowed corruption and abuses of power to fester. And maybe that could be the beginning of the real reforms we've all been waiting for, the reforms you were demonstrating for over the summer. If not for your own self, don't you have a duty to at least try for your country?"

Leila looked pained and confused as she gathered her belongings.

"Anyway," Azar said as she ushered the girl toward the door, "Why don't you go home and talk to your mom about it and decide what you're going to do."

Leila paused in the doorway. "My mom doesn't know anything about it," she said. "I didn't want to get her hopes up."

"Oh, well, maybe it's better that way." Azar replied with a gentle but firm pat on the back that moved Leila toward the elevator. "Come see me again in a few days and let me know what you've decided."

Azar gave Leila a bright smile as the girl turned slowly to push the elevator button. Azar felt a bit bad about pushing her off, but she had to turn her attention to her family.

The elevator door opened almost immediately, and Leila stepped aside as Ali, Hossein, and Muhammadreza tumbled out of the tiny lift and filled the hallway with the sound of tears and shouting.

"My God, these boys are—" Ali stopped abruptly when he saw Leila.

"Sorry Ali-jaan, I had a visitor," Azar apologized. "Leila-khanoom, this is my brother. Ali, Leila-khanoom is the daughter of one of my . . . Shhh! Quiet down boys! . . . Leila-khanoom is . . ."

Azar paused, confused by the way Ali and Leila's eyes were darting from her to one another and then back to her as if they were witnessing something out of place and looking to her to explain.

"Leila-khanoom is my . . ." Azar began again but abandoned the introduction once more as her boys screaming had reached such a pitch that conversation was no longer possible.

"My precious children, why are you crying?" Azar asked. Go inside before the whole building is disturbed."

"He made me drop my ice cream!" Muhammadreza wailed.

Leila waved her goodbyes and stepped into the elevator, and Azar dragged her boys inside.

"It was *my* ice cream!" Hossein responded.

"No! Uncle Ali gave it to me."

Hossein turned on his younger brother, "Only because you're such a baby!" Then, to his mother he explained forcefully. "He didn't like his own ice cream so Uncle Ali made me give him half of mine. But he started slurping it in front of me and making faces like he was happy he got my ice cream . . ."

"I did not!" Muhammadreza interjected.

"So I shoved him! It's not my fault he's so clumsy and dropped it."

Muhammadreza threw his head back and bawled. "I want my ice creeeeeeam!"

"Shut up or I'll hit you again!"

Azar had heard enough. "Stop it, both of you! There's plenty of ice cream in the world for everyone. Muhammadreza, that's enough. Quiet down and I'll get both of you a treat on our way home."

The boys swallowed their tears and anger and looked at her expectantly.

"Can we eat out at Pizza Hat for dinner?" Hossein asked mentioning the popular restaurant that, Azar had heard, was a copy of an American pizza chain.

"If you're good. But first, go to the bathroom and wash off the tears."

The boys cheered and, squabble forgotten for now, raced to the bathroom.

Azar turned to her brother, apologetically bringing him into the waiting area.

"I'm sorry they were so much trouble. Take a seat. Should I bring some tea?"

Ali sat in the same spot that Leila had been just moments earlier. He shook his head indicating he didn't want anything and asked, "Who was that girl?"

"Oh, sorry, I didn't introduce you properly. She's Ms. Tabibian's daughter."

"Your secretary?" Ali asked.

"Well yes, although of course Ms. Tabibian doesn't work for me anymore. Why? Have you seen Leila before? It seemed like maybe you knew each other."

Ali looked at her a moment and then shook his head and said, "*Khaharam*, my sister, you need to be careful."

Worried he was about to say something sensitive, Azar pointed to her still disassembled phone on the table to inquire silently as to whether he had a cellphone with him.

Ali shook his head again to indicate there was no reason for concern. "I left it in the car," he said. "Listen to me, Azar. I don't agree with you and Ibrahim on everything, but I respect and admire the way you stand for your principles. At the same time, you're my sister, and I want you to be safe. They let you out, but that doesn't mean they're finished with you. You can't trust anyone. And I mean anyone. You never know who's working for them.

This again. It irritated Azar to be lectured by her little brother as if he, more than she, understood the oppressive nature of the regime and how to protect oneself. And Azar couldn't understand how her brother's experience of unjust imprisonment had actually made him even more deferential to the system. Didn't they who knew what this regime was capable of have an even greater duty to inform others and work for change?

But, as Azar's thoughts flashed to the sensitive documents she needed to secure, she realized Ali's very deference and apoliticism made him the perfect person to hold on to them. They wouldn't be watching him the way Azar feared they might be watching her. Plus, he could keep the file at his condo, where he seemed to be spending most of his time these days anyway and which wasn't too far from her home if she needed to retrieve them.

"You're right Ali-jaan," Azar agreed, stifling her counterarguments. She couldn't afford to pick a fight with him right now. "Ali, look I have a big favor to ask of you. I need you to—"

Before she could finish her request, the kids came racing back ready to go.

"I have to talk to your uncle for a minute," Azar said to the boys. "Go watch TV in my office until I'm ready."

After a bit of grumbling and Azar promising she wouldn't be long, they trudged reluctantly to her office.

Azar turned to Ali to continue their conversation and held out the white envelope. "I need you to hold on to this for me."

"What is this?" Ali asked.

"You won't believe it!" Azar couldn't help crowing a bit. "These are medical documents that prove a cover up of Arman Tamimi's death due to—"

"No!" Ali interjected. "Don't tell me any more. I . . . I shouldn't have asked."

"Okay, okay. Relax. Just, I need you to hold on to these for a while and keep them safe for me at your condo. They're the only copies I have."

Ali was shaking his head. "No, Azar, I can't. Believe me. You don't want to give them to me."

"What do you mean? You just said I have to be careful. I can't trust anyone. I can't keep these here or at home in case we get raided again. Even our parents' home isn't safe. I need you to do this for me, Ali. You're my brother. You're the only person I can really trust."

Ali closed his eyes and took a deep breath. Azar was irritated. What was his problem? He'd been in jail for barely a month, and no one had touched a hair on his head. He hadn't been sentenced, and even if he had, he didn't have to worry about little children that depended on him. Why was he the one that was such a coward?

"It's just for a few days," Azar cajoled.

Ali opened his eyes. "Okay. Fine. I'll take them."

"Mersi! Put them someplace safe, okay?"

"Yes, of course," Ali said as he rubbed the back of his thick neck. When Ali was a toddler, one of Azar's friends had said his fat neck made him look like the walrus in their science text. Azar had stopped talking to the girl for a month, but she had secretly agreed.

"I'd better go," Ali finally said.

"Didn't you have something you wanted to talk about? Do you want to join us for dinner?" Azar asked.

"No, I have a lot to do. But, yes, I do need to tell you something."

"What is it?" Azar asked.

"I've been . . ." He paused and began fiddling at the chip on his tooth that he'd gotten, along with a broken arm, when he was fifteen and tripped into the deep *joob*, or gutter, that ran alongside her parents' street.

"What?" Azar prompted.

Ali looked at the floor and mumbled, "I've been seeing Sarah."

Azar didn't understand his meaning and looked at him quizzically.

"We ran into each other almost two months ago" Ali explained as he looked up. "Azar, it was so improbable. I was near Laleh Park and went into the very café she just happened to be at with her friends. And then the next week, we found each other there again. There's no way something like that could have happened unless God wanted it. So we've been seeing each other regularly since then."

Azar was indignant. "Are you stupid?"

Ali looked taken aback.

"Have you forgotten who her family is? Have you forgotten what they did to us? How much pain and suffering all of us have had to endure because of that ridiculous girl and her venomous family? Do I have to remind you of their role in your arrest? And maybe in my arrest? Ibrahim is still in that hellhole Evin. Those people are two-faced traitors to us and to this country. I hate everything they stand for!"

"Stop!" Ali's voice was angry. "You don't know her. She isn't like her family. She isn't political. She's . . . I love her!"

"You think you're only marrying her?" Azar railed on. "Families marry each other. Look at me and Ibrahim. We were a good match because our families were a good match. It didn't matter how I felt about him. And it doesn't matter how you feel about Sarah. You think you love her, but there are a thousand girls you could love. It's the family that's important."

"No! I don't agree," Ali protested. "Sarah is the only one for me."

Azar ignored him. "It doesn't matter. You need to end this,

Ali. My God! Now I see why you've been dragging your feet to finalize the divorce. You need to stop immediately. In time, you'll see what a simpering foolish girl she is and—"

"Don't you dare talk about her that way!" Ali's voice was raised now. "She is my wife! She will always be mine. She . . ." Ali's voice suddenly dropped to a whisper. "She's pregnant."

PART THREE
TWO DAYS IN DECEMBER

The rulers, however, say that people do not understand, that they are ignorant and that they do not really understand their interests. They argue that they have been appointed by God and His representative to rule over this mass of people.

—Mohsen Kadivar, prominent critic of the Islamic Republic, August 31, 2009

CHAPTER 7

Friday, December 18, 2009, Midday—six months after the election

Normality hasn't been practiced in Iran . . . The new
generation understand they need to have a normal life.
—Former senior Iranian official[6]

Sarah felt her phone vibrate in her jeans pocket as she leaned over
the bathroom sink, waiting for the ultimate outcome of another
bout of nausea.

She pulled the phone out. As expected, it was Ali.

"*Allo?*"

"Sarah, it's me. I'm just looking for parking outside. Should
I come in?"

"No, Ali-jaan, I . . ."

Sarah's stomach lurched, and she put the phone down to lean
closer to the sink. But it turned out to be a false alarm. She put
the phone to her ear again.

"Sorry, Ali . . ."

"Are you okay?"

Sarah loved that he sounded so worried.

"I'm fine, azizam," she reassured him. "I'm just sick again. Today is the worst it's been."

Ali chuckled softly, "If this kid is causing so much trouble before it even arrives, we're in for a rough ride."

"Ugh . . . I feel too awful to even joke about it."

"You're right, dearest. I'm sorry. Anyway, I'm here."

"Yes, Ali-jaan, I was saying . . . I've been so sick, and my father only just got here. I . . ."

"You haven't told them yet?"

"No, but I'll do it right now—as soon as I get out of the bathroom, okay? I'll text you. Just wait a bit for me."

"Okay. Are you sure you want to do this today?"

"Yes! Don't be mad. I'll text you soon. I've got to go. I'm gonna be sick."

Sarah flipped the phone closed, leaned over, and pulled back her hair with one hand as her body finally released her lunch into the sink.

Sarah felt better with her stomach emptied. She rinsed her mouth, washed her face, and critically examined her small eyes and wide nose in the mirror. Did she look different? In books and movies, pregnant women were always recognized by a certain "glow" about them. But even with all the morning queasiness, her own mother hadn't seemed to notice anything, much to Sarah's combined relief and disappointment.

Sarah smoothed back her thick black hair and fastened it with a hairband before retrieving her headscarf from where it hung on a hook beside her chador. She tugged the headscarf over her hair and tied it firmly under her chin. Then she reached for the light-green cotton chador and draped it over her head, careful to keep the ends from trailing onto the bathroom floor by gathering the folds and tucking them under her left elbow. She opened the bathroom door and shook her right foot loose of the bathroom slippers. Then she set her foot down in the hallway and swiveled to do the same with her left.

But rather than moving toward the salon where her family was enjoying post-lunch tea and sweets with Aunt Mehri's family, she moved toward her bedroom. She was going to tell everyone about Ali. But first she had something to take care of.

*   *   *

Sarah had been shocked, bewildered, overjoyed, and utterly horrified to discover she was pregnant. She had noticed a few subtle changes in her body, but had initially chalked them up to the effects of having lost her virginity. But when her period, which like clockwork normally arrived on the eighth or ninth of the lunar Arabic month, failed to appear twice, she knew something was up.

When she mentioned her concerns to Ali, he got her to a doctor's office for a pregnancy test within the hour. And when they received the positive result, his eyes glistened with joy as he pinched her cheek with his thick fingers.

Sarah was the one with reservations.

"What are we going to do?" She asked Ali in the car on the way back from the doctor's office.

"We're going to have the most beautiful little baby on the planet!" He reached across the gearshift and pulled her hand to his lips for a kiss.

"I mean about our parents."

"We were going to have to tell them eventually," Ali shrugged. "In some ways, this makes it easier. They can't try to keep us apart now."

"No, Ali. I'm so . . . embarrassed. How can I tell them I'm pregnant?"

"There's nothing to be ashamed of. I'm your husband! We haven't done anything wrong."

"But they . . ."

Sarah started weeping as she imagined her mother's and father's likely reactions. They would be so disappointed in her. Not just for being pregnant but also for all the deception. Just last week she'd lied for the first time to her mother's face when she told her she'd been nowhere near Tajrish Square, where one of her mother's friends claimed to have seen her. Sarah had been lucky the friend hadn't seen or recognized Ali and that her mother had let the matter drop relatively quickly.

Ali pulled the car over to comfort her.

"Azizam, my beloved. My little *golli*. My sweet rose. Don't cry. It's going to be fine. You'll see. Your parents love you, and they want you to be happy. And once they see how happy I make you, they'll forget everything else. And when they see the babies . . ."

"What do you mean babies?"

Ali squeezed her hand and smiled mischievously. "I think we should have twins!"

"Are you crazy? I'm still in school! That's another thing . . . How am I going to finish my studies?" Sarah's tears were coming faster now.

"Okay, okay." Ali recanted quickly. "No twins! And we'll get someone to help you with the baby. Don't cry, Sarah darling. And don't worry. It's all going to be okay. You'll see. This is a good thing. Trust me."

But Sarah couldn't stop sobbing.

"Ahh . . . You know what this is?" Ali asked and then answered his own question. "This is all those extra hormones that women get when they're pregnant. That's what's making you cry over such good news. It's okay, azizam. You just let it all out."

He sat with her, awkwardly patting her hand until she started to feel better. He was right. Her parents would understand. And a baby! As scary as it seemed, it would also be fun to be a young mother. She hoped for a girl. She would get to dress the baby in cute outfits her friends would admire, and then her little girl would become a friend and confidant as she grew. Oh, and Ali would be such a wonderful father.

She blew her nose and gave Ali a watery smile.

He smiled back and asked, "You okay, my love?"

She nodded, and he started the car to take them home, where they talked about where to set up a nursery. The master bedroom was on one side of the condo while the three other bedrooms were so far away, on the other side of the guest salon, that Sarah couldn't imagine leaving an infant all alone in one of them. They decided the master bedroom was large enough to add a crib and even a rocking chair for nursing at night. But they would also set up the closest bedroom for the baby. Sarah couldn't wait to finally move in so she could start decorating it and filling the baby's closet with tiny, frilly clothes.

They had told his family the following weekend. Ali took his parents, sister, and nephews out for a late breakfast on the grounds of the Niavaran museum complex, and Sarah met them a bit later, after he texted that he'd broken the news. Sarah felt nervous as she entered the complex and walked along the grassy lawn toward the outdoor restaurant. She wanted so badly for them to love her. But what if they were angry? Or unkind? She wasn't used to being anything other than the doted-upon daughter of loving parents. How would she handle being the target of his family's ire? She was glad they had decided to do this in public, where everyone's behavior would have to be polite and constrained by the watchful eyes upon them.

She needn't have worried so much. Ali met her at the entrance to the restaurant and smiled warmly as he took her hand and walked her toward the traditional low tables at which his family sat picnic-style around their meal. Everyone rose immediately, and his mother came forward to kiss her cheeks, saying, "I hear we have wonderful news! Congratulations, my darling girl." Ali's father bowed his head formally until his mother pushed him closer, teasing, "Don't be so shy! She's your daughter-in-law. Give her a hug and kiss." Sarah felt that Azar was still a bit cold as she greeted her, and they sat down to eat. Azar didn't seem particularly surprised by or even that interested in the news of Sarah's pregnancy. But perhaps she was simply distracted by her boys, who were wreaking havoc as they chased a couple of stray cats around other people's tables.

Ali's mother urged her to eat, asked questions about how the pregnancy was going, and shared a few of her experiences with her own babies, whose colicky screaming was always calmed by a combination of olive oil and rosewater she would rub on their bellies. Sarah was amazed at how natural and easy it felt to be part of this new family and wondered why she and Ali had ever thought it was a good idea to hide their reconciliation.

The plan had been for them to break the news in similar fashion to Sarah's family that very afternoon over dinner. But Sarah's father had an urgent last-minute business trip to Dubai, and they'd put the announcement off until today.

It had been a tough week. Things had gone so well with Ali's family that Sarah couldn't wait to tell her parents too. Ali's mother had started calling her every day to ask after her health and see if she was craving any particular foods that she could prepare for her. Sarah basked in the glow of her mother-in-law's solicitousness but felt guilty and sad to be missing similar moments with her own mother. The morning sickness had kicked in full force, and she felt nauseous most of the time but was trying to hide it. It would be such a relief to finally share her news.

This morning, however, her mother had announced that since today was the first of Muharram, she'd invited Aunt Mehri and the whole family to their house so they could do a series of special prayers and *duas* together after lunch. What to do?

In a whispered telephone call from her bedroom, she and Ali considered the options. They talked about putting off their announcement until another time when it was just Sarah's immediate family and they could go out to a restaurant or other public place. But Sarah didn't think she could keep the secret much longer and knew it would be much worse if her parents guessed the news or, even worse, heard it from someone else. The longer they tried to keep it under wraps, the more likely it would slip out in a way that was potentially disastrous.

It was Ali who decided that they should go for it.

"I don't see what else we can do. We keep trying to wait for the perfect time, but maybe this is the best we can get."

Sarah was still nervous. "I just wish my aunt wasn't going to be here. She's sure to make a scene."

"Would you rather tell your mother right now, on your own?"

Sarah thought about it. No. She was going to need Ali's help to get through this. His arrival right after her announcement would help cut short any unnecessary drama. She also hoped the sight of them together as a couple would help convince everyone that there was no use protesting against it. Besides, it would be kind of fun to tweak her irritating aunt a bit.

She sighed, "I suppose you're right. Let's do it."

*   *   *

Sarah moved swiftly down the hallway. She could hear laughter from the salon, where it sounded like her father was still entertaining everyone with the latest jokes he'd added to his collection about Isfahanis, Rashtis, Turks, and other Iranian regional and ethnic groups living up to stereotyped behavior as cheapskates, cuckolds, and more. She passed her brother's bedroom, where all the youngsters had gathered to watch TV.

In her own room, Sarah locked the door behind her before she opened her closet and dug past hanging clothes to pull a heavy box from the back of the roomy wardrobe. Sarah removed the top of the box and dug through the papers it contained to find the big white envelope she was looking for. She set the envelope on her bed while she replaced the contents of the box and pushed it back to its place in her closet. Then she picked it up and opened it to pull out a manila folder. She left the empty envelope on the bed and hid the folder under her chador. Then she left her bedroom and walked back down the hall toward the den.

Sadegh's briefcase was still where she'd seen him lean it up against the couch when he'd sat down to visit with the men before lunch. The soft leather bag was already overflowing with papers and books. Sarah turned the folder sideways and wedged it into the middle opening so that one end was sticking up a bit. She was sure he couldn't miss it. She wished there was a way to pass this on to someone she hated a little less than Sadegh. But the important thing was to get it out of her own house and make sure it got back to the authorities so she and Ali would be safe.

"Sarah, are you okay?"

Sarah whirled around and found Sumayeh at the entry to the den. Sarah's heart started pounding at the unexpected intrusion. Had Sumayeh seen her fiddling with Sadegh's bag?

"I was worried," Sumayeh smiled. "Your mom said you haven't been feeling well."

Sumayeh had always been kind to Sarah, so Sarah wasn't sure why she'd never been able to warm to her. Maybe it was because of that weird scar. Or maybe because Sarah had still had a bit of a crush on Sadegh when he'd married Sumayeh. Or maybe it was just that Sumayeh was always so serious, had no sense of humor, and never laughed at Sarah's attempts to be funny.

"I'm fine," Sarah said, more coldly than she'd intended. "I was just looking for something."

"Can I help you find it?" Sumayeh offered in a voice so sincerely helpful that Sarah decided she must not have seen her shoving the file into Sadegh's bag.

"No, it's not important," Sarah said with relief. "I was just about to go and rejoin everyone."

Sarah brushed past Sumayeh and headed toward the salon. God, she'd given her a fright. Not that it was really that big of a deal. Sumayeh was probably quite well-informed about all of Sadegh's activities, so she would understand about the papers. But it had startled Sarah nonetheless.

Sarah headed across the salon toward the chair where she'd earlier been sitting between her mother and father, who were bridging the male and female sides of the room. Halfway there, however, she decided it would be better to simply address everyone from the middle of the room. She stopped in the center of the massive carpet her father had purchased from Qom last month, right where the bud of a lotus flower grew between two men on horses in pursuit of a beautiful stag. Sarah cleared her throat and announced, "I have something to say."

A few of the men looked briefly in her direction but the ladies ignored her entirely as they continued their conversation.

Zainab was speaking. With one hand, she held a ribbed glass of tea while the other held a cream puff with a bite taken out of it.

"I was there to pick up Nafiseh's school uniform when I saw her." Zainab used the cream puff to point in a general eastward direction to, Sarah presumed, indicate where she was when the event in question occurred. "She tried to talk to me, can you imagine? Of course, I ignored her entirely. Mr. Akbari's shop is certainly serving a much lower type of clientele these days. We'll have to find a new tailor now!"

A few of the ladies tittered and the men turned back to their own conversations. Zainab took another bite out of her cream puff. Out of the corner of her eye, Sarah saw that Sumayeh had rejoined their gathering.

Sarah had no idea what they were talking about and took a deep breath to try again. But before she could speak, Fatimeh said softly. "That's not nice."

Zainab answered sharply, her hawk eyes zooming onto Fatimeh as if she were prey. "What do you mean? After all that woman has done to our family? I have nothing to say to her . . . None of us should have anything to say to her." Zainab leaned forward and set the remaining half of the cream puff on a small plate before her and then raised her glass of tea to her lips.

"*Vallah!*" Aunt Mehri harrumphed her agreement to Zainab's sentiments.

Sarah gathered herself to try interrupting again but was distracted by the strained look on Fatimeh's face as she opened and then closed her mouth several times in succession. It looked like she was struggling to decide whether to speak or keep quiet in the face of the usual alliance between her strong-willed sister and mother. Fatimeh started chewing on her bottom lip, and it looked as if she'd lost her nerve. But just as Sarah decided to speak up and started saying, "I have to . . ." Fatimeh rallied her courage and spoke. "Well . . . she's been hurt too, hasn't she? Isn't it punishment enough that she lost her son?"

Sarah realized that the conversation must be about Sadegh's real mother. She'd heard the whole story after the mix-up about Sadegh taking flowers for his half sister. What an unlikely coincidence that had turned out to be! Sarah still couldn't quite believe that the beautiful girl she and Ali had given shelter to had turned out to be her cousin's half sister.

Ali, of course, had strongly disputed this interpretation of events. "It's too much of a coincidence to have happened by chance," he'd argued. So far as he was concerned, it was much more likely that the girl had been working with Sadegh all along to entrap him and get to Azar and Ibrahim through him.

Sarah disagreed but chose not to push the point. It wasn't just that Sadegh hadn't even met his biological mother until after Ali had already been arrested. It was also that Sarah still remembered so vividly the moment when Leila realized she was trapped in the alleyway. Sarah didn't think it was possible for anyone to fake the combined fear, resignation, and determination evident on the girl's face. And how could anyone have known, when Sarah herself had no idea, that this exact mix of feelings would elicit Sarah's impulsive decision to invite Leila into their car and create the false premise of Ali's arrest?

Sarah tuned back into the ongoing conversation, or monologue rather, in which Aunt Mehri was chastising her cringing daughter while peeling an orange. "My God, Fati, sometimes you surprise me." It was strange to hear Aunt Mehri use God's name in a way she usually avoided out of respect for Sumayeh's feelings. "Don't you realize what type of lying filth that woman is? And how she nearly destroyed our family?" The knife in Aunt Mehri's wizened hand made several quick slices through the orange peel. "It was only through God's great mercy—" Aunt Mehri pointed the knife heavenward, and resumed shouting. "—that I was able to make it through at all. *Kheili sakht bood!* It was nearly unbearable . . . You have no idea what it did to me!" Aunt Mehri set the knife down with a clang.

Sarah's telephone vibrated. She retrieved it carefully from her pocket and saw a text from Ali: *Should I come now?*

She texted back: *Five minutes.*

Sarah put the phone back in her pocket and readjusted her coverings. She was still standing awkwardly, like a bullseye in the middle of the salon with the whole family sitting on couches and chairs lining a ring around her. She was getting tired of standing on this stiff rug, whose woolen and silk fibers still hadn't gotten enough foot traffic to fully soften. She needed to make her announcement quickly and get to the door for Ali.

Aunt Mehri had continued her tirade as she ripped pieces of the orange peel from its flesh "How that woman managed to fool your father and get her hooks into him, I will never under-stand." *Rip.* "I knew what she was from the moment I laid eyes on her." *Rip.* "My heartbreak wasn't for me . . . it was for your father! I couldn't bear it that such a good, kind, and pious man was being fooled by a snake like her." *Rip.* "And I thank merciful God every day for protecting us from her. It could have been so much worse." *Rip.* "But He heard all my prayers for my children and my husband and my family. And then one day, just like a gift from heaven, he delivered the proof I needed to convince my husband. You wouldn't believe the letters I found from this woman to . . . I can't even say the word!"

Aunt Mehri paused for effect and then ripped the final piece of peel from the orange.

Sarah used the pause to jump in. She spoke loudly as she turned in a slow semicircle on the rug's woven lotus flower to include all the male and female relatives in the room. "I have something to say. I hope it won't be too much of a—"

"No! I . . . oh! . . . I can't . . ."

Sarah lost her audience at once as all eyes turned toward Fatimeh who looked as if she were having some sort of a mental fit. She was shaking her head and making sharp monosyllabic attempts at communicating. With her sunset-colored chador over her round

body, Sarah thought she looked a bit like the orange Aunt Mehri
had just peeled. Although about a thousand times bigger.

Sarah tried to take back the floor. "Please, it's important. I
have a guest joining us today and—"

"She didn't write those letters!" Fatimeh managed a shrill
but coherent sentence before she burst into tears. She pulled her
chador over her face as if to hide in shame.

"What?" Aunt Mehri looked sharply at Fatimeh who, wracked
by sobs, didn't seem capable of further communication. "What is
wrong with you Fatimeh? Take a deep breath and calm yourself!"
Aunt Mehri dug her thumbs into one end of the peeled orange
she still held to split it in two.

Fatimeh readjusted her chador and obediently took two deep
breaths, during which time Sarah wondered whether she ought to
jump in again or, instead, text Ali to wait for the present drama
to pass.

Fatimeh's voice was shaky but clear when she spoke again. "She
didn't write those letters. I know because—" Fatimeh blinked her
long bovine eyelashes twice before continuing. "—I did."

Aunt Mehri looked irritated as she set the two halves of her
peeled orange onto a plate and reached for a tissue to wipe her
hands. "That's impossible! What are you talking about? Most of
the letters I saw were from that . . . man."

Fatimeh's face looked drained of color but resigned. "Yes.
Babak Islami. He was the grocer in the neighborhood."

"Right! See!" Maman-Mehri made her point. "That's the
man she had a . . . relationship with. Disgusting!" Maman-Mehri
returned to her orange. She pulled one section off, bit the end,
and started chewing.

"No, Maman, listen to me," Fatimeh protested. "I was the
one writing to him."

Sarah was confused. Fatimeh wrote *love* letters to a grocer?

Such a brazen and shameful activity was entirely out of character with the sweet, proper, and timid woman she knew. Sarah glanced at Fatimeh's husband to see what he thought of this sudden admission and was intrigued to note that he looked a little embarrassed, but not surprised.

Aunt Mehri, meanwhile, looked indignant and angry. "You're making no sense, Fatimeh. The letters were all addressed to her."

Fatimeh shook her head. "I signed her name on the letters I sent to him. I was a silly teenage girl pretending to be her."

Aunt Mehri shook her head. "Don't be stupid, Fatimeh. You were just a child!" She still held the second half of the orange section she'd bitten into.

Fatimeh had resumed her tears but managed to get words out, nonetheless. "I know. I was a stupid, stupid child playing at something I didn't understand. Roksana, Ms. Tabibian I mean, was so beautiful. But she was lonely. I don't think she was hardly ever allowed to leave her apartment. It was fun to imagine a . . . friendship for her."

Sarah was trying to connect the dots. Aunt Mehri was saying that Sadegh's biological mother, her husband's second wife, had had some sort of illicit relationship. And that she'd learned of the relationship because she'd seen love letters belonging to the woman and the grocer she was in love with. But Fatimeh was saying that she was actually the one who'd sent those letters?

"That's enough!" Maman-Mehri snapped. She dropped the rest of her orange section onto the plate before her and pulled her chador tighter as if to use it as protection against Fatimeh's story.

"I could tell the grocer was in love with her," Fatimeh continued desperately. "So I sent him a note. It was easy enough to deliver. He'd seen me shopping with her, so when I gave it to him, he assumed it was from her. And then he gave me notes to give back to her."

Aunt Mehri made as if to interrupt Fatimeh, but Fatimeh kept talking louder, holding the floor.

"It only went on for a week or so. I got scared when it got serious and he started pushing to meet. I hid all the notes and tried to forget about them. Didn't you wonder why love letters like that would have ended up in my room? I had no idea . . ." Fatimeh turned now to Sadegh. "I had no idea that Maman-Mehri found them or that the letters led to the rupture with our father. I'm so sorry and embarrassed. I don't expect Ms. Tabibian's forgiveness, but only hope God can forgive me."

Sarah thought Sadegh looked pretty calm given the implications of Fatimeh's revelation that his real mother had been ejected from the family based on a horrible misunderstanding. He opened his mouth to speak but was cut off by Aunt Mehri.

"Harm? My dear child . . ." Sarah noticed that Aunt Mehri's tone toward Fatimeh had changed quite dramatically from harsh and dismissive to sweet and cajoling. "It is obvious to me that you are confused. Clearly, she must have manipulated and involved you somehow in this disgusting romance of hers in a way that made you think you were the one instigating it. That woman is more clever than you can imagine."

Fatimeh shook her head to indicate her disagreement, but Maman-Mehri went on.

"It wasn't just the letters, you see. When I found them, I did some additional investigating. I . . . watched her. You wouldn't believe how often this woman went out for groceries!"

"It was one of the only places she was allowed to go!" Fatimeh interrupted.

"You wouldn't believe how much makeup she would pile on to see this man," Maman-Mehri went on.

"She *always* wore a lot of makeup," Fatimeh said.

"Stop defending her, Fatimeh! You were a thirteen-year-old

child. You didn't see things. You don't know how these two would look at each other! You don't know how easily he took a key to her home. As if he was expecting it! He would never do such a thing, let alone actually go to her house, unless she had made him aware that she was completely available for him." Aunt Mehri stamped her foot for emphasis and bumped the edge of the serving table, lightly jiggling her forgotten orange.

The room went silent. Fatimeh blew her nose.

BZZZZZZ.

Sarah had been so engrossed in the conversation between Aunt Mehri and Fatimeh that she'd entirely forgotten about Ali. The sound of the doorbell was an urgent reminder that Sarah needed to do some explaining of her own before Ali walked in the door.

"Like I said, I—" Sarah started but was once again interrupted, this time by Sadegh, who had a question for his mother.

"Wait. What did you say about a key?" he asked as he stroked his beard with his long, thin fingers. Sarah was distracted from her own news once again as she watched Sadegh's eyes narrow and his face darken, as if he suspected something. Sarah tried to remember what Aunt Mehri had said about the key. What was Sadegh implying?

"*Khodaya!* My God, it doesn't end!" Aunt Mehri threw up her hands. "I'm too tired to talk about this anymore. Really, I don't feel good. I need something to drink. Somebody get me some water."

Sumayeh jumped up, and Sarah saw her shoot Sadegh a meaningful look as she left the room. Sumayeh had always been close with Aunt Mehri.

But Sadegh didn't back down. "Maman-Mehri, how do you know how those two would look at each other? How do you know that the grocer took the key to Ms. Tabibian's house so easily?" Sadegh wasn't shouting. But to Sarah's ears, his voice was

so intense he might as well have been. And the implication was
now clear. Sadegh thought Aunt Mehri was involved somehow in
giving the grocer a key to his mother's house.

Aunt Mehri hitched up her chador and pulled it close. When she
spoke, her voice was high-pitched and whiney. *"Sadegh, to ro khoda
vellemoon kon!* Please, don't make me talk about this anymore!"

Sumayeh returned with a glass of water. Again, she shook her
head at her husband to, Sarah assumed, indicate he should drop the
subject for now.

But Sadegh ignored her and spoke to his mother. "Did you
give him the key?" he asked the question directly now.

Sarah wanted to hear Maman-Mehri's answer. But the sound of
the front door opening pulled her attention toward her own drama.
Sarah turned to face the salon entrance and saw Ali being ushered
in by her little brother. Both of them looked confused. Ali held a
bouquet of colorful daisies.

Sarah heard Sadegh ask his mother again, this time with anger
in his voice. "Maman-Mehri, I'm not going to stop asking until
you tell me. Did you arrange for the grocer to have a key to her
apartment?"

Sarah locked eyes with Ali, who gave his head a quick shake and
widened his eyes as if to ask what was going on. Sarah had no idea
what to say or do. Should she try to get the room's attention again?
Perhaps she could pull her mother and father aside for a private conversation instead? At a loss, Sarah simply shrugged her shoulders.

"You still don't understand!" Maman-Mehri shouted. "That
woman was a liar and a cheat and a . . . whore—God forgive me
for saying such a word—from the beginning! God himself guided
me toward doing what I had to do to make your father see and to
protect this family from her. I prayed and prayed over what I was to
do, but the ultimate outcome was so swift and easy that it was clear
confirmation I had understood his will correctly."

The last time Sarah had seen Aunt Mehri so agitated was at her wedding. But this time, there was a nervous edge to her voice that was quite unusual in a woman who was always completely confident in her indignation and self-righteousness. Aunt Mehri knew, Sarah realized, that she'd done something terribly wrong.

"Sarah, what is going on?" Sarah's father's stern voice cut through the conversation. "Mahdiyeh!" Sarah's father called her mother and, gesturing to Ali, said, "Do you know what this is about?"

Sarah felt the blood rush to her face and looked down, wishing she could disappear into the hunting scene on the carpet. In her peripheral vision, she saw her father and mother join her in the center of the room, each stopping on one of the horse heads on either side of the lotus flower Sarah was still standing on. Then Sarah saw Ali's thick, socked feet appear before her on the head of the stag the horsemen were hunting.

"Maman, Baba, I've been trying to tell you . . ." Sarah began as she looked up into each of their worried faces. "Well, we ran into each other a few months back. At a coffee shop, can you believe it? And, well, we were still married, so we thought it was okay to talk for a bit, and then we realized we still want to be . . . together. So we told his family, and I've been trying to tell our family today. Actually, we were going to tell you last weekend, but Baba had his work. So . . ." Sara swallowed hard and looked at the floor. "We want to start our lives as a married couple and . . ."

Sarah knew she was babbling but didn't know what else to do in the face of her parents' silent anger. She stopped talking and allowed herself to be distracted by the sound of Sadegh's quiet declaration, "How could you? I don't know what to say. I need to think. Sumayeh, get the kids. We're leaving."

Aunt Mehri responded with an anguished cry of, "Sadegh! No! Please, don't let this woman tear us apart. Oh, dear God!"

Ali took her hand into his thick palm and gave it a squeeze.

Perhaps he meant to give her courage, but Sarah found the gesture irritating and embarrassing in front of her family and wondered how many of them were paying attention to her and Ali versus Sadegh and Aunt Mehri.

Ali leaned forward to offer her mother the bouquet of flowers. She took them awkwardly, careful not to inadvertently touch his hand.

"These are for you. To celebrate the good news." Ali squeezed Sarah's hand again and announced with a warm and happy smile, "Our little one will be here before we know it."

Sarah could hear Aunt Mehri crying piteously for Sadegh, issuing warnings that her heart couldn't stand this sort of trauma. But Sarah's attention was occupied by the sight of her father's face, which seemed to have turned several shades darker under his beard. It didn't look like he was breathing and his hands were clenched in tight fists.

Ali stretched his hand toward her father for a handshake as he went on. "Mr. Bagheri, I want to assure you that I—"

"Nooo!" Sarah cried as she suddenly realized what was coming. But she was too late.

Her father punched Ali in the face.

CHAPTER 8

*Friday, December 18, 2009, Late Afternoon and Evening
—six months after the election*

I never thought that these matters could be contaminated
like this. I thought that I was continuing the path of my
uncles and our martyrs . . . We really believed that what
we did was correct, that we were serving the people, that
we were serving God and that our mission was nothing
but worshipping God. But now I am ashamed in front of
people, even say that I was mistaken, and I am ashamed
in front of my religion. I committed crimes, knowingly
and unknowingly.
—Anonymous former Basiji interviewed
   by a Western reporter

Sadegh paced outside the half-open door of Sarah's home, where
he'd been waiting for his wife and kids to join him. Sumayeh
stood across the threshold, still in her house chador.

"I think you should get a cab." Sumayeh shrugged as she said
this. It was a small subtle movement that made Sadegh feel she

couldn't care less about the maelstrom that had just upended him.

"What?"

Sumayeh shrugged again as she handed him his jacket and briefcase. "I need the car to get the kids home. Maybe someone will give you a ride. I don't know what to say."

"Are you kidding me?" Sadegh yanked the briefcase and jacket from Sumayeh's hands. "Come on, let's go."

Sumayeh's voice was calm. "I don't feel right about it. Your mother . . . I've never seen her like this. If the kids and I leave, it will be as if she's lost all of us. Besides, it's the first of Muharram, and I want to join in the prayers."

Sadegh wanted to throw his overstuffed briefcase against the wall but controlled himself with difficulty, knowing his situation wouldn't be improved by an explosion of papers, pens, and other contents into the hallway. "Sumayeh, stop it!" Sadegh shouted. "Go get the kids. Now." In a softer tone he pleaded, "I can't stay here. I need you with me."

"I know Sadegh-jaan," Sumayeh looked genuinely sympathetic but entirely unmoved. "I wish I could go with you, but it wouldn't be right. You're upset. I understand that this is all a shock, and it probably is better that you leave and cool down before you say something that will hurt her even more. But I think—"

Something clicked in Sadegh's brain and he interrupted his wife. "You blame me?"

Sumayeh closed her mouth and looked at him evenly. When she started speaking, the words came slowly, as if she was taking her time choosing them.

"You had a shock, Sadegh. Many people would have reacted the same way or worse. But, azizam, my dear, we hold ourselves to a higher standard. The Prophet himself, peace be upon him, spoke of how much respect and obedience we owe our mothers."

"Are you even listening to yourself?" Sadegh fumed. "What

about the woman I threw out of my house? Don't I owe her anything?"

In almost exactly the same tone she used with their son when he was throwing a tantrum, Sumayeh said, "Sadegh, you need to calm yourself down and then find a way to respect and obey both of the women that are your mothers in the manner they each deserve."

Sadegh stared at the unyielding woman before him and then spat words he knew would hurt her. "My God!" Sadegh blasphemed with satisfaction. "Are you even human?"

Sumayeh lifted her eyebrows and flattened her mouth against his disrespectful use of God's name. Her scar was tugged from both sides so it looked tight, shiny, and a deeper purple than usual. Without saying anything further, she closed the door in his face.

Sadegh's breathing came in sharp gasps. He considered pounding on the door for his wife. Instead, he turned and jogged down the stairs to the courtyard, where he pushed through the heavy gate and heard its satisfying slam behind him. He walked briskly, almost running through the alleyways, not entirely certain of his route. His briefcase bumped awkwardly against his knees. Sadegh knew, instinctively, that movement would help his body work through his competing emotions.

Sadegh headed toward the main road, where he turned right toward the square. It wasn't long before he heard the *beep-beep* of a cabbie looking for a passenger and a battered, boxy orange Paykan car pulled over for him.

"Hello. *Khaste nabashid.* How much for a ride to Shahrak-e Gharb?" Sadegh asked.

"For you? Ten tomans." The driver used the common shorthand of "ten" for his asking price of 10,000 tomans.

It was too high, but Sadegh didn't feel like haggling and got in. The inside of the car was in worse shape than the outside and reeked of cigarette smoke. Sadegh could feel the hard wire springs of the seat under his bottom and wondered if they might rip through the upholstery and into his backside.

As the cabbie started driving, Sadegh thought about the events of the last hour. He didn't know what to think of the disturbing revelation that Maman-Mehri had orchestrated Ms. Tabibian's ejection from the family. Maman-Mehri had claimed she'd only been following God's direction. But as she'd been speaking, Sadegh had for the first time noticed the spittle packed into an ugly crack where her upper and lower lips met. The beatific face he'd always known to be especially loved by God had suddenly transformed into that of a petty and ugly old woman.

And now he had to figure out what to do about Ms. Tabibian's calls. He felt bad for her, he really did, especially now that he'd learned how unfairly she'd been treated. But he still didn't have any desire to rekindle that relationship. He felt a surge of anger at Maman-Mehri for putting him in this position.

The worst of it was how he'd snapped at Sumayeh and spoken to her in a manner deliberately intended to inflict pain. Now that he'd calmed down, he needed to apologize and explain things better so she'd understand.

He rummaged through his briefcase for his phone and dialed his wife. It took a long time for her to pick up, and when she did, there was a lot of background noise. Sadegh could hear agitated women's voices and, more distantly, the baby's whimpering.

"*Allo?*"

"Sumayeh," Sadegh said. "I'm sorry. I didn't mean it. I was just—"

"Here, give her to me."

"What?"

"Sorry," Sumayeh apologized. "Fati was handing me the baby. Look, it's okay. Let's talk about it at home."

The baby's whines were much louder now.

"No, it's not okay," Sadegh insisted. "I had no right to ask you to go against what you believe is right without any explanation. You see . . . Ms. Tabibian . . . I didn't tell you . . . she's been calling and leaving such sad messages. I felt cruel for ignoring her, and now . . . Hello?"

As he'd been speaking, the baby's shrieks had escalated. Sadegh, straining to be heard above them, was yelling into the phone even as he tilted the receiver away from his ear to protect his eardrum. But he wanted to be sure Sumayeh was listening.

"Sadegh," Sumayeh answered, "I can't really hear you . . . Fati-joon, I'll be right there. Sadegh, let's talk at home."

"I need you to understand. I've been avoiding Ms. Tabibian out of loyalty to Maman-Mehri, but . . . Can you just put the baby down for a minute?"

"Sadegh, it sounds like you're breaking up. I really have to go."

She was right. Her voice, and the baby's screams, had gone staticky.

"Okay. I just . . . I love you. Please come home soon."

"Sadegh. I can't hear you but I'm going to hang up now. I hope you're feeling better, and I'll see you at home."

"I said I love—"

The line cut off.

Damn. Sadegh flipped his phone closed and looked out the window at the street traffic.

He opened his phone again. He had four bars. Perhaps it had just been a bad line. He should try calling again.

Instead, Sadegh pushed buttons to get to his voice messages. He'd gotten seven calls and three messages from Ms. Tabibian since yesterday. The woman had been persistent in calling every few days since he'd kicked her out of his house two weeks ago, but this was a new level of harassment. He felt bad for her. But he wasn't sure he had it in him to manage this whole new set of obligations. One mother was plenty.

Sadegh punched the button to listen to the first message.

"Sadegh-jaan!" Her voice was almost a shriek. "My dear, dear son. Please, I am begging you, by all that you hold dear, call me. I need to talk to you today. Immediately. I . . ."

There was a pause and then her voice continued, lower now but still urgent.

"Your sister is in grave danger. She's done something . . . so stupid. I'm going to try to fix it, but I . . . I need your advice. And your help, Sadegh-jaan. I know you are angry with me, and you have every right, but please, for your sister's sake, call me!"

This was certainly different than any of the other messages she'd left. He wondered whether he could take this as confirmation that Leila really was pregnant and that they'd finally decided to be honest with him about it.

He owed her a call and an apology anyway. Sadegh pushed the Call Back button. As long as she and Leila would be honest about what was going on, Sadegh would try to help.

"*Baleh?* Yes?"

The shrill female voice wasn't one he recognized.

"I'm sorry," Sadegh said, "is this the home of Ms. Tabibian?"

"*Befarmayeed.* Go ahead."

"May I speak with her?"

"She isn't here," the shrill voice informed him. "Who's calling?"

"Is Leila there?" Sadegh asked. "Can I talk to her?"

"*Na.* Leila isn't here. Who is this?"

"This is Sadegh. Ms. Tabibian's . . . son."

There was a pause. "Ms. Tabibian doesn't have a son."

Sadegh thought about how to answer and resorted to a question. "Who is this?"

"I'm Ms. Tabibian's neighbor. Who are you?"

He ignored the question. "Why are you at her house if she isn't there?"

"I'm not at the house. Miss Leila brought the phone over for me to answer in case her mother called. She's missing."

"Who's missing?" Sadegh asked.

"Ms. Tabibian," the woman answered. "Miss Leila went down to the police station to see what to do."

"What?" Sadegh shifted forward and felt the springs in the seat shift beneath him. If Leila had gone to the police station, she must be really worried. Sadegh felt an additional pang of guilt as he thought of how alone his mother and sister were without a man in their lives to depend on. No wonder they'd clung to him.

"*Hala*, now who is this?" the woman asked.

"I told you." Sadegh answered. "I'm her son. How long has she been missing?"

"I'm not sure I should be talking to you about this," the woman said. "Why don't you call Leila? Poor thing is worried sick."

Sadegh, irritated, repeated his question. "How long has Ms. Tabibian been missing?"

Another pause. Longer this time. Sadegh wondered if the woman had hung up. "Hello?" he said.

"If she really is your mother,"—the woman paused a beat for emphasis—"why do you call her Ms. Tabibian?"

Sadegh groaned inwardly. "Look, it's a long story and, frankly, isn't any of your business. But you've got me worried. Can you tell Leila to call me when she gets in?"

"Why don't you call her yourself?" the woman asked. "She has her cellphone."

"Oh, yeah, okay. Give me the number."

"You don't have your sister's phone number?" the woman asked. Sadegh could hear the suspicion in her tone.

Sadegh clenched his teeth. "It's complicated! Could you give me her number please?"

"I'm not going to give Miss Leila's number out to a strange man," the woman retorted in her shrill voice. "When she gets home, I'll tell her you called, and she can call you herself. If she wants, that is."

Without waiting for any further response, the woman hung up on him.

Sadegh brought the phone down away from his ear and looked at it. Ms. Tabibian was missing? What could the woman mean? The last call he'd gotten from her was—Sadegh checked his phone—just this morning. There was a voice message at 9:08 and a missed call at 11:15. How could she have gone missing since then?

He listened to the voice message from the morning.

"Salam, Mr. Sadegh," Sadegh realized immediately that it was Leila, not his mother, who had called. *"Kheili bebakhshid baraye mozahemat.* I'm so sorry to disturb you again. But . . . I don't know where my mother is. She didn't come home last night. And I'm so . . ." Sadegh thought the message might have cut off but realized once Leila's voice went on that she must have paused to compose herself. Her voice continued in a whisper, ". . . worried. Please call. I don't know what to do."

There was a silence of several seconds before she had hung up.

Sadegh listened to the third message. This one had come late the night before and was also from Leila, who wanted to know if he'd heard from their mother and had any idea what might have kept her out so late.

Sadegh thought a moment. All the calls had come from Ms. Tabibian's house phone. He dialed her cellphone and was immediately routed to her voicemail.

"Agha," he addressed the cab driver. "I'm going to a different destination. Take me to Laleh Park."

*　　*　　*

"Thank you, sir, for your trouble." Sadegh held a 10,000-toman note toward the driver.

The old man twisted toward the back seat and tilted his head respectfully. "Please, be my guest. No payment is required." It was typically insincere Tehran cabbie *taarof* double-speak.

"I insist." Sadegh set the bill on the passenger seat as he opened the vehicle door. He wondered whether Leila was back home yet or whether he should try to find her at the police station. Where was the police station in this neighborhood?

The driver cleared his throat. "In that case, you should know that the price is fifteen tomans. You changed destinations, and I had to spend a lot more time in traffic. But of course"—the man went back to his *taarof*—"you're still welcome to be my honored guest and pay nothing."

Sadegh looked at the driver. He was an old man with deep wrinkles, dark skin, and yellowed eyes. He considered objecting to this outright thievery but he didn't have the time or heart for it. Instead he rifled through his wallet and pulled out another 5,000 tomans as he chided the driver. "*Khejalat bekesh*. You should be ashamed."

"Thank you agha, *raazi bashid*. You understand, of course, I have a family to support."

Sadegh got out of the car, walked up to the intercom outside the gate, and pressed the button for Ms. Tabibian's home. There were fifteen units in the shabby building, three on each of five floors.

There was no answer. Sadegh was about to try again, when the heavy metal door suddenly opened from the other side and a short round woman in a cheap black chador and brown plastic sandals shuffled out. He held the door open and waited for her to exit, but she stopped and examined him with black, beady eyes.

"*Shoma?* Who are you?"

Sadegh winced. He recognized the shrill voice that, in person, was like a pin in his eardrum. "I'm a guest of one of your neighbors."

"Is that right? Who are you visiting?"

Sadegh was stuck. "Um . . . Ms. Tabibian."

"Humph! I told you on the telephone that Ms. Tabibian isn't here." The woman's voice notched upward in energy and intensity until it was a knitting needle in his ear. "*Befarmayeed!* I'm not going to let you in."

"Please," Sadegh pleaded. "I need to see Leila. Is she back?"

"*Befarmayeed, agha!* Be on your way sir!" She trundled toward him so he had to back up and let go of the door to avoid a collision. The door shut behind her with a loud clang.

Sadegh turned and almost bumped right into Leila.

"Oh! I'm sorry," Sadegh said.

"Sadegh-agha, thank you for coming. I wasn't sure you got my messages." Leila's eyes were red. It looked like she'd been crying and might start up again.

The neighbor pushed in between them. "Leila-khanoom, do you know this gentleman? He says he's your brother, but I've never seen him before or heard your mother mention him."

"Yes, Ms. Noori," Leila said. "Thank you so much. This is my brother—well, my half brother—Sadegh. We've only recently been reacquainted and . . ."

"Humph! Well, he looked suspicious." The woman wagged a finger as she spoke. "And you never can be too careful."

"Yes, thank you Ms. Noori," Leila said. "I'm sorry for the trouble. No one called?"

"Just this—" Ms. Noori eyed Sadegh. "—gentleman." She turned toward Leila. Not quite enough to completely have her back toward Sadegh but enough to signify what she thought of him. "Leila dear, I have to do some shopping for Mr. Noori's dinner, but I left the phone with him and gave him strict instructions to answer immediately if anyone calls. What did the police say? Were they any help? You know you can stay with us tonight again, and as long as you need to. Okay, azizam, I need to go or dinner will be late. If you'd be more . . . comfortable,"—she eyed Sadegh again and dropped her voice, as if doing so would prevent him from hearing—"you can take him up to our apartment. Mr. Noori is there, so you wouldn't have to be alone."

At this she paused.

Leila answered, "Thank you, Ms. Noori, for your kindness, but I—"

The woman interrupted with a wave of her hand. "*Hala*, however you're most comfortable. I'm just thinking about the neighbors. You know how they talk. Anyway, I've got to go."

With a curt nod to Sadegh, Ms. Noori left them and headed down the sidewalk. With her black chador and side-to-side waddle, her receding back looked a bit like a plump penguin strolling the streets of Tehran.

*   *   *

"*Kheili lotf kardin oomadin.* It was kind of you to come. I'm . . . sorry for the imposition. I know you didn't want us to contact you, but I—"

"Yes, well," Sadegh interrupted. He cleared his throat. "About that. I may have been hasty. You see, I just found out that, well, I was mistaken. Or really, my mother—Maman-Mehri, I mean— was mistaken. And, well, it's unfortunate."

Leila looked at him from the tiny kitchenette, where she was pouring tea. "I don't understand," she said. "What's changed?"

"Ah, well." Sadegh's fingers drummed his knees as he looked around once again at the astonishing little apartment. An entire woodland scene had been painted in silver over aging walls black-ened by the radiator and gas lighting. Cracks in the cheap plaster had been transformed into tree branches over which small wooden figures of birds and other forest creatures had been hung to look as if they were resting. The floor was covered with colorful cheap *qelims* and big red cushions with traditional geometric patterns that were piled against the walls for sitting purposes. The first—and only—time Sadegh had previously visited Ms. Tabibian at her home, he'd felt as if he was stepping into the luxurious tent of an ancient Persian prince on a hunting trip in the middle of a moonlit forest.

It was a type of décor Sadegh had never even imagined was possible. And he marveled again at how the women had trans-formed what could have been an ugly and depressing space into something so beautiful. The thought occurred to him that if he'd been raised by Ms. Tabibian, perhaps his love of colorful patterns would have been nurtured into an artistic sensibility he didn't even know he had. Despite his confused feelings toward Maman-Mehri, Sadegh still felt pretty lucky to have been raised by her. But perhaps there were things he'd missed out on.

Pulling his attention from the scene around him, Sadegh con-tinued. "I don't know how much you know, and it's silly really, but, well, that grocer, the one that entered her house unannounced, it seems my sister somehow childishly encouraged him to think that your mother was interested in him. And then my mother caught wind of this and alerted my father and, well, it's too bad really, but this is what seems to have led to their rupture."

Leila sat cross-legged and leaned thoughtfully against the wall perpendicular to the one Sadegh leaned against. A little silver squirrel painted on one of the low branches seemed to be whis-pering in her ear. "I don't understand. Your sister gave this man a key? Why would she do that?"

"No, no, that wasn't my sister." Sadegh massaged his kneecaps.

"It was Maman-Mehri who offered the man a key. But only as some sort of test. You see, she didn't think the man would actually go to the house unless he'd been encouraged. And, well, it turned out he *had* been encouraged by my sister, who was playing at some sort of strange child's game of writing him love notes from your mother. But Maman-Mehri didn't know that, and she simply wanted to protect my father, you see. It was all just a mistake." Sadegh smiled and shrugged, lifting his hands and turning his palms upward.

"A mistake," Leila repeated. She looked down at the teacup in her hands. "That's what my mother said. It must have been some sort of mistake. But your father wouldn't believe her. And he cast her out like some sort of leper, warning her that if she ever tried to see her son, he'd have her arrested and imprisoned for adultery."

"Well, you can hardly blame him when he saw . . . Anyway, all's well that ends well." Sadegh clapped his hands on his knees. "Now that this whole thing has been cleared up, she's . . . well, she found her son after all, didn't she?" Sadegh tried to smile, but it felt more like a grimace. There was no way to defend what his father, or Maman-Mehri, had done. But Sadegh couldn't bring himself to criticize his parents in front of Leila. Anyway, it was all in the past.

"She spent years looking for you," Leila said, her glassy eyes still fixed on the teacup. "Despite his threats. She went to his store with hopes of following him to his home, but he was careful and had his men on alert to intervene. And then they moved the store, and she lost track of him."

Sadegh tried to imagine what it would be like if Mahdi or little Sana were taken from him. He'd never get to hold their wriggly bodies again. He wouldn't get to see them grow into the worthy and God-loving people he was raising them to be. The thought filled him with sadness for what Ms. Tabibian must have experienced. He was eager to change the subject.

"Anyway," he said to Leila. "Ms. Tab—your mother . . . I mean, *our* mother. Sorry, I'm still not sure how to refer to her."

"It's okay," Leila said but didn't offer a suggestion. She still wasn't looking at him.

"Anyway, she said that you were in danger and, well, I think I know what—"

Leila's crystal-green eyes snapped toward him. "You talked to her? When?"

Sadegh was startled by her intensity. "I didn't talk directly to her. She left a message saying she was worried about you and there was some sort of danger. I assumed, frankly, that it had to do with . . ." Sadegh's voice trailed off, but he looked pointedly at Leila's midsection as he rubbed his knees again.

Leila didn't seem to notice his insinuation. She asked again even more insistently, "When exactly did she call?"

Sadegh pulled out his phone. "Let's see. She left a message at eleven thirty-six yesterday morning. Then I got three more calls from the same number over the next thirty minutes, but no other messages. And then there were the messages you left last night and this morning."

"Let me listen to her message," Leila demanded.

Sadegh didn't like being ordered about. And he didn't like feeling that he had no control over the conversation. But he knew Leila was distraught and didn't want to upset her further, so he put his phone on speaker and played the message.

Again, Sadegh listened as Ms. Tabibian breathed heavily into the phone. "Your sister is in grave danger. She's done something . . . so stupid. I'm going to try to fix it, but I . . . I need your advice . . ."

At this, Leila took a swift inward gasp of air and covered her mouth with her palm so that her nose was squeezed in the space between her thumb and index finger. She didn't seem to breathe until the end of her mother's message, when she released her nose and took several shaky, shallow breaths that turned into sobs.

"What's going on, Leila?" Sadegh demanded. "You need to be straight with me this time so I can help."

Leila grabbed tissue paper from a box in the corner between them. She wiped at her eyes and blew her nose. She took a deep breath that seemed intended to control her crying.

"Okay, let's start with this," Sadegh took charge. "Leila, don't be embarrassed, but I need you to tell me. You can just nod the answer. Are you . . . expecting?"

Leila looked at him with such an immediate expression of disgust that Sadegh felt almost embarrassed. The squirrel on her shoulder looked at Sadegh with beady, angry eyes.

"What are you talking about?" Leila asked. Her voice was muffled under the tissue she was using to wipe her nose, but Sadegh registered the disdain it held and struggled to remember why he had arrived at the conclusion that she must be pregnant.

"Well, you . . . your mother, I mean, she was in such a rush to get you married. Why else would she—"

"I'm not pregnant," Leila snapped.

"Then what's going on?" Sadegh's shame at incorrectly guessing something so indelicate turned to anger. He leaned toward Leila and pointed his finger in her face. "You and your mother show up and start pushing me to find you a husband. And then your mother says your life is in danger and goes off to who knows where. I'm not a fool!" Sadegh clenched his hand into a fist and slammed it into the soft pillows beside him for emphasis. "If you want my help, you start talking now and tell me what's going on."

At that moment, a familiar whistle rang through the room. Sadegh searched for the source of the sound and found it on one of the high branches painted on the kitchenette corner. It was Maman-Mehri's cuckoo clock. Or, rather, one just like it. How had he not noticed it before? Perhaps because it was somewhat obscured by numerous wooden birds, relatives of the one flying out to announce the time, that surrounded it like a shared nest. Was this, like the one hanging in Maman-Mehri's dining room, a gift from his father?

Leila remained silent until the cuckoo returned to its home for the fifth and final time. "You're right," she conceded. "I'm sure this has all been confusing, and I'm sorry about that. But it's not what you're thinking. It's just hard to explain."

Sadegh, his anger weakened by the surprise of the cuckoo clock and Leila's conciliatory tone, relaxed back into the cushions and waited for Leila to continue.

"I'm not sure where to begin," Leila went on. "There's a Mr. Heydari that works with the Revolutionary Guards and the Basij. You know who I'm talking about?"

"Small man with a short beard?" Sadegh asked. "I've met him once or twice. What about him?"

Leila nodded at Sadegh's description of Heydari. "Yes, that's him. Well, he's from my mother's village up north. And when I was born . . . see, my mother was engaged to my father, but . . . it's kind of complicated."

Leila stopped talking and seemed to be thinking.

"Go on," Sadegh encouraged her. He was intrigued to hear that Heydari was from his mother's village. He wondered what the man would have been like as a child. All Sadegh could imagine was a small boy with cartoonishly big purple lips.

"Eventually, when my mother realized there was no way to find you, she went back home to her parents. My father . . . he was a year younger than her and had loved her even as a child, so when he saw her back in the village, he wanted to marry her right away. But Maman was still mourning the loss of her son. And my father's family didn't want him to marry an older divorcée who was clearly *torshide*, like sour milk. For five years he tried to convince my mother to marry him until finally she agreed. See how much he loved her? Anyway, despite his parents' opposition, they got engaged.

"They could have been so happy." Leila's voice cracked. "She always tells me the best time of her life was the six months they were together. But it wasn't to be. Before they could marry, there was the earthquake."

Sadegh assumed Leila was talking about the 1990 Rudbar-Manjil earthquake that killed more than forty thousand people and left a half a million people homeless. Sadegh had been nine years old and remembered that it happened the night of the World Cup match between Scotland and Brazil. Sadegh didn't care much for soccer, but Alireza did, and Sadegh, trying to keep up with his older brother, had watched along with him until he'd fallen asleep. The next day, the television was awash with scenes of the carnage from towns and villages in Zanjan and Gilan provinces, which had been entirely destroyed.

"My father died under the rubble along with my mother's parents and her two brothers," Leila said. "The only reason she survived was that she happened to be outside, on her way back from the outhouse, when it happened."

Leila shook her head and sighed. "My poor mother. Her first husband kicks her out over unjust accusations of infidelity. She's separated from her son. Then she finally finds happiness again, only to lose my father and her own family. I don't know how she was able to bear it." Leila shook her head sadly in a way that made it look as if the painted squirrel was now stroking her head to comfort her.

Leila squeezed her eyes shut, as if to prevent more tears from flowing. She paused a moment, and Sadegh made what he hoped were sympathetic noises.

"Anyway," Leila went on, "she found out she was pregnant

shortly after the earthquake. The problem was that they'd never officially registered the engagement. And my father's family . . . well, I suppose they were in a bit of shock, having just lost their son. They blamed her. Maybe they thought he would have left the village if it hadn't been for her. Anyway, they refused to acknowledge the engagement or help my mother get the papers she needed. So here she was . . . no husband, no family, and pregnant with an illegitimate child."

It would have been an awful predicament, Sadegh thought. "What did she do?" he asked Leila.

"I don't know all the details," Leila went on. "She only told me this part of it recently. Apparently, Mr. Heydari, well, as I said, he was from her village and had gotten to know a lot of powerful people during the war, when he was at the front with the Basij. My mother went to him, and he somehow arranged documents so I could get a proper birth certificate. Then she left her village and moved to Tehran to raise me by herself in a place where no one knew her story." Leila's breath caught and she shook her head. "And I've never wanted for anything . . . She made sure of that, no matter how hard she had to work or whatever else she had to sacrifice."

Sadegh thought about the young woman Ms. Tabibian must have been. By the time she was his own age, she'd lost three families. He tried to imagine what it would be like to lose so much. When his own father—the man who'd triggered this tragic chain of events—had died, it felt as if Sadegh had suddenly lost a protective shield he hadn't even known he'd been counting on to keep him safe. What would it be like to also lose his mother, his brother and sisters, and Sumayeh and the kids?

Aloud he said. "She's a lion of a woman, a *sheerezan*. I'm sad for everything she's had to go through. And I'm sorry I wasn't more . . . understanding and kind. I'm glad you've had someone like Heydari to look out for you all these years."

Leila shook her head. "No, we've only been recently reacquainted. And that's when all our troubles started. Oh, God,"
Leila gasped. "It was all my fault." She looked at Sadegh as if
beseeching him to grant a pardon that would lessen her blame.

"Leila," Sadegh said gently but with real exasperation. "I still
don't know what you're talking about."

Leila looked up at the ceiling and blinked several times.

"You know, agha Sadegh, I was always aware of the sacrifices
my mother made for me to make sure I had everything. So I really
tried to be good. I never wanted to cause her any trouble. But
recently . . . well, we had some political differences. You might
not like to hear this, but I felt the government went too far in
the election and that ordinary people had to be willing to make
sacrifices for change."

Sadegh tried not to let his irritation show. It was astounding
how cleverly this propaganda had been spread by the enemy. Even
now, almost half a year after the Iranian people had rallied behind
their leaders and defeated the threat from outside, young people
were still vulnerable to these arguments. Just a few weeks ago, after
many months of calm, a group of infiltrators had tried to hijack
the annual Student Day commemorations with offensive slogans
like "Death to the dictator." Ganjian and other Basijis had been
called in to help control the crowds and remove the offenders
before they managed to recruit others to their misguided cause.

"Anyway," Leila continued, "over the summer I went to a few
demonstrations. My mother didn't know . . . I was staying at a
friend's house. But at the last one, I was taken in by the police.
Actually, it's a very strange coincidence, but it turned out that it
was your cousin who tried to help me. It was her wedding night,
and she was in bridal clothes, and they—she and her husband—
hid me in their car. The Basijis had chased us into an alleyway, and
I got separated from my friend. I'd given up any hope of escape,

when they told me to get in. It was kind of her to risk so much for a stranger. I didn't realize it was your cousin until later. I felt bad about her husband's arrest on my account."

Sadegh's brows crowded together as he digested this. He remembered Ganjian telling him Ali had been taken in for hiding protestors in his car. Leila had been one of them? It was indeed a strange coincidence. And it was an inside-out feeling to know and even be related to rioters and demonstrators. Typically, Sadegh's only interaction with such people was while making arrests.

Leila went on. "Anyway, that night, well, Mr. Heydari interrogated me. I didn't know who he was, but when I told him my name and my mother's name, he recognized us."

Sadegh wondered whether Heydari had had the same inside-out experience. It must have been awkward to find an old friend among people you've arrested.

Aloud he asked, "What did he do?"

Leila paused before answering. "Well, he helped us . . . They only held me that one night before I was freed. Others weren't so . . ."

Her voice trailed off, and Sadegh prompted her. "Yes?"

Leila gave him an ironic smile. "I was going to say lucky, but I don't think I was lucky after all. Mr. Heydari, well, he's not a good man."

Sadegh felt piqued again. "Leila-khanoom, Heydari is a very good man who is fighting, just like me and my friends, against a very big evil. I've seen him be harsh, but it's only because he cares so much about our people and country and religion that he gets angry with those who put us at risk. Don't you see what dangerous times we are in?"

Leila shook her head and twisted a tissue in her hands. "No, it's not that," she whispered. "He wanted to marry me."

This was so unexpected that Sadegh let out a disbelieving laugh.

"He wanted to make me marry him," Leila repeated as she looked at him with serious, unblinking eyes. "And he didn't care that I had no interest in marrying a man more than twice my age."

Sadegh had trouble processing what Leila was saying. It was hard to imagine that small, severe man thinking about anything other than the security of the Islamic Republic and his beloved *velayat*.

"Leila, come on," Sadegh chided. "You must have misunderstood."

"He wanted a second wife," Leila insisted again. "We tried to put him off gently. Maman-joon told him I was already engaged. He didn't believe her and kept pushing, so she was trying desperately to find me a real fiancé. Eventually, he started hinting that if we didn't accept his offer, he would go to the authorities and reveal my ID papers as fraudulent. He is a . . . an evil man, Sadegh. I could see he got pleasure out of our desperate struggle."

Sadegh had a sudden thought. "This is why your mother was in such a rush to find you a husband?"

"Yes," Leila confirmed. She said no more but simply looked at him with steady, familiar eyes. It was surprising, Sadegh thought for the first time, how much they looked like each other and their mother. As if their respective fathers had little part in their genetic makeup.

"Leila-khanoom," Sadegh said softly. "It still seems to me that there must have been a misunderstanding." Leila started shaking her head, and Sadegh spoke more forcefully. "Maybe he thought you would welcome such an arrangement. Maybe he thought this was a kindness and that you were in need of protection. Why didn't you say something to me earlier?"

Leila puckered her lips and looked down before answering. "I'm not sure. I told Maman to tell you, but she didn't want to bother you or cause problems between you and Heydari."

A new concern flashed through Sadegh's mind. "Does Heydari know? About us being related, I mean."

Leila looked up. Not at him but at the kitchenette corner where the cuckoo clock hung. She shook her head and said, "Maman-joon was very . . ."

Leila paused and Sadegh tensed. All things considered, he would prefer to keep his private family drama away from and unknown to the Basij. There was a certain amount of prestige that came from being a Hojjati, from being in such a well-regarded family, and he didn't want to sully his reputation with rumors of a potential scandal.

". . . discreet," Leila finished her sentence. "She didn't want to cause any problems for you."

Sadegh felt relieved and annoyed and ashamed all at once. It annoyed him that Leila and Ms. Tabibian assumed he might be embarrassed for people to know about them. And he was ashamed that they were at least partly right.

Sadegh's cellphone rang. He was glad for the distraction. "*Allo?*"

"Sadegh-jaan, *kojaee.* Where are you?"

It was Sumayeh. And she didn't sound pleased.

"Didn't you get my message? I'm at Ms. Tabibian's house."

"Ms. Tabibian's house? Why would you go there? And right after a fight with Maman-Mehri? Do you have any idea the state you left her in?"

"No, Sumayeh, it's not like that." Sadegh glanced briefly in Leila's direction to see if she was listening and wondered how she might interpret his words. "There's been an emergency. I'll be home soon."

"What kind of emergency?"

"She's missing, Sumayeh-jaan. I'll tell you about it when I get home."

There was a silence.

"*Kaari nadari?* If you don't need anything else, I need to go."
Sadegh said. "I'll be home soon."

"Fine. Just . . . real quick, do you have Mahdi's matchbox fire
truck?

"What?"

"He's been crying about it since we got home. He said he put
it in your briefcase.

"I don't know, but I can't look right now."

"Okay," Sumayeh sighed. "Just call me when you leave."

"*Chashm, azizam.* Of course, my dear," Sadegh promised.

Closing his phone, Sadegh addressed his sister. "I have to
leave soon, but I want to help. And I still don't understand what's
going on and where *Madaremoon*"—Sadegh stumbled over the
word for *our mother*—"has gone."

Leila exhaled and drew her arms in and around herself as if
willing her body to shrink.

"Heydari was threatening us," she said. "And we didn't know
what to do. It looked to me like we didn't have any options and
I was going to end up married to that man. But then, something
happened, and it seemed like maybe there was a way to get rid of
him. You see, he left some papers here."

Sadegh was surprised. It would be inappropriate for an unrelated male to visit two women at their home. "Heydari came here?
To your house?"

Leila sighed. "Yes. Many times. He would show up unannounced late at night. Anyway, the papers he left were medical
records that proved Heydari had mistreated a prisoner and that
the government had covered up his cause of death by beating."

Sadegh grimaced. The enemy was so clever in the lies it spread
to undermine trust in the system. Sadegh wished the Basijis were a
little less humble about advertising the many ways they served and
protected the people.

Leila went on. "So I thought that maybe there was a way to use these papers to get him to leave us alone. Like tell him that if he doesn't back off, we would make the records public or something."

"This was your plan?" Sadegh scoffed. "Leila, all these accusations of abuse are lies spread by our enemies. I've had friends in the Basij and worked with them off and on for years now. If there was really abuse, I would have seen it. You must have misunderstood whatever you saw."

Leila shook her head at him in disagreement, and Sadegh considered the possibility that she'd really found something that suggested foul play. "Even if you're right," he said, "and there was some unfortunate event, well, Heydari and his superiors would have had good reason for keeping it private. It's a sensitive time right now, Leila. There are people actively working to overthrow our government and to throw it into the type of chaos we see in Iraq. If you make private documents like that public, you'd be working with the enemy. You could be taken in for treason."

Sadegh had been getting more and more worked up as he spoke, so he was practically yelling by the end. Leila reacted by seeming to shrink even further into the cushions as she hung her head and began to shake with what Sadegh assumed were sobs. He felt bad for having berated her.

"*Hala.*" Sadegh spoke more softly. "Don't cry. I think I understand. So your mother threatened Heydari, and he probably picked her up for questioning. This is definitely serious, Leila, and I'm disappointed that you would think of doing something like this over such a . . . misunderstanding. But . . . I know it was partly my fault for not helping you to begin with. And if what you're saying about Heydari is right . . . well, it's very strange behavior. I'll do what I can to help."

Leila wiped at her eyes with a tissue but continued to weep as she thanked him. "Mersi, agha Sadegh."

"*Vazifame.* It's the least I can do, Leila. Now, I need to go. But why don't you give me the papers you got from Heydari."

Leila took a deep breath and shook her head. "Maman-joon took them. See, Heydari didn't pick her up. She went to see him herself yesterday afternoon. She just never came back."

It was all starting to make sense. Aloud Sadegh said, "I see. So she went to threaten Heydari, and he kept her. I'm not at all surprised that—"

"No, she didn't go to threaten him," Leila interrupted. "Honestly, I don't know exactly what she wanted to do. She was so angry with me when she found out about my stupid plans. She didn't know anything about the papers or anything until yesterday."

"You threatened Mr. Heydari yourself?"

She shook her head. "No, I didn't threaten him. Actually, the opposite. I was trying . . . I was hoping to find more documents like the first one. To see if there was a larger government cover-up. I called him and pretended that I, well, that I'd come around to the idea of marriage and that it was only my mother who was opposed. We made plans to see each other, but I was so nervous I could barely sleep the last few nights. And Maman-joon, she knew something was going on and finally got it out of me. I was stupid to tell her. She went to Heydari to try to clean up my mess and now she's . . ." Leila's voice trailed off.

Sadegh closed his eyes for a moment before speaking. "Let me see if I understand. You were purposely leading him to believe you changed your mind and wanted to marry him in order to steal documents to prove the government is involved in a cover-up?"

Sadegh opened his eyes and looked at Leila, who nodded.

"But . . . why? How would evidence of a larger government cover-up"—Sadegh gave the word a sarcastic lilt to indicate he didn't believe there was any such cover-up—"help you discourage Heydari's interest?"

Leila opened her mouth, but Sadegh made a connection before she could speak.

"You couldn't have come up with this on your own!" he exploded. "Who are you working for? Leila, what is going on?"

Leila looked alarmed as she spoke in a rush. "No! It's not like that. I just wanted him to leave us alone. I went to Ms. Rahimi for help, and she . . ."

"Ms. Rahimi?"

"The lawyer Maman-joon used to work for. You know her."

Sadegh rubbed at his face. Yes. Of course he knew her. The first time he'd met Ms. Tabibian, she'd told him she worked for Ali's sister and that she was trying to get information about his arrest. Sadegh had been glad he hadn't told Ms. Tabibian anything, especially when he heard later that Ms. Rahimi had been arrested herself. Clearly the woman and her husband had been intimately involved in the post-election *fitneh*. The real pity was that she'd been let out at all.

"Yes, of course I know her. She put you up to this?"

"Just listen a moment," Leila said. "See, I needed her help. I hoped the papers I'd found could be used to pressure Heydari, but I didn't know how to use them or who to show them to. She thought it would be better to have a few more of these cases to be able to show it wasn't just a single instance. She thought this way Heydari might lose power, so he couldn't bully us anymore."

Sadegh was furious. "So you were spying for her? My own sister is spying for a woman who is working to embarrass and overthrow the leaders I would sacrifice my life for?"

"No! It's not like that," Leila protested. "I just wanted him to leave me alone! I didn't know what to do. And since when did I become your sister?" Leila looked at him defiantly. "Until an hour ago, you wanted nothing to do with me! Or even your own mother, who sacrificed so much. Ms. Rahimi is a good woman! At least she was willing to help."

Sadegh took a deep breath to control his rage. He looked around at the animals in the moonlit forest, listening in on their conversation. He wanted to smash their faces. But he knew he needed to control his temper.

"Leila, I'm sorry." Sadegh tried to sound sincere. "You're right. It's just . . . this is so much bigger than you. Maybe you're too young to understand, but there are bad people in the world that are seeking to destroy Islam and our country and the supreme leader. Yes, perhaps our government makes mistakes, but what these people are advocating—overthrow of the government—will only lead to chaos and subjugation to the West. It's possible that Ms. Rahimi and her husband and even some of the leaders of the Green Movement don't understand that they are being used as American pawns. But they must be stopped, nonetheless. And it saddens me that they managed to use you as well. It's my own fault, Leila. I should have been there for you. I'm here now and will try to help. But you have to be clear about who the enemy is. If you choose to continue working with people like Ms. Rahimi, there is nothing I can do for you."

Leila said nothing.

"Leila, tell me honestly. Was our mother involved in this . . . plan?" Sadegh asked, afraid of the answer.

"No," Leila insisted. "She was livid when she found out what I'd done."

"Okay, good. Now, you said she took the documents back to Mr. Heydari. That was the only copy, right?"

Leila looked at him steadily. "Ms. Rahimi made a copy in her office."

Sadegh sighed. "Leila," he said aloud. "It's going to be harder for me to help if something actually gets leaked. Can you get that copy back? And make sure there aren't any more?"

"How is this going to help Maman-joon?" Leila demanded.

"Don't you understand? She went to see Heydari yesterday and never came back. He's done something to her. I called him last night and he wouldn't tell me anything. He laughed at me and told me to call when I was ready to be serious." Leila looked close to tears again.

Despite his anger, Sadegh felt a flush of disgust at Heydari's reported behavior. "Look, I'll deal with that," he said. "My guess is that he kept her for questioning, so there's nothing to be so worried about. But I need you to get those papers back. I can't do anything for you if something that is intended to be private gets into the wrong hands. You understand?"

Leila nodded.

"Okay." Sadegh stood up. "I have to go."

It occurred to him that, so long as Ms. Tabibian was still missing, Leila was a young woman, entirely alone.

"Would you like to come with me?" he asked. "You could stay with us until she's found."

"No," Leila shook her head. "This is my home. I want to be here in case she tries to get in touch."

Sadegh wondered whether he should offer to stay with her. But he needed to get back to Sumayeh. There was only so much he could do.

"Okay, well, I have to go. Be in touch as soon as you get the documents or if you hear from her. Oh, and give me your cellphone number."

Leila recited her number, and he entered it into his phone.

Sadegh took his leave and rushed down the five flights of stairs. Two flights down, he saw Leila's neighbor.

"*Darin mirin?* You're leaving already?" she asked.

The plump little lady filled the narrow stairway, so Sadegh was forced to stop a few steps above her. As he did, he heard his cellphone ring.

"Yes, *kar daram*, I have things to do," Sadegh said and rifled through his bag for his phone.

The woman didn't move, so Sadegh asked, "*Ejaze midin?*"

The woman looked at him steadily and then asked in her shrill voice, "Did you find your mother?"

Sadegh ignored the woman and answered his phone.

It was Sumayeh.

"Sumayeh, I'm on my way."

"Did you find the fire truck?" Sumayeh sounded annoyed.

"No. Sorry. I forgot to look."

"Can you check quick right now? He won't stop begging for it."

"Okay. Hold on."

Sadegh took the phone away from his ear and set his briefcase on the steps to rifle through it, taking out a few files to do so.

The woman asked again, "Did you find your mother?"

Sadegh was irritated by the woman's persistence. "No, unfortunately, but I'm sure she's fine and she'll be home soon . . . Ah!"

Sadegh found the tiny red fire truck and put the phone to his ear again. "Sumayeh, I've got it. I'll be home in thirty minutes, depending on traffic."

"Okay. Please come quickly."

Sadegh hung up. He put his phone and the files back in his briefcase.

The woman was still in his way.

"Leila's welcome to stay with us again tonight," she said. "That way she won't have to be all alone in that apartment."

"Thank you. I appreciate it," Sadegh said. "Now I really need to go."

"It's no trouble. She can stay as long as she wants. I just hope she won't be disappointed by our meager meals. Meat is simply so expensive these days I can hardly afford to cook for Mr. Noori and myself."

Sadegh checked a sardonic reply as he realized what it was the woman was after. Silently he rifled through his briefcase again, moving files aside to find his wallet. He handed the woman a 50,000-toman bill.

"I hope this helps. Thank you again for your trouble."

The woman flattened herself against the railing, and Sadegh grabbed his stuff and squeezed by.

"Oh, like I said, it's no trouble. She can stay as long as she likes. I hope we'll get to see you again soon. You should come for dinner one of these evenings. I'm a wonderful cook, if I do say so myself. Mr. Noori especially loves my *ghorme sabzi* . . ."

The woman continued prattling as he raced down the steps and pushed through the doors at the bottom of the stairwell.

On the street, Sadegh raised his hand for a taxi and was lucky when one stopped almost immediately. He hopped in and set down his soft leather briefcase, which was a jumbled mess after his search for Mahdi's fire truck. He put his wallet in one of the briefcase's front pockets and then started going through the stuff in the big middle opening.

Sadegh had always been rather meticulous about categorizing his files, so the thin label-less one on top caught his attention. He rummaged through the briefcase pockets to find a small box of labels, then opened the file to examine its contents for guidance as to which color ought to be used.

The papers it contained were totally unfamiliar. Sadegh looked closer. They were some sort of medical record. The patient's name, Arman Tamimi, was vaguely familiar, but Sadegh couldn't immediately place it. He flipped through the pages.

Arman was twenty-one years old and had been admitted with severe bruising, swelling, and a skull fracture that indicated he had been beaten. Cause of death was listed as blunt trauma to the head.

Oh God! Sadegh remembered why he recognized the name

and slammed the file shut. Several months earlier, Mehdi Tamimi, a reformist parliamentarian from Karaj had publicly accused the government of covering up the cause of his nephew's death—a nephew whose name, Sadegh was pretty sure, was Arman. At the time, Sadegh had been outraged by MP Tamimi's misuse of live parliamentary proceedings to publicly accuse the government of wrongdoing. Was it possible that these were medical records for that very case? Or, more likely, false records designed to make the government look bad.

Sadegh's heart thumped as he opened the file again. Where had it come from? Was this the document Leila had taken from Heydari? Was it a forgery? Clearly, it was a copy and not an original document, as all the signatures were in the same ink as the print. Where were the originals? How had it ended up in Sadegh's briefcase? Had Leila slipped it in while they were talking? He couldn't imagine how. In that tiny apartment, she'd been in sight the whole time they'd been together. Could he have mistakenly picked it up somewhere else?

Sadegh thought a moment. He pulled out his phone and started punching digits but changed his mind before connecting the call. This wasn't something he would want to talk about on an open line.

Sadegh looked out the window. The streets were relatively *khalvat* with few cars on the road, and they were moving fast.

"Agha," he spoke to the driver, "Take Niyayesh to the left."

"Aren't you going to Qeytariyeh?"

"Yes, but I want to make a quick stop in Sa'adat Abad first."

*   *   *

"Hey! What're you doing here on a Friday?" Ganjian demanded with mock anger when Sadegh opened the door to his office in Sa'adat Abad mosque, where he was sitting at his desk alone.

"Didn't I tell you not to drop by on weekends anymore? Every time you do, things go to shit. You're bad luck, man!"

Despite his worries, Sadegh couldn't help cracking a smile at his friend and former teacher.

"Am I interrupting?" Sadegh asked. "I have a quick question."

"Yes, you're interrupting, asshole! Come on in, take a seat."

Ganjian stood to shake hands and pointed him to a chair across from his desk. He was dressed surprisingly neatly, all in black, and his generally unruly hair had been combed and gelled back.

"What's up?" Ganjian asked.

Sadegh placed the file on Ganjian's desk.

"*In dige chiye?* What the hell is this?"

"Take a look," Sadegh told him.

Ganjian rifled through the papers in the file. Sadegh watched as his joking demeanor drained away and was replaced by a serious expression. Sadegh could guess he'd gotten to the part about Arman Tamimi's death by blunt trauma.

"Where did you get this?" Ganjian asked as he fiddled with the top button of his crisply ironed collarless button-up shirt.

"I'm honestly not sure," Sadegh replied. "I just found it in my briefcase today." Sadegh willed Ganjian to dismiss the document as a forgery.

"Well, it didn't come from here. This is a copy," Ganjian said instead.

Sadegh swallowed, "You mean . . . you have originals?"

Ganjian looked at him quizzically but remained silent as one of his men entered the room with a silver tray laden with two cups of steaming black tea and a bowl of sugar cubes. The man set the tea in front of Sadegh and Ganjian and turned to go.

"Hajji, close the door behind you," Ganjian called to him. The man silently complied.

Ganjian looked at Sadegh. "I don't know if we have that one. But I have . . . others."

Sadegh tried to process this information. His mind flashed on Maman-Mehri's mouth at the moment he realized that her spittle-encrusted lips, so often busy in prayer, were busy preserving an untruth. Was Ganjian to be transformed in the same way?

Sadegh could hear the whine in his own voice as he asked, "So all these accusations . . . they're true?"

Ganjian's black eyes flashed. "Which accusations? We're torturing and raping and murdering people's children?"

Sadegh didn't know what to say. He'd certainly never witnessed anything like that when he was around Ganjian. He'd been sure the rumors were lies and propaganda. But now . . .

Ganjian ran his fingers through his hair and scratched at the top of his head, mussing his gelled hair. When he spoke, his tone was softer. "*Na, Sadegh-jaan,* those accusations aren't true." Ganjian paused and patted down his hair before going on. "But . . . well, every once in a while, something happens. Look, if we hadn't brought these people in and they were out walking the street, a certain percentage would die in . . . like, car accidents or something, right? People die when God calls for them. You know the saying . . . 'Your time of death is written on your forehead.' So it shouldn't be a surprise that for some people that time of death happens while they're under our care."

Sadegh thought carefully. What Ganjian was saying would make sense if a person died of heart attack or some other illness or accident that had nothing to do with being taken in.

Aloud he said, "*Aghaye* Ganjian, forgive me for being so stupid, but I still don't understand why you . . . we would have medical records for these cases."

Ganjian rolled his eyes and pulled at his hair again. "Come on, Sadegh . . . What would our enemies do if we let these out?

They would comb through them looking for any tiny detail or scrap of evidence that they could use to prove we are sadistic torturers and murderers. And the fact is that . . . yes, sometimes mistakes happen."

Ganjian leaned forward as he continued. His wiry curls were sticking up at strange angles from the combination of gel and his vigorous pawing. "Sadegh, you've known me and volunteered with us for years, right? You see how we treat the kids we take in. I don't touch a hair on their heads unless they're resisting or doing something dangerous, and even then I tell all my people to be careful. But even as careful as I am . . . well, sometimes mistakes happen." Ganjian looked down, and Sadegh remembered the day after Sarah's wedding, when he had visited his friend in this very office. Hadn't Ganjian said something about one of his prisoners needing a doctor? Sadegh wondered if he was about to hear what happened to that prisoner. He wasn't sure he wanted to know.

"Sometimes you give someone a little push, and they trip and hit their head and end up in a hospital looking like they've been beaten nearly to death or the like. Or you're transporting prisoners and don't realize how hot and stuffy it is in the convoy van, and someone suffocates. Things *happen* when you're dealing with this many people."

Ganjian paused and then looked right at Sadegh. Sadegh could see the anguish in his eyes as he continued. "These aren't hypothetical examples, my friend. These things really happened, and I'm sick about it, I really am. But then I remember who's really responsible for these deaths, and I know my conscience is clear. Goddamn Americans think they can stop the spread of Islam by throwing all of our countries into chaos, and"—Ganjian pounded on the table as he shouted—"they're using these stupid kids and throwing away their lives to make it happen!"

Sadegh took an easy breath as he nodded. Ganjian's

explanation made sense, and his anguish was testament to his sincerity. It wasn't deliberate cruelty that had taken prisoner's lives but unfortunate accidents. Yes, these types of accidents could happen just about anywhere.

"Thank you, my dear friend," Sadegh said, "for your explanation. I'm sorry I doubted for a moment. It's been a very strange day. You're right, these deaths are on the heads of our American and Zionist enemies. But" —Sadegh voiced a question that was still bothering him—"why not just release the information and explain what happened? I mean, well, don't families deserve to know how their kids died?"

Ganjian shook his head as he patted down his thick hair again. "Come on, Sadegh . . . think! How old is your boy now?"

Sadegh wished Ganjian wouldn't change the subject but answered, "Mahdi? He just turned six."

"Okay, do you tell him that when you were a teenager, you would hide in the bathroom during the school *salat* time because you didn't feel like saying your prayers?"

Sadegh grimaced and shook his head.

Ganjian went on. "Do you tell him that you and your friends brought pictures of your female relatives without *hejab*, head coverings, to school to trade among the boys?"

"*To ro khoda,* please, Mr. Ganjian, I was a kid . . . You're embarrassing me."

"See, you don't tell Mahdi these things. Why?"

Sadegh was going to say it was because he was too young and wouldn't understand, but Ganjian answered for him.

"Because he's too young. And he wouldn't understand. And because you're supposed to be an example for him. If he learns about all of your mistakes, what is he going to do when he is the same age? He'll think it's okay to stop praying altogether or, *khodaya nakarde*, God forbid, he might get involved in some sort of sexual perversion. He'll think that if his father did this sort of thing, it's okay for him to go even further. Or, even worse, he might think that his father doesn't have the moral authority to tell him to do anything since he has made so many mistakes."

Sadegh was starting to get Ganjian's point.

"The blessed *velayat-e faqih*, our supreme leader," Ganjian went on, "is like the father to the whole *ummah*. And most people are like your Mahdi . . . They don't understand. Not because they are too young, but because they don't have the religious understanding necessary. So they can be manipulated and misled into thinking that any mistake we might make can be attributed to the supreme leader. And then they lose respect for the institution of the *velayat* altogether. Don't you see? We can't let this happen!

"I agree with you," Ganjian went on. "The death of a young man is a tragedy. I know the name of each and every kid that has died under my care. I know where their homes are. I know what their fathers do. You can't imagine how often I can't sleep at night because all I want to do is go to their families and kneel before them to apologize and beg forgiveness. But I don't, because I know that would be the most selfish thing I could do. I'd be making myself feel better by destroying people's faith in the only legitimate Islamic authority in the world. You see?"

Sadegh still wasn't completely sure. He didn't doubt Ganjian's sincerity. And he couldn't find any flaws in his arguments, but something didn't quite sit right.

"I don't know," Sadegh said aloud. "I guess I have to think about it. It's just . . . a bit of a shock. In all the time I've been working with you, I've never seen this sort of thing."

"*Akh!* This is just a hobby for you Sadegh. You come in every once in a while, hang out with us and do a couple raids, and then you're out of here."

Sadegh was hurt. His work with the Basij wasn't a hobby. He

wanted to make a real contribution to the religion and country that he loved. If he didn't spend as much time with Ganjian as he would have liked it was only because of his obligations to the family business.

Sadegh stood to go. "*Khaili bebakhshid az mozahemat.* I'm sorry to have taken your time with this. I'll get out of your way now. Shall I leave these papers with you?"

"Sit down and don't be so damn sensitive, Sadegh." Ganjian said as he rolled his eyes. "You're more valuable to us this way. You think I don't know how much of the money you collect from your Bazari friends actually comes out of your own pocket? Thank God for your shops. Besides," Ganjian leaned back in his chair and ran his hands lightly along the edge of his desk, "working this way gives you a certain, well, freedom that someone like me will never have."

Ganjian looked pointedly at Sadegh who was still standing. Then he reached up to run two hands through his hair, scratching at his scalp so forcefully his whole forehead was pulled up and down.

"There are things you can do, Sadegh-jaan, that I . . ." Ganjian's voice trailed off and he stopped rubbing his scalp.

Sadegh's hurt feelings had dissipated at his mentor's kind words. But now he felt Ganjian was hinting at something that he didn't understand.

Ganjian stood up. His hair stood on end like he'd had an electric shock. He shook his finger at Sadegh and barked, "Hey, don't you go anywhere."

Ganjian went to the door, not the one that opened to the hallway, but the one in the corner behind his desk that led to a tiny adjoining room. Sadegh didn't know what the room was originally intended for when the mosque was built. But ever since he could remember, it had been used as storage for items needing a bit of extra security. Ganjian opened the lock and went inside.

Sadegh felt impatient. This visit had already taken longer than he'd expected. Sumayeh wasn't going to be pleased. He noticed an open prayer book on Ganjian's desk and remembered that today was the first of Muharram. Ganjian was probably going to an event to commemorate the coming anniversary of Imam Hossein's martyrdom. That's why he was dressed so neatly.

Ganjian returned with two files in his arms. He didn't bother closing the door behind him but came around his desk to hand them over to Sadegh.

"What are these?" Sadegh asked.

Ganjian's eyes darted around the room. "You'll know what they are when you see them, my friend. Like I say, there are things you can do that I . . . well, you know how things are for my father. I have my family to support, you know that. So I can't be a hundred percent sure. I stand by everything I said to you. But"—Ganjian's voice dropped to a whisper—"what if I'm just trying to protect myself?"

Sadegh was shocked to see Ganjian blinking back tears.

"What—" Sadegh started to ask Ganjian what he meant but was cut off before completing his question as Ganjian put his hands to Sadegh's cheeks and pulled his face close so that their foreheads were touching.

"I can't have this weighing on me anymore, Sadegh." Ganjian breathed into Sadegh's face as his tears began to overflow. "Despite everything I said, their families have a right to know." Ganjian released Sadegh's face and wiped at his eyes. Then he shook his head. "Or at least I think they do. I don't know. See, my thinking is clouded. But you." Ganjian clapped Sadegh's shoulder and shook it lightly. "You can think it through without any worries. You can do whatever you think is right, and I know you'll do the right thing. Just . . . before you do anything . . ." Ganjian pulled Sadegh close again. "Think and pray carefully about the consequences for the country, for the families of these kids, for me, and . . . for yourself."

*   *   *

Sadegh could hear the wailing as he fit his key to the lock but didn't feel the full impact of the auditory assault until he opened the door. He kicked off his shoes and headed toward the kitchen. He hoped Sumayeh wouldn't be angry with him for having taken so long to get home.

"Salam, azizam," Sadegh greeted his wife. "Tell me how to help."

Sumayeh handed him a bowl of rice and stew and directed him to feed the baby so she could turn her full attention to Mahdi, who was in the midst of his own meltdown. Sana was screaming as she twisted over the tray of her high chair reaching toward a soft plastic Snoopy figure that was on the floor. Sadegh bent and picked it up but Sumayeh stopped him before he handed it to the baby.

"No. It's a game. She keeps throwing it on the floor and expects me to get it for her."

"Okay," Sadegh said. "I'll only give it to her one more time."

"Sadegh, she's already thrown it down twice." Sadegh could tell from her tone that Sumayeh was on edge. "Leave it on the floor. She needs to learn."

Sadegh looked at Sana who had quieted her whimpering as she anticipated receiving the toy from her father. He sheepishly set it back on the floor instead, and Sana, realizing she'd been double-crossed, resumed her screaming with the additional anger of the betrayed.

Sadegh wasn't sure what Sumayeh wanted him to do now but tried to calm the baby by offering a spoonful of food. Sana shook her head vigorously but then, a wicked gleam in her eye, grabbed at it and threw it on the floor beside Snoopy. Sadegh wondered whether it would be hypocritical to pick the spoon up now.

Sumayeh didn't seem to be having much luck with Mahdi either. Sadegh listened as she offered him a choice.

"Mahdi dear, I'm sorry, but you can't be here if you're going to yell at me. Do you want to walk to your room, or should I carry you?"

"I'm not going anywhere!" was his response.

"Okay. I'm going to carry you . . . Ouch!"

Mahdi had kicked his mother.

Sadegh's protective instincts were provoked. He grabbed his son's shoulder roughly and scolded him. "Hey! Shame on you, you bad boy. Apologize, right now!"

Mahdi squirmed against his father's hold, and unbelievably, Sumayeh intervened on his behalf.

"He is not a bad boy," she said. "He made a bad choice. And now he's going to make a better one and go to his room and stay there until he's feeling better."

Sadegh held on to Mahdi. "So he should get away with kicking you? What's going to happen when he's twice this size?" Sadegh directed his next words to Mahdi as he delivered a light shake. "You apologize to your mother or maybe I'll kick you so you see what it feels like."

Sumayeh's voice was sharp as she intervened. "Sadegh, a forced apology and threats won't accomplish anything. Let him go to his room. I'm sure he'll apologize when he's ready."

Sadegh finally let go and Mahdi ran out of the kitchen crying, "I hate you both!"

Sumayeh sighed and turned her attention to Sana, who was still yelling in her chair. Sadegh felt bad for having further irritated his wife. He had wanted to smooth things over, but it seemed he'd made it worse.

"I'm sorry, azizam," Sadegh apologized. "I just hated to see him hurt you. What can I do to help?"

Sumayeh took another deep breath as she picked Sana up. "I know you want to help, but it's harder for me when you interfere like that. I'm going to put Sana to bed."

Sumayeh left the kitchen, and Sadegh, penitent, started cleaning up.

*   *   *

By the time Sumayeh returned, Sadegh had washed the dishes, wiped the counters, and was in the midst of sweeping the floor. It was a more thorough job than he normally would have done, and he was hopeful it would help smooth things over.

"Mersi, Sadegh-jaan. Sorry that took so long. I was trying to settle Sana down and fell asleep myself."

Sadegh was relieved that her tone wasn't unfriendly. Maybe they could finally put the events of the day behind them. It would be good to be friends again. Sadegh needed his wife's advice.

"I'm almost finished." Sadegh said as he swept crumbs into the dustpan. "Did you already eat dinner with the kids?"

"No." Sumayeh answered. "We've got some leftover *kookoo sabzi*. I'll make it into sandwiches for us."

Sadegh finished the sweeping, put the broom and dustpan away, washed his hands, and started setting the table as Sumayeh rummaged in the refrigerator.

"Sumayeh-jaan, I'm really sorry about what I said at my aunt's house. It was inexcusable. I was angry and confused, and I lashed out."

Sumayeh nodded as she set the green herb patties on a plate and started rolling them into flatbread sandwiches. "Thank you for apologizing, Sadegh. Taking the Lord's name in vain is absolutely not something I'm willing to tolerate. What was going on with you?"

Sadegh sighed as he sat at the kitchen table. So far as he was concerned, the way to make up after a fight was to let it go and move on. But Sumayeh always felt the need to review exactly what went wrong and who was responsible. She said the purpose was to figure out how to avoid similar problems in the future, and Sadegh didn't doubt her intent, but he felt like such discussions were just as likely to cause renewed bad feelings.

"Sumayeh-jaan, I'm really so sorry. It will never happen again. I'm just under incredible pressure. I need your help, azizam. You have no idea what is going on."

Sumayeh set two plates on the table and sat across from Sadegh. She tucked her caramel-colored American hair behind her ears and focused her black Iranian eyes on her husband.

"Okay, so tell me," she said.

Sadegh did his best to tell the story. It wasn't easy. He'd been frustrated with Leila's telling, but, if anything, he did a worse job as he struggled to relate Leila's nonpregnancy and everything else he'd learned that afternoon about Ms. Tabibian being missing, Mr. Heydari's strange interest in the women, and Leila's plan to find government secrets to scare Heydari away. He was about to explain how he'd found the file of medical documents in his brief-case, when Sumayeh interrupted him.

"Sadegh, you need to cut these people out of your life."

"What? Wait, I haven't finished yet."

But Sumayeh had more to say.

"When I was twelve, we went to the US to visit my mom's family. I think I told you that they weren't very happy that she became Muslim and moved to Iran. Anyway, at one point my uncle was talking to me and kept repeating this phrase, 'By their fruit shall ye know them.' It's in the bible, and he was trying to argue that you could tell Islam was an evil religion because it had resulted in so many horrible things."

Sadegh tried to interrupt, but Sumayeh set a hand on his arm to indicate she wasn't finished.

"Just listen a minute. See, I've thought a lot about that phrase, and I think my uncle was right. Not about Iran—he didn't know what he was talking about and had no idea about all the evil things that have been done in the name of Christianity—but I think it's true that you can tell if a person is good or evil based on the impact they have on the people around them. And Ms. Tabibian is one of those people that leads others astray. It would be best to cut her off completely."

"Really? But . . . she's my—"

"Yes, absolutely," Sumayeh squeezed his arm as she barreled on. "If Ms. Tabibian had been a different sort of woman, I would have been the first to welcome her into the family. But I've seen her impact on Maman-Mehri, who I know to be a woman of God. I look at her impact on you . . . Sadegh, in our years of marriage you've never lied, or hidden things, or disrespected me or God in the ways you have since you met this woman. And now Leila has come right out and admitted that she was trying to, well, seduce someone so that she could find something to use against the government. That is disgusting on so many levels. And if she could engage in something like that, she wouldn't hesitate to use you to get at more secrets. Sadegh—" Sumayeh stroked the hairs on his forearm. "—this may be difficult, but I think you should turn her in. Turn her in before she manages to do some real harm."

Sadegh was at a loss. How had his wife arrived at such a firm conclusion so quickly, while he remained lost in confusion over what was going on and what he should or shouldn't do? He reminded himself that she still hadn't heard about the file or his conversation with Ganjian.

"Sumayeh dear, perhaps you're being hasty. There are things

I still haven't told you. See . . . on my way home, I found an unfamiliar file in my suitcase."

"What do you mean by unfamiliar?" Sumayeh cocked her head so that her hair fell against her neck on the right while brushing the top of her shoulder on the left.

"I mean, I'd never seen it before and have no idea how it got in my bag. But it seemed to confirm what Leila was saying."

"Okay," Sumayeh tucked her hair behind her ears again. "So she probably planted something in your bag to make her story more convincing."

"Let me finish. I went to see Ganjian—that's why it took me so long getting home—and he told me it's true. Some of the young people and college students that were taken in last summer, and even more recently, ended up getting hurt. But the authorities don't want people to know, so they've been confiscating medical documents. Look . . ."

Sadegh left the kitchen to retrieve the two files Ganjian had given him plus the one he'd found in his bag. He dumped them on the kitchen table before Sumayeh.

"Ganjian gave me these two. They're for kids that he personally knew who died for various reasons. One of them fell and hit his head. The other one suffocated, probably in a van during transport. None of the families know the real cause of death."

Sumayeh rifled through the papers slowly. When she came to the one that Sadegh had found, she paused.

"Why is this one different?" she asked.

"It's a copy. The others are originals. That's the one I found in my bag. I still don't know how it got there."

Sumayeh turned a few more pages then closed the files and stacked them back into a pile. Sadegh waited for her to say something, but she was silent.

"*Nazaret chiye hala*, what do you think now?" he asked.

Sumayeh traced a finger lightly over her scar as she spoke. "I don't see how this changes anything," she said. "Leila was spying on the government. The fact that she found something that is actually true only makes her more dangerous. You should tell the authorities about her immediately."

Sadegh struggled to understand. It would be a relief to share Sumayeh's certainty.

"Really?" he said. "You don't think that maybe . . . since she was telling the truth about what she found, she was also telling the truth about Heydari? So maybe the only reason she was trying to find something was to stop him from pursuing her."

Sumayeh's reply was quick. "No. That whole story is completely ridiculous. If a man like Heydari wanted a second wife, I'm sure he would have lots of options. Why would he insist on someone that doesn't want him? And, more importantly, how would digging out and publicizing government secrets help Leila decline his offer? It's a pretty weak story."

Sadegh agreed on that point. "Yes, you're right. If it really was her plan, it wasn't a very smart one. But it just, well, it kind of bothers me to learn that the government and people I know were involved in this sort of thing. I think it bothers Ganjian too. I think that's why he gave me those files. He wants me to do something about it. Maybe he wants me to tell the families how their children died."

Again, Sumayeh did not hesitate. "It doesn't bother me a bit. Sometimes, sadly perhaps, sacrifices are required for the greater good. I sacrificed my own face to fulfill my commitment to God. Abraham was willing to sacrifice his own child—imagine! It should come as no surprise that the Islamic Republic has to make some difficult sacrifices as well. It may be sad for those individuals and their families. But, *alhamdulillah*, God is big and is able to compensate them for their sacrifices in this world or the next.

So no, this doesn't bother me at all, and it shouldn't bother you either."

Sadegh couldn't disagree with anything his wife was saying, but something still bothered him. Yes, the story of Abraham was beautiful and inspiring, but only because he was a prophet that was sincerely following God's command. If a madman were to do the same thing . . . Ah! Sadegh realized what the problem was.

He spoke slowly, as he was still sorting his thoughts. "Sumayeh, you're right. And I agree with you . . . mostly. But what I'm stuck on is this: What if a bad man were to get into the system? And what if he did things not because the *velayat* wanted them but because he is evil? How can we recognize and stop such a person from abusing the system and abusing the people's trust?"

Sumayeh looked at him intently, and Sadegh went on. "Two people died under Ganjian's command. I know Ganjian and what a good person he is. I have no doubt he did everything he knew how to do to keep the people in his charge safe. Heydari . . . I don't know anymore. I've heard things and even seen some behavior from him that is surprising. And then, taking into account Leila's accusations . . . well, what if he *is* an evil man? Shouldn't there be a way to tell? Wouldn't it be better, perhaps, if, instead of trying to cover these things up and disposing of medical documents, the government investigated them to root out bad people?"

Sadegh stopped talking. It was an important point. He'd have to think about it more, but he was pretty sure he was right, and at the very least, he was relieved to have finally identified what had been bothering him all along. He looked at Sumayeh. He wondered, with a little spark of pride, whether he'd stumped her. She'd probably never considered this angle.

He prodded her. "What are you thinking?"

Sumayeh closed her black eyes and took a deep breath.

"Sumayeh?" Sadegh asked again.

"Sadegh, I don't know what to say," Sumayeh replied as she opened her eyes and examined him. "I'm just so . . . disappointed. What happened to the man I married?"

"What?" This was not the reaction Sadegh had expected.

"What happened to your *iman*? Your faith? These things you bring up . . . this talk of evil men . . . they aren't our concern. Our job is to have faith in God, in the *velayat*, and in the Islamic Republic. Surely they who are so much bigger and more powerful and more knowledgeable can take care of these problems without our help. Our job is to trust God and be obedient to his dictate and the dictate of those who have been granted his authority. You used to know this!"

"But . . . Sumayeh, that is the whole point! I am happy to be obedient to God's dictate, but not to the dictate of a charlatan! How are we to know the difference?"

"It's like I said in the beginning, Sadegh. You can tell from the fruits of their actions. Look at Maman-Mehri for example. How many prayer meetings does she hold in her home? How much money does she give to the poor? How many prayers does she say every day? How many times has she read the Quran? Clearly this is a woman that is close to and guided by God. Had I realized the depth of her feelings about Ms. Tabibian, I would never have encouraged a reunion. And I'm sorry about that. But now . . . well, if Maman-Mehri—who I know to be a woman of God—feels that Ms. Tabibian is evil, then who am I to question that? And if the Islamic Republic—which has done so much to awaken Iranians, and Muslims, and even non-Muslims like my mother—conducts business through the use of people that, to me and you, look like they are making mistakes, again, who are we to question that?"

Once again Sadegh had the uneasy feeling of agreeing and disagreeing at the same time. His head couldn't find any flaws in his wife's steady reasoning, but something still didn't feel right. Perhaps she was right and his faith was wavering. Maybe this was exactly how the enemy worked. What he needed was a pilgrimage to Mecca or Mashhad or somewhere that he could once again feel the certainty of God's guidance and the relief of submitting to it.

Sadegh was tired of turning this over in his mind.

"Sumayeh . . . maybe you're right. I . . . I'm so confused." He reached across the table and took her hand. "I need your help, azizam."

Sumayeh pulled his hand to her face and snuggled it against her scarred cheek.

"I know Sadegh-jaan. You've been under a lot of pressure. Tonight's the first of Muharram. Let's go pray together . . . It'll help us both."

Sadegh stood and pulled his wife into his arms. He stroked her hair and kissed her cheek. "I love you Sumayeh . . . What would I do without you?"

Sumayeh gave him a tight squeeze in response, and they stood together for a moment swaying slightly in the middle of the kitchen.

The sound of Sadegh's cellphone interrupted the moment.

Sadegh groaned. "Who could that be?"

Sumayeh pulled away and said, "Go ahead and answer. I'll put things away in here, and then we can go pray. Just don't be long."

Sadegh hurried to his phone. The caller ID said Tabibian Home. *Damn.* Sadegh paused a moment as he considered letting the call kick to voicemail. He didn't want anything to interrupt his reconciliation with Sumayeh. But then he hit the Answer button and raised the phone to his ear. It would be better to face this head-on. Perhaps he should even invite Leila and her mother to come talk to him tomorrow in Sumayeh's presence so that his wife could help judge their story and character.

"*Allo?*" Sadegh answered.

"Mister Sadegh? *Shomayee*, is it you?"

It wasn't Leila. Sadegh recognized the shrill voice immediately as the neighbor woman he had met.

"Yes? *Befarmayeed*," Sadegh answered with a sigh. He wished he'd ignored the call after all. "What can I do for you?"

"*Mibakhsheed az mozahemmat*, I'm sorry for the imposition. Ms. Leila asked me to call. The police were just here. Oh, it's so sad. I'm just beside myself. I can feel my blood pressure rising already."

"They came for Leila? It was the neighborhood police? Or the Intelligence?"

"It's unbelievable, I tell you. We've been neighbors for so many years. And she was always good to me. We didn't see each other that much . . . you know how it is with neighbors. But she was a good, decent woman, and it's just so hard to believe I'll never see her again."

"What do you mean? What did they say to you? What has she done?"

But the woman prattled on, ignoring his questions.

"Don't you worry, my son. We will help with all of the arrangements. And Leila is welcome to stay with us just as long as she needs. Oh . . ." The woman's voice broke down. "She was just so young . . . so young!"

Sadegh felt a rising sense of alarm that translated into fury at this woman's refusal to communicate clearly.

"Listen to me!" he hollered into the phone, "What are you talking about?"

"Sadegh, *shhhhh!*" Sumayeh leaned her head out of the kitchen as she shushed him. "You'll wake the children."

Sadegh strained to hear what the neighbor woman was relaying through dramatic tears.

"It's your mother," she sobbed. "She's dead."

CHAPTER 9

Saturday, December 19, 2009—six months after the election

I could smell him before I saw him. His scent was a mixture
of sweat and rosewater, and it reminded me of my youth.
—Maziar Bahari, writing about
his Evin Prison interrogator[7]

Azar awoke with a start to the sound of her cellphone. Could it be
Ibrahim? Every so often, he was allowed to call home from prison,
always at odd hours. What time was it anyway?

Azar squinted at her phone. It was 5:24 a.m., and she didn't
recognize the caller's number, which was a good sign. Azar flipped
the phone open, heart pounding with the happy anticipation of
hearing her husband's voice.

"*Baleh?* Hello?"

"Salam, Ms. Rahimi. It's Leila. I'm sorry to be calling so early."

Leila? Azar felt like she'd just stepped into a warm shower
only to be doused with ice water. She wanted her husband.

Struggling to contain her disappointment, Azar assured the

girl that it was okay. Then, remembering their telephone conversation from the previous day, she asked if Leila had heard from Ms. Tabibian.

"Yes, well," Leila continued in a flat voice. "She's . . . passed. They say it was an accident. She was crossing the street and—"

"Oh my God!" Azar pushed her bedcovers off and sat up, Ibrahim momentarily forgotten.

Leila seemed to be struggling to control herself but finally managed to complete her sentence: ". . . she was hit by a car."

"That's awful! How did it happen?" Azar asked.

"They say she was hit and died immediately," Leila repeated. "I'm sorry. I know I should have called as soon as I found out. I'm so distraught . . . I wasn't thinking. I should have called sooner. I know you would have wanted to know immediately so you . . . I'm sorry."

Azar immediately wondered whether Leila was trying to tell her something between the lines. She seemed to be saying it would have been better for Azar to know Ms. Tabibian was dead as soon as possible so Azar would have more time to . . . what? Secure the file? Like yesterday, when Leila called to tell her of Ms. Tabibian's disappearance, Azar's challenge was to understand the girl's meaning without expecting her to spell things out on a possibly tapped line.

"When did this happen?" Azar asked. Yesterday Leila had told her that her mother had been angry with her and had gone to meet a "friend" to make things right. Azar had taken this as warning that Ms. Tabibian knew everything and intended to tell Heydari about Tamimi's medical documents. It would be helpful to know whether the accident had happened before or after Ms. Tabibian saw Heydari.

"They weren't sure. Thursday night or yesterday morning," Leila replied, her voice still dull. "They found her body in the Ne'mat Abad neighborhood of Tehran. But they haven't been able to find the driver or anyone else who saw it happen. And I don't know what she would have been doing in that part of town."

Hmmm, so it was possible that the accident took place before Ms. Tabibian had even gotten to her meeting with Heydari. But then, Leila wouldn't have called at this hour if she thought that was the case. Clearly, she was trying to warn Azar that Heydari would be looking for the file.

"Well, I need to go," Leila interrupted Azar's thoughts. "I'm sorry I didn't call earlier."

Aloud, Azar offered the girl her condolences in as natural a voice as she could manage and then thought to ask, "Leila dear, are you by yourself at home? Do you have any family to call?"

"Don't worry about me," Leila said. "I'm at my . . . brother's house. He's been very kind."

Azar wondered whether it was Ms. Tabibian's death that had brought about this reconciliation. When Leila had visited her office a few weeks back, she and Mr. Sadegh didn't seem to be on speaking terms.

"I have to go," Leila repeated and said her goodbyes before hanging up.

Azar's mind raced. She had to get to Ali to tell him how to pass on the file. Yesterday, after Leila's call had alerted her, Azar had gone to one of the Foundation's advisors, who'd told her who and how to give the documents for safekeeping. Azar's intent had been to relay this to Ali, but he hadn't been returning her calls, and she hadn't been able to get to him.

Azar looked at the time: 5:47. Still early enough that there wouldn't be much traffic. She could get to Ali's condo in ten minutes and then return in time to get the boys up and off to school. The only issue, of course, was whether she was being watched. Azar considered the possibility and then decided it was still less risky than trying to relay information to Ali over the phone.

She dressed quickly and wrote a note for her boys, which she taped to the TV screen. "I have a quick errand to run. You can watch something until I get back. If I take too long, call your grandma."

Needles from an icy wind stabbed her exposed face and fingers as she stepped into the December air. Azar got into her car and turned it on. While waiting for it to warm up, she checked her phone to make sure she'd turned it off and removed the battery. The streets were quiet and dark but not entirely deserted. The *sangak* bakery on the corner had its lights on, but the usual long line of customers was absent. It would be good to stop by on her way back, she thought, to get some fresh bread for her boys' breakfast.

After a few minutes, Azar released the brake, and slid onto the road. She glanced in her rearview mirror several times as she drove but didn't see anyone behind her. Probably it was too early and cold even for the Guards or Intelligence officials to be on the street. Azar started to relax. She blasted the heater, which quickly warmed her little car. When she turned onto Ali's street, the sound of the morning call to prayer started from the nearest mosques. Perfect, she thought, he'll be getting up already.

Azar parked the car. She waited for a moment to see if another car would appear. Once she decided it was safe, she got out into the cold again and walked to the high-rise condo entrance to push the buzzer for her brother's unit. Another blast of wind hit her as she waited. Ali's neighborhood was farther up the Alborz foothills just enough to be even colder than hers. Azar pushed the buzzer again, this time holding it a bit longer.

"*Befarmayeed.* Who is it?"

The sound of the sleepy young woman's voice gave Azar a start.

"I'm sorry. This is the home of Ali Rahimi?" Azar's face and lips were so cold and stiff she could barely form the question.

"*Baleh. Befarmayeed.* Yes, who is this?"

Ah, of course, it was Sarah. Six months after their wedding, the young couple had finally moved in together. No wonder Ali hadn't been answering her calls.

"Oh, Sarah-jaan," Azar shivered into the intercom. "This is Azar. I didn't realize you'd be here. Let me in. I need to talk to Ali." Another gust of air blew through Azar's many layers of coverings to freeze her flesh and bones.

"*Ali khabe hanooz. Hal nadareh.* He's still asleep. He's not feeling well." Sarah said. The door remained locked.

Azar felt she couldn't take the cold much longer and wondered whether she ought to run back to the warm car like a diver returning to the surface momentarily to catch a breath before trying again. "*To ro khoda,*" Azar pleaded like a beggar at the door. "It's an emergency. Please, can you let me in?"

The door latch finally opened, and Azar stumbled into the building. She took a few deep breaths in the warm lobby air and felt her cheeks tingle as the blood returned. What was Sarah thinking to make her beg like that to enter her own brother's home? Azar took the elevator to the tenth floor and then navigated the hallway to Sarah and Ali's unit. When Azar tapped lightly, Sarah pulled the door open, careful to remain hidden behind it from the eyes of neighbors that would be scandalized, Azar noted, by the sight of the flimsy cherry red lingerie that clung to her swelling belly.

"Salam, Azar-jaan."

"Salam, Sarah."

Azar stepped into the apartment, and the door closed behind her. She held her hand out to Sarah in greeting but didn't lean forward for a kiss. She expected that Sarah would lean in for the friendlier gesture and wanted her own brief hesitation to send a small, but meaningful message that she was irritated with the girl for the interaction over the intercom. To her surprise, however, Sarah held her ground, blinking her small eyes, and the two women simply shook hands in an awkward silence that was broken when Ali came into the room.

He came forward to greet her with a hug and kiss.

"What's going on, Azar?" Ali teased. "You wanted to make sure I'd wake up for my prayers this morning?"

"*Vagh'an bebakhshid,*" Azar apologized. "I'll just be a—Oh my God! What happened to your eye?"

Ali's left cheek was purple and swollen and his left eye was red and glassy.

Azar felt Sarah tense, but Ali's voice was playful. "It's nothing. It looks worse than it is. But it's part of the reason I didn't get back to you last night."

"How did it happen?" Azar asked. "Did you ice it? Are you sure nothing's broken?"

"Seriously, don't worry about it," Ali assured her. "It's nothing. Anyway, what's going on? Come, sit down. Where are my favorite nephews?"

"No, I can't stay," Azar remained standing with her shoes on in the entryway. "I left the boys sleeping at home and have to get back. I just . . . There's been a bit of an emergency, and . . . I need to tell you something."

Azar gave Sarah a sidelong glance to indicate she'd prefer to speak to Ali in private.

Catching on, Ali turned to Sarah. "Sarah, azizam, if it's not too much trouble, would you mind pouring some tea? I put the kettle on a few minutes ago, so it should be ready."

Sarah raised an eyebrow but said nothing and, as requested, left the two of them at the door.

Ali asked again, "So, what's going on?"

Azar spoke quietly. "The . . . thing I gave you for safekeeping—I need you to deliver it to someone as soon as possible. He'll

know what to do with it. Just . . . You need to make sure you get it
to him. Use a driver you trust completely. The address—"

Ali interrupted her, "No, Azar, don't tell me more. I can't do it.
I'm sorry."

Azar hadn't considered the possibility that her brother might
refuse her request.

"What do you mean? It's urgent. Something's happened. I
don't have time to explain but it's possible that they're going to be
looking for it soon."

Ali sighed. "Azar-jaan, you know how I feel about all of this.
I don't entirely disagree with you and Ibrahim. If I could snap my
fingers and change parts of the regime, I would. But these things
you're involved with have serious risks. I don't know what you're
involved with, but I don't want to get dragged in. I need to think
of my own family now."

"My God, Ali!" Azar was beside herself and had trouble keeping
her voice low. "This isn't just about me or you. Those papers prove
that Tamimi was tortured and killed and that all of this has been
covered up by the Guards and Intelligence officials. This needs to
be made public so we can have some hope to putting an end to
this sort of thing. You think you're safe now just because you aren't
behind bars anymore? They could pick you up again at any moment
and do whatever they want with you. Same with me or anyone else.
But maybe, if these papers get out . . . we can change things."

Ali's eyes were hard, and the veins on his thick neck were
beginning to bulge. "Believe me, I know all too well that they can
do whatever they want with me. And I'm not going to provoke
them by working with you to embarrass them. I've already suffered enough because of you and Ibrahim."

"You blame me?" Azar raged at her brother.

"Yes!" Ali cried. "What other reason did they have to hold me.
Even now, they won't leave me alone because of you."

"What do you mean they won't leave you—"

"Enough! I've said too much already."

Azar looked at her brother closely. She saw anger and fear, but also shame in his eyes.

"My God!" Azar exhaled. "Ali, you've been working with them?"

"No!" Ali protested. "It's not like that. I'm just saying that . . . I'm sorry, but I can't help you. I mean . . . even if I tried to help, it wouldn't help."

He's been spying on me, Azar thought. *My own brother.* She wondered how long it had been going on and what sorts of information he might have passed along.

"I see," Azar tried to keep the bitterness out of her voice. "And the file? Did you tell them . . ."

"No." Ali shook his head as he sighed, dropping the pretense that there wasn't a *them*, "I probably should have. But it's safe."

Azar wanted to slap him. Did Ali actually regret not telling the Guards about the file? It was with great effort that Azar kept her composure and said, "Well, I'm sorry I burdened you with it. Why don't you give it to me now, and I'll take it?"

Ali nodded. "Yes, I think it's for the best."

He turned and walked out of the room. Azar stood by the door waiting and trying to plan her next move. She needed to get that file out of her hands and to the right people as soon as possible. But its intended destination was a good thirty minutes away, and she had to get back to her boys. Maybe her mother could get them off to school while she took care of this. If Leila's call had been a warning, Azar probably didn't have much time.

Azar suddenly felt hot. The heat seemed to be on full blast in the apartment. Probably, Azar thought with what she knew was unfair disgust, so that Sarah could walk around in an outfit much too ostentatious for an expectant mother. Azar took off her chador and headscarf to get some air.

Sarah came out of the kitchen with a small tray of steaming cups. She started toward Azar but then paused and turned toward the sitting room.

"Come in and sit down," Sarah invited. "We can drink our tea together."

"No, Sarah dear, I don't want any tea. I'll be going as soon as Ali gives me what I've come for."

Azar's reply was stiff enough that Sarah didn't insist any further. Instead, she set the tray on the coffee table and picked up her own cup of tea.

It was hard to believe, Azar thought, that this frivolous young woman had once risked her own safety for a protester. Azar had finally heard the whole story from Leila. She'd talked about how scared and trapped she'd felt in that alleyway, how grateful she was when Sarah invited her into Ali's car, how bad she'd felt when she saw the Basiji confront the couple that had tried to save her, and how surprised she'd been to realize, at Azar's office, that the groom was Azar's brother and that the courageous and generous bride was Sadegh's own cousin. Hearing the story had made Azar feel slightly more sympathetic toward Sarah. But not today.

Ali called to Sarah. "Sarah . . . *Ye lahze biya.* Come here a second."

"*Al'an.* I'll be right there." Sarah took a sip of her tea before setting it down and heading down the hallway.

Azar waited with increasing frustration. It was starting to get light outside. She needed to get back to her boys. On Saturdays, their school bussed them to an aquatic center for swimming lessons. If they were more than fifteen minutes late, the bus would leave without them. Azar sighed. She supposed she could drive the kids straight to the aquatic center if needed.

Azar wondered what could be taking Ali so long. She kicked off her shoes and wandered into the apartment down the hall toward the master bedroom. The door was closed, but she could hear Ali speaking.

". . . can't believe this. I don't even know what to say. How could you even consider doing something like that?"

Sarah's voice was testy. "Well, how could you even consider keeping something that could put our family at risk. *To ke hamash migi siyasi nisti.* I thought you weren't interested in politics!"

"I'm not!" Ali responded. "But my sister asked me to do something as a favor to her. You had no right to take it without talking to me first."

Azar realized with a start that they were talking about the file.

"Well you had no right to keep it in my home without talking to me first!" Sarah huffed.

My God! Azar thought. What had that girl done?

"What am I going to tell my sister?" Ali's voice sounded defeated.

"Tell her the truth," Sarah answered. "Believe me, Ali, it is better for her this way too."

Azar had heard enough. She knocked on the door but opened it without waiting for an invitation.

"What's better for me?" Azar demanded.

Ali and Sarah looked startled. They stared at her silently for a fraction of a second.

"What did she do with it?" Azar shouted. "Tell me! It's the least you owe me!"

Ali moved forward and positioned himself between Azar and his wife.

"Calm down Azar. Sarah was worried about us. She gave it to her cousin."

Azar's mind reeled. "The one who works with the Basij? The one who got you arrested?"

"Azar, you don't know—"

"No, Ali," Azar cut him off. "*You* don't know. You are a stupid, stupid child and I can't believe I ever trusted you. I'll never forgive you for this betrayal. Never! Not just because I may rot in Evin or because my children may grow up motherless. But because you're so worried about your stupid business and your ugly home and making more money that you were willing to destroy the truth. I'm disgusted with both—"

"That's enough!" Ali hollered. "I'm sorry about what has happened, but you're going too far. Sarah had the best of intentions—Hey!"

Azar had turned on her heel to walk down the hallway and out of the house. She'd had enough and just wanted to get out of there. Ali followed her and yammered on as she stalked to the doorway and started putting on her shoes and outdoor coverings.

"You're making too big a deal of this, Azar. Sarah didn't tell Sadegh the file came from you. She just slipped it in his bag. He isn't going to connect this to you. You don't have anything to worry about."

It was at that moment, with Ali murmuring apologetic reassurances and her hand turning the doorknob, that Azar was shaken by a frightening realization. Leila had called her so early in the morning because she didn't think Ms. Tabibian's death was an accident. Ms. Tabibian had been murdered, and Leila thought Azar was in danger too.

"I hope you're right," Azar said simply. Then she turned and walked out of her brother's home.

The streets were still clear on Azar's way home, but there were enough people lined up at the *sangak* bread bakery that she knew she didn't have time to stop after all.

Despite her realization of Leila's concern for her safety, Azar was surprised at how little panic she felt. Panic, she decided, is only possible when one can guess and frantically try to stave off what is coming. Azar felt so profoundly ignorant of how things would play out that she felt liberated to focus on the moment she was in.

Azar suddenly ached for her boys. She hoped they would still be asleep in the bed they shared when she got home. She wanted to snuggle in between them and stroke their soft hair and watch them dream while she inhaled the aliveness of their scent. With one hand, Azar fumbled to reassemble her cellphone and turn it on. If her boys did wake up, she wanted them to be able to call if they needed her.

Almost as soon as she reassembled the phone, she got an incoming call.

It was her mother.

"Salam, Maman," Azar answered.

"*Azar-joon, kojaee?* Where are you? I've been calling and calling. I called the house, and you didn't answer. I woke the boys, and they didn't know where you were."

"I'm almost home, Maman. I had to get something for their lunches," Azar lied.

"You left the boys alone?" Azar could hear the reproach in her mother's voice.

"Just for a moment, Maman. I'm almost home." Azar tried to change the subject. "Did you need something?"

"I was calling with some sad news. Nargess-khanoom called this morning to tell me Ayatollah Montazeri has passed."

"Oh my God! What happened?" Azar asked.

"They still aren't sure," her mother replied. "He passed in his sleep. The doctors are still there. Nargess is beside herself."

"What a tragic loss," Azar said. She was thinking mostly about the loss to the country. Grand Ayatollah Montazeri had been a significant chink in the propaganda of the Islamic Republic, reminding the country time and again what true Islamic governance could be. Who else had the stature to challenge these people?

On the other hand, Azar thought with a small flutter of hope, perhaps Montazeri's funeral and commemoration could provide the inspiration and opportunity for Green Movement supporters to show their strength once again. It would be satisfying to make the authorities see that the voice of the Iranian people, though temporarily quieted by the regime's bullying tactics, wasn't silenced forever.

"I know," her mother was saying. "It's so sad. We're going to Nargess's house this morning to offer condolences. Do you want to join us?"

"Yes, of course," Azar answered. "I'll come over right after I get the kids off to school."

"Yes, come quickly," her mother urged. "We don't know how . . ." Her mother hesitated a moment. Had she finally learned to be careful when speaking on the phone? ". . . things will go once the news gets out. It's best to go early."

The regime often interfered after the deaths of important critics. Families would be told they had to bury their loved ones in secret and in undisclosed locations so as to prevent funerals from turning into a launching pad for more demonstrations. Azar assured her mother she would come as quickly as she could, and then she hung up.

Standing on the sidewalk, as Azar fit her key into the lock of her condo's gate, she felt, rather than saw, the two men approach her. The panic finally set in as she tried to figure out the best outcome for her boys. Should she beg the men to wait so she could go in and explain and maybe even get them off to school? Should she call her mother back quickly so she would come get them?

But there was no time for any of these options. As the men ushered her toward their waiting vehicle, Azar simply spoke to God, begging and beseeching him to look out for her boys.

*   *   *

Azar entered the back seat of the black SUV. Inside, a small woman in a black chador was waiting for her. She had a large brown growth, possibly an overgrown wart, directly in the middle of her chin.

The men closed the door behind her and waited outside.

"Salam, *khahar*," the woman said. "Come closer, my sister."

Azar scooted across toward her.

"The windows are tinted, so no one can see inside. I need you to pull your chador back and take your scarf off so I can check you."

Azar silently complied.

"*Natars, azizam.* Don't be afraid my dear," the woman said kindly.

The woman ran her hands over Azar's legs and hips and made her lift her bottom off of the seat so she could feel her backside as well. Then she ran her hands over her back and arms, around her neck and across her chest, where she paused and gave Azar's breasts a little squeeze.

Azar pulled away.

"Sorry, dear, just checking," the woman said, laughing. "*Vali heykalet khoobe, azizam.* You have a good figure. Not skinny and flat like me. Okay, put your things back on and give me your purse."

Azar pulled her scarf and chador back over her head as the woman rifled through her belongings. The men tapped on the door, and the woman called to them.

"We're almost finished."

The woman set Azar's purse on the other side of the back seat. Then she pulled out a black cloth and turned to Azar.

"Okay, azizam, I have to put this blindfold on you. So turn your head. There we go."

The woman slipped the blindfold over Azar's eyes then called to the men.

"*Tamoom shod. Biya too.* We're finished. Let's go."

Azar heard the men get in the car and turn it on.

They traveled mostly in silence. From the slight tilt of the car, Azar guessed they were heading north, toward the mountains. She had no idea who these people were working for. If she was lucky, and this was an official arrest with approvals and some hope of oversight, they might be headed to Evin. Her greatest fear, however, was that they might be going to an unmarked station, where she might once again be at the mercy of a madman like Heydari.

The car hit a pothole.

"*Okh, kamaram!* Slow down, my back is killing me." The woman next to her said to the driver.

"Sorry," he replied.

No further words were exchanged until the car stopped and, Azar guessed from the sound of the door opening and closing, the man in the passenger seat got out. A moment later, Azar heard a gate open, and the car pulled forward, stopped, and turned off.

"*Akheysh, residim,*" the woman exhaled. "We're here."

The woman opened the door on her side, then took Azar's hand and guided her out of the car.

"*Movazebe saret bash, azizam.* Watch your head, dear."

The woman's shoes clicked as Azar was led along what she guessed was a garden pathway and then up some stairs and into a building.

"Stop here," the woman told her.

Then, addressing someone else, she called "*Agha Mustafa, koja bebaramesh?* Where should I take her?"

Azar heard a creaking and rolling sound and guessed someone was moving around on a chair with rollers.

A man's voice answered.

"*Payeen dige.* Downstairs, of course."

"*Okh.* All those stairs bother my knees. There's no one in the back room. Can't I put her there?"

"Sure. I don't mind."

"*Khoda hefzetoon bokone, agha-Mustafa.* Thank you, Mr. Mustafa. May God always keep you safe from harm."

The woman pushed Azar forward and guided her through a few turns before stopping her again.

"Take off your shoes."

Azar complied.

"Now walk forward."

The woman had let go of her arm and was no longer guiding her. Azar moved forward but raised her hands to make sure she didn't hit anything. She felt carpeting under her feet.

"Okay, that's enough. You can stop."

Azar heard a door close behind her and the woman called through it. "You can take your blindfold off now, dear."

"Wait!" Azar called to the woman as she swiveled around and ripped the blindfold off. She was in what looked like a large bedroom that was entirely devoid of any furniture. This was definitely not a prison cell in Evin.

Azar pounded on the door.

"Khanoom, please!" Azar pleaded wondering whether she'd be able to get any useful information out of the woman. "Where am I? How long am I going to be here? Why have you brought me here?"

"Calm down dear." The woman answered through the door. "I'm sure you know better than I do why you're here."

"No," Azar cried. "I have no idea why you've brought me here. Please, help me!"

"Only God can help you now. *Tavvakol be khoda.* Trust in him."

The woman's shoes clicked as she walked away.

*   *   *

The noontime call to prayer was Azar's first concrete indication of how much time had passed. It felt like she'd been there for weeks, but it had only been about five hours. Azar was famished and thought longingly of the *sangak* bread bakery.

The bedroom was about fifteen by fifteen feet with an attached bathroom that was missing its door. Some sort of metal sheeting covered what Azar assumed must be windows. The walls and carpeting were grimy with a film of dust and dirt. Azar tried to avoid contact until they became so familiar and she so tired of standing that it didn't matter anymore and she sat on the floor.

She got up and went to the bathroom to make her ablutions. She said her prayers using a cracked prayer stone she found in a corner of the room. She recited the Arabic verses quickly and tried not to focus too much on the meaning of the words that implied a love for and trust in the divine that she did not feel. She finished the eight *rakat*s of prayer and sat against the wall, hugging her knees to her chest. In the distance, she could hear a telephone ringing and the sound of muffled voices.

Azar wondered where Ibrahim was and what he was doing at that moment. He would be horrified to know where she was, but a part of Azar felt closer to him, knowing that neither of them was free. They'd always done everything together. When she was choosing her school major, Azar had even considered joining him in economics so they could study and work together, but he'd encouraged her to go into law. "You'll win every argument in court like you do with me," Azar remembered him saying as they'd cuddled in a postcoital conversation on the topic. "Besides,"—he'd lightly slapped her naked buttock—"I can't have you showing me up in my own profession!"

Azar smiled at the memory.

One of Ibrahim's favorite poems came to her—*Why struggle to open a door between us when the whole wall is an illusion?* Who was the poem by? Rumi? Hafez? Attar? Azar had always thought the point was to comfort believers that their God was nearby. Now, for the first time, she thought of the implications for two people separated as she and her husband were. Perhaps, on some level, they *were* actually together, and if Azar could only see past the illusion of this dirty room, she could find a connection to her husband. Perhaps, on some level, Azar thought with a sudden *aha* of insight, everyone in the world was connected despite the illusion of separation one felt due to distance or even different religions, cultures, and political views.

Azar's thoughts turned to her boys. She often, and perhaps to their detriment, thought of them as a unit, but their personalities were actually quite distinct. Hossein, strategic and driven, was more than willing to put in the long study hours necessary to keep his position at the top of his fourth-grade class. Muhammadreza—just as smart as his brother, but only willing to make an effort on topics and projects that actually interested him—saved his competitive streak for his Ping-Pong matches. But, even there, he wasn't ruffled by a loss in the same way that Hossein might be devastated by a test he hadn't aced.

Azar wondered how long the boys had waited before calling her mother. Smiling wryly, she guessed they wouldn't have called until all their favorite morning shows were over and there was no danger of being interrupted before they'd had their fill. Oh, they were getting so big and independent. She felt confident they would be okay no matter how this ended.

And how was this going to end? Azar turned the possibilities over in her mind again. She could only guess that she was in Heydari's station. She thought back to her previous interaction with the man and immediately felt nauseous. Heydari was unpredictable, evil, and possibly even a murderer. With rising panic, Azar wondered whether she was going to die in this place. Would she never hold her boys again or tell them how much she loved them and how they deserved a better mother than she? Would she never again hear the man she loved whisper of his desire for her.

Stop it! Azar scolded herself. There was no reason to imagine the worst. Yes, Heydari might be evil, but he wasn't stupid. Azar wasn't like Ms. Tabibian. She wasn't an unknown single mother without any family. Heydari would have to be more careful with her. There would be consequences for her death.

She had to prepare herself for an interrogation and possibly a beating. But, unlike her previous interaction with the man, she had two advantages. First, she already knew who and what he was. Second, she had nothing to hide and no one to protect. She didn't have the file, and Ibrahim was already in jail. All Azar had to do was be smart about how she answered the man's questions, to avoid admitting she'd ever had the file. Ali said the file had been slipped into Sadegh's briefcase. Azar wondered whether he'd found it yet, where he would think it had come from, and what he would do with it. Perhaps she could tell Heydari that Leila had put it in his briefcase for safekeeping? That would protect Leila by making it seem as if she'd done the responsible thing by giving it to her Basiji brother. And it would leave Azar out of the whole thing altogether. Yes, that could work!

Although, Azar reconsidered, surely he would check the story out with Leila—perhaps he was interrogating her already—and would be looking for any differences in their stories. If only there was a way to coordinate with her or be sure that Leila would also realize this was the best story to get both of them out of this.

Perhaps the best approach would be to probe the man with questions of her own to try to figure out what exactly he knew or suspected, whether he'd already spoken with Leila, and then adjust her story as needed on the spot. She'd have to do it carefully so he wouldn't realize what she was doing. She'd need to be respectful and deferential so he could enjoy feeling powerful and perhaps even relax a bit and let his guard down. And then, well, it was impossible to know how this would play out, but maybe, just maybe, Azar could talk her way out of this. She'd often managed to do the same when representing clients in family court. So much of the outcome depended on attending to the relationship with the judge and trying to figure out and influence his priorities. She could do this.

Having decided how she would handle Heydari, Azar felt almost impatient to see him. Anything would be better than staying in this room another second.

She didn't have much longer to wait.

Azar heard the familiar click of footsteps outside her door, and then a key was inserted into the lock.

"Turn around so your back is to the door and you're facing the wall."

It sounded like the same woman who'd brought Azar to the room, but the voice had a different quality to it.

Azar stood up, tightened her headscarf, wrapped her chador around herself, and then turned toward the wall with the metal sheeting. She heard the door open behind her.

"Good," the woman said. Her voice was sharp and clear without the door between them. "Do you have your blindfold?"

Azar pulled it from her manteau pocket.

"Put it on," the woman instructed.

Azar did as she was told.

"Now, I want you to move forward slowly and put your hands up on the wall."

Again, Azar followed the woman's instructions. She hitched her chador up so it would hang around her without slipping off her head and shoulders.

"You will stay in that position until you are told you can move. Understand?"

"Yes," Azar replied, "but please, can you tell me what is going on? Why am I here? What am I accused of?"

"*Basse!* That's enough!"

The woman's words were accompanied by a sharp rap to Azar's head with a hard object, possibly some sort of baton. Azar let out a cry more of surprise than pain.

"You will be silent until you are asked a question."

Azar heard bumping and scraping noises behind her, as if someone were moving large objects into the room. Then came the sound of more footsteps outside the door that were muffled as a second person entered the carpeted room.

The woman took Azar's arm and guided her toward the center of the room. Azar grabbed at her chador with her free hand to keep it from slipping.

"There's a chair behind you," the woman told her. "*Beshin*. Sit down. Pull your chador up so you don't sit on it."

Azar felt the edge of the chair against the backs of her legs and sat. She felt the woman lifting the back of her chador over the chair so that it draped around it.

"Let go of your chador and put your hands behind the chair."

Azar hesitated. She didn't know if the other person who had entered the room was a male and didn't want to compromise her modesty.

"*Ya'allah!* Get moving," the woman demanded.

She did as she was told and felt the woman clip her chador under her chin so it would stay in place. Her hands were bound under the chador and behind the chair with some sort of plastic material. A moment later, she felt the woman bind each ankle to the leg of the chair.

"*Daresh biyaram?* Should I take it off?" The woman asked and, apparently receiving approval from someone, fiddled under Azar's chador to undo the blindfold.

The blindfold slipped away, but Azar's field of vision remained entirely black. The woman leaning over her was wearing a full face veil, which was extremely unusual among Iranian women. Up close,

Azar could barely make out the woman's eyes under the black cloth that hung over her face like a fencing mask. Was this the same woman with the ugly wart on her chin? Why was she wearing a face veil?

The woman backed away slowly, her chador sweeping aside like a magician's cape to reveal the man sitting in the chair behind her.

Mr. Heydari.

The fear clenched her belly and rode the explosion of air it produced out of her throat in a scream that sounded inhuman even to Azar's ears. Her back arched and her arms and legs bucked against their restraints, refusing to believe there was no escape. Azar felt the clip under her chin release and her chador begin to slip, but her fears of exposure were entirely overwhelmed by her visceral drive to get away. The restraints around her wrists and ankles bit into her skin as she twisted against them.

Even when her lungs were emptied of air, Azar's stomach muscles couldn't relax enough to allow an inhale. Her head swam, her vision dimmed, and Azar thought she might faint. Instead, she was revived with a slap.

"*Khaffe sho!* Quiet!"

The woman hit her again. Azar tasted blood. She cringed and squeezed her eyes closed as the woman raised her hand for another blow.

"That's enough for now," Heydari said. His voice was smooth and comfortable, reflecting confidence in his control.

Azar kept her eyes closed. She took deep breaths as she struggled to control her panic and clear her mind. What had happened to all her mental preparations for this moment? She had to keep it together. She felt the woman's hands readjust her chador into place and fasten it again, more tightly this time.

"Don't be such a baby," the woman chided as if she was speaking to a child. "You scream like that again and I'll have to give you something to scream about."

The baton tapped Azar on the head again—a warning.

"Now open your eyes," the woman commanded.

Azar steeled herself and opened her eyes.

The sight of Mr. Heydari once again generated an automatic fight-or-flight response, but this time Azar managed to suppress any outward signs of her distress. Heydari was sitting across from her in a folding chair with one leg crossed over the other. His fingers were interlaced and wrapped around his knee. He wore dark slacks and a white pinstriped shirt that was open at the collar. He wore his amber agate ring and his dark purple lips were smiling.

Heydari bowed his head respectfully in greeting.

"Salam, hajj-khanoom. Hello, good lady."

How dare he speak to her with such mock deference! Azar looked at him with angry defiance. Heydari made a small motion with his head, and the woman flew at her. Azar ducked but realized, too late, that her head wasn't the intended target when she felt the sharp rap of a baton across her shins. Azar clenched her jaw to keep from making any noise and bore the pain silently.

"*Bitarbiyat!* Show some respect!" the woman yelled and hit Azar's legs again.

"That's enough," Heydari said. The woman fell back immediately.

"I apologize for my colleague," Heydari addressed Azar. "She's quite devout and devoted to our beloved *velayat* and can't stand this sort of disrespect to the institutions of his government." Heydari's pretense was obvious. It was clear that the woman was merely a puppet operating under his command.

"Anyway," Heydari went on. "There is no need for this to be unpleasant. You have something of mine. I want it back. Where is it?"

Azar needed to get things on track. Her overblown physical reaction to seeing the man had been unexpected. *Concentrate*, she told herself. She tried to orchestrate her facial muscles to convey deference as she said, "I'm sorry, sir, but I have no idea what you're talking about."

The woman in black took a step toward her, and Azar cringed. But Heydari raised his hand, and the woman backed off.

Heydari sighed as he uncrossed and then recrossed his legs so that the other knee was on top. He folded his arms, leaned over them, and peered at her.

"Listen to me closely. I know Ms. Tabibian gave you something of mine, and you are going to tell me where it is. There are many different . . . approaches we can use to get this information out of you. I assure you that in the end you will tell me everything I want to know and then some. The only question is how much time it will take and how unpleasant it will be for you."

Azar was surprised. Heydari thought Ms. Tabibian, not Leila, had brought the file to her? Why would he . . . Azar thought and then quickly landed on a plausible answer. Ms. Tabibian must have wanted to protect her daughter by leaving her out of the whole thing. Yes, that was smart. But why would she have implied that Azar had the original? And where was the original?

"Should I loosen her tongue?" The woman asked Heydari, interrupting Azar's long silence.

"No, please," Azar said. "I'm just trying to think of what you might be referring to." She needed a few more clues as to what Heydari was thinking.

Heydari looked displeased. Azar wondered whether his patience had run out and she needed to start talking. But then he relaxed. He smiled a friendly smile and stroked his neatly trimmed beard.

"Let's try a different approach," he said. "Allow me to explain your situation. Perhaps when you understand it more clearly, you'll be able to make a better decision. You see, hajj-khanoom, we have been watching you for some time. We know about your work for the Foundation. We know you have contacts with Westerners. We know where you shop for food and clothes and makeup and jewelry. We know where your children go to school and how often you leave them with your parents so you can pursue your . . . plotting."

It was a strange mix of truths and untruths. Azar had never been in touch with Westerners, and she couldn't remember the last time she went shopping for makeup or jewelry, so the man was clearly lying and trying to make it seem as if he knew more than he did. On the other hand, he knew at least a little about her work with the Foundation. And he knew she frequently left Hossein and Muhammadreza with her parents. Ali, she thought bitterly, why did you have to tell them about my boys?

"If you've been watching me so closely," Azar said aloud, "you should know I have nothing of yours."

"Oh, *we* haven't been watching," Heydari's smile broadened. "It's the good people around you who have been concerned about what you are up to that have come to us. People you work with. Family members. Your . . . brother."

Heydari looked quite pleased with himself. Clearly, he expected Azar to be distraught at the news of all the spies around her.

"I don't believe you." Azar tried to respond as she imagined she would have had her brother not confessed his betrayal that very morning.

"Oh, I assure you it is true," Heydari smirked. "He's been working with us since the summer."

"And he told you I have something of yours?" Azar probed.

Heydari frowned. "No, that was Ms. Tabibian. She told me she gave you a file that belongs to me."

A small victory. Azar had guessed correctly that Ms. Tabibian had lied and said she herself had brought the file to her office. Azar suppressed a smile.

"But how could Ms. Tabibian tell you anything? She's dead!" Azar pushed further.

The woman in black stirred from her spot by the wall and shook her baton at Azar. "*Por roo!* Who said you're allowed to ask questions?"

Heydari raised his hand and waved it gently in front of the woman as if to restrain her. "It's okay," he said. "I'll answer her question. And then she will answer mine."

He nodded his head at Azar. "Yes, I heard about the unfortunate accident. She was in my office on Thursday and told me all about your trying to recruit her to spy on me and get information to pass on to your American contacts."

"That's a lie!" Azar cried. Would Ms. Tabibian really have said all those things? Or was Heydari making things up to scare Azar or, rather, to suit beliefs about her that he'd already formed.

"Come now, hajj-khanoom," Heydari responded. "I've been open with you. Now it's your turn. All I want is that file. You tell me where it is, and you walk out of this room right now."

It was at this moment that Azar decided what her story was going to be and set her energy to believing the sequence of events she was about to relate. It shouldn't be too difficult as it would contain a good dose of truth. And the story had the advantage of protecting everyone by laying all the blame on someone who had nothing more to lose.

"Mr. Heydari, you know my situation better than I do." Azar hoped her voice sounded respectful. "My husband is in jail. I have two small children, and I'm barred from working to support them. There is no way I would do something that might create more trouble for my family. I'm telling you, Ms. Tabibian came to me. She wanted to give me a file, but I refused."

Heydari pursed his lips. "Ms. Rahimi, you are beginning to try my patience. I don't have time for this."

"It's true!" Azar protested.

"Why would she lie to me?" Heydari asked.

"Maybe she was trying to protect her daughter," Azar answered. "She told me you wanted to marry Leila."

"What?"

Azar noted with satisfaction that she'd hit a nerve. Heydari flicked a glance at the woman in black and looked almost embarrassed.

"Shame on you . . . trying to force that poor girl to marry you. She's half your age!" Azar knew she didn't sound deferential anymore. She was hoping to get more leverage from shaming the man in front of his colleague.

Heydari rose swiftly from his chair, and Azar wondered if she had gone too far. With her hands tied behind her, she wouldn't even be able to shield her head from his attack.

But Heydari simply stood there a moment, looking at her angrily.

Azar spoke up, returning to the previous topic and her submissive tone, "I didn't take the file. I told her she should give it back. And I think she gave it to her son."

Heydari didn't seem to hear her. He walked around his chair and stood behind it with his hands resting on its back. When he spoke, his voice was soft.

"Yes, I offered to marry her daughter," he acknowledged. "But it isn't what your disgusting mind thinks. Leila-khanoom has some . . . deficiencies that limit her prospects. I've known Ms. Tabibian since she was a child and was simply looking for a way to help the two of them. Unfortunately, she was too stupid to understand. She lived her life following such base animal motivations, she couldn't recognize my pure intent. Anyway, *khoda ra shokr*, praise God, Miss Leila hasn't been infected by her mother's nature. She will need me now more than ever."

Azar hesitated, not wanting to provoke him. Gently, she asked. "Does Miss Leila want to get married? Nineteen is still quite young."

Heydari smiled proudly. "Yes, she is quite young . . . and beautiful!" He shook his finger at Azar with a mischievous look. "My intentions are pure, but I'm still a man after all."

Heydari took a breath before continuing. "She will adjust to her fate."

Heydari walked toward Azar. He stopped right in front of her and leaned down so they were face-to-face. She could see the clipped ends of his thick nose hairs move as he exhaled.

"Now, I'm getting tired of all this conversation." Heydari breathed his words down on her. "All I want from you is a one sentence answer to this question. Where is my file? We've already searched your home and office, and it isn't there."

They'd searched her home? Where were her boys when they'd barged in? Azar was afraid. She needed to connect the dots of her story for Heydari without delay.

"I don't have your file. I think Ms. Tabibian gave it to her s—"

In one swift motion, Heydari wrapped his hands around her neck and began to squeeze through her chador and headscarf. Azar could see the frustration and rage in his eyes as he leaned close and screamed in her ear "I said one sentence!"

Azar couldn't move. Her lungs kept trying to suck air, but her intake was blocked by Heydari's thumbs on her windpipe. Heydari started shaking her, and the back of Azar's neck cracked painfully. Heydari put one knee on her lap as he leaned closer and continued yelling and shaking her. "*Meslinke hanooz nafahmidi ba ki tarafi!* It seems you still don't know who you're dealing with! You stupid cow! Bad things happen to people who stand in my way. Just ask Ms. Tabibian! I can make you disappear as easily as she did."

Azar saw spots swimming before her eyes, and then the light in the room seemed to dim. In her narrowing peripheral vision, she saw the woman in black come close and murmur. "Mr. Heydari, I think she's had enough . . . Mr. Heydari, listen to me please. Be careful, sir."

"*Akh!*"

Heydari released his hold on Azar's throat and pushed her away. Her chair tipped over, and Azar crashed onto her shoulder but barely felt the impact; she was so grateful to breathe again.

Heydari turned on the woman in black. "*Khaffe sho!* Shut up! Shut up! Who told you to interfere, you incompetent idiot?"

The woman cowered, and Heydari gave her a swift kick. Then he turned and grabbed the chair he'd been sitting on and threw it to the ground as he continued to rant. "You think this is some kind of a joke? The enemy is surrounding us, and you protect her? This is war! A war between those who are on God's side and those who are against. There can be no mercy in such a moment!"

The woman in black murmured apologetic bleatings that Azar couldn't understand. Now that the fear of strangling had receded, she could feel the sharp pain in her shoulder where she'd landed. From her position on the floor, she watched Heydari carefully.

Heydari continued shouting. "I've had enough! There's only one way to deal with this."

He stalked to the door and yanked it open. Then he turned and spat "*Eeno bolandesh kon!* Get her off the floor!" before walking out the door.

The woman in black limped over to Azar, took hold of the back of her chair, and heaved her up.

"*Okh, kamaram!*" the woman complained about her back pain as she lifted Azar. The momentum of her push caused the chair to tip again, and Azar worried momentarily that she might fall in the other direction, but after a few wobbles the chair settled upright.

"Please," Azar said to the woman in a choking voice that burned her bruised vocal chords, "help me!"

The woman in black was fixing Azar's chador around her again, but said nothing.

"Khanoom, please!" Azar repeated.

"You need to help yourself!" the woman snapped. "Believe me, there's nothing I can do for you. Answer his questions, or it will get a million times worse."

The woman clipped Azar's chador so tightly that it scraped and stung her skin where it had been crushed by Heydari's choke hold. Azar grimaced but didn't complain.

"Listen," She spoke urgently to the woman in black. "I'm not lying. Ms. Tabibian gave the file to her son. Her son works with Heydari. You must know him. Mister Sadegh."

At that moment, Heydari reentered the room, pushing a blindfolded young man before him. He held a small paring knife in his right hand.

The young man looked familiar, but his presence in this context was so alien and unexpected that Azar's mind struggled against accepting it even as she identified the bright-blue Nike shoes she had purchased two weeks ago.

This was no young man.

This was a child.

This was her son.

Azar's instinct was to scream and shout and fight against the impossible scene of ten-year-old Hossein standing next to this evil man. But she had just enough presence of mind to hold herself in check so as not to scare her son any further. What sort of nightmare was this? She'd never heard of the Islamic Republic using children in this way.

Azar spoke in a low voice. "What are you doing with my son? Why have you brought him here? He's a child!"

Heydari flicked an angry look at Azar and said "One sentence. That is all I ask of you. One lousy sentence."

"Maman, is that you?" Hossein asked.

"Yes, my love." Azar answered, grateful that he couldn't see her. "Don't be frightened. This is just a mistake. Be brave, my boy."

"Where's my file?" Heydari demanded.

"I don't have it! Sadegh Hojj— Oh my God! Please! No!"

Heydari had taken Hossein's head in his hands and tilted it. He lifted the paring knife toward Hossein's face, and as Azar begged for mercy, he sliced off Hossein's right earlobe with one swift motion.

Hossein screamed and wriggled against Heydari, but Azar could barely hear him so loud was the bellow issuing from her own injured throat. She yanked against her restraints. The woman in black grabbed her arms and pulled them up painfully behind her, forcing Azar to be still.

Over the screams of mother and child, Heydari yelled. "One sentence! That's all I ask. What kind of mother are you to let your own child suffer in order to save yourself? Stop your lying and admit you took the file! I ask you again: Where is it?"

"Sadegh Hojjati has it!" Azar screamed. "Please! I'm telling the truth. I admit everything. Yes! I took it, but I gave it to Mr. Hojjati. Please! Oh, God, I'm begging you. Don't hurt my son! Don't hurt him!"

Heydari looked suspiciously at Azar. Hossein was still screaming and struggling against his grasp.

"Who's Mr. Hojjati?" Heydari demanded. "Is he with the Foundation?"

Azar tried to get the words out as quickly as possible. "He works with the Basij! Sadegh Hojjati. His cousin is married to my brother. I took the file from Ms. Tabibian. I admit it. Or actually, I took a copy. But I didn't keep it. I wanted to get rid of it and put it in his briefcase. Or, rather, I asked my sister-in-law to do it for me. I wanted to return it to the authorities. But she just slipped it in there. He might not have even found it yet, but it's there. Please! Ask him."

Heydari pushed Hossein to the floor, where he curled into a tight ball in the corner and whimpered as he clutched his ear. Blood trickled through the cracks between his fingers and down his arm.

Heydari took a few steps toward Azar and stopped right in front of her.

"I don't know any Sadegh Hojjati. What makes you say he works with me?"

"Please!" Azar pleaded. "Maybe he works with a different unit. Let me make a few calls, and I'll find him for you. I swear to God I'm telling the truth. Just, please, my son has nothing to do with this. He—"

"Shut up!" Heydari snapped. He cocked his head at the woman in black. "Go see if anyone knows this Hojjati."

The woman released Azar's arms. She walked to the door, opened it, and leaned out the doorframe. Azar heard her call to someone. "Do you know a Sadegh Hojjati? No? Go see if anyone knows him. Mr. Heydari wants to talk to him. Hurry!"

Azar could hear footsteps going down the hall. The woman in black turned back into the room but left the door slightly open behind her.

"You said Ms. Tabibian gave you a copy?" Heydari asked. "I don't care about a copy. Anyone could have doctored it. What I want is the original. Where is it?"

"I don't know!" Azar insisted. "All I know is that I had a copy and I arranged for it to be put in Sadegh Hojjati's briefcase. I don't know anything more than that!"

"You know this will be easy to verify," Heydari said softly to Azar. "If you're lying, it's going to be bad for your son!"

"I'm begging you!" Azar cried. "You have to believe me. Just talk to Mr. Hojjati. Tell him to check his briefcase. You'll see I'm telling the truth!"

Unless, Azar thought in a panic, Sarah had lied about what she'd actually done with the file.

Heydari looked toward Hossein. "Bring me a towel or something," Heydari instructed the woman. "This kid is bleeding all over the place."

The woman in black walked behind Azar and out of her field of vision to, Azar assumed, the bathroom. She returned with a roll of toilet paper. Azar wondered how clean it was and what the risk of infection would be to Hossein.

"Please," she implored Heydari, "let me help him!"

Heydari calmly took the toilet paper from the woman in black and wrapped it around the bit of flesh that was still attached to his knife. He crumpled up the paper and handed it to the woman in black.

"Get rid of this," he said.

The woman took the small package and walked toward the bathroom again.

"Please, no!" Azar couldn't bear the thought of a piece of her son's body being disposed of as if it were trash. "He needs to see a doctor! A doctor can reattach that."

Heydari chuckled, "That's funny. You want to reattach an earlobe? Ha!"

Heydari pulled off another longer section of toilet paper and shoved it into Hossein's hand. "Here, hold this up to your ear to stop the bleeding. And stop your whining, kid! You better hope your mother is telling the truth, or the next piece that goes is going to be a lot more important than an earlobe! You hear me?"

Hossein held the paper to his ear as he slumped miserably against the wall with his knees drawn up to his chest. His eyes were still covered by the blindfold. If he was still crying, he did so silently.

"Please!" Azar begged again. "Let me help him."

"You can help him as soon as I find out if you're telling the truth," Heydari answered.

Footsteps sounded from outside the door.

A male voice said *"Befarmayeed.* Go on in."

The door pushed all the way open and Azar could see a guard ushering in two men. It was Sadegh Hojjati and a big bear of a man that Azar didn't recognize.

Azar could see the surprise and discomfort in Heydari's eyes as he swiveled his body to block the men's view of Hossein on the floor. Would they stop him if they saw what he'd done?

"Ganjian," Heydari addressed the man that Azar didn't recognize with a tight smile and forced greeting. "What a nice surprise. What are you doing here?"

As he spoke, the woman in black had swiftly taken up a position beside Hossein so that the boy was entirely hidden from view by her chador as Heydari moved forward to greet the men with handshakes and kisses.

Azar watched Sadegh take in the scene. She couldn't read his expression and wondered if he recognized her. She wondered what he thought of what he was seeing. He couldn't see her restraints under her chador or her bleeding boy behind the woman in black. But perhaps he wouldn't be surprised anyway. Perhaps he'd seen many similar scenes before. Perhaps what happened in the interrogation centers of the Islamic Republic was far worse than Azar had ever imagined.

The man Heydari had referred to as Ganjian spoke first. "Sorry, we didn't know you were in the middle of something. This is my colleague Sadegh Hojjati."

"Ah, the famous Mr. Hojjati." Heydari was smiling, but Azar sensed he was nervous.

"We've met before," Sadegh said. He didn't return Heydari's

smile. "Anyway, we had some questions and were waiting in your office, but they said you wanted to talk to us."

"What perfect timing," Heydari said. "I have some questions for you as well. But let's go back to my office. It's much more comfortable there." Heydari held out his hand to usher the men out the doorway.

Azar decided to take a gamble. She had no way to know whether this would save her son or seal his fate but knew she had to act.

"Mr. Hojjati! Please! It's me, Ali's sister. Help me, please. This man is torturing my son! You can leave me here, but please, *to ro khoda, to ro Imam Ali,* take my boy!"

Sadegh paused and looked at her. Azar thought she saw shocked recognition in his green eyes.

Heydari continued to push the men out of the room.

"Ignore her, my friends," Heydari said. "She's crazy. Let's go to my office so I can explain."

Azar screamed, "Mr. Sadegh, take my boy. You don't know who this man is. Please, oh God, please! Take my boy!"

Heydari closed the door firmly behind him as he joined the men outside the room. Azar continued to yell.

"*Aghaye Hojjati!* Please don't leave my son, my Hossein, here! He's going to kill us like he killed your moth—"

She was silenced by a slap to the face from the woman in black.

"You stupid woman!" she hissed at Azar. "You have no idea what you've done! Even I who have worked with this crazy man for three years don't want to think about what he will do to you now!"

Azar hung her head and sobbed. She cursed herself. She cursed Ibrahim. How stupid they had been not to realize the extent of the dangers they faced. They'd been willing to risk imprisonment and other dangers for themselves, but never for their boys. Was this torture of children a new tool of the regime, or was Heydari acting without authorization?

"Oh, Hossein!" Azar cried. "Hossein, my boy, I'm sorry. I'm so, so sorry."

Hossein piped up from the wall where he still sat. "It's okay, Maman. I'm fine. It doesn't even hurt anymore, Maman. Don't cry!"

Her son's brave words broke Azar's heart further, but she would not deny his request and calmed her tears.

"Yes, my son. I'm sorry," Azar apologized. "Thank you. Thank you for helping me be brave."

As she calmed down, she realized she could hear Heydari, Ganjian, and Sadegh arguing in the hallway.

"I told you I have your file. Why do you still need to keep her?" Azar recognized the first voice as Mr. Sadegh's.

Heydari answered. He sounded angry. "I have more to question her about. And I don't need to explain myself to you!"

"I have an idea," the third man—Ganjian—seemed to be trying to strike a compromise. "Why don't I take her and keep her at my station. Then whoever needs to can come question her there."

A glimmer of hope began to warm itself in Azar's chest. Was it possible they might get away from this man?

"No!" Heydari answered. "She's *my* prisoner. She isn't going anywhere until I am finished with her."

"And the boy? What did he do?" Sadegh demanded.

Azar's heart leaped again. They *had* seen Hossein despite Heydari and the woman's attempts to hide him.

"Ganjian, you need to teach your friend some respect for his superiors!" Heydari shouted.

"You're right Mr. Heydari. Sadegh, calm down," Ganjian reprimanded his companion. "But I'm curious too. Why is the boy here? He's too young for this."

"I just wanted to scare his mother a little," Heydari explained. "She wasn't being straight with me."

"*Na dige*, come on Heydari," Ganjian chided. "It's going too far to bring a *bigonah*, innocent, kid into it."

"If you knew what this woman had been up to, you wouldn't say that. I tell you she has been in direct contact with foreigners and has been trying to collect secret government documents to pass on to them. Sometimes sacrifices need to be made. You know that."

"Okay." It was Ganjian again. "Let's do this. If you need to keep the woman, fine. But let us take the boy and return him to his family. Okay? Can we all agree?"

There was a silence.

Finally, Sadegh answered. "Fine. But since we're here, I have a couple of questions for her myself. It won't take long."

"No!" Heydari objected. "I'm at a sensitive point in the interrogation. And I'm not finished with her!"

"*Aghaye Heydari, kootah biya.*" That was Ganjian again. "Give us a break here. Let's give Sadegh five minutes to ask his questions and then we're out of here, okay?"

"I'm telling you this woman has obviously had training in resisting interrogation. She's a master of deceit!" Heydari's voice was on edge.

"Ahh, don't worry so much," Ganjian said. "Five minutes and we're gone."

The door to the room opened and Heydari entered, followed by Ganjian and then Sadegh. Ganjian walked directly to Hossein and sat on the floor beside him.

"Salam, *amoo!*" he said. "Hey kiddo, how are you?"

Hossein said nothing but shrunk away.

"Hey, don't be afraid," Ganjian tried to reassure Hossein. "I'm going to take you away from here, okay?"

"No!" Hossein cried defiantly. "I don't want to leave my mother!"

Ganjian swallowed. "You're a brave little guy, I can tell. And if your mother tells me to let you stay here, I will, okay? But I think she wants me to take you to visit your grandma. What do you think about that?"

Ganjian looked meaningfully at Azar, and Azar spoke up. "Yes, Hossein-jaan. My brave, strong boy. I need you to go with him, okay? Don't worry about me. I'm fine. And don't be afraid. He's going to take you home. I'll be there soon, okay?"

"Okay, big guy, you heard your mother," Ganjian said. "Take my hand and let's get up together. Whoa, what's going on with that ear?"

Ganjian pulled Hossein's hand away from his head and saw the bloody ear missing it's lower quarter. Azar watched his eyes grow hard with anger and felt gratitude and relief that her son would be safe with this man.

Ganjian led Hossein, still blindfolded, out the door and called to the guard. "Agha Mustafa, get an ice cream for this little guy." Then, presumably to Hossein, Ganjian said. "Sit here for just a minute, and we'll go, okay? Be a good boy."

Ganjian returned to the room. Sadegh had picked up the chair that was still lying on the floor where Heydari had thrown it. He set it in front of Azar and sat down. Azar thought Sadegh looked nervous but also angry and determined. Heydari and the woman in black stood right behind Sadegh. Ganjian stood behind them, leaning against the door. He still looked angry over what had been done to Hossein.

"Mrs. Rahimi," Sadegh began. "I'm very sorry to see you here."

Azar didn't know how to respond and said nothing.

"I have a couple questions for you," Sadegh said. "I understand you arranged to get some sensitive documents to me." Azar looked at Sadegh closely, and he continued, this time enunciating every word as if it had particular meaning. "I spoke with Miss Leila this morning. It seems she knows nothing about all this."

Azar caught on quickly. It was almost as if they had coordinated their stories to protect Leila. She nodded, "Yes, that's right."

"Wait a minute!" Heydari exploded. "What the hell were you doing talking to the girl? This is my investigation."

"She's my sister," Sadegh answered without turning to the man. Heydari eyes widened briefly, but otherwise digested this new information without much of a physical response.

"So, Mrs. Rahimi," Sadegh went on, "I understand your secretary, my mother, God rest her soul, she gave you these documents. Do you have any idea why?"

"This is all highly inappropriate," Heydari spoke up. "If you're related to these people, then you definitely shouldn't be involved in an investigation."

Sadegh turned and looked at Heydari. "I understand you and my mother were old friends. Perhaps you shouldn't be involved either."

Azar watched Heydari's jaw tighten as the two men stared each other down. Finally, Ganjian broke in, "That's enough. Sadegh, ask your questions and let's go."

Sadegh turned back to Azar. "Ms. Tabibian died this morning. I have reason to believe the circumstances of her death were suspicious. Why did she give you these documents?"

Azar looked at Heydari. He didn't actually perform a cut-throat gesture but his face clearly communicated his intent to cause harm if she said something he didn't like.

"I'm sorry to hear about your mother's death," Azar turned her gaze back to Sadegh. "But I don't know why she gave me the documents. She didn't say anything about her reasons. But maybe she had some . . . political reasons."

"Are you sure?" Sadegh's voice sounded disappointed.

Azar looked at Heydari again. His face had relaxed a bit and he gave a subtle nod. He was pleased by her answer. He didn't want her to talk about his desire to marry Leila with his newfound brother. A brother with connections to the Basij.

"Ms. Rahimi, look at me," Sadegh said. "You have nothing to fear. Just tell me honestly. Why did she give you the documents? And what do you know about her death? Earlier I heard you say something about someone killing my mother."

Azar looked at Heydari again. She looked at the woman in black. And then she looked at the floor. She heard Hossein from the hallway. "Mmmm," he said. "It tastes even better blindfolded."

Azar was not even a little tempted to tell Sadegh what Heydari had implied about his role in Ms. Tabibian's death or about his intent to pursue Leila. Her only goal was to get her son out of here safely and away from the madman before her.

She looked Sadegh in the eye as she answered. "I'm completely sure. I'm sorry about what I said earlier. I was just trying to get your attention."

"You see!" Heydari crowed in triumph.

Ganjian came forward and clapped Sadegh on the shoulder. "Okay, my friend," he said. "Let's go."

Sadegh looked a bit lost in thought but stood up. He and Ganjian said their goodbyes to Heydari, who was standing tall and proud. Azar's spirits sank a bit at the realization that she would soon be alone with this man. But she comforted herself with the knowledge that she could bear anything so long as her children were safe.

Ganjian stepped out of the room, and Azar heard him address her son. "You ready to go? How was the ice cream?"

Azar didn't hear Hossein's reply, however. Just as Sadegh was closing the door behind him, the woman in black suddenly called out.

"Wait! *Agha-yoon*, Wait!"

Sadegh turned and opened the door. He and Heydari both looked at the woman in black. Her voice trembled as she spoke.

"He killed her! Yes! He killed your mother. And there were others. Most of them were traitors. But . . . I'm not so sure. Please, you have to protect me! I wanted it to stop, but didn't know how."

Azar realized Heydari still held the paring knife as he raised his arm to attack.

"Watch out!" Azar screamed.

Heydari took hold of the woman's shoulder with one hand, pushed her against the wall and plunged the knife into the mass of black fabric. He pulled the knife out and brought it down again as he screamed.

"You liar! How dare you! You traitor! You corrupt stain on earth! You will go to hell for your blasphemy!"

It was horrific to watch Heydari stabbing the woman with abandon. The man was bloodthirsty. What if he went after Azar next? Or even Hossein?

Sadegh ran toward Heydari. He grabbed Heydari's arm and wrenched the woman free. Then Sadegh pushed Heydari back and stood between him and the woman who slumped down the wall to the floor.

Azar realized with panic that Sadegh thought Heydari would come to his senses once confronted by a colleague. Sadegh still didn't know, as she had quite painfully learned, that Heydari's rages didn't end until he reasserted control.

"Watch out!" Azar shouted as Heydari brandished the knife toward Sadegh.

"You stupid, stupid boy," Heydari raged, spittle frothing from his purple lips. "You're cut from the same cloth as your whore of a mother. You *haramzadeh* filth! I'm going to kill you like I killed her!"

Heydari slashed his knife at Sadegh, narrowly missing his throat, but coming down on his defensive left forearm. Sadegh bellowed in pain as his shirt stained red. He backstepped away from Heydari's next lunge but tripped and hit the ground. Heydari jumped on top of him, arm raised and ready to attack. Azar couldn't believe that this little man was overpowering Sadegh, who had at least a head and twenty pounds on him. But Sadegh still didn't seem to fully recognize the intent and ability of his adversary. As Heydari rained down insults and struggled to bring the knife to his target's neck, Sadegh's main focus seemed to be calming the man down rather than defending himself from a deadly attack.

"*Aghaye Heydari, aroom bash!* Be calm, Mr. Heydari." Sadegh said as he grasped at Heydari's knife hand. Heydari said nothing in response but used both hands and his body weight to push the knife down closer to Sadegh's chest. Azar screamed as the knife point approached and appeared to pierce Sadegh's jacket right over his heart. Sadegh, finally seeming to recognize the danger he was in, kicked his feet to try to get some leverage.

He was saved, not by his own efforts, but by Ganjian, who had returned in the midst of the commotion. He pulled Heydari off of Sadegh and shoved him to the floor. Heydari fell near Azar's chair and the paring knife, covered in blood, clattered beside him.

Ganjian hovered over Sadegh, checking his wounds.

Too late, Azar realized Heydari had risen and was approaching the men. Her scream accompanied the paring knife's thrust into Ganjian's side. The big man didn't make a sound but turned, looking startled. Heydari had pulled the knife out and moved to strike again. Ganjian caught Heydari's knife hand, and then, with his free hand, delivered a punch to Heydari's face. Heydari spun, cartoonlike, before collapsing with a thunk on the floor, finally releasing the knife. He might have risen again except that the woman in black crawled toward him, grabbed the paring knife, and buried it in his heart.

PART FOUR

A YEAR LATER, ANOTHER WEDDING

Governmental brutality and intimidation can withstand the march of history for years, but not indefinitely. Whatever becomes of the Green Movement in the short term, millions of courageous Iranian protestors made clear to the world last summer that their country's centennial quest for a democracy is an idea whose time has come.

—Karim Sadjadpour, Iran Expert with the Carnegie Endowment for International Peace, Project Syndicate, June 2, 2010

CHAPTER 10

Thursday, June 17, 2010—one year and five days after the election

Azar couldn't take it anymore.

"*Dari divoonam mikoni!*" she shouted. "You're driving me crazy! That's it! I'm going to drop you off at your grandparents."

"Nooooo!" came a chorus of pleading from the back seat.

"I can't drive like this with you two fighting back there!"

"We're not fighting!" Hossein answered immediately. "We're playing."

"Then why was Muhammadreza whining?" Azar demanded.

"I was just pretending." Muhammadreza explained. "I'm the bad guy, and Hossein threw me in jail."

"We'll be good, we promise! Please let us come to the wedding." Hossein pleaded.

Azar's threat wasn't serious, but she continued to pretend that dropping the boys off was an option, hoping to leverage some assurances of good behavior out of them.

"I don't know," Azar said. "I still remember all the trouble you caused the last time we were at a wedding. I thought you'd grown up since then, but here you are yelling and screaming in the back seat while I'm trying to drive in this traffic. And we're already an hour late! Grandma's house is on the way. I'm just going to drop you off there."

"No! No! No! No!" Muhammadreza kicked the back of Azar's chair with each exclamation.

"*Shhh!* Stop it!" Azar heard Hossein restraining his younger brother. "You're just making it worse! Maman," Hossein addressed his mother now, "We're sorry. We didn't realize we were bothering you. We can be quiet, I promise. And I think you know that I've grown up a lot since the last wedding. I know how to behave around adults, and I can watch Muhammadreza too."

Azar smiled to herself at her older son's attempts at maturity. Ibrahim would be so proud of them. She couldn't wait for the three remaining months of his sentence to pass so that they could be a family once again.

Aloud, however, she kept her voice stern. "Well, I don't know. Let's see how you behave on the way there."

In the rearview mirror, Azar saw Hossein flash a victory sign to his younger brother. Clearly, the scamp thought he'd won.

"I can always change my mind . . ." Azar warned, reasserting her authority.

"We'll be good!" Hossein promised promptly.

In the mirror, Azar saw Hossein whispering something to his brother, his ragged right ear clearly visible.

Yes, Azar thought sadly, he'd grown up a lot more than she would have ever wanted. She wondered, as she had so often since the nightmarish encounter at Heydari's station, whether that madman's brutality had affected her son in ways she couldn't yet perceive. Once again, she cursed herself for not having been more careful. What sort of a mother was she to so casually risk her sons' well-being for abstract notions like justice and truth? What sort of mother was she to have abandoned her children in the middle of the night to try to save a bunch of useless papers? What sort of person was she to have risked Leila and Ms. Tabibian's lives by pushing them to look for more documents? What sort of feeble-minded thinking had allowed her to imagine she could affect the direction of the Iranian regime? What sort of—

Stop! Azar commanded the voice in her head that sounded suspiciously like Heydari's. Even from the grave he seemed to be waging a battle to destroy her, this time with the help of her own psyche. For a time, it had even looked as if he'd succeed.

In the weeks following Heydari's final attack, Azar had fallen into a blackness she'd never experienced before. She and the boys moved in with her parents, where Azar, afraid to return to her office, spent most days in bed. Sleep was her only escape from the stream of vicious words and insults hammering into her skull every moment of the day.

It was her father who finally shook her out of it.

He'd shuffled into her room one morning and gently pulled the blanket off her face.

"*Dige basse*," he said. "That's enough. It's time to get up."

"I can't," Azar moaned.

"You can and you will!" her father insisted. "You're going to get up and be the fighter you are. Your boys need you to be strong."

"They're better off without me. The world is better off without me!" Azar cried.

"No," her father gently shook her. "That's what they want you to think. Azar, my daughter, resistance isn't only about pouring into the street. Their greatest success is when they can destroy people from the inside and make them turn on themselves and forget who they are. That's what you need to resist!"

Her father sat on the bed next to her and stroked her hair.

"I should have told you more often," he said in a whisper,

"how proud, truly proud, I am of you. There is nobility in the work you have done. Such courage in the way you stood up for those women despite the judgement of other people. Sometimes, it is true, I wished you were a little less brave. But I've always been proud. How could you ever doubt that the world needs you? Your family needs you. Don't let them win!"

*   *   *

Azar parked the car in the hotel's lot. She opened the door and gathered her chador around her as she awkwardly exited the car.

"Hossein, bring the flowers." Azar instructed her son.

"That's not fair! Why does he get to bring them?" Muhammadreza objected.

"I'm the oldest." Hossein explained with a smug grin as he hopped out of the back and opened the passenger door to take the flowers from the seat.

He was too slow. Muhammadreza lunged from the back seat over the gearshift to grab the flowers just as Hossein's fingers closed in on them from the front. A tug-of-war ensued that Azar feared the flowers would lose.

"Stop it!" Azar hissed.

The boys ignored her. Azar plopped back onto the driver's seat and reached across to grab the flowers.

"*Bedesh man!* Let go and give them to me! What is wrong with you two? Do we need to go to your grandmother's after all?"

"No!" Muhammadreza shouted.

"Then behave yourselves! I'll bring the flowers myself."

Azar pulled the corners of her chador into her teeth and then exited the car again with the now-bedraggled flowers in her arms. She bumped the car door awkwardly to close it with her hip and then led her boys across the parking lot toward the hotel, doing her best to ignore their continued bickering. They'd better let Ibrahim out of jail soon, or he wouldn't have any sons to come home to!

Inside, they walked toward the banquet hall, where a uniformed hotel employee in a blue overcoat and *maghnaeh* head covering told them where to set the flowers and directed them to the ballroom entrance.

"The boys can't go with you," she said.

"What do you mean?" Azar asked.

"They can go in the men's section with their father," the woman informed her.

Her words pinched. Azar wondered with a heavy sigh how Ibrahim would be spending the evening and what type of food he would be eating in jail as she and the boys enjoyed a wedding feast.

Aloud she complained, "You've got to be kidding me. They're only ten and eleven. My husband isn't with us tonight."

"*Sharmandeh*," the woman apologized. "I'm sorry, but the ladies want to be comfortable. I've been told that boys school-age or above have to go in the men's section. Don't you have any other family here with you?"

"This is ridiculous," Azar snapped.

The woman shrugged her shoulders. "*Be har hal*, there's nothing I can do about it."

Azar pulled out her phone to call her brother.

Ali picked up almost immediately.

"Ali-jaan, are you at the wedding?"

"Yes," her brother answered. "Are you here?"

"Great," Azar said. "I'm going to send the boys in to you. They won't let them in the women's section."

Ali groaned. "You brought the boys with you?"

"What was I supposed to do with them?" Azar asked. "Come on, don't worry so much. They'll be good. Besides, I'm not planning on staying long. I just have to make an appearance. If they do anything bad, I'll take them home immediately, okay? I'm going to send them in now. *Mersi, baradaram.*"

Azar hung up and turned to her boys, but they had disappeared.

"They went in," the hotel employee told her.

"To the men's section, right?" Azar asked hopefully.

The woman confirmed with a nod. Azar sighed. She stepped into the room adjoining the banquet hall that was the designated area for ladies to remove their coverings and touch up their hair and makeup before entering. Azar handed her chador, manteau, and headscarf to a woman who hung them up and handed her a number in return. Then she stood before the full-length mirror and studied herself.

With Ibrahim away and her hands full with work and the kids, Azar had little reason or time to dress up. She couldn't remember the last time she'd worn a gown, styled her hair, or put on makeup. Azar leaned forward to apply lipstick and pressed her lips together to even out the color. Pleased with the effect, Azar wished her husband was around to appreciate her efforts. She closed her eyes briefly as she thought of the one night they'd had together after she'd gotten out of prison. He'd held her in his arms and stroked her hair as he whispered "Beautiful . . . so beautiful . . ."

"Ejaze midin?"

Another lady had entered the small room and wanted to use the mirror.

"Oh, of course. I'm all finished," Azar said.

Azar entered the ballroom. Her heart was warmed to see how nice the room looked. It was a much smaller crowd than Sarah and Ali's wedding, and there weren't quite as many predinner treats loaded onto the tables. But the relatively drab ballroom had been transformed with low lights and thick candles glowing from crystal centerpieces. And what Azar could see of the bridal spread at the head of the room looked quite elegant in its display of all the necessary elements without the gaudy extras that had marked the one Mehri Hojjati had fallen onto last year.

Sadegh and his family had been generous.

Azar made her way to the bridal spread. The groom hadn't yet entered the room, so the ladies were busy dazzling one another in the bright, tight gowns they'd purchased for the occasion. Azar quickly found Sarah, who was wearing a low-cut royal-blue sleeveless dress that clung to her belly and accentuated her enhanced cleavage. Azar couldn't have imagined wearing something so tight this late into her own pregnancies.

Sarah saw her and came to greet Azar with a kiss.

Azar embraced her sister-in-law and said, "Look at you! I've never seen such a beautiful pregnant woman."

"Oh my God," Sarah said, gesturing to her belly. "I'm so fat!"

"You're stunning, azizam," Azar assured her. She remembered how huge and insecure she'd felt when she was pregnant with her own two boys. Whatever she thought of Sarah's dress, Azar wanted to be kind. "Enjoy it. It'll be over before you know it and then you'll have a screaming baby boy to take care of."

Sarah smiled and squeezed Azar's hand before letting her go to greet Sarah's mother and aunt and the rest of the ladies who had now become family. It was nice, Azar thought as she kissed cheeks all around, how the enmity between the families had been smoothed over by the imminent arrival of a shared grandson. Not that Azar didn't still get irritated by Sarah's lack of interest in anything serious or her mother's obsessive worrying about ridiculous things, like whether the baby outfits she was purchasing matched the colors of his car seat. Sarah's Aunt Mehri also continued to annoy her with her matriarchal dominance, which was supported and enforced by the younger women in her tribe. And the last time Azar had seen her, Sadegh's wife had been especially insufferable in her smugness over her perfectly behaved children. In fact, Azar thought as she kissed her, Sarah's cousin Fatimeh, with her unfailing friendliness and good cheer, might be the only one of the lot that she genuinely liked. But it didn't matter. They were family. And if there was one thing that religious and respected families like theirs knew, it was how to interact with civility and dignity no matter what you thought of one another. Anyway, it wasn't as if she had to see them every day.

Azar ended up on the outskirts of the group, standing next to Fatimeh, who squeezed her hand, pulled her close to her pillowy body, and exclaimed, "Isn't she the most beautiful bride you've ever seen!"

Azar turned to look at Leila, sitting demurely at the head of the *sofreh aghd*. Even under a chador, Leila was a pretty girl, but tonight she was something else altogether. This was the first time Azar was seeing her with so much makeup, and of course, in a gorgeous lace wedding gown. But there was something else that added to her allure in a way Azar couldn't quite identify. She had no trouble agreeing that Leila was indeed the most exquisite bride she'd ever laid eyes on.

"I just wish"—Fatimeh's voice dropped to a whisper intended only for Azar's ears—"that her mother could have been here to see this. It breaks my heart that she died so young and before she and Sadegh had a chance to reconcile. Truly—" Fatimeh's big brown eyes became glassy with tears. "—I blame myself. Not only for what I did as a child but for taking so long to confess. If only I'd told Sadegh earlier, perhaps there might have been time for him to intervene and she would be here today, celebrating with us."

Azar had never considered this, perhaps because she'd been so busy blaming herself for endangering Ms. Tabibian and Leila. But thinking on Fatimeh's role in Ms. Tabibian's ouster from the Hojjati family—a story she'd learned from Sarah and Ali—Azar realized it was true. Had Fatimeh been quicker to absolve Ms. Tabibian of the charges of infidelity, Sadegh might have reconciled with her in a way that would have protected her from Mr. Heydari.

Azar felt a flush of relief. How freeing it was to shift the weight of blame to someone else's shoulders. And yet, recognizing the pain in Fatimeh's eyes, Azar's relief was quickly followed by empathy for the large woman and a flash of anger directed at the source of misfortune they'd both taken misplaced responsibility for.

"You can't think like that, Fatimeh-joon," Azar said drawing on her father's words. "It's not your fault. You did the best you could and never intended to hurt anyone. If you've been told the full story, you know there's only one person truly responsible for her death. A monster that the regime promoted and, even in death, protects. If we want to honor Ms. Tabibian's memory, we need to work to make changes so that such men can't gain power. We need to make sure there won't be more Ms. Tabibians in the future."

"Oh," Fatimeh's sigh rippled through her body. "You're so strong and brave. I don't know how you do it. Especially now when there seems to be so little likelihood of change. Even Mousavi has finally given up."

Fatimeh was, Azar assumed, referring to the large protests planned for last week's one-year anniversary of the stolen election. In the end, Mousavi had canceled them to "protect people's lives and property." Despite the cancellation, small groups of protestors had dared to gather in the streets, only to be promptly arrested.

"I don't think Mousavi's given up," Azar said. "He's just being strategic about deciding when and where to challenge the system in a way that doesn't lead to more loss of life.

"Forgive me, I'm sure I don't understand these things," Fatimeh's heft seemed to shrink a bit as she apologized. "But what's the point of continuing to challenge the system when there's so little hope of winning? The government forces are so much stronger."

It was an important question. One that Azar had struggled with herself as the darkness of depression threatened to envelop her. What was the point of resistance when there was no hope of winning? Why waste one's life striving for something that would never be realized?

But when Azar spoke, it was with the conviction born of having survived a hard fight for her truth. "It's not just about winning, Fatimeh-joon. It's about the life I want to lead and how I want to contribute and who I want to spend time with. I don't know if we're going to win, but I know what side I want to be on, because all the people I most admire are on that side too. And I do have hope that my small efforts will move the wheel of the world in the right direction. If not me or my children or my children's children, perhaps some future generation will enjoy a better life because of my choices. But even that modest hope will die if we stop trying."

Fatimeh blinked several times. Her eyelashes were so long they seemed to tangle together whenever her eyes closed so that one expected her to have to struggle in opening them again. She opened her mouth, but before she could say anything she was interrupted by Zainab, who was shepherding the ladies toward the head of the bridal spread so they could be in position, once the groom entered the room, to rub cones of sugar over the bride and groom's heads and sprinkle sweetness over their union.

Azar took the opportunity to greet Leila with a warm two-cheek kiss.

"Congratulations, azizam," Azar said. "May you grow old together and enjoy many happy years."

Leila smiled warmly at Azar and gave her hand an extra squeeze before turning to the next well-wisher. Once again, Azar noted that there was something different about the young woman.

Perhaps it was the way she carried herself with a different sort of confidence now that she was part of the respected Hojjati family.

Fatimeh and Azar took their places behind the bride, where they would take turns rubbing the sugar cones and holding the lace canopy over the new couple. Azar watched as Mehri-khanoom, Sarah's aunt, fussed over the train on Leila's dress so that it would sweep properly along the side of the bridal spread.

It was sweet to see the old woman's attentions. At every family function in the past six months, Mehri-khanoom, forgetting that Azar already knew her, would reintroduce Leila. "Do you know Sadegh's sister Leila?" Mehri-khanoom would ask. "I can't tell you how happy we are to have her with us. It's as if she was supposed to be in the family all along. *Vallah*, she's just like Fatimeh and Zainab for me."

Mehri-khanoom clearly meant well. But Azar couldn't help wondering whether Leila ever thought about how her mother might feel to know that she, like her brother Sadegh before her, was now being cared for by Mehri-khanoom as if they were her own.

"You know, I saw her that day," Fatimeh whispered into Azar's ear.

Azar didn't know what Fatimeh was talking about.

"Roxana," Fatimeh whispered again. "She came to my house before going to see . . . him."

Azar realized Fatimeh was talking about Ms. Tabibian.

"She'd been trying to get in touch with Sadegh but, well, he still wasn't talking to her then. So she came to my house." Fatimeh leaned even further into Azar's ear. "She had some papers she wanted me to keep for her."

Fatimeh backed up and looked at her meaningfully. Azar understood immediately. Fatimeh could only mean the original file on Arman Tamimi. The one that Leila had shown her in her office and that Azar had copied. Leila had said she'd given it to her mother and had assumed she was going to return it to Heydari. But Heydari had behaved as if he'd never gotten it. Had Fatimeh had the file all this time?

"My God!" Azar struggled to keep her voice low as her excitement soared. "You understand what this means? I can get it to the right people. We can make sure the Iranian people know without a doubt what the government is doing. What a miracle . . . I thought that file was lost forever."

In her excitement, it took a moment for Azar to notice Fatimeh looking increasingly abashed.

"*Chi shode?* What is it?" Azar asked.

"I'm sorry," Fatimeh said, flustered. "I didn't mean that . . . I didn't want to . . . I don't have it anymore. See, I thought the best thing was to pass it on to Sadegh. He's been trying through different channels to get answers about what happened to his mother and . . . well, the file was his mother's after all."

Azar was silent as she watched Fatimeh's eyelashes fluttering again

"I'm so sorry," Fatimeh said again. "I probably shouldn't have said anything. I just wanted you to know that Sadegh was working on it, and *insha'allah*, those involved will be punished."

Azar swallowed this disappointment, as she had so many before, and managed a small smile. "*Insha'allah*, if God wills it," Azar agreed aloud, although recent history didn't give her much hope that God actually cared to punish those who abused their power.

Wanting to distract herself, Azar turned her attention to Leila, who was greeting yet another guest who had come to wish the bride well.

"*Vagh'an*, he was always a good boy," the woman said with a knowing shake of her head. "The best. So good and kind and warm hearted and always taking care of everyone."

The guest must be talking about the groom.

"My heart broke," the guest went on, "the way things turned out for him. But you're such a good girl, it's clear. *Insha'allah*, you'll be happy together for many years."

Leila bowed her head with a smile to agree with the guest, and this time Azar realized immediately what was different about the young woman. She looked happy. Her smile went beyond the corners of her mouth to shine through all her features, and even the way she carried herself seemed to exude joy.

Was it because of the marriage? Was Leila truly in love? Azar didn't know Leila's groom well, but he did seem like a good man. In fact, Azar owed him a special debt for the way he'd once cared for her son. And she'd heard that he'd recently left the Basij, perhaps because he was troubled by some of their actions. A man like that could be a kind husband and father and exactly the sort of friend and protector Leila needed.

Leila's joy lifted Azar's own heart as she recalled the love of her life, Ibrahim, standing before her in a mess of broken glass and kabobs. With a man like that, a woman could survive almost anything.

* * *

Sadegh saw the boys as soon as they entered the room. "Salam, *amoo*," he used the familiar term that signified he was Hossein's uncle or a good friend of his father's.

Azar's older son looked up at him with serious eyes. "I'm looking for my Uncle Ali. Do you know where he is?"

"Hmmm . . . Let's look for him together, huh?"

Sadegh put a hand on Hossein's neck as he scanned the room, looking for his cousin's husband.

"I don't see him. But why don't we go over to the kids' table. You can hang out with my son, Mahdi, until your uncle comes along."

"How old is Mahdi?" Hossein's brother asked, eyeing Sadegh suspiciously.

Sadegh chuckled. "You're right, he's a little young for you two. But there are other children with him."

Sadegh steered Hossein and his brother around the room, surreptitiously examining Hossein's ear as he did so. At the children's table in a corner of the room, more than a dozen boys between five and fifteen years old were crowded around one child playing video games.

"See, I told you there were kids your age." Sadegh said to the boys as he delivered them.

"Wow, what is that?" Hossein's brother asked as he pushed his way through the pack of boys to hover over the gamer's shoulder.

Sadegh, too, was intrigued by the flat device that seemed to operate with no controller other than the boy's own fingers. He watched for a bit as the child positioned a red cartoon bird on a slingshot and then released it to sail through the air and crash into a pile of blocks.

Sadegh's son, Mahdi, was standing at the edge of the group. He saw his father and used the opportunity to press his case again.

"Baba, can I?" he asked.

"I'm still deciding," Sadegh answered his son.

Sadegh decided he'd better make a speedy exit before his son pestered him again.

"I'm going back to my table," he told Hossein. "I'll let your uncle know he can find you two here." But Hossein was so engrossed in the video game that he didn't seem to hear.

"Hey." Sadegh reached out and tugged on the sharp corner of Hossein's deformed ear. This got his attention immediately and Hossein scowled at Sadegh as he pulled away and rubbed at his ear.

"Sorry," Sadegh apologized.

But it was too late. One of the boys at the table had noticed.

"Oooh, Gross! What happened to your ear?" His question was interesting enough that several boys looked up from the video game.

Hossein's expression changed immediately to one of confident indifference.

"Whaddya think? The barber cut it off."

The boys laughed and turned back to the game.

"Sorry," Sadegh apologized again. "I just wanted to make sure you'd stay here until I can send your uncle over."

Hossein nodded and turned his attention back to the game, still absentmindedly fingering his ear.

Sadegh wondered as he made his way back to his own table, how much Hossein remembered of the night he'd lost his earlobe. Did he even realize that Sadegh had been there? After Azar had been freed from her restraints and rushed to hold her boy, she'd insisted that he keep his blindfold on. She didn't want him to see, Sadegh assumed, the bloody scene in the room or the dead man with the knife in his heart.

In fact, it had been incredibly lucky for Hossein and his mother that Sadegh and Ganjian had decided to drop in on Heydari. Actually, Sadegh reflected, it was really Leila who'd saved the boy. She'd been so certain Heydari had something to do with her mother's death that she'd made Sadegh promise to go find the man immediately. It wasn't until Sadegh had walked into that room and seen the cowering child and his terrified mother that he began to share Leila's suspicions as well.

Heydari's female assistant eventually confirmed everything in a later debrief with Sadegh and Ganjian at the Sa'adat Abad mosque office. She'd been in the room when Ms. Tabibian, clearly trying to protect Leila, told Heydari she was the one who'd taken the documents to try to pressure him to leave her daughter alone. Ms. Tabibian told him about the documents and had begged for Heydari's forgiveness. In response, Heydari bludgeoned her to death with the wooden leg of a chair.

Sadegh had been horrified and enraged to hear the story of his mother's death. He was touched to see Ganjian's eyes fill with tears as well. When the woman had finished telling her story and left, Ganjian got emotional again. "Oh, Lord, it's just so awful. I'm sorry this happened to your mother, God bless her soul. It's such a shame, Sadegh-jaan."

"It's criminal is what it is!" Sadegh hissed as he paced the room. "Who else did that man murder? How many others are there like him? We've got to do something about this."

Ganjian shook his head. "Sadegh-jaan, be careful. You have every right to be upset. But things like this happen. Maybe they even happen for a reason. Maybe almighty God was simply ready for your beloved mother to return to him. It's horrible, but this is the world we live in. You need to let it go. Promise me you won't do anything stupid."

But Sadegh couldn't let it go. Sadegh was smart enough not to say anything to the investigator that was looking in to Heydari's death but kept pestering Ganjian until he got Sadegh a meeting with someone he promised was influential.

Sadegh met the man in his office off of Bobby Sands Boulevard. His dark skin was weathered and wrinkled, but his thick beard didn't have any grey. He wore clerical robes and a black turban to indicate he was a descendent of the prophet Muhammad. The man smiled kindly when he stood to greet him, his lips and fingers moving silently as he chanted continuously on his prayer beads.

Sadegh was careful in how he told the story of Heydari's misdeeds to avoid any mention of the medical documents. Instead, he focused on how Heydari had tortured Hossein, pressured Leila into marriage, and possibly killed their mother. It was hard to tell if the cleric was really paying attention. As Sadegh spoke, the man took no notes, continued his quiet chanting, and even closed his eyes.

When Sadegh stopped speaking, the man opened his eyes and nodded.

"Good. I'm glad you came to me," the cleric said. "We'll be sure to look into this. I'll let you know what we find out."

Sadegh felt he was being dismissed but wasn't ready to go.

"Hajj-agha, the concern I have isn't just about Heydari. I'm worried that there may be others like him that are doing . . . inappropriate things in the name of the Islamic Republic. I'm worried that we might not have a strong enough system for making sure that deviants don't get into the system and behave in a way that can shake people's faith. I'm worried that—"

The man interrupted him with a raised hand.

"*Pesaram*," he said. "My son, why don't you leave the worrying to me."

"But what's going to happen?" Sadegh asked. "I don't understand."

The man smiled at him, the corners of his eyes crinkling like an accordion. "Well, dear boy," he chuckled softly, "there are many things in this world that we will never understand."

"But"—Sadegh couldn't stop—"Heydari was a bad man. If bad men take over a good system then won't it become bad as well?"

The man sighed. He put his prayer beads in a small dish on his desk and leaned onto his forearms.

"How do you know he was a bad man?" he asked Sadegh.

Sadegh was taken aback.

"He . . . I just told you. He tortured a little boy. He . . . may have murdered someone."

"Was Khizr a bad man?" the cleric asked.

Sadegh shook his head. He was familiar, of course, with the story of Khizr in the eighteenth chapter of the Quran. Khizr was a mystical being or prophet who had agreed to take Moses on as a student. During the course of their travels together, however, Moses had objected to some of Khizr's actions including his killing of a small boy. In the end, Khizr lost patience with Moses's doubts and explained that all of his deeds were in accordance with God's will and toward a good end. He had killed the young boy as he would have become a rebellious and defiant unbeliever who would have guided others, including his parents, off the path of righteousness.

"And what about Montazeri, a man that the blessed Imam Khomeini once called 'the light of my life,' was he a good man? You know better than I what his followers are doing in the streets."

Montazeri's death had sparked a series of protests all around the country that the authorities had had to deal with for weeks. Things had gotten so bad in Najafabad, Montazeri's hometown, that authorities had imposed martial law for the first time since the 1979 revolution.

The man continued his questioning. "If our precious Imam Khomeini was unable to judge Montazeri . . . if the prophet Moses, peace and blessings be upon him, was unable to judge Khizr, what makes you think that you can judge Heydari? Maybe there are things about Heydari and this child you say he hurt or these women that you don't know."

"I just . . . I don't understand." Sadegh was surprised to note that he was close to tears. "How am I supposed to know who is a good or bad person? How do I know what is wrong or right? What is the standard by which to judge even my own behavior?"

The man smiled and reached for his prayer beads as he stood up to dismiss Sadegh.

"You must trust in those who know more than you," he said.

AS HE APPROACHED HIS TABLE, Sadegh noticed that the groom had joined his brother, brothers-in-law, and other male relatives at their table.

The groom stood as he approached, and Sadegh greeted him with a three-cheek kiss. "How're you holding up?" Sadegh asked.

"This suit is so tight I can barely move," the groom growled. "And I can't eat a thing or the vest will pop a button. My God, how long do I have to wait before we can get things going? The ladies need to move things along before I rip this crazy outfit off, and your sister changes her mind about marrying such a slob."

Sadegh chuckled.

Ganjian actually looked quite presentable. His wild hair had been beaten into submission by the combination of a good cut and copious gel. His three-piece suit—minus a tie—slimmed his belly while accentuating his broad shoulders. Besides, Leila wouldn't notice or care, even if he'd shown up in his usual outfit of relaxed khakis and an oversized button-down shirt.

Sadegh thought back to the family luncheon when he'd introduced Leila to his friend and mentor. Ganjian, not usually at a loss for words, had gone quiet and even stammered a few times as Leila pointed out that they'd met before on the night she was arrested. When Ganjian asked, some weeks later, if he and his family could come *khastegari* courting of Leila, no one was surprised.

What had been surprising, to Sadegh at least, was how quickly Leila seemed to return his affections. Ganjian had no money to speak of, especially now that he'd left the Basij and had gone back to teaching full-time. His family situation was awkward, with an invalid father and two younger sisters depending on him. And, as well as Sadegh could judge, Ganjian wasn't exactly good-looking.

When Sadegh had asked Leila whether she wanted to accept an engagement proposal from Ganjian, she'd blushed and agreed immediately. "He's a good man," she'd said. "He has a kind heart."

Sadegh would be sad to see Leila move out. It was hard to remember that there was a time he didn't want her in his life. As they'd gotten to know one another, he'd been astonished to find so many familiar gestures, habits, and preferences in someone he'd only just met. It was a completely different relationship than he had with Zainab and Fatimeh. Leila was younger, of course, so Sadegh felt protective of her. But she also seemed to understand him in a way that was more intense than either of his other half sisters. He would be sad to see her go.

Even so, Sadegh agreed with Leila's assessment of Ganjian. She would be loved, protected, and cared for. And she would be married to a man of faith who would keep her on the right path. He had no trouble encouraging the match and even supporting the new couple with a generous dowry and, with Maman-Mehri's help, a respectable wedding party.

"Well, you know how it is," Sadegh teased his friend. "The ladies have to get things just perfect over there before they'll let you in for the ceremony. Never forget, my friend, that despite appearances, women truly are in charge of the world."

Ganjian laughed and shook his head.

Sadegh felt a tug on his sleeve.

"*Mishe, Baba?* Can I, Daddy?"

It was Mahdi, come to pester him again.

Ganjian reached out and pinched Mahdi's cheek.

"Look at this young man. He starts at Adab in the fall, right?" Ganjian asked.

Ganjian was referring to the K–12 private school that Sadegh himself had attended and where Ganjian had once been his teacher.

Mahdi squirmed away from the man's attentions and yanked his father's sleeve again. "Baba, when are you going to answer me?"

Sadegh leaned down to kiss Mahdi's forehead and then pushed him on his way. "Go play, kiddo."

Mahdi complied but stomped his feet as he walked away to convey the depth of his conviction that life was unfair.

"Well," Ganjian said. "I'd better go too. I'm told I'm supposed to stop at every table to talk to everyone. God, when will all of this be over?"

Sadegh clapped his friend on the shoulder, and Ganjian took his leave.

Sadegh was about to sit, when he noticed his cousin's husband, Ali, squeezing between two tables on the right.

"Ali-agha!" Sadegh called to him.

Ali stopped and looked around but then continued on his way. "Ali!"

This time Ali saw Sadegh and responded as he walked toward him.

"Salam, Sadegh-jaan. *Chetori?* How are you?"

Sadegh took Ali's hand and kissed his cheeks in greeting. The young man had grown on him in the months since Sarah's marriage had finally been settled by news of her pregnancy. Sadegh had been particularly touched and abashed to learn that Ali's time in jail had resulted from his and Sarah's generosity to Leila.

"I'm good." Sadegh said. "I wanted to tell you your nephews were looking for you. I sent them over to the kids' table in the corner."

"Oh, great, thanks. I couldn't find them and was starting to worry. Those two get into trouble pretty quick. I should go check on them."

Sadegh pointed Ali in the direction of the children. As he headed off, Sadegh watched the boys at the table. Someone must have brought a second gaming device since the pack of boys had divided into two separate groups, each of which was centered around the lucky player. Sadegh saw his son standing at the outskirts of one of the groups.

Sadegh wondered with a sigh how long it would be before Mahdi would head over and pester him for sweets again. This was a definite downside to his recent rebellion against his wife's rule.

Up until six months ago, Sadegh had generally been happy to go along with Sumayeh on pretty much anything she felt strongly about. He had so much faith in her purity of intent and the process by which she deliberated God's will that he knew she would make good decisions. Even when he secretly disagreed or felt resentful, it was much easier to comply and comfort himself with the knowledge that it would be Sumayeh's fault if things went wrong.

But it wasn't working for him anymore. Sumayeh had been so utterly wrong about Leila, Ms. Tabibian, and Maman-Mehri. Sadegh couldn't help thinking, perhaps unfairly, that things might have turned out differently for Ms. Tabibian if he hadn't been so eager to please his wife and mother. And Sumayeh's conviction that any questioning of government policy was a sign of weakened faith had caused a disturbing rift in their once rock-solid friendship. Sadegh had become increasingly disillusioned by the authorities' seeming endorsement of Heydari's operation. Their differences on these big issues had trickled down into squabbles over less important day-to-day hassles. Sadegh seemed to have developed an uncontrollable compulsion, which the children had swiftly noticed and begun to use to their advantage, to constantly question his wife's views and consider the pros and cons of every single decision in an effort to figure out what he thought was right.

It was exhausting. And scary. If he was wrong, Sadegh would have only himself to blame.

Like his decision to start sharing the medical files of people who had died in custody. That could blow up in his face at any minute, and Sadegh wasn't even entirely sure he was doing the right thing. He had no desire to publicly embarrass or harm the Islamic Republic which, contrary to Sumayeh's accusations, he continued to feel a strong loyalty and sense of duty toward. But he also felt an unyielding conviction that these families had a right to know how their children had died. That was why he'd met the three families privately to let them read through the medical files of their loved ones.

The hardest visit was with the family of Arman Tamimi. His mother had wept as she'd read the medical evidence that her son had been sodomized and burned before being beaten to death. And his father had demanded a copy of the file, which Sadegh had refused.

Sadegh still wasn't sure that the path he'd chosen was a good one. But it was better than any of the alternatives he had been able to think of. And he couldn't think of any better way of divining God's will than using the mental faculties God had given him to make his own best guess about which path to take.

Sadegh noticed Mahdi waving at him. Having caught his father's attention, he raised his eyebrows and nodded vigorously as if to say, "I can have another sweet, right?"

Ugh! This again. It was time to devote some mental energy to the question of sweets. Sumayeh was always insistent that the children have no more than twenty grams of sugar per day, a number she'd pulled from some United Nations guidelines about healthy eating. Mahdi was surely well past that number for today, but Sadegh generally felt that weddings and other special events ought to constitute occasions for leniency.

As Sadegh watched, Mahdi reached for the platter of cakes and other sweet treats at the center of his table. Mahdi chose a small cream puff and raised it up to his mouth. He paused there looking at his father expectantly, waiting for his final approval.

But Sadegh shook his head to indicate he would not give permission. Sumayeh was right. Not because of her insistence on following UN food guidelines, but because Sadegh had seen for himself how Mahdi's behavior deteriorated when he had too much sugar.

Mahdi's eyebrows knit in indignant anger as he brought the cream puff down. Suddenly, however, his arm reversed course, and he smashed the whole sweet into his mouth.

Sadegh almost laughed out loud at his son's blatant defiance. Clearly, the boy thought he had the right to make his own decisions too. Good for him. But now, Sadegh thought as he walked toward his son to administer parental discipline, Mahdi was going to have to learn that the power to make choices carries with it the responsibility to deal with the consequences.

*   *   *

Sarah spoke into her phone, "*Allo?* Ali?"

"*Janam*, Sarah. Yes, my beloved." her husband answered.

"How's it going over there?" Sarah asked.

"The ladies' section is where all the action is at. I'm dying of boredom over here." Ali spoke quietly, and Sarah guessed he was covering the phone with his hand to make sure he wasn't overheard. "Next time, I'm sneaking in with you!"

"You just want to be on this side to see all the ladies in their revealing clothes," Sarah teased her husband.

"No! That's not what I meant," Ali protested. "What would be the point anyway, since I wouldn't be able to keep my eyes off the most beautiful woman in the room."

"You're such a liar! I look like a blue cow." Sarah pouted.

"What can I say? I like blue cows." Ali laughed.

"*Vagh'an ke!* I can't believe you said that!" Sarah said with mock outrage.

"*Shookhi bood, azizam!* Just kidding! You're right, I prefer red cows. Do you have a red dress you can change into?"

"That's it! I'm telling my father," Sarah threatened.

"That again? Oh my God . . . I'm finally figuring it out! You arranged all that with your father on purpose so I'd be terrified of him and have to listen to your every command for fear of another beating. What sort of woman am I married to?"

Sarah was laughing so hard she realized she had to pee.

"Oh my God, you're killing me. I have to go to the bathroom," she said.

"Okay, azizam. My beautiful wife. My one and only *golli*. We'll talk later."

"Wait!" Sarah exclaimed. "I almost forgot why I called. Azar's phone died, and she wanted to check on the boys. Are they doing okay?"

"Actually, tell her they've been great tonight. Some of the kids brought those new flat computers and they've all been mesmerized."

"Oh, okay, I'll tell her," Sarah said before hanging up.

After informing Azar, who was relieved to hear that her boys were behaving, Sarah slipped away from the bridal spread to find the bathrooms.

When she returned, her mother fussed over her. "Are you okay? Where did you go by yourself? I turned my head to talk to your aunt for one minute, and suddenly you were gone."

"I just went to the bathroom!"

"By yourself?" Sarah's mother objected. "At this point, you shouldn't go anywhere alone. You never know when things will start. I think this little one is ready to come meet his wonderful mother."

Sarah's mother moved a hand to her belly and gave the little one inside a squeeze.

The baby kicked back and punched a bony appendage into Sarah's pelvic bone.

"Ouch!" Sarah said.

"Are you okay? What happened?" Her mother was automatically on high alert.

Sarah leaned to one side to adjust her position and get more comfortable as she spoke. "It's nothing, *Maman*. This little rascal is just moving around."

"*Chi shode?* What happened?" nosy Aunt Mehri called from her place beside Leila.

"Nothing. The baby just kicked me," Sarah reassured the ladies, many of whom were now looking at her with concern.

"Your time is getting close, dear," Aunt Mehri went on. "You need to be very careful now to make sure you don't overexert yourself. Mahdiyeh," Aunt Mehri directed her words to Sarah's mother, "she should have someone with her all the time now. Did you finally find someone? Batul-khanoom is very experienced. I sent her to be with all my girls. And she knows how to help after the birth too."

Although Aunt Mehri had addressed her mother, Sarah answered for herself. "Our housecleaner's daughter is coming from Karaj to stay with me starting this week."

"Her housecleaner's daughter?" Aunt Mehri directed her words to Sarah's mother again. "How do you know she can be trusted? It's your decision, of course, but I certainly would never entrust my daughter and grandchild to just anybody. Mahdiyeh-jaan, I strongly recommend you think this through carefully."

Sarah's mother spoke up. "Yes, Mehri-joon, you might be right. It seems Sarah already promised the job, unfortunately, but I'll keep a close eye on the girl when she comes."

"I'm surprised at you Mahdiyeh-jaan," Sarah's aunt chided her mother. "A decision like this shouldn't have been left to Sarah. What does she know about what is needed? I'll talk to Batul-khanoom tomorrow, and she can come over and meet the girl and make sure she's acceptable."

Sarah gritted her teeth to keep from saying anything. Leila's wedding wasn't the place to cause a scene, but there was no way she was going to let Aunt Mehri decide who she would or wouldn't have help her.

Luckily, Sarah was spared from further advice by the announcement that the groom was about to enter the salon. The ladies all began donning the indoor chadors they carried. Sarah couldn't find hers and panicked before her mother reminded her she had it. Sarah shook out the folded chador and wrapped it around herself just as the groom entered the room.

Sarah still didn't understand the match. Leila was stunning. Yes, there was the fact of her being an orphan of unknown parentage, and she certainly didn't have much money or property to her name. But it didn't seem right that Leila should end up with someone so ordinary. And Sarah still couldn't forgive Ganjian, the red-eyed man, for arresting Ali all those months ago.

Ganjian made his way to sit next to Leila on the raised platform at the head of the bridal spread. He kept his eyes down low so as to avoid seeing the ladies, but Sarah saw him flick his eyes toward Leila, and for a moment, the bride and groom smiled at one another.

Thankfully, and unusually, the mullah officiating the ceremony kept his comments brief. When he asked the beaming bride whether she would marry the groom, Leila cocked her head playfully toward the roomful of women who obliged with a roar.

"*Aroos rafte gol bechine!* The bride is picking flowers!"

ACKNOWLEDGMENTS

I'd like to start by thanking my parents, Ali Naghi Sadr Hajj Seyed Javadi and Allison Dewey Vail Sadr, for bravely and lovingly knitting together two sprawling tribes, one from Qazvin, Iran, and the other from Salt Lake City, Utah. You taught us that the "other," if not already a family member, was likely a potential friend and made it possible for me to move forward in the world, excited to meet them all.

I'm grateful for my five brothers—Iman, Issar, Azad, Taher, and Nurraddin—who have been with me from the beginning as a source of love, joy, camaraderie, and Speed Uno. Azad, a fellow writer, has advised and encouraged me at every step.

I am blessed with many wonderful aunts and feel incredibly grateful for the community of women I've gotten to grow up in. Sarah Carlson and Holly Javadi, from opposite sides of the family, have been particularly involved with and supportive of me at all phases of the writing. Thank you both for the long chats and the helpful feedback on my book and my life.

For befriending and guiding me during my years in Tehran, I'd like to thank my cousins, especially dear Niloufar, who left us too soon, Salman, Salmeh, Asieh, Mehrnoush, Soroush, Farnoush, Simin, Elahe, Sedigheh, Pardis, Iman, Kareem, and Kimia as well as my uncles Ahmad and Mansour. Thank you also to my friends at Rahmate-lel-alamin, including Nassim, Minoo, Alireza, Maryam, Sharareh, Tayebeh, Azita, and Shahriar. Thank you to Taghi, Katrine, and other coworkers at CENESTA and to my colleagues at the Ministry of Jihad, with whom I have so many fond and funny memories, not the least of which was chasing chickens in Hamedan.

I'm grateful to my in-laws, who welcomed me into their family with a warmth that was all the more touching given the reasonable reservations they might have had about their son marrying so far outside their traditions. It was an all-too-short joy to get to live with them for periods of time in both Tehran and New York.

Although I felt compelled to tell this story, I had little confidence in my ability to do so and would have likely aborted the project altogether were it not for the encouragement and prodding of my dear friend Sarah Lane. Sarah read every single chapter as I completed it, managed to ignore all the embarrassing flaws of a first draft, and made me feel like my voice and story had value.

During much of the writing, my family was embraced by the beautiful Village Community. In addition to teaching and loving my children, Village friends read early drafts, helped me practice my "pitch," and watched my kids so I could write. I'm especially grateful to Anna-Maria White and Michelle Longosz for their editing advice; Lynn Offenhartz, Amy Dalziel, Elizabeth Adinolfi, and Matt Hammer for reading the full manuscript and saying nice enough things that I felt confident to start querying; Jennifer Birnbaum, Jeri Vasquez, Shelly Dorai-Raj, Lila Lam, Gina Koepf, Steve Smith, Rob Rothrock, and Stephanie Snow for letting me practice my "pitch" on them before heading to the San Francisco Writer's Conference; and Diana Joseph and Aine O'Donovan for helping me figure out social media.

Thank you to friends in Iran who read the book and gave me feedback to make sure I got things right including Zahra, Samira, Bijan, and Maryam. Thank you to Morvarid, Bahareh, Nassim, and Parisa not only for reading (and rejecting!) the Farsi translation but also for being my adopted Iranian sisters and family in California. Thank you to Javaneh and Mohsen for helping me figure out my "audience" and saving me from a few embarrassing flaws.

Thank you to Jenny Ballif (a.k.a. Science Mom!) for being my writing buddy and champion, for improving the book through your insightful edits and thoughtful questions, and for making me query beyond the three agents I was initially planning on. Thank you to Zaha Hassan and Lara Kain for helping me figure out how to organize the first chapter. Thank you to Heather Lazare for being the first professional to encourage me and for providing so much thoughtful and useful feedback. Thank you to Ausma Zehanat Khan and Persis Karim for paving the way for voices like mine.

Thank you to Shiloh Ballard, Jessica Waite, Allison Greenlee and the rest of my colleagues at the Silicon Valley Bicycle Coalition who have supported a project whose relevance to our goal of getting folks on bikes may not have been obvious.

I've heard it said that finding the right agent is like falling in love and can attest that in my case, at least, the aphorism rings true. I knew Danielle Burby of the Nelson Literary Agency would be a perfect match from the moment I stumbled across her website and read of her interest in social justice themes that were a central element of my novel. My esteem for her has only increased as I've seen the professionalism, confidence, and wisdom with which she's shepherded and gone to bat for this project. Thank you Danielle! Thank you also to Kristin, Brian, Samantha, and other members of the NLA team.

Addi Black, Jennifer Pooley, Megan Wahrenbrock, Zena Coffman, Jeff Yamaguchi, Greg Boguslawski, Ember Hood, Josie

Woodbridge, and the team at Blackstone Publishing have been a dream to work with. Thank you for believing in and making so many important contributions to improving this story and getting it out. And thank you for supporting me when I needed it most.

Finally, Hamed, Sobhan, Matine, I love sharing my life and home with you. Thank you for putting up with me during the ups and downs of a writer's life. I hope I can support your projects with as much enthusiasm and grace as you have always supported mine.

NOTES

CHAPTER 1

1. Roger Cohen, "Iran: The Tragedy & the Future," *New York Review of Books* 56, No. 13 (August 13, 2009).

CHAPTER 3

2. Kalame, "'If a Nation Wants to Change Its Destiny': Zahra Rahnavard on Women's Rights and the Green Movement," in *The People Reloaded: The Green Movement and the Struggle for Iran's Future*, eds. Nader Hashemi and Danny Postel (Brooklyn: Melville House, 2010).
3. Maziar Bahari, "Newsweek Reporter's Ordeal in Iran," *Newsweek*, November 21, 2009.

CHAPTER 4

4. Golnaz Esfandiari, "Student Protests against Ahmadinejad Continue in Tehran," *Radio Free Europe / Radio Liberty Online*, September 29, 2009, https://www.rferl.org/a/Student_Protests_Against_Ahmadinejad_Continue_In_Tehran/1839076.html.

CHAPTER 5

5. Stephen Adams, "Iran Confirms Capture of Five British Sailors," *The Telegraph*, December 1, 2009.

CHAPTER 7

6. Roula Khalaf, "Iran's 'Generation Normal,'" *Financial Times*, May 29, 2015.

CHAPTER 9

7. Maziar Bahari, *Then They Came for Me: A Family's Story of Love, Captivity, and Survival* (New York: Random House, 2011), xi.